THE THIRTEENTH GATE

GASLAMP GOTHIC #2

KAT ROSS

The Thirteenth Gate

First Edition

Copyright © 2017 by Kat Ross

Cover design by CYK Publishing and Conrad Teves Art

ISBN: 978-0-9972362-9-3

For Mom

PART I

I trembled, and my heart failed within me; when, on looking up, I saw, by the light of the moon, the daemon at the casement.
   — Mary Wollstonecraft Shelley, *Frankenstein*

CHAPTER 1

R ain drummed on the roof of the carriage as it raced up Wickham Hill Road. Just ahead, the Greymoor Lunatic Asylum crouched at the end of a long, treeless drive, its peaked slate roof silhouetted against the sky. The black brougham drew to a halt before the wrought-iron front gate. Following a brief exchange with the occupants, two officers from the Essex constabulary waved it through, immediately ducking back into the shelter of a police wagon.

The asylum made a grim impression even in daylight. Now, in the darkest hour of the night, with water coursing down the brick façade and thunder rattling the turrets, Greymoor looked like something torn from the pages of a penny dreadful, hulking and shadowed despite the lamps burning in every barred window.

"I told them to watch him," Lady Vivienne Cumberland muttered, yanking her gloves on. "To keep him isolated from the staff and other patients. Clearly, they didn't listen. The fools."

The carriage jolted forward down the rutted drive. It had been a little over a month since her first and last interview with Dr. William Clarence. Afterwards, Lady Cumberland had taken a hard look at those bars and strongly suggested to the asylum superintendent that he move Dr. Clarence to a room with no window at all.

Her companion, Alec Lawrence, gripped the cane resting across his knees. He had been present at the interview, had looked into Dr. Clarence's eyes, a blue so pale they reminded him of a Siberian dog. The memory unsettled him still, and he wasn't a man who was easily shaken.

"We don't know what happened yet," he pointed out. "Superintendent Barrett can hardly be faulted considering we withheld certain information. I rather doubt he would have believed us anyway."

Vivienne scowled out the window at the rain-blurred grounds. "You may be right, but it was only a matter of time. I've known that since the day Clarence was brought here. The S.P.R. made a bad mistake entrusting him to Greymoor."

"We still don't know for sure—"

"Yes, we do. The killings stopped, didn't they?"

"That could be for any number of reasons," he said stubbornly.

"Including that the creature who committed them is behind bars. Or *was*, at least."

Alec Lawrence buttoned his woolen greatcoat. This was not a new debate. "Perhaps. But there's not a scrap of hard evidence against him. Nothing but a single reference in a report by some American girl and Clarence's own odd demeanor. Had there been more, he would have been locked up tight in Newgate Prison."

Vivienne turned her obsidian gaze on him. With her unlined skin and full lips, she might have been thirty, or a decade in either direction. Only Alec and a handful of others knew better.

"That *American girl* is Arthur Conan Doyle's goddaughter and she seemed quite clever to me. It wouldn't have mattered anyway," she added quietly. "Walls don't hold Dr. Clarence's sort for long."

"Look," he said, softening. "For what it's worth, I think we did the right thing taking him off the streets. I just...." He trailed off, unsure how he meant to finish the thought.

"You don't trust my judgment anymore. Since Harper Dods."

"That's not even remotely true. I simply think we need to keep open minds on the matter. The signs aren't there, Vivienne. I'm the first to admit Dr. Clarence is an odd duck, perhaps worse. But that doesn't mean he isn't human."

Vivienne arched a perfectly sculpted eyebrow. "And yet here we are, summoned by Sidgwick in the middle of the night. I wonder if he's regretting his decision?"

The note from Henry Sidgwick, president of the Society for Psychical Research, had arrived in the form of a small, bedraggled messenger boy pounding on Lady Vivienne's front door in St. James an hour before. It was both vague and ominous, citing an "unfortunate incident" involving Dr. Clarence and urging all due haste to the asylum.

"I suppose we'll find out in a minute," Alec said, turning his collar up. He swiped a hand through chestnut hair and jammed a top hat on his head. "Off to the races."

A gust of rain shook the carriage as it slowed at the front entrance. A six-story tower capped by a Roman clock and white spire anchored two wings extending on either side. Unlike most asylums, which had separate annexes for men and women, Greymoor's residents were all male. The north wing housed those poor souls suffering from garden-variety disorders like dementia and melancholia. The other was reserved for the so-called "incurables," a euphemism for the criminally insane. Violent, unpredictable men deemed unfit for prison.

Despite his doubts, Alec Lawrence would have happily had the lot of them over for tea rather than spend five minutes in the company of Dr. William Clarence. In his heart, he wondered if Vivienne's instincts were correct. But he wanted her to be wrong because the alternative was far worse.

The jouncing of the wooden carriage wheels ceased. A pocket of silence descended, broken only by the steady hiss of the rain on the roof. He watched Lady Cumberland compose herself, smoothing a stray curl into place. The pearl grey gloves seemed to glow against her dark skin. They had been together for many, many years, and frequently disagreed, but he'd never grown tired of looking at her.

Vivienne unclenched her jaw and took a long breath through her nose.

"Shall we, Mr. Lawrence?"

He nodded once, girding himself for what waited inside. The young coachman, Henry, jumped down and opened the carriage door, offering his hand to Vivienne. Freezing rain swept sideways across the heath, soaking them both despite Henry's best efforts to subdue a wildly flapping umbrella. Alec ducked his head against the downpour and used his cane to clamber down. The winter damp always worsened his knee, but he limped swiftly up the stone steps to the welcome shelter of the portico. A tall woman, Vivienne's stride matched his own. Henry snapped the reins and the carriage moved toward the rear stables. Somewhere off in the darkness, Alec heard the mournful baying of a hound.

Moments later they stood dripping on the carpet of Greymoor's small entrance hall. The sour aroma of mutton and boiled cabbage emanated from a distant kitchen. Through the door of an adjacent parlor, Alec glimpsed a fire crackling in the hearth, but the air in the hall was still uncomfortably cold.

A knot of police stood at the end of the corridor. They turned at the newcomers' arrival. Alec recognized the shrewd gaze of Detective Inspector Richard Blackwood. He acted as the liaison between Scotland Yard's Dominion Branch and the S.P.R., of which Alec and Vivienne were members. They'd worked together on several previous cases of a delicate nature, and Alec liked D.I. Blackwood. He was discreet and open-minded, embracing modern methods of investigation while at the same time accepting there were things in the world the general public would be better off staying in the dark about.

"Lady Cumberland," he exclaimed, rushing forward in his usual energetic manner. Blackwood was small and wiry, with prematurely thinning black hair parted on the side and a faint Yorkshire accent. The buttons of his navy uniform had been done up crooked, as if he'd put it on in a hurry. "Mr. Lawrence. I've been waiting for you."

Blackwood steered them into the parlor, which was marginally warmer, and closed the door. Fading rose-printed wallpaper provided the only color in the room. The rest of the furnishings were dark wood, and the paintings arranged above the fireplace —all of bearded men with somber expressions who were either alienists or benefactors of the asylum—did little to enliven things. Alec assumed the parlor served as a waiting room for the patients' relatives, although the place had such an untouched, almost desolate air, he suspected visitors to Greymoor were a rare event.

Alec shrugged off his coat and hung it on a rack. Vivienne leaned against the mantel, letting the heat of the flames dry her sodden cloak. For an instant, he envied her ability to bask in the warmth and light. It was an experience he would never share.

"I have a dead orderly upstairs," Blackwood said unhappily. "And if you two are here, I suppose I can expect things to get worse. Barrett says the patient who did it was voluntarily admitted at the personal request of Mr. Sidgwick."

"Has Clarence escaped?" Vivienne asked.

Blackwood nodded. "Through a window. He must have used a prying tool. We have bloodhounds combing the grounds, but the rain isn't helping any. Time of death was about eleven o'clock. The body was only discovered two hours ago. He's had a head start."

Alec and Vivienne shared a look. "You must tell your men not to approach Clarence under any circumstances," she said. "Should they find him, we'll deal with him ourselves."

"I already did, as soon as I heard the S.P.R. was involved. We know the protocols."

Alec nodded approvingly. Commissioner Warren had been astute to put Blackwood in charge of the Dominion Branch. He didn't take chances.

"What have they told you?" Vivienne asked. "About Dr. Clarence?"

"Practically nothing," Blackwood muttered, dropping heavily into an armchair. "Only that he was admitted four weeks ago after complaining of migraines. No one seems to have an adequate explanation of why he was placed in South Wing. He was the only patient there without a criminal record." He gave them both a level look. "If this is a matter of interest to the S.P.R., I would like very much to know why the Yard wasn't informed earlier."

"The short answer, Inspector? Dr. Clarence is a surgeon with the New York Police Department. Or was, until a few weeks ago." She paused for dramatic effect. "It would cause them a great deal of embarrassment should the newspapers learn he's a suspect in the Whitechapel killings."

"What?' Blackwood sat up straight. "The *Ripper*? I hope you're joking. We've been tearing the city apart for weeks—"

"He's not an official suspect," Alec interjected, shooting Vivienne a quelling look. "There's no physical evidence. None at all. Only circumstantial, and of a nature that cannot be made public, if you get my meaning."

D.I. Blackwood took his cap off and sighed. "Let's have it then."

Vivienne withdrew a cigarette from a silver case and tapped it twice on the lid. Blackwood waited with barely suppressed impatience while she produced a Magic Pocket Lamp, then took a long drag and exhaled a wreath of smoke. "There's a connection between Dr. Clarence and the Jekyll and Hyde case in New York."

"I heard about that," Blackwood said thoughtfully. "Nasty business. They caught him with a little boy in the Beach Transit Tunnel. But I thought it was solved?"

"The man's name was Leland Brady," Alec said, taking a seat on a sofa by the window that was about as cozy as a slab of granite. Lightning flashed in the low skies outside, followed by a rumble of distant thunder. "A perfectly respectable real estate agent who killed five people. Dr. Clarence was present when Brady took his own life. He was treating the suspect's gunshot wound. Shortly afterwards, the doctor quit his post and boarded a ship for England." Alec hesitated. "He arrived just before Polly Nichols was butchered on August 31st."

D.I. Blackwood said nothing. He knew there was more to it than that.

"Before he died, Brady wrote a letter to his wife," Vivienne said, flicking ashes in the general direction of the fireplace. Alec, ever fastidious, tried not to wince. "It expressed his belief that he was possessed by a demonic entity, and contained the words 'From Hell.' The letter was written in early August. You do see the significance?"

Blackwood rubbed his chin. "Aye. The note with that same phrase from the Ripper wasn't sent until weeks later. Christ, it was the one with the piece of kidney, wasn't it? What else?" He rested his hands on his knees. "Are you saying Clarence is a ghoul? That Brady somehow infected him?"

"He passed the iron test," Alec said quietly.

"Definitively?"

"Yes. He also spoke to us quite normally, although he admitted to suffering from headaches. What about the dogs? How did they react to his scent on the bedclothes?"

"No frenzied barking, not like they would for a ghoul. One or two did whimper rather strangely. I wasn't sure how to interpret it. But you say Clarence passed the iron test. And he carried on a conversation. Doesn't that settle it, then?"

"Not for me," Vivienne said. "There are too many oddities in the Brady case. Evidence that doesn't quite add up. And now we have another killing."

Blackwood stared at her uncertainly. "But if it's not a ghoul and it's not a man…what is it?"

"Something different."

"Such as?"

"I've no idea, Inspector."

Vivienne's tone remained level, but Alec sensed her frustration. This was essentially the same conversation she'd had with Sidgwick a month ago.

"All right." Blackwood pressed a hand against his forehead as if it pained him. Alec understood. It was a lot to digest in one lump. He still wasn't sure what to make of it all himself. "You say there were oddities in the New York crimes."

"A few. The report claimed that fingerprints were burned into one victim's throat," Alec said, earning a grateful look from Vivienne. "An actress named Anne Marlowe."

The inspector leaned forward. They'd caught his interest. "Have you seen anything like that before?"

"Never," Alec conceded.

"Who wrote the report?"

"An amateur detective in New York named Harrison Fearing Pell."

"Fearing Pell? As in Myrtle Fearing Pell?"

"Harrison is the younger sister."

"I've heard of Myrtle. The Yard called her in last year on a rather bizarre extortion case involving the Duke of Argyll. Solved it in record time, apparently. Is the sister any good?"

"Well, she managed to catch Mr. Brady, so I'd say she's quite competent," Vivienne said. "Her summary of the case came to us through Arthur Conan Doyle. He thought the Society would be interested because of the occult features." Her mouth tightened. "Unfortunately, Miss Pell's report sat under a heap of papers on Mr. Sidgwick's desk for nearly three weeks before he read it and passed it on. Had we known about it sooner, Mary Jane Kelly might still be alive."

They were all silent for a moment. Kelly had been the last of the Ripper's victims, and the most savagely treated. She'd died on November 9th, bringing the number of confirmed murders to five. Fear still gripped the city of London, although the man who called himself Jack appeared to have vanished as suddenly as he'd arrived.

"We found Dr. Clarence on November 12th in Cheapside," Alec said. "He wasn't hard to trace. The lodgings had been rented under his own name."

Alec had a sudden memory of that night. Kicking open the door of a squalid room. William Clarence sitting on the edge of his bed, neatly dressed in a dark suit, black leather bag between his feet—the same bag Leland Brady had seized a scalpel from to cut his own throat.

The doctor slowly lifted his head. He didn't seem surprised or alarmed at the sudden intrusion.
Yes?
You're to come with us, sir, Alec said firmly.
Dr. William Clarence smiled.
Certainly. If you say so.

"He came along readily enough," Alec continued. "That in itself was rather peculiar, considering he claimed to be on holiday. But in light of the fact that we had no case against him—either on the Whitechapel murders or anything else—Mr. Sidgwick suggested he be committed to Greymoor. For observation."

"He's been locked up here ever since, against my strenuous objections," Vivienne said.

In fact, she had wanted to cut his head off, but Sidgwick wouldn't permit it. Not without proof; not after the Harper Dods fiasco.

"The timeline of Ripper killings does fit." Blackwood thought for a moment. "With all due respect, it's still rather thin, milady. But I'll send some extra men to Whitechapel. If nothing else, Dr. Clarence is a confirmed murderer now. Where were his lodgings?"

Alec recited the address and Blackwood went into the hall to notify the officers waiting there.

"The Met will check out Cheapside," he said when he returned. "Where else would Dr. Clarence go?"

"I haven't a clue." Vivienne tossed her cigarette into the hearth.

"What about you? Would Dr. Clarence hold a grudge for bringing him here?"

"I doubt it. He has all of London to terrorize. No, I'm afraid we'll find out soon enough where he's gone. Now, perhaps we should see this poor orderly. What was his name?"

"John Davis Pyle. We've already taken statements from the staff, but I ordered the police surgeon to leave the body as it is until you had a chance to examine it."

"Where's Superintendent Barrett?"

"Upstairs with Dr. Cavendish. He was Clarence's attending physician. Cavendish arrived just before you did, I haven't spoken to him yet. Do they know about any of what you've just told me?"

"No," Vivienne said with disgust. "Sidgwick insisted on complete secrecy. I suspect there was some pressure from the S.P.R. in New York. They're all convinced the iron test is infallible. Anyway, Sidgwick and Barrett were school chums at Eton. I'm sure it helped grease the wheels."

"Well, I suppose that explains the South Wing. But next time, I'll thank you to take me into your confidence sooner. I'm not sure what we could have done to prevent Pyle's murder, but we don't need another incident like Buckingham Palace. Her Majesty would not be amused."

"You're right, Inspector, and I apologize," Vivienne said. "We should have come to you straight away."

Somewhat mollified by the sincerity in her voice, Blackwood led them to twin curving staircases at the end of the hall. A grandfather clock on the landing sonorously chimed the hour: half past three. They turned right, away from the quiet, airy north annex toward South Wing where Dr. William Clarence had spent the last thirty-three days in solitary confinement. At the top of the stairs, a burly attendant waited by an oaken door. He seemed to expect them and produced a ring of iron keys.

"I hope you catch him," he said, unlocking the door. "Pyle was a good man. Didn't deserve such an end as that brute gave him."

"Don't worry," Blackwood said firmly. "We won't rest until Clarence is found."

The attendant shook his head. "He's the last one I would've expected to snap like that. Never gave us any trouble. Quiet as a mouse." He gave a resigned sigh. "Sometimes I wonder if we aren't mad ourselves, working in this place." The attendant stood aside to let them pass. "The other patients have been riled up since it happened. Don't pay 'em any mind, milady."

The heavy door closed behind them, the tumblers echoing in the silent corridor. They passed an empty day room and several offices for the resident physicians. Around a corner, the cells began. Despite the wave of reforms that had swept England's mental institutions mid-century, Greymoor's secure wing harkened back to an earlier era when the mad were treated like feral beasts. Alec understood this was less a reflection on the asylum itself than the character of the men it was entrusted with.

Slack, unshaven faces pressed against the small grates of the cells. When they saw Vivienne, a collective howl went up, like chained dogs catching the scent of a hare. Blackwood flushed at the lewd and venomous suggestions hissed through broken yellow teeth. Vivienne didn't appear to notice. Alec, on the other hand, gripped his cane with such force the silver falcon on the handle bit deeply into his palm.

"Black African whore," one of the inmates growled.

Alec's stride didn't slow as he passed the man's cell. He kept his eyes straight ahead. But a smile spread across his face as he heard a soft thud and cry of surprise.

"Witchcraft!" the man choked from the dark recesses of his cell. "She done hit me with an invisible cudgel!"

The other inmates erupted in loud laughter at this, and the vicious mood seemed to lighten. "Shut up, the lot of you!" an excited voice yelled. "She'll think we're all as barmy as poor Hobbes. Fer feck's sake, mind yer goddamn manners. There's a lady present."

"I ain't barmy," Hobbes moaned. "Somethin' clobbered me."

His fellow inmates began to debate the relative merits of Hobbes' sanity as they reached the end of the corridor.

"Really, Alec." Vivienne glanced over her shoulder.

He raised an innocent eyebrow. "What?"

"I think Mr. Blackwood would agree that we should exercise discretion."

Blackwood shrugged, sharing an amused look with Alec. "I didn't see anything. The fellow's quite mad, of course. I doubt anyone will believe him."

They turned another corner. The smell of boiled cabbage grew stronger, then faded away. The cells in the furthest part of the ward sat empty, except for one at the very end, where a pair of constables guarded a door that stood slightly ajar. The light of a lantern spilled through the crack. Vivienne rushed ahead, long skirts rustling like dry leaves in the wind. There'd been no time to change and she still wore the sea green evening gown she had on when the messenger boy arrived.

"It's not a pleasant sight," Blackwood warned. "Not at all.

Perhaps Mr. Lawrence…." He trailed off under Vivienne's cool gaze.

"I'll be perfectly fine, Mr. Blackwood."

The inspector nodded to the constables, who stepped aside so Vivienne and Alec could enter.

The cell was bare save for a rusted iron bedframe and mattress. Someone had placed a lantern just inside the door. Rainwater pooled on the floor where it swept in through a broken window set high in the opposite wall. The bars had been bent to either side, leaving an opening just large enough for a man to squeeze through and drop to the ground outside.

Alec had a sudden vision of Dr. Clarence wiggling between them like an eel, his light blue eyes fixed on the damp grass below.

John Davis Pyle sat against the bedframe with his chin resting on his right collarbone. He would have been handsome in life. Strong jaw, dark wavy hair. A boyish face, with faint laugh lines at the corners of his mouth that spoke of an amiable disposition. Pyle's eyes were half-open, lips parted, in a posture that suggested a man dozing off in his favorite armchair.

Vivienne cautiously approached the body, skirting the large pool of blood. The attendant's navy blue uniform had soaked up a good deal of it. The only visible blood on his person was a large swath on the left side of his neck. It had flowed down from the ear, where a fountain pen had been embedded to a depth of five inches or so.

"Goddess," Vivienne murmured. "It looks like Clarence must have caught him by surprise." She studied the angle of the wound. "He attacked from the side and slightly behind, I would think." Her face softened with pity. "Oh, Henry Pyle. What on earth did he say to convince you to open the door?"

Alec turned away from the gruesome sight and moved to the window to examine the bars.

"There are no tool marks," he observed. "Bring over the lantern, would you?"

Vivienne obliged, while Blackwood watched from the door. Alec's keen eyes took in every inch of the twisted iron. What he saw made his breath catch in his throat. He stared at the patterns, willing them to go away or rearrange themselves into something less horrifying.

"What is it?" Vivienne demanded.

"There are finger marks burned into the bars," he said in a low voice. "Clarence did this with his bare hands. Some sort of heat transference, just like the Brady case."

Blackwood laughed weakly. "But that's—"

"Impossible?" Vivienne let the word dangle in the air.

They turned at the sound of footsteps approaching in the corridor.

"Lady Cumberland!" A small man with a wispy ginger mustache that quivered like a shy animal peered over Blackwood's shoulder. His gaze landed on Pyle and darted quickly away. "Terrible business. Where is Mr. Sidgwick? I'd expected him to come personally."

"Superintendent Barrett," Vivienne said, moving quickly away from the window. "Mr. Sidgwick has been unavoidably delayed. He asked us to come in his stead."

They returned to the hallway, where a second man in a tweed suit stood wringing his hands. "I see." Barrett gestured to his companion. "I believe you know Dr. Cavendish?"

Vivienne inclined her head. "We met briefly following Dr. Clarence's admission."

Barrett introduced D.I. Blackwood, and Dr. Cavendish shook the detective's hand. He was tall and grey-haired with a perpetual look of injured surprise, as though someone had just slammed a door in his face.

"There was no indication he would do something like this," Dr. Cavendish burst out in a defensive tone. "He stopped speaking entirely three weeks ago, but he never behaved in an aggressive or self-destructive manner. Quite the opposite. The man was practically catatonic."

"If I may ask," Blackwood said politely. "Where did he get the fountain pen?"

Dr. Cavendish studied the ceiling. "I'm afraid it came from my office."

"He was to be kept in total isolation," Vivienne said, her voice cold. "I thought that was unambiguous."

"This is a mental institution, Lady Cumberland, not a medieval dungeon." He puffed his chest out, a primate asserting home turf dominance. "It's my duty to carry out periodic assessments of my patients. I assure you, he was accompanied by four attendants at all times. I'm not sure how he managed to steal it."

"No one's blaming you, Dr. Cavendish," Barrett said, frowning at Vivienne.

"I last saw Clarence this afternoon. Very briefly, for fifteen minutes perhaps. I asked him a series of questions and received no response. Frankly, I couldn't say if he even heard me." Dr. Cavendish paused. "Something rather odd did happen. I was just signaling to Pyle and Stokes to take him back to his cell when he mumbled a phrase."

"What was it?" Blackwood asked eagerly.

"I can't be certain, but it sounded like, 'They're here.' That's all. Then he resumed his catatonic state."

"They're here," the inspector repeated. "Was he looking at anything in particular in your office when he said it?"

"I believe he was looking out the window."

"Did he have any visitors while he was at Greymoor?" Alec asked.

"None."

"Do you know how he spent his days?"

"Whenever I looked in on him, he'd be sitting on his bed, hands folded. Staring off into space. We only had one troubling incident, near the beginning of his stay here. The patients are not permitted writing materials of course"—he seemed to remember Pyle and paled a bit—"but that doesn't prevent them from... communicating in other ways." Dr. Cavendish glanced at Vivienne with obvious discomfort. "I don't think it's appropriate to relate in front of a lady, begging your pardon."

"It's all right, Doctor," Vivienne said in an amused tone. "I won't be offended. Please go on."

He took a breath. "Well, he did write something on the walls of his cell. In..." Cavendish coughed. "I'm afraid it was his own feces. Over and over. It was at that point that Mr. Barrett and I agreed he should be kept indefinitely."

"What did he write?" Blackwood asked.

"A Latin phrase." He searched his memory. "*Pervadunt oculus*, I believe it was."

"They come through the eyes," Alec said softly.

"I see you know your Latin, Mr. Lawrence," Dr. Cavendish said approvingly. "I assumed he meant the headaches. Migraines are often accompanied by a phenomenon we call auras. It's a shimmering light viewed in the peripheral field of vision. They commonly precede onset."

D.I. Blackwood shot Alec a questioning look. Alec gave him the barest nod.

"Well, you've been very helpful, Dr. Cavendish," the inspector said briskly. "If there isn't anything else, I think we're done here for now. I'll write up your statement. You can sign it later."

Dr. Cavendish seemed relieved to be off the hook. "Indeed. Such a tragedy. I do hope your men find him quickly. Good day, gentlemen. Lady Cumberland." He gave a brief bow and fairly scampered off down the corridor, eager to get away from the macabre scene lurking behind Clarence's half-open cell door. Alec didn't blame him in the least.

"The morgue wagon is waiting downstairs," Blackwood said to Superintendent Barrett. "I'll have Mr. Pyle removed now."

"Poor Pyle." Barrett shook his head. "He has three children, you know. I'll organize a collection for the family."

"Please allow me to contribute," Vivienne said immediately, offering him a card. "I…well, we brought him here. I feel responsible."

"That's kind of you, Lady Cumberland, but I don't blame you, nor Mr. Sidgwick. I've been superintendent of this asylum for more than twenty years and know better than anyone how difficult it can be to predict human behavior." He stroked his mustache. "The soul of man is larger than the sky…ah, deeper than ocean or…or…."

"The abysmal dark of the unfathom'd centre," Alec finished quietly.

"Yes, that's it! You're an admirer of Hartley Coleridge, Mr. Lawrence?"

"I enjoy poetry," he admitted. *"Though my soul may set in darkness, it will rise in perfect light. I have loved the stars too fondly to be fearful of the night."*

"Splendid. I'm not sure I know that one. What's his name?"

"It's a woman, actually. Sarah Williams."

"Indeed." Barrett seemed to lose interest. "Well, I can vouch that the mind is a strange and confounding place. We may never know what drove Dr. Clarence to this unspeakable act."

"Perhaps. But I still wish to help his family," Vivienne said, and Alec understood that she would carry her burden of guilt no matter what anyone said.

"I'm sure it will be appreciated, thank you, Lady Cumberland. Shall I accompany you out?" Barrett looked down the corridor, in the direction of the other occupied cells. "They've been worse since Clarence came. I can't fathom why. He kept to himself."

"Thank you, but we can see our own way," Blackwood replied. "Good day, Mr. Barrett."

They made their way back through the cells. Dim wall sconces cast pools of alternating light and darkness. No bright electric bulbs, Alec thought. Not here, in this forgotten place. The usual cacophony of deranged voices accompanied their progress, but it was more subdued this time around, as though the men shared their foreboding.

It was in one of the pools of shadow that he heard a whisper from the cell next to him. Alec stopped, facing the grill set into the door at head height.

"What did you say?" he asked softly.

Ahead, Vivienne and D.I. Blackwood turned to stare at him.

"Alec?" Vivienne called.

He could see nothing beyond the grill but more darkness. Whoever was inside didn't respond.

"Never mind," he said.

Alec limped toward them, the iron tip of his cane clacking on the stone floor. Vivienne watched him for a moment, then followed Blackwood to the stairway. Alec glanced back once. The ward had gone quiet again, but he was certain of what he'd heard.

Two words.

They're here.

Alec retrieved his coat and hat from the parlor. Barrett paused at the front door. "Pervadunt oculus. You've heard that phrase before."

"It was in the Brady report," Alec said. "He scratched it on the walls of the Beach Transit Tunnel."

"What in blazes are we dealing with?"

"Not a ghoul." Alec needed to think. To talk with Vivienne. "Something worse, I fear."

"It might not be in Dr. Clarence anymore," Vivienne said. "You should be aware of that possibility."

Blackwood swore under his breath. "Then how do we catch it?"

Neither of them replied. Alec leaned heavily on his cane. His knee throbbed from all the stairs. For some reason, going down was always worse than going up.

"Well, that's the problem," he said at last. "I think we'll have to get very lucky."

"I'll need a copy of that Hyde report," Blackwood said.

"I'll have it sent over straight away."

"Stay in touch. If you come up with something."

Outside, the rain had eased to a light mist. Alec scanned the grounds as they waited for Henry to bring the carriage around. He could still hear the faint baying of the dogs, but knew in his bones Clarence was gone.

"What do we tell Sidgwick?" he asked at last.

"The truth," Vivienne replied, lighting another cigarette.

"Those are bad for you, you know," Alec pointed out. "No matter what they claim."

Vivienne rolled her eyes. Alec turned away, but a faint smile played on his lips.

CHAPTER 2

Dawn broke as they joined the flow of traffic back into London. Even at this early hour, the streets were jammed with carriages and omnibuses and people walking to their jobs in factories or shops. At Vivienne's request, Henry took the Bow Road back into the city, which became Mile End Road and finally, Whitechapel Road. The thoroughfare itself was broad and busy, but the maze of alleys and side streets to either side concealed some of the worst slums in London. Clarence's old hunting ground.

Neither of them spoke much. Vivienne stared out the carriage window, scanning the faces of the people on the street. The sober ones who had just woken up for work looked tired already, stoically ignoring the drunk ones who hadn't gone to bed yet. Barefoot children played in the muck before rows of drab brick buildings. Vivienne's gaze lingered on the children. Alec knew Brady had killed a boy in New York. An organ grinder.

She'd been right about Dr. Clarence all along, but she didn't rub it in his face, which Alec found surprising given Vivienne's propensity for gloating. It occurred to him that perhaps she hadn't wanted to be right, either.

A few minutes later, Henry deposited them at the front door of 19 Buckingham Street off the Strand where the Society for Psychical Research kept a suite of rooms. It had been formed in January 1882 to investigate growing claims of spiritualist phenomena using rigorous scientific methods. That remained its primary mission, but following certain dire events at Buckingham Palace in 1886, a small and entirely secret subcommittee had been formed to deal with more dangerous aspects of the occult. This coincided with the creation of the Dominion Branch of Scotland Yard, and the two entities worked in tandem—with the Queen's blessing—to contain the undead ghouls that plagued Britain.

Vivienne and Alec went straight to the library, where Henry Sidgwick waited with a tray of tea. He sat erect, bushy black beard falling down his chest, a sheaf of papers held loosely in his large hands.

"Well?" he inquired without preamble. "How bad is it?"

"We have a problem," Alec said, pouring himself a cup and dropping into a wing chair. "Potentially quite serious."

"Potentially?" Vivienne repeated. "I'd say it's very serious indeed."

She removed her cloak and tossed it carelessly on an ottoman. Her ball gown was sleeveless. Gold glinted in the light of the lamps—a thick bracelet circling her right wrist. Words flowed across the metal in a script that had not been spoken aloud for more than two thousand years.

"Do you know what this says?" she asked Sidgwick, holding up the cuff.

"I've always wondered," he replied dryly.

"*We are the light against the darkness*. And now we've failed in our duty. Clarence is gone," she said bitterly. "Escaped. He murdered an orderly. There's no doubt it's the same creature that ran loose in New York. None at all."

"Dear God." Mr. Sidgwick turned to Alec, who could usually be relied on not to embellish the facts. "Is this true?"

Alec nodded wearily.

"Tell me everything."

So he did, while Vivienne paced the room like a caged lynx, skirts swishing.

"What exactly do you think we're dealing with?" Sidgwick asked when he'd finished.

"Your guess is as good as mine."

Sidgwick shut his eyes. "I'm still coming around to believing in ghouls. Not that I doubt it anymore, their existence is an unfortunate fact of life in England, it seems. Now you're telling me we have a creature that looks and sounds human but can burn iron bars with its hands and do God only knows what else. Is it undead?"

"Probably." Vivienne snapped her lighter shut and blew out a stream of smoke.

"Most definitely," Alec added cheerfully. The hot, strong tea—three cups of it—had worked its humble magic. It was one of the few English customs he embraced with open arms.

"Dear God," Sidgwick said again.

Vivienne dropped onto a settee and crossed her ankles. "We need to consult Cyrus. He might know something."

"Agreed. I'll send Mr. Ashdown a cable. When can you leave?"

"It would be better if he came to London," Alec said.

"He won't want to," Vivienne pointed out. "You know he hasn't left Ingress Abbey in more than eight years."

"If Barrett's men do manage to find the good doctor, or whoever he's taken, we need to stay close."

"Do you think you can kill it?" Sidgwick asked.

"It's already dead," Alec reminded him.

"That was a figure of speech."

"We can try to banish it back to the Dominion through a Greater Gate." Alec had rolled up his shirtsleeves and propped his

24

feet on the edge of the ottoman. He idly traced the curving script on his own cuff, a match of Vivienne's. "So, The Serpentine. It's by far the closest one."

Sidgwick swallowed. "I went boating in Hyde Park just a few months ago. Are you saying—?"

"That there's a portal to the Underworld beneath the lake? Yes, but only in parts."

"And they're safely warded." Vivienne looked at Alec. "Aren't they?"

"Most assuredly."

"How do you know the wards haven't been broken?" Sidgwick persisted. "I don't find your explanation to be the least bit comforting."

"Because I know." Alec gave a thin smile. "I have the only talisman."

Sidgwick grunted. "You should have told me all this before."

"It didn't seem necessary. Nothing comes through the Gates anymore."

"So you believe it was summoned?"

"Had to be. By a powerful necromancer, I'd say."

"But if it came from New York, that would be the American branch's problem." Sidgwick brightened.

"The necromancer, not the whatever-it-is."

"True. I'll send a cable to Orpha Winter. Any chance this"—he consulted the papers—"Becky Rickard was the one who brought it through?"

"Brady's first victim?" Vivienne said. "She was a medium, but that's hardly the same thing as a necromancer. In fact, she was disgraced as fraudulent. It doesn't seem likely."

"Whoever brought it through, the thing is loose now," Alec said. "And the usual rules don't seem to apply."

"We'll have to tell the Queen." Sidgwick's tone was funereal.

"I suppose you will." Alec's choice of pronoun was not lost on Henry Sidgwick, whose dark, close-set eyes narrowed.

"She won't like it one bit."

"Not much to like, is there?"

"I need to be able to tell Her Majesty truthfully that we have the situation under control."

Alec picked up his teacup, saw with disappointment that it was empty, and replaced it in the saucer. "Of course. I don't see a problem as long as you omit the word *truthfully*."

"Gentlemen," Vivienne interrupted. "This is getting us nowhere. When Dr. Clarence is found, which we all hope will be sooner rather than later, Alec and I are fully capable of disposing of him."

Sidgwick brightened again. "Well, that's good news."

"We are?" Alec said, earning a withering look from Vivienne.

"Yes. So we'll put off visiting Cyrus for now, at least until we hear from Inspector Blackwood. Do send that cable though, Mr. Sidgwick. Cyrus can search the archives. They go back quite a long way, as you know. Perhaps he can find a reference to something similar."

"What about your original interview with Dr. Clarence?" Sidgwick sifted through the sheaf of papers. "I have it here somewhere. Ah, yes...."

He began to read the transcript aloud. Alec knew it all first-hand. Vivienne had conducted the interview in the empty dayroom at Greymoor while he stood by at the door, ready to unleash a whip-crack of power should Clarence do anything Alec found objectionable.

The doctor had sat in a chair facing Vivienne. He wore a woolen suit and held a small valise on his lap. It contained toiletries and a change of clothing. Alec had kept his black surgeon's bag, with its syringes and vials and other tools of the trade. Including a set of exquisitely sharp knives.

Even as Henry Sidgwick's pleasantly deep and learned voice recited the transcript—he was a professor of moral philosophy at

Trinity College, after all—Alec heard the echo of two other voices in his head....

"WOULD YOU STATE YOUR NAME, PLEASE?"

"William Howard Clarence, of 34 Greenwich Street, New York."

"Do you know why you're here, Dr. Clarence?"

Clarence raised a hand to his forehead. "I...I've been suffering from headaches."

"Why did you come to England?"

"I had a difficult case. A man used my scalpel to..." His fingers fluttered limply. They were small, delicate hands. "May I have some water? My mouth is very dry."

Alec signaled to the attendant who waited outside. A minute later he returned with a glass.

"Thank you."

"You mentioned a difficult case," Vivienne resumed. "Do you mean Leland Brady?"

"Yes. I wished for a change of scenery."

"You booked passage on the RMS Umbria, which arrived in Liverpool on the 25th of August. What did you do then?"

His eyes grew vague. "I don't know. I walked around. Looked for lodgings. I think I visited St. Paul's Cathedral."

"Where were you on the evening of August 31st?"

"What day of the week was that?"

"A Friday."

"Well, I'm not sure. If my head was very bad, I might have gone to bed early."

"Have you experienced lost time?"

"What do you mean by that?"

"Periods in which you cannot recollect your own actions. Places you might have gone."

"No." The sun crept across the floor. A shaft of light fell across

Dr. Clarence's face and his pupils suddenly contracted. "Just the headaches."

"What about the evening of September 8th?"

"I've no idea."

"September 30th?" Vivienne persisted.

"Why are you asking me these questions?"

"Mary Ann Nichols. Annie Chapman. Elizabeth Stride. Catherine Eddowes. Mary Jane Kelly. Are you familiar with these names?"

Clarence held her gaze. "Of course I've heard about the murders. They're all over the newspapers."

"What sort of man do you think the police should be looking for?"

"Are you accusing me of these heinous crimes?"

"Not at all. I'm simply curious about your professional opinion. Having just concluded the Hyde case."

Clarence folded his hands atop the valise. "He must be reasonably clever to have eluded the police. Whitechapel is a busy area."

"Have you been there?"

"No. I read about it in the newspaper. I wouldn't frequent that sort of place. It sounds like a cesspool."

"Why do you think he does it?"

"Why?" A ripple passed over his features. "I'm not sure that question has a satisfactory answer, Lady Cumberland. Why does the earth suddenly slip its moorings and crush the little ants crawling across the surface?"

Vivienne's jaw tightened. Alec sensed the fury simmering beneath her calm exterior.

"Are you saying these women are insects, Dr. Clarence?"

He sighed. "You misunderstand."

They looked at each other for a long moment.

"Or are you saying Jack is a force of nature?"

Dr. Clarence smiled. "That might be overstating it. I merely mean that these killings strike me as perfectly senseless. There's no more meaning to them than the eruption of that volcano in Japan last summer." He grew solemn again. "I do hope they catch him."

"As do we all."

Dr. Clarence rose and walked to the window. It looked out across the grounds, brown fields meeting white sky in the soft, monotonous palette of midwinter. "Will I be staying here?"

Vivienne looked at Alec. They'd reached the tricky part. Dr. Clarence had committed no crime, not that could be proven. He was an American citizen and member of the New York City Police Department. If he refused to admit himself to Greymoor and the consulate got involved, it would be a diplomatic nightmare. And Clarence would almost certainly end up slipping the net.

Fortunately, he had no wife or children. No one looking for him. By all accounts, his life in New York had been quiet and solitary.

"Dr. Cavendish believes he can help you with your headaches," Vivienne said. She forced a smile. "A nice rest might do you good."

Dr. Clarence raised a hand and curled it around the iron bars. Something in the gesture struck Alec as calculated, deliberate, although Clarence kept his back to them.

He's toying with us.

Alec pushed the unbidden thought aside.

You're letting Vivienne's emotions cloud your judgment. Don't.

"That would be most amenable," Dr. Clarence said, returning to his chair.

Vivienne leaned forward and offered him a piece of paper. Their hands brushed and despite his misgivings, Alec's heart beat faster.

"Thank you." Dr. Clarence laid the form on his valise. He

patted his pockets. "I'm sorry, but do you have a pen I might borrow?"

Vivienne gave him one. She waited, eyes fixed on the form.

Dr. Clarence paused, pen hovering over the paper. "How long would I be at Greymoor?"

"Just a short time," Vivienne lied. "For observation. You can leave anytime you like."

"All right, then." Clarence didn't bother to read the form. He signed with a flourish and handed it back. "Here you are."

Vivienne scanned the document. It gave the doctors at Greymoor full legal authority to commit Dr. William Howard Clarence to the asylum until such time as they deemed him no longer a danger to himself or others. Alec knew that if Vivienne had her way, that day would never come.

"Thank you." She stood up. "The attendants will see to you now. Good afternoon, doctor." She'd reached the door before she stopped and turned back. "I believe you still have my fountain pen."

Dr. Clarence looked down at his hands. "Oh, I'm awfully sorry. Here you are."

He rose and gave Vivienne back the pen. His eyes met Alec's for a single instant. They seemed to sparkle with some private amusement.

The attendant closed the heavy door. Alec waited to make sure he locked it.

Later, when they delivered the admission forms to Superintendent Barrett, he'd asked if sedation would be appropriate….

"OH YES, give him everything you've got," Vivienne was saying. "We promised Inspector Blackwood we'd share the full report from Miss Pell."

"I'll see it's done right away," Sidgwick said.

Alec came back to the present with a start.

"Send the report to Cyrus too," he chimed in, hoping no one would notice his long absence from the conversation.

Sidgwick frowned. Vivienne sighed. "English, Alec. You're lapsing into Greek again."

"Sorry." He repeated the request.

"He does that all the time." She stabbed her cigarette into a heavy bronze ashtray. "It's not even modern Greek. Some obscure third-century dialect only a handful of scholars have ever heard of."

Alec smiled apologetically. He'd probably forgotten more languages than he remembered, and he knew dozens fluently. Hundreds. Different places, different times. Different lives. It all swirled together in his head sometimes. Vivienne was much better at keeping the past neatly arranged. She was a perfect chameleon. It had only taken her a week to acquire a posh British accent, while Alec still sounded vaguely "Continental."

Alec spun the cane in his hands, suddenly full of restless energy. Outside the window, he could hear the clamor of London's five million souls rushing through their day. He had been many places in his long life, but never had he seen a city quite like this one. He'd watched it grow from a backwater of the Roman Empire to the undisputed capital of the world. Watched the factories rise like smog-belching dragons. Stood under the bright glare of electric lights, Vivienne on his arm, to see one of her plays. The pace of scientific progress was as swift as the steam trains that fascinated him so. The only thing that hadn't changed was the weather, he reflected.

It was still lousy.

"So what do we do now?" Sidgwick asked.

"Either Blackwood and his men will find Clarence," Vivienne said. "Or he'll do something to draw attention to himself."

Kill again, she meant.

"So we wait."

"Yes." Vivienne lit another cigarette. "We wait."

CHAPTER 3

Vivienne's townhouse on Park Place was a five-minute carriage ride from the Society's offices. The butler, Quimby, greeted them at the door. Tall and large-nosed with a rumbling baritone, he had served Lord Cumberland's family for more than thirty years and was the soul of discretion.

"Do you care for breakfast, milady?" he inquired.

"Just coffee, Quimby, thank you," Vivienne said with a tired smile. "We'll take it in the conservatory."

Alec followed her through the black-and-white tiled entry hall to a glass-enclosed sunroom facing the rear garden. It was Vivienne's favorite room, filled with comfortable wicker furniture and a riot of potted plants. Alec inhaled the honeyed scent of cymbidium orchids, their pink and white blossoms nodding like drowsy children.

"I miss the old days when we were free agents," Vivienne said. "The S.P.R. is well-intentioned, but they don't seem to grasp the fact that this is a war—and we're losing. Clarence was in our hands, Alec. Now he's gone. We may not get another chance."

Alec sighed. "Even if we do, this thing can use fire. That puts me at a major disadvantage."

Vivienne said nothing, but her face could have been carved from stone. Alec knew she feared fire above all things, not for her own sake, but for his.

"You'll have to hold my power," he said.

She nodded. "As much as I hate doing it, I don't see any other choice."

"So the question now is how to track him." Alec sat down, resting his cane across his knees. "If only there was some pattern. But the murders in New York and London were random, senseless. Just as Dr. Clarence said. There's no connection between any of the victims."

"The Ripper's were all prostitutes."

"Because they're easy prey. Drunk, alone on the streets late at night. That's all. He killed them for entertainment, Vivienne. But what if he's looking for someone or something specific now?"

"Such as?"

"Clarence stayed quietly at the asylum for nearly a month. Something set him off." He stared unseeing at the garden. Just a few feet away, beyond the warmth of the greenhouse, everything lay dead and dormant, waiting for spring. "On our way out, one of the inmates whispered the same phrase to me, Viv. *They're here.*"

"Barrett said he had no visitors. Could it be something inside the asylum?"

"I don't think so. He went straight out the window, even though the cell door was open. Heading for London."

"Well, that narrows it down." She picked up a figurine of a squat woman with pendulous breasts. Vivienne still believed in the old goddesses. She kept a small shrine to them in the conservatory. Mami Natu, who had made humanity from the flesh of her left buttock. Vengeful Kavi of the nine flails. Innunu, her crocodile-skinned patron, the goddess of justice. Alec thought it quite possible that Vivienne was the last person on earth who remembered their names.

"Thank you, Quimby," she said, as the butler returned with a silver tray bearing a pot of coffee and yesterday's mail.

"You have a letter from Lord Cumberland," he replied, pouring them cups—black for Vivienne, cream and two sugars for Alec. "Does her ladyship care for anything else?"

She gave him a warm smile. "That's all for now."

The butler nodded and withdrew.

"How's Nathaniel?" Alec asked, as Vivienne scanned the letter.

"Sounds happy. He wants to know if we're coming up for Christmas."

"Two weeks from now? Unlikely."

Vivienne began to uncoil her braid. Freed from its prison, her hair puffed up like a black thundercloud. "Nathaniel says he won't speak to me if I miss our anniversary again." She sounded amused.

Nathaniel Cumberland, the dashing young Marquess of Abergavenny, had proposed to Vivienne on Christmas Eve two years before in a burst of enthusiasm fueled by mulled wine and the dire state of his bank account. They had been close friends for several years, though not romantically involved (Nathaniel discreetly but emphatically preferred the company of men). Like much of the old aristocracy, he was rich in land and poor in actual money.

Vivienne, on the other hand, happened to be very rich and the match appealed to her. Titles opened doors that would otherwise be closed, especially for a woman of African descent. So they were married, with Alec's blessing, and Vivienne became Lady Cumberland. She and Alec took possession of the St. James townhouse while Nathaniel promptly returned to his family seat of Eridge Castle, a gothic pile in Sussex.

Everyone assumed that Alec Lawrence was Vivienne's lover, although she claimed he was her personal secretary. It was all more than a bit scandalous. But once the dust had settled, and Nathaniel put it about that Vivienne was descended from the last of the Malian emperors, invitations began to roll in. Hence the ball gown. She'd been at a soiree hosted by the Earl of Lindsay earlier that evening. Alec had stayed home. He wasn't much for parties.

"I'll tell him we have a complicated case," she said. "It's the truth."

"You're taking this awfully well," Alec said.

Her slightly tilted eyes narrowed a fraction. "What does that mean?"

"It means I thought you'd hold a grudge for being overridden on Clarence."

"It's not my style."

Alec laughed. "Right."

Vivienne stood up, annoyed. "I'm going upstairs. This corset wasn't mean to be worn for nine hours straight."

Alec put his leg up on the chair she'd just vacated.

"Think I'll stay down here for a bit. Can I read Nathaniel's letter?"

"Go ahead. He asked after you."

Alec smiled, pleased with himself. She knew he liked Nathaniel, although not in precisely the same way Nathaniel liked Alec. It was an old joke between them.

Vivienne retired to her large bedroom on the second floor. Her maid, Claudine, helped her strip off the evening gown and undergarments. She knew she should go to bed but couldn't stop thinking of Henry Pyle.

We did that. Brought a monster into their midst with no warning. He never stood a chance.

"Shall I draw a bath?"

"Not just yet. I'll take the black tunic and trousers."

Claudine smiled, one side of her mouth lower than the other from the scar there. "Going a round with Mr. Lawrence?" she asked in a lilting West Indian accent.

"If I can lure him into it."

"Ah, he's always game, isn't he?"

"Because he's a show-off."

This wasn't fair and Vivienne instantly regretted saying it. Despite the fact that Alec was stronger and faster by several magnitudes, he never used it against her. Quite the opposite. But he'd always been able to read her. In fact, she *was* angry at him for not taking her side about Clarence when it might still have mattered.

"I'll wait," Claudine said, suppressing a yawn. "In case you want the bath after."

Vivienne squeezed her hand. "Go take a rest. I know you were up all night waiting for us. I can see to myself."

Claudine protested but not too strenuously.

"Everything all right, milady? You tore out of here in a terrible rush earlier."

Claudine knew some of what Vivienne and Alec did for the S.P.R. Vivienne had rescued her from a dockside brothel six years before and there was an unquestioned loyalty between the two women. A shared understanding of what it meant to have brown skin in a white country. The English were perfectly civilized except when it came to women, poor people and foreigners, and God forbid one happened to be all three.

"Not all right, but nothing we can do about it now," she said. "Just leave the lavender salts by the tub, would you?"

Claudine did and said goodnight. When Vivienne finished dressing, she lit a lantern and went downstairs to the pantry. She pushed aside burlap sacks of flour and sugar and pressed a hidden panel in the wall. It swung open soundlessly, revealing a winding stone staircase. She padded down, the stone cold against her bare feet.

The space below had last served as a wine cellar. Before that, Nathaniel had told her with some glee, it was a secret chapel where Catholics held Mass during Elizabeth's bloody purge. The current mansion had been built atop a much older structure that dated at least to the 16th century. Upon taking possession, Vivienne shipped the wine off to Eridge Castle and converted the space to a more useful purpose. Now, she held up the lantern and surveyed the rough walls.

Light glinted on a dizzying array of weapons, neatly arranged in metal brackets. There were swords for stabbing and clubs for bludgeoning, wicked half-moon axes and wooden poles of every length, some with daggers attached to the end. There were weapons you fired, and weapons you threw.

Vivienne's first sword had been a scimitar, but she'd lost it in the sea a long time ago. After, when she and Alec were bonded, she'd done a great deal of traveling. These were her souvenirs, and she'd learned to use every one of them.

The Japanese samurai had their iron fans, the Madurese dueled with sickles, and 14th-century German knights favored the spiked mace called a morningstar. Vivienne picked up a set of bagh naka, which resembled knuckle dusters but with five curved blades like tiger claws affixed to a crossbar. The Rajput clan of India would poison the tips and use them for assassinations. Each culture devised their own unique style for killing, she reflected, though the end result was the same.

Her gaze paused for a moment on a macuahuitl, a wooden sword whose sides were embedded with jagged blades of obsidian. Too nasty, she decided. She wasn't *that* angry. No, they were both tired. Better to stick with a weapon they knew well.

She went to the far end of the cellar and lifted a Japanese katana sword from its bracket. A slightly curved blade with a single cutting edge, the katana was made of steel that had been folded and beaten four hundred and forty times by a master swordsmith. This one had taken five weeks to forge and polish. She'd commissioned a custom-made pair from Nagasone Kotetsu, a famous swordmaker, when she and Alec had passed through Edo. The steel derived from iron sand, and ghouls despised it.

Vivienne admired the lacquered wooden sheathe but didn't draw the blade yet. There was an entire art devoted to that too—and to flicking your opponent's blood from the edge.

Alec would know she was down here by now. He'd sense it through the bond. An invitation.

Will he come?

Vivienne stretched like a cat. A moment later she heard Alec's light tread descending the hidden staircase. She moved to the clear space in the center of the chamber.

"I thought you were going to bed," he said, lingering on the stairs.

"I changed my mind."

He studied her a moment, inscrutable. Then he took his jacket off and hung it from the tip of a harissa pike. He set his cane against the wall.

"What do I get if I win?" she asked.

"You never win." This was said with a grin to take the sting out, although it was true.

"But if?"

"How about a groveling apology for Clarence?"

"That suits."

Alec unbuttoned his waistcoat and rolled up his shirtsleeves. He was slender, a middle-weight at best, but Vivienne knew it was no indication of his true strength.

"I'll need to hold the power," he said. "It helps my leg."

"As long as you just hold it."

He limped over and selected a second sword from its bracket. He drew it in one fluid motion and returned the scabbard to the wall mount.

"I don't cheat," he said.

Vivienne drew her own sword, gripping it with two hands but leaving a fist's breadth between them. Lamplight shimmered on the edge of the blade, which she kept polished to a mirror-like sheen with choji oil.

"First cut wins," she said.

They began to circle each other. Alec's sword wasn't even up. He looked deceptively relaxed, sleepy almost. Waiting for her to make the first move.

Vivienne flicked her wrist and the blades met in a blindingly fast exchange. It sounded almost musical, the gentle *plinking* of rain on a tin roof—nothing like the clashing of broadswords designed for crude hacking. The katana was a slender blade, fearsomely sharp and light.

Rather like Alec Lawrence.

He wielded his sword one-handed as a handicap, but it still took everything Vivienne had to keep him at bay. They broke apart, circled, then met again. Sweat rolled down the back of her tunic.

Just once, O Cunning and Frightful Innunu, Mother of Battles. Let me beat him just this one time.

The swords swept together again, edges kissing and parrying with little flicks. Alec's power swirled at the edge of her consciousness, but he kept his word and didn't touch it. His only weakness was his leg. A small, evil part of her was tempted to exploit it, but that would be unforgiveable. So she mustered every scrap of skill she'd acquired, every trick she'd learned from the old masters.

Had Vivienne faced a mortal opponent, blood would have been spilled at first contact. With Alec, she was always half a beat behind. Even so, she suspected he was holding back on her. Irritated, she leveled her blade for a slashing sweep—and Alec spun neatly inside her guard and punched her in the side with his hilt hand. They both heard the crack as a rib snapped. She dropped to one knee, muttering oaths in the liquid tongue of her homeland.

"Are you all right?" He crouched next to her.

Vivienne drew a painful breath. "Been worse."

"I'm sorry, I didn't mean to hit you so hard. I must be tired."

Alec placed his hand on the curve of her hip. Searing heat

rushed through the damaged tissue and bone. Vivienne rolled to her back, trying not to gasp. No matter how many times he healed her, she never got used to it.

"Drink plenty of water." He staggered to his feet and found the cane propped against the wall.

"You always say that." She felt suddenly angry and didn't know why. Or perhaps she did and didn't want to admit it. When bonded touched each other, the sensation could be...intense. Vivienne was careful to avoid it, except in emergencies. He hadn't even asked her if she wanted to be healed.

"Because it's true."

She stared at him stubbornly. "That was a cheap shot."

Alec turned away, sheathing the swords and returning them to their brackets. "I didn't feel like bleeding you, Vivienne."

"Call it a draw then."

"Fair enough." He studied her, the faint lines beneath his eyes betraying his exhaustion. "Are you coming up?"

"In a minute."

Vivienne watched him limp up the stairs. He moved like an old man again. She touched the cuff around her wrist and felt her anger dissipate, followed by the familiar savage bite of guilt.

He lives this way for you. How much longer can you let it go on?

She lay there, unmoving, until Claudine came down and coaxed her into the bath.

CHAPTER 4

Alec changed into a clean set of clothes and made himself a pot of Darjeeling. He couldn't shake the feeling that things were changing. Rearranging themselves in ominous new formations.

The problem of ghouls coming through from the Dominion had improved markedly since he and Vivienne managed to close the last of the twelve Greater Gates. The ones they faced now were summoned by necromancers—humans as old as Alec himself who knew the Art. They were a scourge too, but the terrible, endless flood of undead had abated. Until now.

Perhaps Clarence was an anomaly. A ghoul that happened to be more intelligent than the others.

And impervious to iron. And able to work fire.

It didn't bear thinking about.

Alec rarely slept, and he felt too restless to read a book. He piled the tea things on a tray and made his way upstairs. He spent much of his time at various London clubs and societies related to the advancement of science, but his laboratory was where he studied the elements, manipulating them in the service of devices driven by earth, air and water.

A cavernous space, it occupied the entire fourth floor of the townhouse. Large windows looked out on the neighboring mansions of Park Place. He preferred to work in daylight, without the distraction of gas lamps.

A gleaming pair of metal wings attached to a leather harness leaned against one wall. Others held shelves of beakers and retorts, coils of copper wire and bits of inscrutable machinery. But it was not simply a workspace. The décor reflected Alec's love of nature. Bright, sensuous paintings by Jacques Le Moyne de Morgues hung above the tall windows. *A Thistle and a Caterpillar. A Linnet on a Spray of Barberry.*

Alec felt most at peace when he gave himself over to the ebb and flow of elemental power. He knew this was his nature as a daēva, as much a part of him as the flesh and bone of his mortal body. Hours passed like minutes when he was in the Nexus, and days like hours. On such occasions, Vivienne would come with a plate of food and gently remind him to eat something.

Now he stood at one of his work tables, breath coming in deep, even inhalations just short of gasps. A light breeze ruffled his hair. Rotors spun, pneumatic chambers filled, then emptied. He had ideas about an air-driven motor for a submersible and was studying a set of schematics when a scrap of wet black fur sprung up to the table. Alec poured some milk from the tea tray into a saucer and set it down. The cat gave him a yellow stare, pushed it around with one paw for a minute, then curled her tail over her paws and began lapping at the milk.

He'd never named the cat since she wouldn't answer to it anyway. But they were friends. She came in and out as she pleased, most often on rainy days, when the slick, sooty rooftops were not to her liking. Now, she sat on the windowsill and watched him work through slitted eyes.

Cats fancied elemental power, he'd discovered. They weren't afraid of it as dogs were. Alec thought cats might even have a spark of the power in them but couldn't be troubled to use it. Too lazy.

He knew Vivienne was still awake. It was a side effect of the matched cuffs. Things bled through. Emotions, even physical sensations like pain or hunger. Vivienne felt frustrated because she wanted to act, to do something, and there was nothing to do but wait.

Thirty-six years they'd been in England. He thought of her as Vivienne now, although they'd both gone by other names. In Paris, Hélène and Michel. In Damascus, Amira and Qasim. In St. Petersburg, Tatiana and Aleksander, though everyone called him Sasha. Back and back it went. He was fairly sure even Cyrus didn't know Vivienne's true name. She'd only told Alec once. He had laughed, and she'd gotten angry. Alec had a talent for making her angry.

Zenobia Zumurrud bin Qindah.

She'd changed it to Tijah after she ran away from home. Zenobia was simply too ridiculous. Alec had agreed that Tijah—which meant *sword* in her native tongue—suited her much better.

He forgot other details but he remembered the names.

Now they were Vivienne Cumberland and Alec Lawrence—as English as one could get. It always paid to blend in.

Alec worked through the day, making little progress on his engine. His thoughts kept returning to Dr. Clarence. The finger marks burned into the iron bars. Not a ghoul. Something else. *What?*

Dark came early and Quimby came in to light the lamps at four-thirty.

"Is Lady Cumberland still asleep?" Alec asked.

"She is, sir. Shall I have Claudine wake her?"

"No. Let her rest."

Alec sat by the window for a while, watching a large flock of starlings wheeling in the air above Green Park. He was tempted to try out his new wings, but perhaps the starched neighborhood of St. James was not the ideal location for such an experiment. He would have to take a trip to the countryside. The Ruabon moors in Wales, perhaps. Wild and desolate and covered with purple heather. The thought cheered him.

Alec's reverie was broken by a knock on the front door, four floors below but still audible to him. He was halfway down when he met Quimby on the stairs.

"It's a constable from the Yard, Mr. Lawrence. I asked him to wait in the library."

"Thank you."

Alec made his way downstairs, hoping it was positive news but prepared for the worst. He recognized the officer standing before the cold hearth as one of Blackwood's.

"Constable Graves," he said, shaking the man's hand. "What's happened?"

Graves was in his early twenties, with keen grey eyes and a narrow, almost mournful face. "There's been a death. D.I. Blackwood thinks it could be related to Dr. Clarence."

Alec felt a sting of adrenaline. "Where?"

"Sotheby, Wilkinson, & Hodge of Wellington Street."

Alec frowned. He'd expected it would be another of London's poor lost souls. A prostitute or street urchin. "Who is it?"

"A clerk. The body was found just after closing."

"Why does Blackwood think it's related?" Vivienne asked from the doorway.

Both men turned as she entered the room wearing a high-necked gown of dark blue silk. Her wiry curls had been drawn into a complex knot pinned at the nape. Considering she'd been asleep not ten minutes before, Alec couldn't fathom how she managed it so fast, even with Claudine's help. The constrictive costume of this time was bad enough for men and pure hell for women—although perversely, Vivienne seemed to enjoy the spectacle.

Graves gave her a deferential nod. "Cause of death is still

44

undetermined. The body was not abused in any way, milady. But the clerk"—he glanced at his notes—"a Mr. James Cromwell, had just assisted in an auction of rare books earlier this afternoon. By invitation only."

"What sort of books?" Alec asked, his curiosity piqued.

"Well, that's the thing, Mr. Lawrence. They were all related to the occult. Grimoires." He cleared his throat. "Demonology. That sort of thing."

"There was a grimoire involved in the Hyde case," Alec said. "Give us a moment, Mr. Graves. We'll come immediately."

"I'll have Henry bring the carriage around," Vivienne offered, black eyes shining. "If it's Clarence, perhaps we'll catch his trail this time."

A thick fog had rolled in, muting the street lamps to diffuse yellow orbs. Wellington Street wasn't far, but the poor visibility slowed traffic to a crawl. Henry took the broad, stately thorough-fare of Pall Mall to Trafalgar Square and turned onto the Strand. They passed the newly renovated Adelphi theater, its electric marquis dark.

"They're in rehearsals for a new play called *The Silver Falls*," Vivienne observed, lighting a cigarette. "Another overheated melodrama, although I hear it's a cut above most of the others. Olga Nethersole plays the wicked adventuress Lola. She's one to watch. You should come with me when they open next week, assuming we're still alive."

Alec caught a glimpse of the poster advertising the play. It showed a young man, hand raised as if to strike a girl in a flowing white gown.

"Only if you buy me dinner at Pagani's first," Alec murmured. "It looks awful."

Vivienne's mouth twitched. "That seems a fair trade."

Wellington Street intersected the Strand from north to south, affording access to Waterloo Bridge. Alec could smell the Thames, a witch's brew of mud and sewage and rotting fish. It was better than it used to be, when all of the city's waste flowed straight into the river, but not by much—especially at low tide.

Sotheby's shared the street with an array of book sellers and publishers. Two constables waited at the door of No. 19, a stolid brick building occupied by Messrs. Sotheby, Wilkinson, and Hodge since the turn of the century. They found Blackwood in the Sale Room, a grand space with floor-to-ceiling bookcases stretching along the walls. Two long wooden tables with benches occupied the center of the room, facing the auctioneer's podium. To the right of the auctioneer sat a second railed platform with a desk, where a clerk would record the bidding.

Cyrus Ashdown, a devoted collector of rare books, had attended many auctions there. Alec accompanied him once or twice. Each lot for sale would be taken from the shelves by a porter and placed on the table for examination, and the haggling would commence. It moved at a breakneck pace and even a single instant of distraction could cost a buyer their desired lot.

The room also held a number of chairs, but these were tacitly reserved for the high priests of the rare book trade, who tended to congregate near the shelves on the far left where the lots being auctioned were kept. D.I. Blackwood sat in one of these chairs, reviewing a catalogue. He looked up as they entered, the dark circles under his eyes signaling he had yet to sleep since the night before.

"I take it the search of the asylum grounds turned up nothing," Alec said after they exchanged terse greetings.

"The dogs lost the scent on the Wickham Hill Road. He may have found a ride on a farmer's wagon headed to London. We checked Clarence's rooms in Cheapside, but there was no sign he'd returned and the landlady said she hadn't seen him for a month. I interviewed the new tenant myself. He wasn't any use either. Have a look at this." He handed the slim catalogue to Alec, who scanned it and gave it to Vivienne.

"No one saw a thing," Blackwood continued. "The auction

began shortly after one o'clock and ran until two-thirty. At the close of business, the lots were sent out for delivery. I have a list of everyone who was present, and who bought what. At six o'clock, one of the chars who comes in to clean found Mr. Cromwell stuffed into a closet."

"I'd like a copy of that list," Alec said.

"Of course. Any idea what's he after? If it's even our Dr. Clarence, which is far from certain. I have to consider all the possibilities, although everyone insists Mr. Cromwell had no enemies."

"Dr. Clarence said 'They're here.' What if he didn't mean a person but a thing?"

"You think he might have been referring to one of the books?"

"Possibly. I'll need to show the catalogue to Cyrus Ashdown. He's the Society's resident expert on such things. He probably knows all the people who attended personally."

"Is anything missing?" Vivienne asked.

Blackwood gave a shrug. "It's hard to say. There's a large amount of inventory to account for. But nothing's been reported so far."

"So the auction lots were already out for delivery when Cromwell died," Alec said.

"Yes. But he knew where they were going. He served as the clerk during the auction. I've already sent men to question everyone who was present—and to keep an eye on them in case Clarence decides to pay a visit. Lucky for us, it was an intimate affair. There were only nine people bidding."

"Do you mind if we speak to some of the buyers as well?" Vivienne asked.

Her black eyes roamed over the empty chairs, as if imagining the room as it was earlier that afternoon when an elite group of the most hardcore collectors in England had assembled to dicker over centuries-old manuscripts devoted to the occult.

"By all means." Blackwood paused. "I read the Brady report.

The officers I've sent, most of them have families. They understand the risks, but I still feel like I'm throwing them to the wolves. This creature we're dealing with....Will bullets stop him, Mr. Lawrence?"

Alec held his gaze. "I don't know."

Blackwood nodded. "Then let's hope you find him first." He turned as a constable entered the room.

"Morgue wagon's here, sir."

"Good." He faced Vivienne and Alec. "But I think you should see the body first."

"I'll do it," Vivienne offered.

She sensed his reluctance. Alec didn't mind killing when he knew the thing on the end of his iron blade didn't belong in this world, but he'd never gotten used to the violent death of innocents, no matter how many times he witnessed it. After seeing two of the Ripper scenes, including Mary Jane Kelly, he'd felt permanently soiled.

So Vivienne went and examined the body with Blackwood while Alec waited in the Sale Room. He tried to picture the gathering earlier that afternoon. Invitation only. That meant rich and/or well-connected. He'd always found it amusing, the mortal fascination with the occult. It was all quasi-religious bollocks. The Dominion was real, but it wasn't Heaven, nor Hell either. And the souls that returned as ghouls might have been church deacons for all he knew.

In Alec's view, the last two millennia had been a history of pointless persecutions by men who used their power to terrorize. He himself knew what it was to be called a devil. A witch. Now everything had come full circle, and the very same books that people had been burned at the stake for were valued in the thousands of pounds and squabbled over by collectors.

But Clarence wanted something here. Clarence had *been* here. He thought he might sense a residue of the man, or whatever was inside the man, but there was nothing.

"Well?" he asked when Vivienne returned.

"We need to see Cyrus." Her mouth set in a grim line. "Right away."

"What did you see?"

"No injuries, but the expression on his face, Alec...." She trailed off. "I think the poor man died of fright."

CHAPTER 5

SUNDAY, DECEMBER 16

They caught the early morning train from Charing Cross to Greenhithe, a tiny, bucolic village in Dartford. Cassandane, Cyrus's daēva, met them at the station. A tall, strapping woman, she disdained all forms of frippery, preferring grey flannel trousers and a man's hunting jacket.

She shook hands with Alec and grinned as Vivienne planted a warm kiss on her cheek. Despite their superficial differences, Vivienne and Cassandane had always been close. They were both warriors at heart. Foot soldiers against the darkness that bled through from the shadowlands.

Cyrus was the scholar. Their collective memory. In many ways, he was the most human of them all. Brilliant, complex, acerbic—and prone to black melancholies that might last for days or years. It couldn't be easy to be bonded to such a man, but Cassandane managed it. They were so different, Alec always wondered what held them together. Not sex. Their relationship was platonic. It was something else. An extraordinary kind of love that made no sense to anyone outside of it.

"It's good you come," Cassandane said, tossing their bags into the open carriage. She jumped into the driver's seat and urged the matched pair of chestnuts to an easy trot. "He's in one of his moods. Barely leave the library."

Before coming to England, she and Cyrus had spent many years in Buda-Pesth, and Cassandane still had a thick Hungarian accent. She kept her brown hair just long enough to cover a missing left ear that was also partially deaf. It was the only concession to vanity Alec had ever seen.

"We have an escalating situation," Vivienne said as the carriage bounced through the cobblestoned streets of Greenhithe. "Something's come through, maybe been summoned, we don't know yet. But it's on a bloody rampage."

"Yeah, I hear about this from Cyrus."

"It can burn things with its hands, Cass."

"Fasz." *Shit.*

"We need Cyrus's help," Alec said. "Yours too."

"Sure. I could use some excitement."

"Has it been quiet?"

"Only one ghoul in six months. Terrorized a bunch of nuns in Norfolk. I take care of it."

"This one won't be easy," Vivienne said. "It got away. Could be anywhere by now."

"Or anyone," Alec added.

"Igen." *Understood.*

"How bad is Cyrus? Will he pull himself together?"

Alec knew about the melancholies. Vivienne had them too sometimes. Her solution wasn't to shut herself away as Cyrus did, but to throw herself into a frenetic schedule of charity work and social events. She fought the darkness tooth and nail.

"He seems better already," Cassandane conceded. "Sidgwick's cable cheered him. You know Cyrus. He needs a cause. Then he's happy again."

Ingress Abbey lay about three-quarters of a mile from the village, set on a vast estate of rolling lawns and wooded parkland. It had been built and re-built many times. The latest incarnation was a neo-Gothic heap with towering gables of grey stone—some of it supposedly pilfered from the Old London Bridge—and a central tower facing the Thames.

The Abbey had a colorful history, first as a 14th-century convent and later as a country retreat for King Henry VIII, who confiscated it from the nuns to pay for his invasion of France. Cyrus had bought the estate from a London solicitor and filled it with all the rare and wondrous objects he'd collected over the centuries. Visitors could sip tea from cups made during the Qin Dynasty, the glaze as fresh as the day they were fired, while admiring the skeletons of strange animals long vanished from the face of the earth.

Open a drawer and one might find cringe-inducing Egyptian medical instruments, or yellowed scrolls casting the horoscopes of people long ago turned to dust. There were iron-nickel meteorites and dory spears from ancient Sparta and bags of coins minted with the faces of forgotten kings. The flotsam of a thousand shipwrecked cultures.

Alec always enjoyed his visits to Ingress Abbey. It was the closest thing he had to coming home.

Rain began to fall as they turned up the drive to the house. It was lined with ancient, grey-barked elms, their naked branches dark against the sky. Cassandane stopped the carriage at the bottom of a long flight of weathered stone steps carved into the hillside leading up to the front door.

"You know where to find him," she said. "I go to the stables and meet you inside."

Alec got out and started up the stairs, ignoring the dull ache in his knee. Halfway to the top, he paused, leaning on his cane. He pretended to admire a sailboat cutting through the muddy waters of the Thames, but Vivienne wasn't fooled.

"Take my arm," she said.

"I'm fine."

"No, you're not. Take my arm."

Alec sighed and let her support him for the last three flights. She smelled of tobacco and the scented oil Claudine combed into her hair at night. Something with jessamine.

"It's the weather," he said.

Vivienne looked away. He knew she felt responsible, even though he had chosen the bond, not her.

"Or maybe I'm just getting old."

She barked a laugh, but there wasn't much humor in it. "You're a terrible liar."

The massive front door had been left unlocked. Vivienne pushed it open and gave a theatrical shiver.

"Goddess, how the hell do they live like this?"

Ingress Abbey was impossible to heat, and their breath steamed in the stark, gloomy entrance hall. White sheets draped a dozen marble statues, like an assembly of ghosts. Alec followed Vivienne through a labyrinth of hallways paneled in mahogany carvings of birds and fish and stranger creatures from medieval bestiaries. Another flight of stairs, more corridors, and they reached a heavy door with lamplight spilling through the crack.

Alec opened it, grateful for the rush of warmer air. Cyrus hoarded almost anything that caught his fancy, but books held pride of place. The library at Ingress Abbey contained thousands of volumes, many of them rare first and second editions bound in calfskin with gold leaf lettering on their spines. A treasured few were believed to be forever lost, like Plato's *Hermocrates* and Livy's complete history of Rome in one hundred and forty-two volumes.

Cyrus Ashdown sat ensconced in a large leather armchair, an afghan across his knees. His skin bore the livid sheen of a man who hadn't seen daylight in months, but his predatory black eyes burned as bright as ever.

"My dears!" Cyrus gestured at two chairs barely visible beneath tottering heaps of books. "Sit down, sit down."

Cyrus had aged more than Vivienne, but he still appeared no

older than his early fifties, with silver-streaked hair, thin lips and a patrician nose. Beard stubble roughened his jaw. He wore a tatty dressing gown and fur slippers that looked like something Alec's cat might cough up.

"Magus," Vivienne murmured, kissing his cheek.

Alec cleared the chairs and took the one farthest from the coal fire that burned in an enclosed iron stove. Vivienne immediately lit a cigarette.

"Holy Father, must you?" Cyrus grumbled. He clutched a book in his lap, one finger holding his place on the page.

Vivienne exhaled a stream of smoke toward the ceiling. "I won't burn anything up, I promise."

"Do you have any idea what the contents of this room are worth?"

"Roughly." She looked around for an ashtray. "What are you reading?"

Cyrus pursed his lips but let it drop.

"William Blake. Of course. I find his gloriously mad visions to be quite stimulating, not to mention relevant to our purpose."

Alec suppressed a smile.

Cyrus opened the book. "In the universe," he quoted, "there are things that are known, and things that are unknown, and in between, there are doors."

"Indeed there are," Vivienne said, pouncing on an ashtray that appeared to be made from the skull of a small hominid.

Or, Alec thought, it simply *was* the skull of a small hominid.

"Perhaps you should tell me what's come through one of those doors," Cyrus said quietly.

"You've read Blackwood's cable?" Alec asked.

"Yes."

"This began in New York, there's no doubt of that. But now it's here."

Cyrus raised a bushy eyebrow. "It."

"Yes, *it*. Most definitely not a ghoul. Far more sophisticated."

"How many known victims?"

"Eleven. Twelve counting the clerk at Sotheby's. And I fear it's only the beginning."

The door opened and Cass stomped in. "I hate this English weather," she announced. "Wet all the time. Who wants some pálinka?"

Alec's stomach cringed at the sight of the murky green bottle in her hand, but Vivienne enthusiastically accepted a glass. Technically, pálinka was fruit brandy. The stuff Cassandane brewed down in the Abbey's cellars, however, was more accurately described as Hungarian moonshine. Alec had gone blind for a few brief, terrifying seconds the only time he'd tried it.

He opened his case and took out the Sotheby's catalogue, handing it to Cyrus. "What do you make of this?"

Cyrus put on his spectacles. "I was invited, you know," he said. "But I already own half of these books. And Cassandane refused to attend as my proxy."

"You want something, you go get it yourself," she said. "Otherwise you sit here all day. It's not good."

Vivienne hovered behind Cyrus's armchair, trying to read over his shoulder. She had the glass of pálinka in one hand, cigarette in the other. Alec wondered how flammable the fumes were.

"We believe Dr. Clarence, or whoever summoned him, wants one or more of these books," he said. "The question is which one, and why?"

Cyrus quickly scanned through the pages. "Well, several of them are grimoires. Essentially instruction booklets for the invocation of spirits, as you already know." He tapped the catalogue. "The ones listed here are especially valuable because so many were burned by the Catholic Church during the medieval era."

Vivienne's face darkened. Alec knew how much she despised the Church. They'd all had more than one encounter with the

Inquisition. In most measurable ways, it was worse than the ghouls.

"Of course, the printing press wasn't invented until 1440. Prior to that, all books were copied by hand. Very few from that period survived." Cyrus pushed himself out of the armchair and slid a rolling ladder along its track until he found the shelf he wanted. He removed a slim volume and handed it to Alec.

"Here's one in the catalogue. *The Heptameron*."

"Seven Days," Alec murmured.

Cyrus nodded. "Attributed to the 13th-century philosopher Petre D'Abano. It's an astrological treatise claiming to give precise instructions for summoning angels, one for each day of the week. *The Heptameron* is the source of many later European grimoires. First known edition is Venice, 1496. The one you're looking at is an English translation by Robert Turner dating to 1655."

"There was a grimoire in the Hyde case too. *The Black Pullet*."

"I'm familiar with that one, of course. They all share similarities. *The Heptameron*. *The Magical Treatise of Solomon*. *Le Dragon Rouge*. Et cetera. I could go on for hours, but suffice it to say they're simply texts in the art of invocation."

Alec leafed through the yellowing pages. They were covered in arcane symbols and geometrical figures he found unintelligible.

"Could a necromancer be using this thing to hunt for a text? Perhaps to summon others?"

Cyrus removed his spectacles and gave him a pitying look. "None of the grimoires actually work, Alec."

He smiled. "Right."

"Words and rituals alone are useless, which you of all people ought to know. A talisman is needed to open a gate to the Dominion."

"Or blood price."

"Yes, or blood price—but again, one must have the spark, which is extremely rare."

"What about this?" Vivienne asked. She'd taken over Cyrus's chair and was flipping through the catalogue. *"Discours et Histoires des Spectres,* 1605 edition."

"Ah, yes. Pierre Le Loyer." Cyrus shuffled off to the dim recesses of the library and returned with a thick tome bound in cracked red leather. "This is my English edition, also published in 1605. Loyer was a true daemonologist, devoting a significant portion of his life to the study of undead spirits. He calls them spectres and phantasms. A classic work of its time, but nothing earthshaking. You already know ten times as much as Loyer did."

Alec's eyes roamed over the dusty shelves. They had to be missing something. He felt certain that whatever Clarence sought, it was in the catalogue.

"May I?" he asked Vivienne.

She handed it over, eyebrow raised.

"So we have useless books for summoning spirits. How about the ones for banishing them?" Alec said. "I see a copy of *Manuale Exorcismorum.* And a 1587 edition of the *Directorium Inquisitorum.*"

"Eymerich," Vivienne snarled.

They had all known Nicholas Eymerich. He was a Dominican friar who had been appointed Inquisitor General of Aragon in 1357. The book he wrote was used as a manual for witch-hunters. An untold number of innocents had suffered brutality and death at Eymerich's hands.

"I still regret not killing him in Valencia," Cassandane remarked, tossing back the last of her pálinka. "The man couldn't tell ghouls from his own bony *fenék.*"

"No, he couldn't," Cyrus agreed. "Those books are simply rants on the evils of sorcery and how to torture a *confession* out of heretics. In all honesty, I can't see what Clarence might want with any of them."

Alec flipped to the end and tapped a page. "What about this?"

Cyrus replaced his spectacles, peering over Alec's shoulder at the small print. He frowned. "Now that *is* odd," he murmured. "I wonder what this was doing at auction."

"What?" Vivienne demanded.

"It lists seven pages from a 1480 edition of Claudius Ptolemy's *Geographia Cosmographia.*"

"Isn't that some kind of atlas?"

"It's much more than that. The 1478 edition of the *Geographia* is one of the rarest books in the world. Priceless, really. There are only four known copies. But I've never even heard of a 1480 edition."

"Four copies," Vivienne said. "And I'll bet you own one of them, you old goat."

Cyrus smiled. "As a matter of fact, I do."

He unlocked a glass-fronted cabinet and removed a cloth-bound parcel. Alec hastily made space on one of the tables. With exquisite care, Cyrus undid the wrappings. The book was large, roughly the size of a modern atlas. Alec and Vivienne leaned over his shoulder as he laid open the cover.

"There are four important early printed versions," Cyrus explained in his lecturing tone. "Three originated in Italy, one in Germany. They appeared nearly simultaneously, although uncertainty persists about the dates of the Florence and Bologna editions. But the Rome edition is easily the finest, in terms of quality and fidelity to Ptolemy's original texts."

The first pages were all text, two columns written in Latin, with sketches of Ptolemy's projections. This was followed by a lengthy index of places with cryptic numbers after each entry that seemed to be his own system of latitude and longitude coordinates. At the end came the maps themselves.

The first was titled *Prima Europe Tabula*. It showed the British Isles along with six bodies of water—Oceanus Germanicus (the North Sea), Oceanus Hibernicus (the Irish Sea), Oceanus Vergivius (the Saint George Channel and Celtic Sea), Oceanus

Britannicus (the English Channel), Oceanus Hyperboreus (Ocean beyond the north) and Oceanus Deucalidonius (the sea north of Scotland). It all looked fairly accurate except for the fact that Ptolemy had decided to throw in the mythical Island of Thule at the top corner, somewhere near Norway.

"Ptolemy's maps were cartographical gospel for more than thirteen hundred years," Cyrus explained. "Columbus consulted this particular edition in preparation for his voyage across the Atlantic. Of course, they were mostly wrong, at least concerning places beyond the borders of the Roman Empire. Ptolemy vastly underestimated the earth's circumference, leading poor Columbus to believe it would be a relatively easy voyage to the East Indies. But that hardly matters. This book still represents the first serious attempt to accurately depict the world as a sphere."

His fingertips lightly traced the sketches. "Besides its histor-ical significance, the 1478 edition is probably the first example of copperplate engraving. All the world maps that preceded it were crude woodcuts, like cave drawings next to the Sistine Chapel."

Cyrus pointed to the corner of the page. "Do you see the crossbow within a circle watermark? The 1478 folio was printed in Rome by Arnold Buckinck, and remains the only known work bearing his imprint. His partner, Conrad Sweynheym, set up the very first printing press in Italy in 1464 but died a year before the *Geographia* plates were completed. It's the first edition with maps, twenty-seven to be exact."

Vivienne yawned behind her hand. "That's all fascinating, magus, but is there any connection to the occult?"

"None whatsoever. Not in this edition, at least."

"Then I don't see how this fits with the other books."

"Nor do I," Cyrus agreed. "You should speak to the buyers who attended the auction. They might have an idea."

"That's what we intend," Alec said. "Blackwood gave us a list of names. One lives not far from here. Lady Frances Hake-

Dibbler of Hauxwell Castle. She bought the collected works of the alchemist Alexander Seton."

Cyrus made a face. "Lady Frances is not, in my opinion, a serious bibliophile. She only likes to acquire scandalous texts to show off to her friends at parties." He waved a hand. "But by all means, go see her. The woman's an inveterate gossip. At the least, she can tell you if anything unusual occurred at the auction." He glanced at Vivienne. "You may wish to send Alec on his own for this one. She has a notorious fondness for attractive young men."

"Too bad he's not young."

"Hake-Dibbler won't know that."

Alec sighed and eased himself into a chair. "If I'm being used as bait, can I get a cup of tea first?"

"I make you some," Cassandane offered. "Special Hungarian recipe."

He stood as hastily as his bad leg permitted. "I hate to trouble you, really. I can make it myself."

Halfway to the door, he heard Cyrus emit a bellow of outrage.

"Holy Father, Vivienne, have you been using that for an *ashtray?*"

"What? This skull?"

"It's nearly two million years old!"

"Sorry. I thought it *was* an ashtray."

Cyrus blew into the skull. A cloud of grey flakes erupted from the left eye socket, followed by the smoldering butt of an Oxford Oval. Vivienne looked at Alec and mimed an *oops* face.

"It's okay. Nothing lasts," Cassandane said. She shrugged her broad shoulders. "But eventually, everything comes again."

CHAPTER 6

C assandane drove Alec the five miles to Hauxwell Castle the next morning. He'd spent the night in one of the Abbey's frigid bedrooms, with dusty tapestries of medieval hunts looming over him, and was glad to be outside in the fresh air. It was a rare sunny morning for late December. Fallow fields stretched between lines of hedgerows. They passed two villages even smaller than Greenhithe and a dairy farm with black and white cows standing sentry at the fence.

"I'm not blaming, but I still don't understand why you don't kill this Dr. Clarence when you first find him," Cassandane said.

Alec sat next to her on the driver's bench. He wore a new morning jacket Vivienne had bought for him and a top hat with a red silk lining that she said was all the rage in Paris.

"We weren't sure about him until it was too late."

Cassandane glanced at him. "*You* weren't sure."

"All right," Alec conceded. "I wasn't. Not entirely."

"Why you don't believe Vivienne? She's always right."

Alec looked out at the rolling uplands of the Kent countryside.

"Not always."

"Something happen?"

"You and Cyrus were away at the time. There was a series of child killings in the area around Victoria Park Cemetery. The murderer emptied their bodies of blood. It seemed clear that we were dealing with a ghoul. Inspector Blackwood asked for our help."

"You find this monster?"

"Yes. We caught him with the last victim. A boy of nine. He was bending over the child's body. Vivienne ran ahead of me. You know how she gets. I couldn't stop her. She took his head clean off."

The daēva shrugged. "I don't see problem."

"No gate opened, Cass. The man was mortal. A brick-layer named Harper Dods."

"Still a monster."

"Without doubt. But there are rules now. It wasn't self-defense. He'd backed away from the boy and put his hands up. When he saw Viv with her sword, he started begging for his life. We're supposed to do an iron test before any summary executions."

Cassandane said nothing. She didn't seem to feel sorry for Harper Dods. Neither did Alec, but that wasn't the point.

"Blackwood and Sidgwick hushed it up, but Sidgwick especially didn't trust Vivienne after that."

"He still needs us."

"Yes. It's the only reason we weren't asked to leave London."

"Vivienne okay about it?"

He smiled. "I don't think she understood what all the fuss was about. Man or ghoul, Dods got what he deserved. Full stop."

"*Fasz*. Those men haven't seen the things we have. They don't know."

Alec was quiet for a minute. "Sometimes it seems it'll never stop."

"What, ghouls?"

"Them, yes. This war we've been fighting. It's like bailing a leaky boat. We should be hunting necromancers."

"You hear anything from Anne?"

Anne was Alec's half-sister. A daëva, but never bonded to a mortal. She'd gotten wind that there might be a nest of necromancers in Translithuania and gone haring off to investigate.

"Nothing. She left for the Carpathians two months ago. I'm starting to worry."

"She take care of herself. Anne isn't much for writing letters."

Alec smiled. "No, she isn't. But Vivienne's worried too. Anne's like a daughter to her."

Cassandane turned to him, the reins dangling loose in her strong hands. "Does she ever get sad like Cyrus?"

"Vivienne? Sometimes. But this is a good age for her. She likes the noise, the crowds." He laughed. "The parties. She has her theater friends. And she uses her money to help people."

"Cyrus thinks their kind isn't built to live so long, even with the bond. Not their bodies. Their minds."

"Time passes differently for us," Alec agreed. "As for Vivienne, she never looks back. Only forward. It spares her the misery of regret."

"Cyrus has his books. But it's the hunt that keeps him going, I think. He needs the darkness."

Alec rubbed his knee. "Maybe we all do."

———

INSPECTOR BLACKWOOD HADN'T BEEN idle. Two of his officers stood watch near the front door of Hauxwell Castle. They watched Alec approach with stony faces until one recognized him. His name was Marsten and he'd been called to Buckingham Palace when the ghoul got loose inside, first in the form of a chambermaid, then a second footman. Alec had arrived just as the ghoul was unsteadily carrying a tea tray toward the Queen's chambers. It had achieved a very close facsimile of the footman except for the hair, which was a long and lustrous red.

"Mr. Lawrence," Marsten said, a smile creasing his broad, sunburnt farmer's face. "What are you doing here?"

"Thought I'd have a chat with her ladyship."

The men exchanged a look. "Have fun."

"What have you told her?"

"That the murderer could be a deranged collector and we're taking every precaution to ensure the safety of all parties who attended the auction."

"Did she believe it?"

"Seemed to. I think she's enjoying the excitement."

"Any news from London?"

Marsten shook his head. "We have men watching everyone on that auction list. He'll have to show himself eventually." He paused. "Is it a ghoul, Mr. Lawrence?" His hand unconsciously moved to the pommel of a short iron blade, halfway between a dagger and a sword in size. All members of the Dominion Branch carried one since Buckingham Palace.

"I don't think so," Alec replied. "We're working on it now," he added lamely.

"You believe her ladyship knows something?"

Alec shrugged. "She might. It's worth finding out."

"Godspeed to you then." The men laughed.

Alec lifted the front door knocker—a hideous imp's head with a ring through the mouth—and let it fall. The summons was answered by a gaunt butler who gave Alec a long-suffering look when he presented his card, as if he were a traveling salesman or religious zealot.

"I'm an acquaintance of Mr. Ashdown," Alec said.

"Very good. I shall inform her ladyship. If you'd come this way, Mr. Lawrence."

The butler showed Alec to a large drawing room with French doors overlooking the gardens and retreated upstairs. Hauxwell

Castle was better maintained than Ingress Abbey, if not much warmer. Oil portraits of Hake-Dibbler ancestors sporting stiff Elizabethan collars lined the walls. The furniture was a bit fussy and overstuffed for Alec's taste. He sat with his legs crossed and passed the time making up names for the numerous Hake-Dibbler dogs gazing adoringly at their masters.

Twenty minutes later, the lady of the house sailed into the room like a luxury liner plowing through rough seas. She wore a cream-colored silk gown with tight sleeves and an even tighter corset that elevated her ample bosom to dizzying heights. Alec guessed her age at about fifty. A very well-kept fifty. Her hair was a towering confection of frosted curls that gave him a toothache just looking at it.

Alec rose and offered her a graceful bow. "Lady Hake-Dibbler. I apologize for the intrusion. It's very crass not to have written ahead."

"Not in the least, Mr. Lawrence. I'm always delighted to have unexpected company," she said in a surprisingly deep voice. "Would you care for tea?" Lady Hake-Dibbler bestowed a sly smile. "Or perhaps something a bit stronger?"

Alec looked longingly at the tea service but decided that he ought to take the hint.

"Whatever you're having will be fine, thank you."

The butler poured them both sherries. Alec took an obligatory sip and set the glass aside. He'd never understood the appeal of spirits. They dulled all the things he found beautiful in the world.

"What brings you to Hauxwell Castle, Mr. Lawrence?" she boomed.

"Other than the pleasure of your ladyship's company?"

Hake-Dibbler laughed. "Yes, other than that."

"I understand you're an avid collector of rare volumes on the occult. So is Mr. Ashdown, as I'm sure you're aware."

"Do you represent him?"

"Informally. He hasn't been well. He was unable to attend the recent auction at Sotheby's."

She shuddered. "We all heard what happened afterwards. How ghastly. You must have seen the policemen outside. I hear it was an attempted robbery and the murderer might be on some sort of rampage." She took a nip of sherry. "Kind of them to stand guard, but no one gets past Braithewaite. I'd like to see him try!"

Alec wondered if she meant the skeletal butler, who had to be at least seventy. "Indeed. I suppose you were already interviewed by the police?"

"They came yesterday. An Inspector Blackwood, he said his name was. I'm afraid I wasn't much use. I left as soon as the bidding concluded and returned to Kent." Her sharp hazel eyes appraised him. "What is it you're after, Mr. Lawrence?"

Alec smiled disarmingly. "You own a copy of the *Alphabetum Diaboli*. Mr. Ashdown was hoping you might entertain an offer for it."

She seemed to relax. "I'm afraid it's not for sale. But I'll show it to you, if you like."

Lady Hake-Dibbler gestured to the butler, who returned with a large, well-worn book bound in vellum. Alec opened it. The title page was a woodcut of capering demons stabbing sinners with long knives. Some of them held up wine cups, so drunk they were spewing on the ground. Beneath their feet, more unfortunate souls roasted in eternal hellfire, mouths yawning open in silent screams.

"Johannes Niess was a Bavarian Jesuit," she said. "He actually wrote this book for children, if you can imagine."

Alec could. "It was a dark time."

Lady Hake-Dibbler studied him. "*The Garden of Earthly Delights*. Are you familiar with it?"

"By the Dutch painter Hieronymus Bosch?"

"Very good, Mr. Lawrence. The original triptych is in El Escorial, but there are many copies. It's quite extraordinary. The left panel imagines the innocent paradise of Eden, whilst the center shows the Fall. Naked men and women frolicking in moral abandon. But it is the right panel that is arguably the most studied."

"Why is that?" Alec asked, although it wasn't hard to guess.

"It graphically depicts the medieval concept of Hell. Cities burn in the background, as demonic hordes inflict nightmarish tortures upon those who've sinned and fantastic beasts feed on human flesh. It made Bosch famous, or perhaps infamous. Most people find it disturbing, but to the scholar, it simply represents the Church's shift from a focus on eschatology—the doctrine of last things, such as the Second Coming of the messiah, his resurrection, and final judgment of humanity as a whole—to judgment of individual souls when they pass to the afterlife, as described in the Book of Revelation."

Alec nodded, thinking to himself that Cyrus had underestimated this woman. Her interests clearly ran deeper than the shock value of conducting a few séances at parties.

"There were many first-hand accounts of Hell at that time as well, purportedly written by those near death who had narrowly escaped its clutches," she explained. "Dante's *Inferno* is of course the best known of these. They describe snakes and wheels and seas of burning embers, fields of ice and moving bridges that throw the unfortunate into rivers of sulfur."

She smiled. "In fact, the very same Florentine church in which Dante Alighieri was baptized contains Coppo di Marcovaldo's famous mosaic *Hell,* depicting a horned Satan devouring the damned on a flaming throne. Thomas Aquinas believed that the angels and saints should be made to observe this divine retribution in order to better appreciate their own position in Heaven."

"A veiled threat?"

"Oh, absolutely. The Islamic concept of Hell is similar. They call it Jahannam, and it has seven levels and seven gates, including Jaheem, or blazing fire, Hatamah, that which breaks to pieces, and Haawiyah, the abyss." She took a demure sip of sherry. "Do you believe in God, Mr. Lawrence?"

"I don't know."

"An honest answer. And the Devil?"

"Almost certainly."

She seemed amused by this response, as he wanted her to be. "Some thought Hell was an entity rather than a place, a great beast with seventy thousand reins, each held by seventy thousand angels, that would come on Judgment Day. Still others, like the medieval Cathars, believed in Hell on earth. Considering how they were relentlessly persecuted by the Catholic Church, it's understandable."

Lady Hake-Dibbler laid a hand on his arm. "But I must be boring you to tears. Would you care for a cucumber sandwich?"

Braithewaite brought sandwiches and more sherry. By the third glass, Alec managed to steer the conversation back to the auction. Cyrus was correct on one thing. Lady Frances Hake-Dibbler was a font of gossip about her fellow collectors.

"The auction was rather dull until Mr. Summersbee and Mr. Crawford started bidding on the Ptolemy pages," she confided, reaching for a triangle of bread in such a way that one be-ringed hand brushed Alec's thigh. "There's a long history of bad blood between them."

"Bad blood?" he repeated, crossing his legs.

"Oh, Summersbee snatched a 1616 edition of *Le Fléau des Démons et Sorciers* out from under his nose at the last auction. Crawford had some sort of sneezing fit and had to retire from the room for a minute. Of course, he didn't wish to, but it was so disruptive, Mr. Hodge—he always conducts the bidding—was forced to insist. By the time Mr. Crawford returned, they'd moved on to the next lot." She laughed. "He privately claimed that Summersbee had put something in his snuff. Perfect nonsense, I'm sure, although I wouldn't put it past the man. The 1616 edition is the most sought-after. Summersbee would have sold his own mother for it."

"And the Ptolemy pages?" Alec prompted.

"Oh, Summersbee got those too. At an exorbitant price. Too rich for Mr. Crawford's blood, I imagine."

"What makes them so special? Mr. Ashdown said he'd never even heard of a 1480 edition."

"I didn't pay much attention to the *Geographia*," Lady Hake-Dibbler said apologetically. "I'm more interested in grimoires." She leaned forward and lowered her voice to a conspiratorial whisper. "But from what I understand, those particular pages have unique features that are different from other editions."

Alec raised an eyebrow. "Something related to the occult?"

"You'll have to ask them. They own rival bookshops in Oxford, just a few streets apart. It's like the Wars of the Roses." She placed her glass on the end table. Alec could see traces of lip rouge on the rim. "Does Cyrus have a secret interest in the Ptolemy pages, Mr. Lawrence? You can confide in me."

"Purely academic."

Lady Hake-Dibbler gave a small, forgiving smile as if to say he was a terrible liar, but aren't we all. "Well, if you do make further enquiries, I suggest you start with Dorian Crawford. He's a bit pompous, but he won't turn you away."

"And Mr. Summersbee would?"

"Mr. Summersbee is a paranoiac. He takes all this...this"—she swept her hand to indicate the *Alphabetum Diaboli* and books like it—"*claptrap* literally. I think he's come to believe the demons of Hell are after him personally." Her laughter had a brittle edge. "Though who's to say they aren't?"

"Thank you for your time, Lady Hake-Dibbler." Alec gripped his cane and stood. "You have my card if you ever reconsider Mr. Ashdown's offer."

She gave him a long, frankly appraising look. "I may indeed, if it brings me the pleasure of such charming company." She walked him to the sitting room door. "I hope you don't find the question rude, Mr. Lawrence, but are you a veteran?" She glanced at his cane. "I thought you might have been injured overseas. Afghanistan perhaps?"

"A childhood illness."

"Oh. Well, you've overcome it admirably, Mr. Lawrence." Lady Hake-Dibbler gave him a bright smile. "Do visit again!"

CHAPTER 7

While Alec was sipping sherry with Lady Hake-Dibbler at Hauxwell Castle, Vivienne curled up in the library with Cyrus. He'd caved in and given her a proper ashtray, a bronze turtle with a hinged shell that opened and shut. It was already overflowing.

"You shouldn't live in a house you're too cheap to heat," she said, tucking a second afghan around her shoulders. "This place is a bloody tomb. Get a nice flat in Pimlico, magus. Put your knick-knacks in storage."

Cyrus refused to take the bait. "You look fit, Vivienne. Is it all the parties, or the head-chopping?"

"I thought you were supposed to be a shut-in," she grumbled. "Far from the madding crowd and all that."

"I have my informants." He laughed. "By God, Vivienne, you get more English every day. I think you were born for London. Or maybe the other way around."

"So you know about Dods." She scowled. "I suppose Sidgwick told you. What of it? He's not the first man I've killed and I doubt he'll be the last."

"I don't care about Dods." Cyrus pointed to a stack of metal boxes. "Drag that over here, would you?"

"Which one?"

"All of them."

Vivienne jammed the Oxford Oval between her lips and hauled the first box over. "What's in here?"

"Reports on the Duzakh. Accounts I've gathered on the necromancers. Other light reading."

"You think there's something useful?"

"They know the Dominion better than anyone. Better than we do, as much as I hate to admit it."

Vivienne opened the box. She surveyed the pile of yellowing parchment inside, a jumble of documents dating back hundreds of years, none of it in any discernible order.

"I need some pálinka," she said.

"No, you don't. Bring the lamp closer. I'll take this one. You take the next."

Vivienne chose another box at random and sat down on the floor. She took a sheaf of papers from the top and began reading. All of it appeared to be personal letters Cyrus had stolen or intercepted. Despite the fact that the men who had written them were near-immortal sorcerers who'd devoted themselves to the service of evil, most of it was incredibly boring. Vivienne glanced longingly at the bottle of pálinka as she slogged through the petty rivalries and jockeying for power within the Duzakh, the loose alliance of necromancers that had self-destructed in the late 1700s.

When the dust settled, those still alive had scattered to their secret strongholds. Rooting them out had proven nearly impossible. Now one could only infer the presence of a necromancer by the unusual number of ghouls in a given area. The irony was that the necromancers didn't even summon the undead on purpose. Ghouls came through when one of their human slaves died, five for every fresh corpse. It was a backwash of the binding spell.

"This is pointless," Vivienne complained when she reached the bottom of the box.

Cyrus peered at her over his half-moon spectacles. He said nothing, merely pointing to the stack. Vivienne sighed and hauled over another box.

Two hours and three boxes later, she snapped out of her stupor.

"Magus?"

A weary sigh. "Yes, Vivienne?"

"I may have found something."

Cyrus arched an eyebrow.

"It's a travelogue of sorts from some prat of a necromancer styling himself the Vicomte de Lusignan. Dated…1542? He had awful handwriting. Anyway, it's titled *Voyages Behind the Veil*. He says he used a talisman and a pool of absinthe to open a lesser gate to the Dominion. He was looking for doors to other worlds."

"I wonder how much of it he drank first?"

"Hush. Listen to this."

And on the shores of that Cold Sea, I did meet a thing of Shadow and Flame. It spake in voiceless tongues, and did promise untold power in exchange for Passage. The beast named itself Daemon.

"Oh, yes," Cyrus said thoughtfully. "I remember that one. De Lusignan is dead now. Murdered in the purge of 1680, I believe."

"There's more."

"Go on."

Vivienne squinted at the spidery hand.

It shewed me its layr amidst the desolation of a Great Keepe. A hoole, deep and black. Jörgen did claime the Shadowlands hath many planes, many Doors, and I think it truth. A bargayn was Made, and Passage agreed, but both the Greater and Lesser Gates did reject it. Nether blood nor talisman sufficed. From that place I did flee fore the Daemon did take my Eyes.

"A daemon, you say?"

"And the bit about the eyes. Suggestive, don't you think?"

They combed through the rest of the archives. There was one other reference to a daemon, in a history compiled by a necromancer named Gressius. He claimed one had come through in Rome and started the Great Fire of 64 A.D. that burned half the city. His account had been written hundreds of years later, though, so its credibility was hardly iron-clad.

Alec came in at lunchtime, his cheeks flushed and windblown.

"I hope you had a pleasant afternoon," he said. "I got to look at pictures of Hell while being discreetly felt up."

"At least it was discreet." Vivienne thrust the de Lusignan papers at him. "Think I found something. We may have a name for our Dr. Clarence."

Alec read the paper and let out a slow breath.

"*Shadow and flame.* But the wards turned it back."

"Sounds like he also tried to open a temporary lesser gate with the talisman and that didn't work either."

"So if it is the same creature, or a similar one, how did it get through?"

"That's the question we're stuck on. Now tell me about your Lady Frances. Did she know anything?"

Alec related his visit to the others.

"The Ptolemy pages could be a wild goose chase," Vivienne said. "I still don't see how they fit."

"They could," Alec agreed. "But they're the only item in the catalogue Cyrus isn't familiar with. And Hake-Dibbler said they were unique, although she didn't know exactly how."

Vivienne scanned the catalogue again. The written description was brief.

Cosmographia Geographia. Seven pages, 1480 edition. Printed in Rome. Original volume lost. Engraved color illustrations. Additional annotations based on original treatise by Marinus of Tyre.

"Lady Hake-Dibbler said the bidding got quite hot," Alec said.

"I think it's worth a trip to Oxford. Cyrus can continue to look into the other books in case there's something we missed."

"I suppose that makes sense," Vivienne conceded.

"I'd try Mr. Crawford first," Cyrus suggested. "He's friendly enough. He'll likely tell you what they were after. Summersbee guards his secrets. No one even knows who his buyers are."

"That's what Lady Frances said." Alec looked at the heaps of yellowing parchment piled all over the carpet and sighed. "We're running out of time. Whatever Clarence is looking for, there's a good chance he's already found it."

"Then we should leave right away," Vivienne said, rising. "I'll get Cass and tell her not to bother unharnessing the horses."

"I'm sorry your visit was so brief, my dear." Cyrus gave her a peck on the cheek. "Send a cable if you learn anything. I'll keep digging through the archives." He blinked owlishly. "I believe there are a few other references to daemons. Even the Duzakh feared them, though I was never certain they actually existed until now."

Outside, the rain had turned to snow—small, dry flakes that made Alec think of ashes. Perhaps it was spending the morning with the Lady Frances Hake-Dibbler and her fascination with Hell, but it struck him as an ill omen. As though the very world had caught fire.

CHAPTER 8

Alec and Vivienne caught the next train back to London and changed at Paddington for the Great Western line to Oxford. They hailed a hansom cab outside the station. Alec gave the driver the address of Crawford's on Queen Street. It had snowed here too, and the cobbled lanes and patchwork of ancient honey-toned colleges lay under a blanket of white.

Queen Street was a bustling area of quaint, gabled buildings with businesses occupying the bottom floors. The book shop was tucked between a cobbler and the Empress Tea Emporium. A sign above the plate glass window announced CRAWFORD'S BOOK & PRINT SHOP, and beneath that, *Libraries Purchased*.

Two of Blackwood's men watched the entrance from across the street. Alec tipped his hat to them, getting a nod in return, and opened the door. A bell tinkled somewhere in the maze of shelving. Volumes crowded every inch of space, arranged according to some inscrutable system known only to the owner. Thick tomes on the sciences sat cheek by jowl with cheap yellow-backs by popular writers like Wilkie Collins, whose eye-catching covers favored swooning women and devilish men. The air smelled of wood polish and old paper, which Alec found quite pleasant.

They started for the rear of the shop just as a door opened behind the counter and Mr. Dorian Crawford emerged. He was round and dark-haired and sleek as an otter, with clever little hands that seemed made to curl against his belly as he floated merrily down a river.

"How may I assist you?" he asked, his expression polite but wary. He glanced involuntarily at the front windows, where the constables could be seen.

He's frightened of something, Alec thought. *Though I suppose they all are.*

Vivienne led the introductions, explaining that they were friends of Cyrus Ashdown. Crawford's tense posture relaxed.

"Haven't seen him in a while, but I always valued his opinion. I hear his library is extraordinary!" This was said in a slightly wistful tone, as though he'd angled for an invitation that never arrived. "He's not selling, is he?"

"Nothing like that," Vivienne said with a smile. "Actually, we're interested in the *Geographia Cosmographia.* The 1480 edition."

"Ah. You've missed the boat, I'm afraid. Seven pages were just sold at auction." A shadow passed over his features. "And I was unable to acquire them."

"I understand. But we hoped you might be able to tell us something about the pages themselves." Vivienne paused. "It's unclear why they were included among the other lots."

Mr. Crawford tilted his head, considering. "Well, I can show you one. I bought it at a previous sale. It's currently on hold for a client, but I suppose you might have a look."

"That would be wonderful," Vivienne said, beaming. "We've traveled all the way from London." She leaned in conspiratorially. "And Mr. Ashdown says Mr. Summersbee has a rather prickly disposition. That's why we came to you first."

The mention of his rival's name made Crawford shudder, as though a goose had just stepped over his grave. "An intolerable man," he muttered. "I would compare him to Mr. Dickens' Scrooge, but that does a disservice to the character." His brown eyes twinkled with malice. "Mr. Summersbee," he said, "would have sent those spectral visitors screaming into the night. He is the personification of evil. And I say this as one who always seeks out the good in my fellow man. Unfortunately, in Summersbee's case, it is a futile effort."

With this pronouncement, Mr. Crawford led them into the back room. A large table held several books in the process of having their bindings repaired. Shelves against the wall displayed extra boards, cloth and paper, along with different sizes of needles and thread, and jars of glue. A book press held a copy of Jules Verne's *Five Weeks in a Balloon* clamped between its jaws.

"Very little is known about the life of Claudius Ptolemy," Crawford said, rummaging through a chest of drawers. "He was a Greek who lived in Alexandria around 100 A.D. Besides his interest in geography, he was an astronomer and mathematician."

"I've read the *Almagest*," Alec said. "A brilliant man, even if he did believe the Earth was the center of the universe."

"Indeed. His influence on later astronomers can hardly be overstated. That's why these pages are so unusual."

Crawford removed a binder containing a single large sheet of paper, which he laid on the table.

"Here it is. Cost a pretty penny," he said. "I'll thank you not to touch it. The parchment is quite fragile."

The plate depicted the lands surrounding the Arabian desert: Palestina, Syria, Mesopotamia and Babylonia. Vivienne's home was there somewhere, Alec knew. A land called Al Miraj, although it had vanished from the history books long before Ptolemy was even born.

"Identical to the 1478 edition, but with one small change that makes it priceless," Crawford said. His finger hovered above the point where the Nile River divided in its flow toward the Mediterranean. Egypt's ancient capital of Memphis.

Alec squinted and leaned over the map.

"You see it, right there? *Et portae inferni*. The gate to Hell."

Alec felt the blood drain from his face. Vivenne's own shock echoed through the bond.

"Are you all right, Mr. Lawrence?" the shopkeeper asked. "Would you like to sit down?"

"I'm fine," Alec managed. "Do other pages have this symbol?"

"I only know of this one, and the seven that were just sold. I had a chance to view the pages at Sotheby's. They're all in cities of the ancient world. Rome, Damascus, Jerusalem, Babylon....ah, Samarkand and Bactria. Athens was the last, I believe." He pointed to a symbol next to the ornate lettering that looked like an umbrella with two handles, one longer than the other. "That's an amenta. The Egyptian hieroglyph for the underworld."

Alec shared a long look with Vivienne. Things started falling into place. Very unpleasantly.

"The pages were only discovered recently," Crawford explained. "Scholars and collectors are still debating their meaning. But they're a significant anomaly for a work by Ptolemy because he was so rigorously scientific for his time. There's no hint that he dabbled in darker arts, or had any interest in religious symbolism."

"Where were they found?" Vivienne asked.

"The grandson of some Italian duke found them in his library after he died. The provenance can be proven without a doubt. Each page bears a watermark from the printer, Arnold Buckinck. They've all been exhaustively verified."

"Thank you, Mr. Crawford, you've been an enormous help," Alec said abruptly, steering Vivienne back into the main part of the shop.

"But don't you—"

Crawford's words cut off as the door slammed behind them. Vivienne and Alec broke into a run.

"Revered Mother, we have to get those bloody pages," she muttered, skirts bunched up in her fists.

Alec didn't reply. He was already half a block ahead.

Summersbee's shop was around the corner on St. Aldate's Street. Two bored-looking policemen stood outside. They wore the helmets and dark uniforms of the local constabulary.

"Is the owner in?" Alec demanded, as Vivienne skidded up next to him.

"And you'd be?" The first cop eyed them with suspicion and moved to block the doorway.

"Agents with the S.P.R." Vivienne thrust a card into his hand. When they saw the words "lady" and "marchioness," both of them knuckled their foreheads and backed down. Alec didn't like the rigid British class system, but it had its uses sometimes.

"He's in there," the second officer said. "Though Mr. Summersbee's none too pleased to have us here. Says it's bad for business."

"So no one else has gone inside?"

"Not since we arrived three hours ago."

"Good."

"Expecting trouble?"

"Possibly. Can you get some extra men here?"

The cop nodded and blew his whistle twice. "Shouldn't be long. Kelly, go in with them. I'll wait outside."

"Do you have any men around back?"

"We did, but they were called off an hour ago for a disorderly at a public house."

"Perhaps Mr. Kelly should take the back door then," Alec suggested.

Kelly, a bear of a man with the piercing blue eyes and dark hair of the type sometimes called Black Irish, shrugged and stomped into a narrow alleyway leading to the rear of the shop.

Alec and Vivienne went inside. Summersbee's establishment was much smaller than Crawford's. Gleaming shelves displayed volumes neatly organized by their subject matter, which, Alec noticed, was decidedly darker than ghost stories and adventure tales. Most of the titles were in Latin or French, a few in German. There were several copies of *Mallei Maleficarum*, The Hammer of Witches. A primary manifesto of the Inquisition, it had been a bestseller in the 16th century.

Light spilled through the mullioned windows but it didn't penetrate the rear of the shop, which was bathed in gloom.

"Mr. Summersbee?" Vivienne called. "Hello?"

There was no response. They followed a long runner of worn brown carpet to an archway leading to a second room, also lined with shelves. The low ceilings and dark tones—most of the books were bound in brown and black calfskin—gave Alec the impression of entering a cave.

"He must be in the back," Vivienne said.

A long hallway led to what looked like a parlor. Halfway down, Alec's hackles rose. He smelled blood, newly spilled, still warm, earthy and metallic. He stopped in his tracks.

"Sever me from the power, Vivienne," he said in a low voice. "I'm not safe."

She laid a hand on his arm. An instant later, something slammed down on their bond. He could still sense her emotions, but the river of power that flowed between them had been dammed as though it never even existed. Alec couldn't even remember the last time he'd been forcibly severed. The loss made his skin crawl, made him want to howl in fury.

It was what the cuffs had been expressly designed for all those centuries ago: to permit a human to control a daēva. They were no more than glorified choke collars. Vivienne didn't use hers against him unless he asked her to, but the degradation of it still chafed. Alec bit down hard on his anger and took a steadying breath.

She only did it to save his life. Fire was his Achilles heel. The one element he couldn't work. No daēva could, even though the wild, untamed energy of fire exerted an almost irresistible pull. If Alec lost control and reached for it, if he even got too close, it would char him to ashes.

And the daemon was a creature of shadow and flame.

"Ready?" Vivienne asked.

Alec nodded grimly. They moved forward. The smell of blood grew stronger, almost overwhelming. He heard small clicking sounds he couldn't identify, like insect legs. They came from the parlor.

He turned back to Vivienne and saw she already had her knives out, plain but wickedly sharp blades of iron. Alec flicked a catch on his cane. The outer casing fell away, revealing a slender sword.

"Let me go first," Vivienne said.

Alec didn't argue.

They found Mr. Summersbee in the parlor. He lay on his back, gasping through a terrible slash in his throat. Some of the furniture had been knocked over, indicating a struggle, but there were no hiding places big enough for a man. Vivienne rushed to the rear door and tried the knob.

"Locked from the inside," she said. "Windows too."

"Let me help him," Alec said. And when Vivienne hesitated: "Just do it!"

Her lips thinned. She didn't want to risk it, but she could also cut him off again in an instant. The dam vanished. Molten power surged through his veins. Alec dropped to his knees next to the dying man. He knew how to use elemental magic for healing, had done it for Vivienne countless times. He laid a hand on Mr. Summersbee's chest, felt the feeble heartbeat. If he tried to knit together the gash in his neck, the shock would kill the man, Alec realized immediately. He'd lost too much blood. So Alec took his hand instead, holding it gently. Mr. Summersbee's glazed eyes locked on his own. The bookseller was elderly, small and frail. He had a strong will, though. Alec could see it though the terror and pain.

Holding the power made Alec feel disconnected from his own emotions, but anger battered at the Nexus, largely at himself. If only they had come here first. If only they had been quicker.

"Where did Clarence go?" Vivienne muttered. "He must be inside somewhere. I'll check the front again."

Mr. Summersbee opened his mouth. Nearly gone, Alec thought. He heard Vivienne banging around in the stacks, opening and closing doors, then heading to the front to inform the policeman outside what had happened.

The old man gave a shudder. Summersbee's eyes fixed on a point past Alec's shoulder. For a moment, Alec thought he was dead. Then Summersbee dragged his gaze back. Imploring. Urgent. A single drop of blood bloomed on his white shirtfront. Falling from above. Alec turned his head and looked up.

Dr. Clarence clung to the ceiling, fingers and toes wedged into tiny cracks in the mortar. His expression was empty. An inhuman mask. Alec leapt back with a cry of surprise, fumbling for his sword. Clarence dropped down to hands and knees, crouching like an ape. His eye sockets were shadowed, but pinpricks of light gleamed in their depths.

The doctor had changed since Alec last saw him.

It was nothing obvious. If you'd passed him on the street, you might not notice anything amiss. But the fingers poised on the carpet were tipped with filthy black nails that hooked like talons. The skin beneath his jaw appeared rough, like hide. Clarence smiled. How large and white his teeth seemed in the darkness.

Alec's hand closed around the silver falcon of his sword hilt. Before he could raise it, Clarence sprang past him, smashing through the window. Outside, Kelly shouted something. Then he screamed. Alec clambered over the sill, trying to avoid the shards of broken glass. The policeman rolled on the ground, clutching his face. It didn't seem a mortal wound and Alec didn't stop. Vivienne and the second officer were running down the alley from the direction of St. Aldate's, but Clarence had gone the other way, into the tangle of narrow, snow-slick passageways leading toward Wheatsheaf Yard.

The doctor had no shoes, but it didn't slow him down. His blurred form was already far ahead. Alec's lungs swelled to bursting as he recklessly called to air. Clarence's hair whipped in the sudden headwind and he scuttled like a crab, but quickly regained his footing. He turned a corner. Alec pursued. Crumbling brick flashed past, the sky a thin white ribbon above. There would be hell to pay later for abusing his bad leg, but he wouldn't let his quarry escape a second time.

The wall slammed into place again as Vivienne cut him off. She knew what he'd just done and didn't approve. Probably for the best.

Alec burst from the mouth of an alley and realized he was on the High Street, a continuation of Queen Street. Dusk was falling. Shadows deepened in the crevices between the buildings. He paused beneath the yellow glow of a gaslamp. Could Clarence be headed back for Crawford's page? But no, he could see fresh footprints leading east, the toes oddly elongated, ape-like. They'd melted through two inches of snow, leaving a clear trail.

The handful of people huddled under shop awnings shrank away from the man with wild eyes holding a naked sword. Alec barely registered them. He followed the footprints up High Street. At Oriel Street, they veered toward the gothic spires of University Church of Saint Mary the Virgin. The medieval church sat between two of Oxford's colleges. Alec could see the neoclassical dome and cupola of the Radcliffe Camera looming behind.

He gulped air and ignored the growing ache in his knee. The trail led to the church entrance on the north side of the street, an ornate porch flanked by serpentine columns and a statue of the Virgin and Child. Alec slipped inside the heavy doors into the nave. Archangels holding shields stared down from stone niches, but sadly, they had failed to smite the unholy intruder. Clarence was nowhere in sight. Alec looked around, his eyes gathering the faint light filtering down from the stained glass windows of the clerestory. A dozen candles flickered on the altar.

"Did a man just come in here?" Alec asked a middle-aged woman dressed in widow's black who sat in one of the pews.

She didn't speak, just pointed with wide eyes. Alec padded down the central aisle on his toes, scanning the shadowed archways on either side for any signs of movement. Just past the altar, he saw a single drop of blood. Alec passed through a second chapel and found himself at the base of the tower. A cramped spiral staircase wound upward.

He closed his eyes and listened, daēva senses heightened to an exquisite degree. He heard the whispery patter of snow falling, the gentle creaks of an old building settling under its weight. The drip of beeswax and the rustle of skirts as the woman he had spoken to hurried for the exit to High Street. And the soft slap of bare feet on stone, far above him.

Vivienne would follow. She would track him through the bond as surely as he had tracked Clarence's trail in the snow. Alec wished she were here now, but he couldn't wait for her. He clenched his teeth and started to climb. His leg hurt. Badly. And now stairs, lots of them. He trailed a hand on the rough stone-block walls, fighting a wave of vertigo as the spiral grew even tighter.

Up and up the staircase wound, until Alec finally reached the top. Bits of sleet stung his eyes as he emerged onto a narrow walkway enclosed by a waist-high stone wall. Leering gargoyles jutted from the stonework above, poised as if about to take flight. His knee felt on fire.

All of Oxford spread out below. The old row houses of the

High Street, the spires and towers of other colleges. The horizon was a white smudge.

Six hundred years this tower had stood here. It had survived wars and plagues and being shot up by Cromwell's troops. Alec would have liked to pull it down on Clarence's head but he was severed from the power. All he had was his blade. *I'll have to make good use of it then.*

"Daēva."

The word grated as if spoken through a mouthful of pebbles.

Alec turned. Dr. Clarence stood at the place where the walkway curved around to the far side of the tower. He was little more than a dark shape against the night.

"I know what you are," Alec said, adjusting the grip on his sword. A porcelain-thin layer of ice coated the stone between them. "Daemon."

Soft laughter. "And I know what *you* are. I've trafficked with your kind before."

"Who summoned you?"

"No one." The daemon sounded amused. "I come and go as I please."

"Well, I'm afraid you can't stay."

Alec sensed Vivienne. She tugged at him, like a compass needle spinning toward true north. He knew she'd reached the entrance on High Street. She was afraid, mainly for Alec, but murderously angry too. *Hurry. I'm not so proud to think I don't need help with this one.*

Clarence laid a hand on the balustrade. Snow hissed into steam beneath his fingers.

"They called you Achaemenes, didn't they, slave? And here you are, two thousand years later, still doing their bidding." He made a *tsking* sound, like a mildly displeased schoolteacher. "How pitiful. But you don't know mine, do you? Should I tell you before you die?"

Alec tried to control his shock. He felt suddenly unmoored, as though the rules of a game had been chucked out the window halfway through. It wasn't possible. And yet somehow it was.

This thing knows my real name. Only three people in the world— Vivienne, Cyrus and Cassandane—remember it and they would never tell a soul. What does that mean?

Clarence watched his reaction with malignant delight. "I'm old too. Older than you, daēva. By several orders of magnitude." He cocked his head. "Come closer. I want to see your face."

Alec drew a steadying breath. *Don't let him bait you. Nor touch you either.*

"Give me the maps," he said. "They're no use to you anyway. The Greater Gates are locked and shall never be opened again."

Dr. Clarence took a step closer. The blizzard howled around them. Alec felt the void to his left beyond the wall, a black abyss that dropped at least a hundred feet to the paving stones below.

"Per me si va ne la città dolente," the daemon hissed. *"Per me si va ne l'etterno dolore, per me si va tra la perduta gente. Giustizia mosse il mio alto fattore....Lasciate ogni speranza, voi ch'entrate."*

Through me you go to the grief-wracked city. Through me you go to everlasting pain. Through me you go to wander among lost souls. Abandon all hope, Ye Who Enter Here.

Alec couldn't help it. He laughed. "Are you quoting Dante's *Inferno* at me, Dr. Clarence? The only truly terrifying part is your Italian accent. It's all wrong for the Late Middle Ages, if you're going for authenticity."

Alec raised his sword only to have it knocked away as the daemon closed the distance between them faster than he could have imagined possible. They grappled beneath the blank glares of the stone gargoyles, crashing against the tower wall with bruising force. Smoke rose from Alec's coat where Clarence touched him. The stink of burning flesh filled the air. Alec instinctively sought the Nexus, battering against Vivienne's iron grip. It was futile. Instead, he smashed an elbow into Clarence's face. Bone crunched and red spurted from his nose.

He bleeds just like everyone else. The body he stole still lives. Just snap his neck....

The doctor roared, pupils pulling into themselves like collapsing stars. Darkness gathered there. Something tangible and sentient. It eyed him almost lustfully.

"Look at me, daēva," he hissed. "Why don't you use your elemental power?" The lids narrowed. "Or is it because you can't?"

A faint sound rose above the wind. Alec thought it might be the echo of feet pounding up the tower stairs. Clarence heard it too, eyes flicking to the doorway. Alec seized the chance to slither away. He leapt for his sword half buried in snow ten feet away, every movement precise and economical. The frozen hilt seared his palm but he barely felt the cold. He brought it back for a two-handed sweep. Air whistled against the razored edge of the blade.

On second thought, I'll take his head. That usually does the trick.

Everything in Alec's field of vision snapped into sharp focus. He sprang forward, faster than a mortal eye could track. He was almost there when he hit a patch of black ice. The ground tilted beneath his feet. Agony exploded in Alec's knee as he dropped onto it hard, the impact jolting the sword from his hand. Clarence kicked it over the parapet. A hand seized his coat and pinned him to the low wall so that his back arched out over nothingness. He smelled the daemon's breath, a sulfurous spring.

Alec had never encountered anything, man or beast, stronger than himself. It came as a shock to discover he couldn't break free, no matter how hard he struggled. Clarence's other hand reached into his wool jacket and removed a shiny object.

Alec's chest felt painfully exposed. His heart slammed against his ribcage. Bits of sleet whipped his face, melting on his lips.

A blade through the heart will do me. The daemon knows it. I can see it in his eyes.

Alec stared up at the dark sky, willing Vivienne to come,

knowing she wouldn't make it in time. The centuries of his life spun away into the distance like the void receding at his back. What did it all boil down to? What was the bloody point? Besides his own stupidity and recklessness.

I wish I'd kissed her, just once. And: *I always knew my leg would kill me in the end.*

Dr. Clarence looked at him intently. The darkness behind his eyes flickered. Vivienne was seconds away now. They both knew it. The daemon's arm moved forward and up, almost tenderly, shoulder hitching a little as the knife in his hand struck bone.

The pain in Alec's knee was eclipsed by a terrible *tearing* in his abdomen. His legs felt severed from the top half of his body. Cold and numb. The daemon raised a bloody hand. Alec heard the droplets sizzle as they struck the ice, like butter on a hot griddle.

He tried to find a place of emptiness, but the pain was too vast. It blotted out everything except the sight of Clarence's hand, which paused an inch from Alec's face. The palm curved, a grotesque parody of a mother about to cup the rosy cheek of her infant. An ocean of flame roiled beneath the skin. Alec felt its tidal pull, sucking him deeper out to sea. He closed his eyes. Tried to twist away. Everything seemed swathed in red gauze.

"I'll be back for you, daēva," the daemon whispered.

He yanked Alec away from the abyss just as Vivienne exploded from the tower archway. A knife flew from her hand into Dr. Clarence's back. She was yelling, though Alec couldn't make out the words or even the language. He slid to the ground, leaning brokenly against the tower wall. His head lolled down and he saw the scalpel buried there. Clarence had turned his guts into sausage hash.

"Amán," he muttered in Greek, though he'd meant to say, "Oh, dear."

A dozen uniformed officers jammed the narrow walkway. Arms lifted him up—Vivienne?—and took him in from the cold. The stairs made his head whirl. He knew he was dying when she put her mouth to his ear and whispered, "Stay with me." And then for good measure, "Meíne mazí mou," in case he was still in Greek mode.

Vivienne only said that when he was at death's door, a threshold he had lingered on more than once. He'd said those same words the day he bonded her, when *she* was the one bleeding out on the sand. She had told him to go away. But he hadn't, and he wouldn't.

"Always," he told her now, his voice a ragged husk.

He managed to hold on until the eighty-second step. Then he fainted.

CHAPTER 9

Two constables helped carry Alec to a doctor on Magpie Lane, a few short blocks from St. Mary's Church. His name was Couch and his skills were highly regarded, although Alec lost so much blood on the way, it was obvious no one except Vivienne expected him to live.

A rail-thin housekeeper answered their frantic pounding on the front door. She took one look at Alec and led them straight to the surgery at the rear of the house. Shelving held rows of neatly labeled glass bottles and medical textbooks. A black leather bag perched on a small desk in the corner. It was nearly identical to the one they'd seized from Clarence.

"Put him there," the housekeeper said briskly, pointing to a long wooden table. "Dr. Couch is having his supper. I'll fetch him immediately."

The police deposited Alec on the table, then waited awkwardly in a puddle of melted snow. Vivienne snatched a folded sheet from a pile, wadded it up, and pressed it against Alec's abdomen. Within seconds, scarlet bloomed through the white cotton. He hadn't woken up. It was a mercy, she thought. Vivienne had felt the blade go in. Through their bond, she experienced perhaps a tenth of what Alec did, and still the pain had taken her breath away.

"What's happened?" A man of late middle age bustled in, wavy grey hair sticking out in unruly tufts as though he had a habit of tugging at it. He had shrewd blue eyes and a broad, ruddy-cheeked face with large features that made him seem younger. The buttons of his dark frock coat strained against a prosperous paunch.

"He was attacked by an escaped mental patient," Vivienne said. "The man had a knife."

"Was the assailant apprehended?" Dr. Couch asked in alarm, rushing to Alec's side and checking his pulse.

"Not yet. But the police are combing the streets. It happened over at St. Mary's."

"We'd best join the search, milady," one of the constables said, touching the brim of his cap. He glanced at Alec, then away. "Dr. Couch will see to Mr. Lawrence."

Vivienne nodded distractedly as the officers hurried out the door.

"Let's have a look," the doctor said, gently lifting the wadded sheet. His face grew grave as he unbuttoned Alec's shirt. Vivienne sensed a presence in the doorway. The housekeeper had returned with bandages and a pot of boiling water.

"What's that for?" Vivienne demanded.

Couch shot her a harried look. "I'm a believer in heat sterilization, Lady Cumberland."

She frowned. "What's that?"

"A new technique that seems to reduce infection." He used a pair of forceps to dip a surgical needle in the pot. "Fetch the black thread, Mrs. Bergmann."

The housekeeper moved to comply. She had the same cool efficiency as her employer and Vivienne guessed they'd been together a long time.

"What can I do to help?" she asked.

"Stand over there and try not the get in the way," Dr. Couch replied, not unkindly.

Alec lay still as a corpse while the doctor shot him full of morphine and sewed him up. Couch's demeanor remained calm and competent throughout, but Vivienne could see the resignation in his eyes. All he could do was suture the skin. There was no way to repair the internal damage.

"I'm terribly sorry, but it's unlikely he'll last the night," Dr. Couch said when it was done. He had a direct manner Vivienne respected. "The blade pierced both liver and kidney. I counted seven separate stab wounds. The survival rate for this kind of injury is roughly one in twenty, Lady Cumberland. Even if he does live, there's a good chance he'll be septic within a week." He wiped his hands on a cloth. "He'll stay here tonight. You might wish to remain. Just in case."

"I'll stay. Thank you for what you've done."

Dr. Couch nodded. "I wish it was more, but he's in the Lord's hands now. Call me if you require anything."

The stairs creaked as Dr. Couch went up to his rooms, which occupied the top three floors of the building. Vivienne sank into a chair. She watched Alec sleep. He looked as bad as she'd ever seen him. White and bloodless as the children who'd been taken by Harper Dods. The morphine dulled his pain, but she felt it at the edge of her awareness.

Vivienne didn't blame Alec for not waiting. She would have done the same. But it terrified her to think of what might have happened if she'd been a few seconds later. Vivienne had been bonded to one other daēva before Alec. She had died trying to work fire. Part of Vivienne had never recovered from the loss.

He'll live, she thought. *He's a tough bastard.*

She took his hand. It felt feverishly warm. The daēva blood working to repair ruined tissue. There wasn't a bone in Alec's body that hadn't been shattered at one point or another. Not an inch of skin that hadn't been torn open. Had he been mortal, he would have been dead a thousand times over. He'd always pulled through.

But eventually, there would come a day when he wouldn't. She knew this too. Alec wasn't immortal, just very old. Lucky too.

You're a tough bastard, she thought again, barely aware of the tears on her cheeks.

Alec's eyes fluttered open sometime after midnight. He'd already metabolized a dose of morphine that should have kept him in twilight for a full day.

"Where?" he croaked.

Vivienne brought a glass of water and helped him drink. She understood what he was asking.

"Clarence got away. He scaled down the side of the tower like a bloody spider."

Alec closed his eyes. "He knew...my name."

"What?"

"He called me...Achaemenes. Called me a slave."

Vivienne was silent for a long moment. "When I find him, I'm going to send him back to a pit so deep and dark, he'll never find his way out." She produced a crumpled pack of cigarettes and lit one, snapping the lighter shut with a savage *snick*. "You're in a doctor's surgery, by the way. He plugged the holes. Took hours."

"Oughtn't...smoke in here," Alec managed.

She waved a hand through the nicotine fog. "Couch'll never know."

Alec laughed weakly. "Rots your lungs."

"Not mine." Her full lips curled. "Called you a slave, did he? The tosser." Her language tended to grow coarse when she was angry.

"Thought I still was."

She frowned. "That's interesting. Doesn't get out much, our daemon, does he?"

"He could have killed me, Viv."

"I know. You got lucky."

"Not what I mean. He *chose* to spare me."

She snorted. "I'd say he carved you up pretty badly, Alec."

He coughed, wincing. "Yes. But he knew the wounds wouldn't be mortal. Why not the heart? Only way to be...certain."

Her almond eyes grew thoughtful. "Are you sure?"

"Fairly sure." Alec lay back and closed his eyes. "Need to sleep now."

Vivienne nodded and fussed with the sheet, tucking it around his shoulders. "Heal yourself," she said. "And do a proper job of it."

"I am," he murmured.

She smiled at the thought of what Dr. Couch would say when he came down in the morning and found his patient sitting up.

Tough bastard.

CHAPTER 10

WEDNESDAY, DECEMBER 19

Alec spent two more days in Dr. Couch's surgery. On Tuesday afternoon, he walked out the door, leaning heavily on his cane but otherwise operating under his own steam. Dr. Couch, who taught at one of the colleges, tried to convince Alec to stay on for another week or two. He wanted to write a paper for *The Lancet* about Mr. Lawrence's remarkable recovery.

Couch was disappointed at Alec's polite refusals, but clearly delighted with his own skill.

"You're the case of my career, Mr. Lawrence!" he declared with a grin. "I don't suppose you'd agree to a portrait?" He blushed. "I'd like to hang it on my wall."

Alec agreed, and Dr. Couch found a photographer. They posed him sitting on a tasseled footstool with his top hat on and chin propped on his cane.

He'd told Vivienne everything that happened atop the tower except for the part about slipping on the ice; that his infirmity had betrayed him. She would feel guilty, as she always did, but it was simply the price of the bond. The cuff took a piece of you. In Alec's case, it was a bad knee. For Cassandane, it was a malformed ear. Each daēva endured a different mutilation. Alec

96

would have a limp until the day he died or their bond was broken. He hoped it would be the first.

Back in London, they both stewed. Dr. Clarence hadn't resurfaced. An exhaustive search of Summersbee's shop confirmed that the Ptolemy pages were gone. Blackwood's men confiscated Mr. Crawford's single folio, despite vociferous complaints and threats to sue. He seemed to believe it was all a plot by Mr. Summersbee to steal his clients. That Summersbee was dead failed to persuade him otherwise.

Vivienne sent a cable to Cyrus and Cassandane informing them of the latest developments. Cyrus responded that he would continue searching the archive for anything of use, particularly as it related to the Greater Gates.

And so they waited. Vivienne spent her time prowling around the house, or overseeing her various charities for women and girls. Alec worked in his laboratory, but he was unable to lose himself the way he normally did. He blamed Vivienne. He rarely chafed under the bond, but he did now. No matter how far apart they were, he could sense her growing frustration, like the maddening hum of a fly.

On Wednesday morning, Alec shaved and dressed in a suit of charcoal grey. His woolen greatcoat had been too blood-soaked to salvage, but he found an old ulster that ought to keep the rain off. He placed two objects in the pocket. The first was a stone, the second a shell. He put his top hat on and made his way into Green Park. Stately oak and plane trees framed long, sweeping vistas and acres of manicured lawns.

On fine summer days, people would set out picnic baskets. But it hadn't always been so civilized. Alec remembered passing through on horseback with Vivienne a couple hundred years before. They'd been set on by some luckless bandits with bayonets and terrible teeth. Vivienne had wanted to chop their heads off, but Alec scared them away with a display of witchcraft.

London had been far worse then. A city of plague and decay, suffocating in its own stench. They hadn't lingered.

Alec took Constitution Hill to Knightsbridge and entered Hyde Park. The waters of the Serpentine shimmered a dull grey. Two swans glided along the shore of the lake. Fortunately, the water hadn't frozen over. He slipped a hand into his pocket. The talismans dug into his palm. One for Traveling, one for Locking.

Alec took a quick look around, saw no one, and waded into the lake, his reflection absorbing itself. The substance he entered was more like smoke than water. His clothing remained dry as the gloaming closed over his head. Beneath, a twilight world stretched in all directions. Alec followed a gentle slope leading down. Tall grasses undulated to either side. Within a minute, he saw the luminous glow of the Gate.

A doorway, perhaps twelve feet high and five wide. Had it been open, the surface would flow like a swift river. Alec circled it. The Gate looked frozen, although shadows flickered behind it. Most definitely still locked.

Alec watched the shadows for a moment, battering futilely at the bars of their prison. Shades trapped in the Dominion. If they escaped and found a living host to prey on, they would become ghouls. Undead creatures with the ability to assume the form of their victim. A ghoul would go on killing and changing until it was stopped, either by fire or iron.

The Greater Gate of London was the last of the twelve he and Vivienne sealed. It had taken them centuries to find, which was the primary reason England still had a ghoul problem. So many had come through while they were hunting. But Alec knew now that Clarence had not entered the world this way.

A well-heeled matron was pushing a pram down the shore path when he emerged from the lake. She gave him a startled look. Alec tipped his hat with a smile, and she hurried off.

He didn't want to go back to St. James yet. So he exited the park at Alexandra Gate and walked south, past the Royal Horticultural Society and the Natural History Museum, into the tangle of streets past Old Brompton Road. A light rain began to fall. He turned his collar up.

You ought to go home, he thought.

But his legs kept walking, despite the growing ache in his knee. Alec looked up and realized he was on Symons Street. No, *realized* was disingenuous. Part of him had meant to come here all along. It was why he'd worn a nice suit. He stood on the doorstep, hesitating. Then he rapped twice with the knocker. A moment later, the door swung open. An attractive woman stood on the threshold.

Catherine de Mornay had thick brown hair that she wore in a loose chignon. A velvet gown of deep purple clung to her generous curves, its appeal only enhanced by the high neck.

"Mr. Lawrence," she said coolly.

"Catherine." Alec tried on a smile. "It's good to see you."

"You ought to have sent a note," she said. "I might not have been home. Or I might have been otherwise occupied."

"But you are home." He held her eyes. "Will you invite me inside?"

She waited just long enough to make her point, then stood aside. Alec took his hat off and entered the well-kept brick townhouse. He stood in the front parlor, unsure if he should remove his coat.

"If I'm disturbing you, I needn't stay."

"It's fine. Would you like a drink?"

"Some tea, if you don't mind."

Catherine laughed, a rich, hearty sound Alec had missed very much. "I'd almost forgotten how few vices you have, Mr. Lawrence."

"Alec. Please."

She grinned. "I prefer to call you Mr. Lawrence. It's such a proper English name. Although I doubt that you're an Englishman, despite your addiction to tea. May I take your coat?"

"I've got it," he said, hanging it on a hook by the door. "You make the tea."

He sat down in the front parlor. After a few minutes, Catherine returned with a tray. She poured the tea and settled herself into an armchair.

"How's Sarah?" he asked.

"Much better since you visited. Whatever you did worked wonders. She's still in hospital, but the doctors expect her to make a full recovery. They've never seen a case of consumption pass so quickly."

"I'm very glad," Alec said, although he'd known the child would survive. He'd given her some tablets for the doctors' benefit, but it was a subtle weave of elemental power that had cleansed the sickness from Sarah's lungs.

"You haven't come to see me since. I think I know why."

She'd always been direct. When she admitted a few months before, as they lay tangled together, that her eleven-year-old daughter was dying, Catherine's eyes had remained dry. Even then, she hadn't wanted his sympathy. Just someone to listen.

"Catherine—"

"You think I'll feel I owe you a debt."

Alec said nothing.

"I'm a free woman, Mr. Lawrence. The way I conduct my affairs is my own business. And while I *am* grateful for whatever you did for Sarah, it has nothing to do with us. You enjoy the pleasure of my company, and I happen to enjoy the pleasure of yours. Is that clear?"

"Yes. I'm sorry for assuming otherwise."

In truth, she was entirely correct. Alec felt some of his tension dissipate. Catherine de Mornay made a handsome income from her gentleman callers, enough to live independently in this house and decide who she chose to entertain. She lived life on her own terms, and would despise him if she thought he pitied her in any way.

Catherine smiled and kicked off her slippers. "Now that that's out of the way, there's something I've always wanted to ask. Where were you born, Mr. Lawrence? Your grammar and idioms are impeccable, but your accent...." She frowned. "It's not quite French or Italian. Certainly not American." She blew on her tea, the steam blurring her features. "Let me guess. Say something."

Alec took a sip of his own, felt the warmth blossom in his belly.

"I can smell your perfume."

The corner of her mouth twitched. "I'm not wearing any perfume."

"Your soap, then. Something with lilacs."

"You have an excellent sense of smell. I bathed hours ago."

Alec was distracted by a brief image of Catherine washing her long hair in the tub.

"I thought you were guessing where I'm from," he reminded her.

His hostess closed her eyes. "There's a softness to your vowels. Almost musical. Someplace warm, I think. With palm trees and white sands." Her green eyes flew open. "I've got it. One of the Colonies. The West Indies?"

What would she think if he told her the truth? That he was born in a desert prison more than three hundred years before the infant Christ took his first breath?

Throw him out on the street, if she didn't call Bedlam and have him committed.

Alec smiled. "You're right. My family is from St. Kitts."

"How exotic." She studied him for a moment, then set her cup aside. "Your hair is quite disarranged, Mr. Lawrence."

"I've been working in my laboratory all day. I tried to make myself presentable, but I can see I've failed miserably."

She scrutinized him. "The frock coat is elegant, but the hair simply won't do. Would you like me to comb it for you?"

Alec let her take his hand and lead him upstairs to her

bedroom. Heavy drapes covered the windows. The décor was expensive and tasteful, like Catherine herself. He was aware she had other rooms where she sometimes entertained other gentlemen. But this was *her* bedroom. He knew because there was a framed photograph of Sarah next to the ornate four-poster bed. She was a solemn child, with her mother's dark good looks.

Alec had visited Catherine four or five times in the two years since they'd met at one of Vivienne's parties, and she'd always brought him here. He found it touching.

"Sit, please," she said, patting the bench of a vanity.

Alec sat down facing an oval mirror. He rested his cane against the table. Pots and brushes crowded the polished surface, although Catherine wore little make-up. She picked up a silver comb and began running it through his hair, still slightly damp from the mist outside.

"Most men like to look at themselves," she said, smoothing a lock back from his forehead. "You never do. Why?"

"I'd rather look at you."

Their eyes met in the mirror. The comb paused, then continued its journey around his ear and down the back of his head. Alec closed his eyes. Her fingertips brushed his nape, just above the starched collar of his shirt.

"There's something different about you, Mr. Lawrence. Like a wolf in sheep's clothing." She felt him tense and laughed softly. "I don't mean you frighten me. You don't in the least. Well, I suppose I'm not sure what I mean. Just that you seem like a person with secrets. Are all gentlemen from the Colonies so enigmatic?"

She cupped his cheek and he rested it there for a moment, smelling her lilac bath soap and the pleasantly bitter hint of tea on her breath.

"I don't think so."

"How sad for the ladies. Say something else. Recite some poetry for me."

Catherine knew she could make him say anything she pleased. And she found it romantic that he knew so much verse by heart. Volumes and volumes.

Alec thought for a moment.

> "Lying asleep between the strokes of night
> I saw my love lean over my sad bed,
> Pale as the duskiest lily's leaf or head,
> Smooth-skinned and dark, with bare throat made
>   to bite,
> Too wan for blushing and too warm for white,
> But perfect-coloured without white or red.
> And her lips opened amorously, and said:
> I wist not what, saving one word – Delight."

Catherine laid the comb down. "That's lovely."

"The man who wrote it was a tortured soul."

"It's still lovely."

"Yes."

"Did you choose it because you're a kindred spirit, Mr. Lawrence?" The question was spoken lightly, but there was an intensity in her expression.

"A tortured soul, you mean?" He laughed. "Not like Swinburne. I don't wish to be flogged, thank you."

Catherine didn't smile. "Who is she, Mr. Lawrence?" she asked quietly.

The sudden change of topic caught him off guard.

"I'm not sure what you mean."

She didn't answer. Alec turned his face so his mouth pressed against her palm. She slid her hand to the curve of his jaw, lifting his chin.

"No one, Catherine."

"It doesn't matter." She turned her back on him. "Help me with my buttons."

"Perhaps—"

"No. I'm being ridiculous." She glanced over her shoulder. "Don't leave. I want you to stay."

Alec used the cane to lever himself to standing. One by one, his nimble fingers undid the long row of tiny pearl buttons. Catherine wore no corset beneath. The smooth lines of her bare back unfurled before him like a gift.

He kissed the skin behind her ear. "You're very beautiful, you know," he whispered.

She turned and helped him take off his shirt and waistcoat, running her hands across the plane of his chest. She'd never asked what was wrong with his leg. How he'd injured it. Alec was grateful for that.

"You're beautiful too, Mr. Lawrence," Catherine said. Then she noticed the shiny pink scar tissue on his stomach. Her breath caught. He kissed her before she could speak.

When he pulled back, they looked at each other. Catherine's gaze was steady. She would not ask about this either. She would let Mr. Lawrence keep his secrets, as she kept hers. He kissed her again before she could change her mind.

Her gown fell away, puddling in a velvet shadow around her bare feet, and for the first time in many long weeks, Alec forgot about Vivienne, and dead things that still walked, and the endless river of time he drifted in. There was only Catherine, and the faint smell of lilacs.

HE LEFT her sleeping hours later, and he left a stack of bills on the vanity. If she'd been awake, she might have tried to stop him. Or she might not have. One couldn't be sure with Catherine De Mornay. But despite her great affection for him, Alec would never presume to think he was more than a client. Truthfully, he didn't wish to be more. Anything else was impossible.

He let himself out and returned to St. James Place. It was quite late, but the lamps were still burning in the front parlor. Vivienne lay on the carpet in her silk dressing gown, listening to her new phonograph. She rarely opened a book, but she loved music. The tinny strains of Handel's *Israel in Egypt* broke the silence.

"Where have you been?" Vivienne asked, as if she didn't know.

"I went for a walk."

"And how was your walk?"

"Invigorating, thank you." He tossed his coat on the sofa. "The Gate in Hyde Park is still locked. I checked."

She gazed up at him, head leaning on one hand, her expression unreadable. Alec waited to see if she would pursue it. His relationship with Catherine was none of her business. Vivienne had made her choice a long time ago. He understood and respected it, but he wouldn't live like a monk.

"Hand me my Oxfords, would you?" she said.

Alec spotted them on the mantel. He watched her flick the lighter, felt the pull of the tiny, wavering flame. If he ever grew tired of life, he knew how he'd choose to end it.

"A message came from Blackwood while you were out," Vivienne said. "They found Dr. Clarence."

"What?" He stared at her. "Where? We need to—"

"His body," she clarified. "Fished it out of the Mersey River up north. Throat slit."

"Self-inflicted?"

"Appears that way. The daemon has moved on, Alec. Taken someone else. Could be anyone. Man, woman, child."

He sat down on the sofa. "Damn it."

"Yes. Cyrus has agents watching all the Gates. They'll be ready if he shows up. But at least none have been opened. Not yet."

"The daemon would need a talisman. As far as we know, ours is the only one in existence."

"As far as we know."

"If his victim was reported missing, we might be able to track him that way."

"Blackwood's already looking into it, but Lancashire is a big county. It could take weeks to cover."

Alec felt a wave of weariness wash over him. His brief respite with Catherine had been a balm, but such moments were always temporary. He hadn't yet healed, not completely, and needed more rest than usual. But it wasn't just physical exhaustion. It was a sickness of the soul that weighed on him now. A fear that their best efforts weren't good enough, and never would be.

"I'm going to bed," Alec said, grabbing his cane. "We can talk about it in the morning."

Vivienne blew a smoke ring at the ceiling.

"I'm going to find this daemon and I'm going to kill it, Alec," she said. "If it's the last bloody thing I ever do."

He heard her softly humming along with the Oratorio as he climbed the stairs.

CHAPTER 11

THURSDAY, DECEMBER 20

Alec woke to a landscape of white. Snow had fallen during the night. Across the street in Green Park, children in bright mittens and scarves screamed and waged war with each other. He splashed his face in a basin, then went downstairs and let the cat inside. She arched against his leg.

This particular cat never made a sound, unless she was hissing at one of the neighboring bulldogs. She didn't believe in mewling for her food like other cats. But the significant look she cast at the hall leading to the kitchen indicated that Alec should fetch her something as she had been out in the cold all night.

He obeyed, thinking he might make himself a pot of tea. He still felt strange asking Quimby to carry out such simple tasks. Alec wasn't used to having servants. He preferred to do for himself, even though he knew Quimby found it a bit scandalous that Alec refused a valet to dress him. Apparently, it simply wasn't proper that an English gentleman should button his own trousers.

But Alec wasn't a gentleman, and he wasn't English, and he wouldn't put up with it.

The grandfather clock in the hall issued ten chimes. Quimby was usually polishing the silver in the formal dining room around this time. *He'll never know I snuck behind his back....*

Alec heard voices as he approached the kitchen, which lay at the rear of the house. One belonged to the cook, a sweet woman of middle age who lived in Camden Town. The other was deeper, a rich, silky baritone. There was a moment of silence, then mad giggles from the cook.

Alec pushed open the door. Mrs. Abernathy was kneading dough on the counter, her plump arms floured to the elbows. Seated with his long, booted legs sprawled beneath the well-worn wooden table, the Marquess of Abergavenny, Viscount of Nevill and master of Eridge Castle spooned jam into his mouth with boyish glee. He had dark blonde hair and eyes so electrically blue they were almost unsettling to look at.

He spun in his chair as Alec entered, the smile dying on his lips.

"Where's my wife, you cad?" he demanded stonily.

The cook stopped kneading, looking between them uncertainly. Alec blinked. He opened his mouth, then closed it again. The Marquess roared with laughter. He bounded to his feet and seized Alec in a bear hug. Nathaniel Cumberland had the broad shoulders of a boxer and Alec found himself enveloped in damp wool that smelled of wood smoke and horses.

"By God, Alec, does everyone sleep all day around here? I've been up since five-thirty, and waiting for you to come down since seven." He returned to the jam, pulling out a chair for Alec. "Since you won't visit for Christmas, I had to take a trip to London." He waggled his thick eyebrows. "Viv's letter piqued my curiosity."

"Hold on, Nathaniel. I have to feed the cat."

Alec found a bit of ground meat in the icebox and put it in a bowl. He set it next to the table. A black streak arrived on silent paws, pushed it around for a minute, then began to eat.

"How about a big bang-up breakfast, Mrs. Abernathy?" Nathaniel said, flashing his trademark lopsided grin. "Eggs, toast, bacon, kippers, the whole lot? I'm starving."

The cook brightened. Vivienne existed on coffee in the mornings, and Alec never asked Mrs. Abernathy to make anything at all. If he was hungry, he usually bought a hot pie on the way to wherever he was going.

"A 'course, my lord." She made a shooing motion. "But you mustn't hang about in here. I'll ring Mr. Quimby when it's ready."

Even Alec knew most cooks wouldn't talk to a marquess that way, but most marquesses weren't Nathaniel Cumberland.

"Splendid!" Nathaniel gave the spoon a last lick. "How I've missed your strawberry jam, Mrs. Abernathy. Nectar of the gods."

The cook blushed and waved her rolling pin at them.

They passed Claudine on the way to the conservatory. She gave a curtsy when she saw Lord Cumberland, keeping her eyes fixed on the ground despite his warm greeting. Vivienne refused to talk about Claudine's past, but Alec could guess some of it. It was clear she feared men. She probably had good reason.

"I'll tell Lady Cumberland milord is here," Claudine whispered.

"Tell her she'll miss breakfast if she doesn't rouse herself," Nathaniel said with a laugh. "Party last night?" he asked Alec with a knowing wink when Claudine had gone upstairs.

"Not exactly."

Alec wasn't sure how much he should say. He was still adjusting to this surprise visit. Nathaniel knew about ghouls, of course, and the S.P.R. But he didn't know Alec wasn't human, or any of the rest. He seemed to think they hunted the undead for the fun of it, which, to Nathaniel, made perfect sense.

"Don't hold back on me, Alec. You've got that look. The one you wear when you're trying to decide which lie to tell."

"Unfair. I've never lied to you." Which was true, mostly.

"Another ghoul at the palace?" Nathaniel asked with unseemly hopefulness. "That poor woman."

"Worse."

"Worse?" The marquess rubbed his hands together. "How perfectly awful. Let's hear all about it."

Nathaniel stretched out on one of the extra-long couches, hands interlaced behind his head, while Alec produced a version of events over the last five days that omitted how badly he'd been hurt on the tower and a few other minor details. He laughed long and hard when Alec described his luncheon with Lady Frances Hake-Dibbler.

"Just be grateful your thigh is the only thing she squeezed," he confided. "I was at a weekend party once in Hampshire—"

"We all know that story," Vivienne interrupted. "And frankly, you got off easy. I had to put up with that horrible bore, the Duke of Lancaster. I don't think the man ever brushes his teeth."

Nathaniel unfurled himself from the couch in one serpentine movement.

"My darling," he breathed, drawing her close. "My ravishing angel. How I've pined for you these long—"

Vivienne chucked him under the chin. "I've missed you too," she said. "Breakfast is ready."

"Capital!" Nathaniel dropped her like a hot potato and bee-lined for the dining room.

"What did you tell him?" she whispered as Alec came to her side and they followed the marquess.

"Most of it. He pried it out of me."

Vivienne rolled her eyes. "You just can't resist his charms. It's pathetic."

Alec gave her a wounded look. "Nathaniel can keep a secret. He always has."

"I know." She cast a fond glance down the hall. "I would have told him myself anyway."

The dining table was ridiculously long. They gathered at one end, Nathaniel at the head, Alec and Vivienne on his right and left hand, respectively. Quimby poured coffee all around and retreated to the sideboard. His face rarely altered in expression, but there was an added spring to his step. Alec wasn't the only one who had difficulty resisting Nathaniel's charms.

"So how's life at Castle Blood?" Vivienne asked, reaching for a piece of bacon.

"Oh, you know," he said airily. "Ghosts in the dungeons, icy drafts that arrive just as one steps out of the bathtub. It's like a Collins novel. You ought to visit more often." Lord Cumberland looked at Alec as he said this last part, sapphire eyes alight with mischief. "I promise you won't find it dull."

Alec grinned into his kippers.

"Now, let's hear about your new case, Vivienne." He buttered a piece of toast. "A daemon, eh? Sounds nasty."

"It is." She poked at her scrambled eggs, pushing them about on the plate. "We've no leads to go on. Nothing to do but wait for him to strike again."

Nathaniel laid his knife down. "Haven't you read the papers?"

"Oh God." Vivienne sat stock still. "Don't tell me there's been some grisly killing."

"Nothing like that. But you say this creature has a connection with Claudius Ptolemy?"

"What do you know, Nathaniel? Out with it."

"Well, there's a new museum exhibit opening in New York. Some American chap apparently found his tomb in Alexandria. It's getting quite a bit of international press." He shrugged. "Could be a coincidence, I suppose."

"Or not," Alec said. "Mr. Quimby? Would you bring in today's *Times*?"

"Of course, sir."

A minute later, he was scanning a brief article on page four. Alec felt a surge of excitement.

"It's not opening until after the New Year, but there's a gala planned for December 23," he said. "The article doesn't list the items found, but what if there's a connection?"

"Dr. Clarence's body was found in the Mersey River," Vivienne said. "That's near Liverpool."

"The point of departure for transatlantic steam ships."

"From what you told me, New York is this creature's old hunting grounds," Nathaniel put in. "Perhaps it's going home."

They were all silent for a moment.

"I'd like to speak with Harrison Fearing Pell," Vivienne said. "She might know more than she included in her report."

"And what if we're wrong?" Alec asked. "What if it strikes in London while we're in the middle of the Atlantic?"

"Then Cassandane will come down. She's more than capable, as you well know."

And that seemed to settle the matter.

The rest of the day was a flurry of packing and telegrams to Henry Sidgwick, D.I. Blackwood, and Cyrus and Cassandane, informing them of the latest developments. It seemed their luck had finally turned. A ship was sailing for New York on the following day. At first the agent claimed it was fully booked, but Nathaniel managed to pull some strings and secured them a first-class cabin.

That evening, when Lord and Lady Cumberland decided to go out to dinner at Claridge's and scandalize polite society, Alec locked himself in his laboratory with paper and pen. He felt a foolish urge to write Catherine a letter explaining his sudden departure and that he didn't know when he'd be back, but she oughtn't worry. Foolish because she probably wasn't thinking about him at all, and what they had should have been more than enough.

He could never tell her the truth: that Mr. Lawrence from St. Kitts belonged to another race of beings entirely. That she would grow old and die while he stayed the same. Alec had been down that path before and it always ended badly. It was why he paid for female company. Much better to keeps things businesslike.

Yet he couldn't stop thinking about Catherine de Mornay. Not just her smooth skin and lush hips, but the light in her eyes when she looked at him. Her rich, unrestrained laughter.

Christ, Alec, don't borrow trouble. You've got enough already.

In the end, after a dozen crumpled attempts lay scattered at his feet, he simply sent her the last verse of *Love and Sleep*. Unsigned, but she knew his handwriting.

> And all her face was honey to my mouth,
> And all her body pasture to my eyes;
> The long lithe arms and hotter hands than fire,
> The quivering flanks, hair smelling of the south,
> The bright light feet, the splendid supple thighs
> And glittering eyelids of my soul's desire.

FRIDAY, December 21

THE *ETRURIA* WAITED at anchor in the Port of Liverpool, her two great funnels belching smoke. The lower furnaces had been lit the previous night and the top fires were burning hot since six that morning as she needed to run a full head of steam at least an hour ahead of departure.

The *Etruria* was only three years old and fitted with a new single-screw propulsion system that made her the jewel of the Cunard fleet. She'd set a speed record for the Atlantic crossing earlier that year: six days, one hour, fifty-five minutes. With any luck, the ship would arrive well before the Egyptian exhibit opened at the American Museum of Natural History.

Their first-class stateroom on the Saloon Deck was appointed with every luxury, but Vivienne wasn't looking forward to the trip. Not only was she impatient to get to New York, but Alec had annoyingly forbade her from smoking in their shared suite.

A porter took charge of their luggage on the dock. Now they stood on the forward deck as the great ship prepared to set sail. Crowds lined the pier, blowing kisses and waving white hand-kerchiefs at the departing passengers. The whole scene had an air of suppressed excitement, except for the crewmen, who'd made the crossing many times and moved efficiently about their duties. Windlasses spun, winches cranked. The white-haired captain conferred with a representative of the company on the bridge.

"Watch the man from Cunard," Alec said, checking his pocket watch. "Any moment now...."

The pair shook hands. The man disembarked with a brief salute, and the captain gave a quiet order to the first officer. It was quickly relayed through the chain of command. The capstan began to noisily haul the massive anchor chain back home. Vivienne drew a deep breath of cold salt air. Seagulls wheeled over the bow.

The *Etruria* swung free of her mooring and the great engines thrummed to life. A long blast from the whistle claimed right of way in the channel, which was crowded with sailboats and cargo vessels. The schooner-rigged pilot ship guided them to the harbor mouth. And then nothing lay ahead but open ocean for more than three thousand miles.

"Let's go inside," Vivienne said, turning away from the rail. "I'll never get a cigarette lit in this wind."

Alec laughed. His skin glowed with raw vitality. Air had always been his strongest element. She suspected he'd missed standing under the wide sky, surrounded by nature rather than throngs of people and buildings. It was another difference between them. She preferred cities, but Alec loved the wild places.

"Is that really such a bad thing?"

"Yes."

"You're addicted."

"Don't be an ass." She took his arm. "I know your leg hurts. Come rest it for a bit."

They went to one of the lounges and found a quiet table with large windows overlooking the Upper Deck. A waiter in an elegantly cut jacket brought coffee and a plate of deviled eggs.

"I was thinking, Vivienne. If Claudius Ptolemy knew enough to map the Greater Gates, if he knew about the Dominion, there could be talismans in the collection."

She nodded. "I think he understood all too well how dangerous those pages were. He made only one set and they were lost for more than a millennium."

"Until that duke's grandson found them and they went up for auction."

"So our daemon somehow learns about it...."

"*They're here* could have been referring to the map pages."

"It snaps him out of his hibernation at the asylum." She tapped a cigarette on the table but didn't light it. Addicted? Ridiculous.

"So Clarence escapes and tracks them down. It all fits so far." Alec frowned. "And how does he know about the museum exhibit in New York?"

"The same way we did."

"The newspapers?"

"Why not?"

He shrugged. "All right. The point is, the maps alone are no use to him. Not without a talisman of opening for the Gates."

"Which is why he's going to New York."

Their waiter finally noticed Lady Cumberland fiddling with her cigarette and hurried over to light it.

"Thank you." Vivienne took a long, satisfying drag.

"Can we expect full cooperation from the American S.P.R.?" Alec asked.

"Sidgwick says yes. He'll send a cable warning them that something might be coming their way."

The tinkling notes of a piano served as counterpoint to the muted conversation at other tables. Cunard had spared no expense to create the illusion they were in a fashionable hotel. The décor was modeled after a late-Renaissance Italian palazzo, with gorgeously carved oak paneling and a domed skylight depicting the signs of the zodiac. Without the faint pitching of the deck, Vivienne would never have known she was floating atop a thousand fathoms of frigid water.

"How much do they know about us?" Alec asked.

"Enough."

"That I'm a daēva?"

"Yes, but only the senior officers."

"Who are…?"

"Their president is a man named Benedict Wakefield. He's some sort of wealthy financier. But the ones who manage day-to-day operations are the two vice presidents, Harland Kaylock and Orpha Winter. I've heard they can't stand each other."

"Well, that's promising," he said testily.

Vivienne knew Alec didn't like people knowing what he was. Humans feared any power they didn't share. The truth had been erased from history books, but Alec remembered. As a child, he'd been taught by the magi in Karnopolis to believe he was a demon himself. Impure. *Druj.*

"Do you trust them?" he asked.

"I haven't met them, so no. Sidgwick does. Frankly, I'm more interested in meeting Harrison Fearing Pell and John Weston." She stubbed out her cigarette. "This daemon we're chasing, it was inside Leland Brady for at least a week. He was her *client*, Alec. I'd say she knows it better than anyone."

"That's what I'm afraid of."

"You mean it might go after her?"

Alec didn't answer right away. He stared out to sea, eyes fixed on the flat horizon. "There's a storm coming, Viv. I can smell it. And we need to be in New York when it breaks."

PART II

"If he be Mr. Hyde," he had thought, "I shall be Mr. Seek."
— Robert Louis Stevenson, *The Strange Case of Dr. Jekyll and Mr. Hyde*

CHAPTER 12

TUESDAY, DECEMBER 25, 1888

Everyone agreed it was the party of the year.

Waiters in Egyptian costume plied the buzzing crowd with trays of caviar and frosty magnums of champagne. Hundreds of beeswax candles cast a cozy, flattering light on the cream of New York society, people with names like Vanderbilt, Astor and Gould. Mayor Hewitt chatted with the museum's energetic director, Morris K. Jessup. A thick haze of cigar smoke hung like smog below the high ceiling.

Outside, Christmas wreaths adorned the brick façade of the American Museum of Natural History, but in the spacious entrance hall beyond its front doors, the décor was more exotic. A much-anticipated new exhibit would be opening on January 2nd: Ptolemy's Tomb: The Secrets of Alexandria. The soiree was intended to provide an advance viewing of the treasures brought back by Dr. Julius Sabelline before they went on display to the general public.

Glass cases held amulets and terracotta amphorae and crumbling fragments of papyrus scrolls. There were blue-glazed scarab beetles and solid gold bracelets of writhing snakes. But the thickest knot of party-goers swirled around the six mummies in stone sarcophagi, one of whom was supposedly the famed mathematician and astronomer Claudius Ptolemy.

Speeches were made, more champagne consumed. By midnight, the party started winding down. The long line of lacquered carriages outside ferried their well-heeled (and well-oiled) passengers to mansions across Central Park, or to late-night diversions in less reputable areas like the Tenderloin. The hired staff cleaned up and departed for their own beds in cramped tenements and row houses. At twelve-thirty, the front doors of the museum were locked. Only eight people remained.

Dr. Julius Sabelline, the reclusive Egyptologist who had brought the relics back to New York from Alexandria.

His wife, Araminta, and twenty-year-old son, Jackson.

The socialite Mrs. Orpha Winter and Count Balthazar Jozsef Habsburg-Koháry, financier of the dig.

Nelson Holland, head of Near East and North African Acquisitions at the museum.

Davis Sharpe, Dr. Sabelline's junior colleague.

And lastly, Jeremy Boot, the guard stationed at the front entrance.

Dr. Sabelline retired to his office to return one of the most valuable artifacts to a strongbox for safekeeping. Half an hour later, when he had failed to return, his wife went looking for him, accompanied by Mr. Sharpe. Dr. Sabelline's office door was locked and he didn't respond to their entreaties to open it. Boot was summoned with a spare set of keys.

He unlocked the door, took two steps inside, and promptly vomited on the carpet. Mrs. Sabelline rushed in behind him. A scream of horror echoed through the corridors of the illustrious institution….

"Does it actually say she screamed?" Harrison Fearing Pell interrupted. "I don't remember that bit."

John Weston paused in his dramatic rendering of the police report. "Wouldn't she, though? Finding her husband lying there in a pool of blood, all mangled." He gave Harry a sober look. "I'd shriek like a schoolgirl and I'm not ashamed to admit it."

"I'm sure you would, John, but I believe it says she fainted. Don't muddy the waters. They're thick enough already." She suppressed a smile. "I won't hold it against you for taking liberties with the party. All of that's probably true. But don't embellish the crime itself, please. Or the key witnesses."

The pair reached the corner of Seventy-Third Street and Eighth Avenue. Harry, a solemn, diminutive figure in sturdy boots and a red wool coat, her strawberry blonde hair dusted with melting snow. John, nearly a foot taller with brown hair and lively eyes, shaded now under the brim of a grey Homburg hat.

They had been close friends for many years, but in recent months, the paths of their lives had taken a strange twist. As of that morning, they had signed consultancy contracts with the New York branch of the Society for Psychical Research and been sent off to the American Museum of Natural History to investigate a murder with some very peculiar elements.

It had proven impossible to find a hansom cab so early on Christmas Day, so Harry and John took the elevated train to Fifty-Ninth Street and trudged north from there. To the right, the gentle hills and walking paths of Central Park lay under four inches of pristine snow.

John held his hands up. "Just trying to imagine the scene. Give it a little spice."

Harry shot him a disapproving squint. "What else did you make up?"

"Not a single thing, I swear." He consulted the paper. "Right... time of death occurred between twelve forty-five and one-thirty a.m., when the body was found. Cause was blood loss from six nasty stab wounds, all confined to the neck and upper body. No weapon was found, so the killer must have taken it with him."

"Or her."

"Or her," John agreed. "But the ghastliest aspect is what was done to his eyes."

Harry nodded, gazing distantly into the park. "Without question. It implies a very personal motive. And an aberrant killer. Someone with a point to make, who won't hesitate to commit an act others would find repugnant."

"It reminds me of the Hyde case." John paused. "The way Brady covered his victims' faces. This killer may be taking it a step further, but the result is the same. They can't look at him anymore."

"Or her," Harry corrected automatically.

"Or her."

"It's a fair point, but we don't know why this killer took Dr. Sabelline's eyes. It could be connected to something ritualistic, a burial practice related to his work. Or something else entirely that's of significance only to his murderer. There are no other similarities that we're aware of. No bloody messages. No satanic pacts."

She blinked snow from her eyelashes. Harry's favorite hat—a saucy confection with a single black raven's feather—had blown off on the elevated platform, a casualty of New York's sudden capricious gusts. "Let's hope this one's not a repeat killer too."

They crossed Seventy-Fifth Street, walking along the east side of the avenue and the low stone wall that skirted the park. The lake lay on the other side. Beyond it stretched the woods of the Ramble. Bare of leaves, with fresh snow on the ground, this rustic section of Central Park looked bright and open.

It had been a different place on a sultry August night the previous summer, when Harry chased another killer into its dense thickets. She thought briefly of an archway dark as midnight, and the dull gleam of a blade….

"Let's move on to the locked door," John said. "There were only two keys. Sabelline had one, the guard had the other."

Harry tore her gaze from the Ramble. The terror she'd felt that night seemed so unreal now, with John at her side and the happy shrieks of children in the distance.

"The lock had been changed at Sabelline's request on the morning of the party," she said. "It makes a copy by a third party unlikely, although not impossible. But it does raise the question of why he changed the locks at all. It almost sounds like he expected a break-in."

They'd both read the report on the train, but Harry found reviewing the details aloud helped clarify her thoughts.

"Which is why the police initially arrested Boot, the guard. Even if Sabelline had left his office door unlocked and the killer waltzed straight in, how could he—*or she*—have locked it behind…them?" John thrust his hands in his coat pockets. "Sabelline's key was found in his desk, where he'd placed it when he entered. There were no windows in the office. So Boot is the only person present who could have done it."

They waited as a carriage rolled past on its way downtown, the horses' breath steaming in the cold air. Harry switched the small valise she carried to her left hand. They'd made a hurried stop at her townhouse on West Tenth Street before heading uptown so she could grab the bag. Harry had kept it packed and ready for *years*.

"And yet Boot was released hours later for lack of evidence," she pointed out. "No blood on his shoes, or anywhere on his clothing. And the others all saw him slip out for a cigarette. He was gone only a few minutes, and a smoking butt was observed in the alley when they summoned him back in. I believe the police found it and took it into evidence. Boot simply wouldn't have had time to commit murder." She gave a thin smile. "It's a pretty mystery, John. However, I'm certain that once we are in possession of all the facts, a solution will present itself."

"It had better. I wouldn't want our first case for the American S.P.R. be a dog's dinner." John skipped over a puddle of slush.

"What about motive? The police seem to assume it was a robbery since Sabelline's strongbox was emptied."

"Let us not *assume* anything," Harry said dryly. "The report doesn't even specify what was taken, except that the objects were connected with the Egyptian exhibit. What else?"

"Only the bizarre fact of footprints not belonging to the victim leading into a pool of his blood but not out again. It's what drew the S.P.R.'s attention to the case in the first place. That and the fact that Orpha Winter happened to be there." His voice took on a gleeful sing-song quality. "This one's a stumper, Harry."

Besides her status as one of the shining lights of New York society, Orpha Winter happened to be a vice president of the S.P.R. She was also a potential suspect in Dr. Sabelline's murder. This was almost certainly a conflict of interest, but one Harry had to overlook if she wanted to be an agent for the Society.

"Maybe Orpha did it," Harry muttered.

"We can't rule her out," John agreed cheerfully. "Though the footprints were most definitely male. Size eleven. Both Jackson Sabelline and Nelson Holland are size eleven, but their shoes didn't match the tread."

Harry sighed. "There's much yet to be learned. I'm sure this morning's interviews will shed some light on what happened the night before last."

Having been forewarned by the sad fate of Harry's little French number, John grabbed onto his hat as a gust of wind swept across the park. They weren't far from the fortress-like structure of the Croton Receiving Reservoir. Harry fancied she could feel the chill of that great body of water even from several blocks away.

"I hope so," John said, jamming the Homburg more firmly onto his head. "Rupert's probably opening all my presents right now and handing them out to the other savages."

By mutual unspoken agreement, their steps slowed as the gothic building of the American Museum of Natural History appeared on the north side of Seventy-Seventh Street. Two police wagons stood on the verge.

Harland Kaylock, vice president of the New York branch of the Society for Psychical Research, had promised his newest agents full authority to view the crime scene. But despite her recent success in the Jekyll and Hyde case, Harry felt a twinge of nerves. Working for the S.P.R. was a lifelong dream come true. She didn't want to contemplate what failure on her first official assignment might mean.

Oh, she knew Kaylock didn't expect her to actually solve the murder. That was a job for the police. Homicide lay well outside the bounds of the S.P.R.'s mandate, which focused on apparitions, clairvoyance, precognitive dreams, thought-reading, hauntings, mesmerism and other supposedly supernatural phenomena.

Harry's only task would be to determine whether there were any credible occult elements involved in the case, and to investigate them to the best of her ability. She would then compile her findings in a report almost no one would read, and that would be the end of the matter.

The real problem, which even Harry had to acknowledge, was her own ambition. Growing up in the shadow of her elder sister Myrtle Fearing Pell, whose reputation as the scourge of the criminal classes, both high and low, seemed to grow by the day, Harry felt an acute need to prove herself. Perversely, solving the Brady case had only poured oil on the flames.

A single victory could be chalked up to luck. Now she had the chance to show her new employers she was, if not smarter than Myrtle—*no, never that, Harry thought with a hollow laugh*—at least competent. She could already picture the half-amused, half-pitying look in Myrtle's cool grey eyes if her sister got wind that Harry's case had dead-ended.

John seemed to understand all this, for he didn't rush her. "I haven't been here in ages," he said, surveying the five-story red-brick building. "We came once on a trip when I was in school at

St. Andrew's. Lots of fossils and dusty taxidermied animals, as I recall."

"I've never been, not since it moved from the Central Park Armory," Harry admitted. "Mrs. Rivers took me and Myrtle there when we were children. I don't think Myrtle cared much for it, except for the venomous spiders, of course. And the snakes."

John laughed. "They had live ones too back then, didn't they? I got the impression the museum was more popular before it moved uptown. When my class came here, oh, seven or eight years ago, it was practically deserted."

"I imagine the new Alexandria exhibit is supposed to give attendance a boost." Harry stamped her boots, hoping to regain some feeling in her toes. It had been nearly a mile's walk from the elevated station. "Shall we, Mr. Weston?"

"Off to the races," he said, tipping his hat at her.

A lone guard stood dolefully outside the front doors, his cheeks ruddy with cold. "We're closed," he yelled the moment they came within hearing distance.

"And we're expected." John flashed a toothsome smile. "Merry Christmas, sir."

"Not for me," the guard grumbled. "First time I've ever worked on Christmas Day, and it ain't worth the pay and a half." He eyed them with open disenchantment, and a touch of quiet but heartfelt hostility. "You the pair come to see Mr. Holland?"

"We are indeed." John rubbed his hands together and turned the grin up a notch, undeterred in his relentless spreading of yuletide cheer. "Can you point us in the right direction?"

"Let's see some identification first."

John and Harry produced their spanking new S.P.R. badges—a circle with the Greek letter Psi in the center, which John thought looked a bit like a candelabra—and were ushered inside. The Egyptian exhibits had been moved to the east wing early that morning and replaced with the usual motley assortment of stuffed fur, fowl and scales. Altogether, the museum boasted some twelve thousand birds, more than a thousand mammals, three thousand reptiles and fish, and a large number of corals. Its collection was unrivaled, in America at least, but the lifelike dioramas for which it was to become famous in later years had not yet materialized, and some of its harsher critics compared the museum to a glorified cabinet of curiosities.

Harry felt the gazes of dozens of glass eyes as the guard relocked the door and escorted them up several flights of stairs to the fourth-floor corner office of Nelson Holland, head of Near East and North African Acquisitions.

"Come in," a deep, resonant voice commanded.

"S.P.R. people, Mr. Holland," the guard said, eying them askance.

"Of course. Mrs. Winter mentioned you'd be popping by."

Nelson Holland rose from his desk to greet them. Harry guessed his age at somewhere in the late forties. He sported thick auburn whiskers with his chin shaved clean. Holland had narrow, close-set eyes and a scholar's high forehead and fine bone structure, but his hands and shoulders indicated a powerful build.

Two windows behind the desk overlooked Central Park, where people were venturing out for strolls and sledding on some of the larger hills. Old Latin maps hung on the walls, and a few photographs of Holland posing in exotic jungle locales. Tomes on history and archaeology lined the shelves of a mahogany bookcase. It was a highly ordered room, Harry noticed, with minimal clutter. Even the masses of paper on the desk were organized in neat piles.

"Mr. Weston," Holland said, shaking John's hand. "And Miss Fearing Pell. I've heard of your sister, of course."

"Of course," Harry said with a tight smile. "Who hasn't?"

John leapt into the silence. "Perhaps you're familiar with Miss Pell from the Hyde case?" he said loyally. "She's the one who caught him."

Holland frowned. "Those murders last summer? I vaguely

recall them from the papers. In any event, Orpha spoke quite highly of you both." He gestured to chairs that had been placed in front of the desk. "Please, sit down."

Harry and John shared a brief, puzzled look. Orpha Winter was Kaylock's archrival at the S.P.R. Neither of them had met her yet, although Harry knew her reputation. She was a firm believer in psychic and occult phenomena, unlike Mr. Kaylock, who was known to be a skeptic. Harry couldn't help but wonder why Mrs. Winter would give them such a ringing endorsement.

"Was she here?" Harry asked. "Since the party, I mean."

"Yes, Orpha stopped by early this morning. She was interested in the progress of the investigation. I suppose you know they released Mr. Boot." Holland picked up an inkwell, examined it in a distracted way, then set it back down. "Hard to imagine he'd do such a thing." He gave a humorless laugh. "But I suppose that leaves the rest of us. I honestly don't know what to make of it."

"I imagine the police thoroughly searched the building?"

"Oh yes. They're still at it. Windows and doors locked tight. No sign of any break-in."

Harry gave him a small, sympathetic smile. "What can you tell us about Julius Sabelline?"

"A brilliant man. We're all reeling from the tragedy." Holland leaned back. "Jessup has managed to keep it out of the papers so far, but I expect the murder will be front page news by tomorrow. Quite a disaster for the museum. I'm sure they'll play up the curse angle. It's why you're here, isn't it?"

John visibly perked up. "Curse?"

Holland sighed. "The relic taken from Dr. Sabelline's strongbox was supposed to be cursed. Of course, this wasn't uncommon. In ancient Egypt, curses were often placed on sacred objects and possessions to stop the living from disturbing them, grave robbers mainly."

"Interesting," John said, drawing out every syllable with relish. "And what did this particular curse say?"

"It's a long one."

"We're in no great hurry," John said with an encouraging smile, pulling out a notebook and putting nib to paper.

Holland sighed again, more deeply. "Some nonsense about *They who shall disturb this talisman of the Underworld shall lose their earthly positions and honors, be incinerated in a furnace, capsize and drown at sea, have no successors, receive no tomb or funerary offerings of their own….*Um, *Their bodies will shrivel because they will starve without sustenance, they will be struck blind and their bones will decay to dust.*"

"That does seem quite exhaustive—" John began, scribbling furiously.

"*As for every mayor, every wab-priest, every scribe and every nobleman who shall touch the talisman, his arm shall be cut off like that of this bull, his neck shall be twisted off like that of a bird, his office shall not exist, the position of his son shall not exist, his house shall not exist in Nubia, his tomb shall not exist in the necropolis, his god shall not accept his white bread, his flesh shall belong to the fire, his children shall belong to the fire, his corpse shall not belong to the earth, I shall be against him as a crocodile on the water, as a serpent in the field, and as an enemy in the necropolis.*"

John waited to see if there was any more, but Mr. Holland seemed to have wound down. Harry tried to maintain a sober expression. She had little use for curses unless they were carried out by human agency—which seemed to be the case with Julius Sabelline, unless vengeful mummies had taken to wearing size eleven men's dress shoes.

"How many people knew of the curse?" Harry asked.

"Oh, everyone involved in the exhibit. We thought it was, well, rather funny."

"I'm impressed that you memorized the whole thing."

"As I said, we made rather a joke of it." He glanced meaningfully at a clock atop the bookshelf.

"Just a few more questions, if you don't mind, Mr. Holland. I understand you were in your office when Dr. Sabelline was killed?"

"Yes. I had some grant proposals I planned to take home over the holiday. There are several expeditions in the works for next year and we need to find backers. Mr. Jessup believes strongly that exploration is a key mission of the museum."

"Such as the one Dr. Sabelline conducted in Alexandria?"

"Precisely. That was financed by a private benefactor and the Egypt Exploration Fund."

"By private benefactor, I take it you're referring to Count Balthazar Jozsef Habsburg-Koháry?" Harry asked. Kaylock had mentioned his name that morning at the S.P.R. offices.

"Yes. The Egypt Exploration Fund covered about twenty percent of the costs, and the count generously paid for the rest. He is a collector of antiquities."

"So he was Sabelline's patron?"

"I suppose you could say that. Sabelline worked with Flinders Petrie for many years until they had a falling out. Julius was quite well-connected in Egypt. Spoke Coptic and Greek fluently. A stickler on methodology, not like some of the slapdash archaeologists out there. When his partnership with Petrie ended, Count Habsburg-Koháry approached him about a dig in Luxor. It proved successful and they planned a second expedition to Alexandria."

"Did Dr. Sabelline have any enemies?"

"None that I can think of. Julius was a quiet man, devoted to his work."

John looked up from his notes. As a student at Columbia's College of Physicians and Surgeons, he knew firsthand how bitter academic rivalries could become. "Were any other teams elbowed aside at Alexandria?"

"Quite the opposite. Most of them laughed at him when he said he planned to dig there. Nothing of value had ever been found. The general wisdom is that there was nothing left. Sabelline proved them all wrong. It turned out to be a goldmine."

"He found items belonging to Claudius Ptolemy?"

"Yes, among other things. The city was founded by Alexander the Great in 331 BC. It became the capital of Egypt and quickly grew to be one of the greatest cities of the ancient world, second only to Rome."

For the first time, Holland showed a spark of enthusiasm. It was clearly a subject he enjoyed talking about. "Then, in 641 AD, Alexandria was besieged and fell to the Rashidun Caliphate. The city entered a long decline. Over the centuries, the original granite and marble buildings vanished, but the ancient sewer system remained. There's a network of underground chambers. It was in one of these that the primary find was made. The Tomb of Ptolemy."

"That was about five months ago?" John asked.

"Yes. It took time to transport the relics to New York and prepare them for exhibition. Julius had been working on it night and day."

"Do you know why he went back to his office after the party ended?" Harry asked.

Holland nodded. "He'd gone to lock up one of the objects on display. Sabelline kept a strongbox next to his desk. That's what was emptied. His papers were left untouched, but his attacker took an item Count Habsburg-Koháry Balthazar placed special value on. It was a condition of lending it to the museum that it be secured at night."

"Which item carried the curse?" John asked.

"The amulet of Osiris. It's called a Tet, or Djed. About the size of my hand. I suppose you could say it resembles a pillar with four stacked squares on top. The curse was in Greek on the lid of the box containing it. We don't know who wrote it, although Julius believed it was Ptolemy himself. There are also three hieroglyphs carved into the amulet. One meaning door, or gateway. A second representing a key."

"And the third?"

"The third is an Amenta. The symbol for the Underworld."

"The key to the gates of Hell," John whispered.

"Something like that."

Harry adjusted the small valise on her lap. "Was anything else missing?"

"From the exhibit? No. And some of the items on display were solid gold, worth far more than the contents of Julius's strongbox." Holland tapped his fingers on the desk. "I must say, Miss Pell, the police already asked me all of these questions. I thought you'd be focused on the occult aspects. Isn't that why Mrs. Winter sent you?"

"I'm interested in the facts," Harry said blandly. "All of them."

"Your employer is a great friend of the museum, which is the only reason I agreed to entertain this visit, but I'm afraid there's not much more I can tell you."

"Of course," John said. "We'll just be on our—"

"One last thing. Was anyone with you in your office that night?" Harry interrupted.

"I was working alone. I believe Sharpe was also in his office. But you can ask him that yourself."

"We'd like to see Dr. Sabelline's office first, if you don't mind."

Holland rose with a weary expression. "Yes, I thought you might. The body was taken away yesterday, but otherwise the room was left exactly as they found it."

He escorted them back down to the basement. A young patrolman from the Thirty-First Ward stood outside Sabelline's office. He had a droopy mustache, closely shorn hair, and the beefy solidity typical of New York's Finest.

"Officer Clancy, these are the people I told you about. From the S.P.R." Holland said it with an air of faint awkwardness, like someone pretending to laugh at a joke that had gone on just a bit too long.

Harry presented the patrolman with her card. It still secretly thrilled her to see her name engraved next to those illustrious initials, Holland be damned.

"You worked the Jekyll and Hyde case, didn't you?" Clancy said.

Harry smiled. Clearly, her reputation was growing. "I did."

The policeman nodded slowly. "Are you the poor bugger she shot?" he asked, turning to John.

John made a choking sound that sounded suspiciously like suppressed laughter. "Afraid so."

"It was an accident," Harry said, a red flush creeping up her neck. "He's fine now."

"That true?"

John flapped his left arm. "Right as rain."

Clancy grinned. "Well, Miss Pell, you might be a lousy shot, but you brought that maniac down in the end, so I guess you're okay." He stood aside. "Don't touch anything," he warned. "The detectives have been through twice, but it's still an active crime scene until they say otherwise."

Harry and John nodded assent. Nelson Holland discreetly cleared his throat.

"I'm afraid I have to leave you to it," he said. "As deeply as it pains all of us, the exhibit must proceed without Julius, and there is much yet to be done. If you wish to interview Davis Sharpe, you'll find him at the end of the hall. Just follow it around to the left. He works with his door open."

John thanked him for his time. Harry gave him a card in case he thought of anything else, but the careless way he shoved it into his pocket and hurried off made her doubt they'd be hearing any more from Mr. Holland.

"Ready?" she asked John.

He nodded, hazel eyes dead serious for a change. They'd been to one crime scene together before, an old grain elevator on the East River where an actress named Anne Marlowe had been brutally strangled. When Harry and John arrived, the chain was still wrapped around her slender neck. The killer had slashed open her wrist and used the blood to write *Mors me solum potest prohibere* in backwards Latin on an adjacent wall.

Only death can stop me.

The stranger part had been the fingerprints John found burned into her skin. It was one of several aspects of the Hyde case Harry had never resolved to her satisfaction.

Anne Marlowe had not been an easy sight. In fact, the image had haunted Harry for days. But when she opened the heavy oak door of Dr. Sabelline's office and saw what waited there, she understood that there were far worse ways to die.

CHAPTER 13

H arry felt her bile rise. From the way John stood stiffly next
to her, not venturing any further, she knew he wrestled
with the same emotions—revulsion, shock, a visceral urge to
look away. As a medical student, he was no stranger to death. But
this was something else.

"My God," he said quietly.

The office was roughly the same size as Holland's, although
more austerely furnished. It held a graceful Queen Anne desk of
polished cherrywood and a matching chair, which had been
overturned. A bookshelf occupied the wall opposite the door. In
front of it sat an empty strongbox with the lid open. Reddish-
brown streaks and splashes covered the walls and carpet—even
some parts of the ceiling. The smell was overpowering.

Some of the stench emanated from a pile of sick about two
feet to the left of the door. That's where Jeremy Boot must have
lost the contents of his stomach. It had dried to a congealed mass.
Harry took a deep breath through her mouth and began a slow
circuit of the room, pausing here and there for closer examination. A profusion of footprints crossed in and out of the blood.

"Mr. Boot entered first, but he only made it two or three steps before he was overcome," she said, trying to regain some degree of professional detachment. Going over the basic facts of the police report helped. "Araminta rushed in behind him. You can see her smaller footprints in that bloodstain near the desk as she went to her husband. Then she fainted."

"Who was next on the scene?" John asked.

"Davis Sharpe, but he was smart enough to stay out and go for help," Officer Clancy offered. He stood just inside the door, ready to swoop down if anyone disturbed the evidence.

Harry opened her valise and removed a short ruler. "May I?"

"I'm sure the Society for…what is it? Psychic something?"

"Psychical Research."

"Right. I'm sure the Society for Psychical Research is the pinnacle of criminal apprehension," Clancy said. "But the New York Police aren't complete idiots. The detectives already did that."

"Merely double-checking," Harry said with a disarming smile.

He shrugged. "Commissioner Porter himself gave permission, so go ahead. But I thought you were looking for ghosts." He laughed to himself.

"Mummies, actually," John said. "Probably Ptolemy himself. Most likely suspect in a case like this."

Clancy looked at him uncertainly. John returned his gaze with perfect blandness.

Harry ignored the jibe. Carefully avoiding the bloodstains, she laid the ruler next to a set of prints that stood out from the rest. They followed a clear path across the diamond-patterned carpet to the wood floor by the strongbox, where the largest pool of blood had accumulated.

"Size eleven male dress shoe with pointed toes," Harry confirmed. "Brand new, from the crisp heel pattern. No signs of wear whatsoever."

"Leading into the blood, but not out again," John said, shaking his head.

Harry got down on hands and knees and crept around the edge of the still-damp stain, muttering to herself and occasionally plucking fibers with a pair of tweezers and stuffing them into glass vials that she tucked into the valise. Clancy watched her with a bemused expression. At last she rose and dusted off her skirts.

"Interesting," she said noncommittally. "Let's move on to the rest of the scene. What do you think, John?"

"Based on the position of the body as described in the police report and the arterial spray on the wall, I'd say Sabelline was most likely caught by surprise and stabbed in the neck from behind while sitting at his desk," John ventured. "He rose and staggered across the room, then collapsed next to the strongbox."

Harry nodded. "I'd agree with that assessment."

The box itself was made of cast iron. Using the ruler, Harry called out the dimensions, which John duly noted: height of ten inches, width of one foot, eight inches, depth of one foot, one inch. She approximated the weight at one hundred forty pounds.

As Kaylock had told them that morning, there were no windows. The only way into the room was the door to the corridor, which had been locked when Sabelline was found. Harry looked around, her keen eyes taking in every inch of the room.

High up in a corner to the right of the door, she noticed a small duct to permit ventilation of the gas wall sconces, roughly four inches high and five inches across.

"Did the police examine this?" Harry asked Clancy.

He frowned. "What's the point? It's too small for anything, Miss Pell."

"And yet we'd be remiss to overlook it, would we not?" She glanced around, but the only furniture was bloodied and she doubted Officer Clancy would allow her to use it as a ladder. "Give me a boost, John."

Gingerly picking his way through the minefield of blood,

John crossed to the vent and knit his fingers together so Harry could use them as a platform.

"I don't suppose anyone has a screwdriver?" she asked.

"Try a coin," the cop suggested.

John rummaged through his pockets and gave Harry a penny. With a few twists, she loosened the screws and placed them in her pocket.

"They weren't as tight as one might expect, indicating they've been recently removed and replaced," she observed. "And now...."

Harry lifted the grating away. The shaft was too dark to see into beyond a few inches. She touched a finger inside. It came back with a coating of dried reddish flakes.

"By God, that looks like blood," Clancy said.

"Indeed."

"Best come down, Miss Pell. This is new evidence. We need light."

Clancy returned a moment later with a portable police lantern. He and John dragged the strongbox over. Clancy used it as a stepstool and trained the light inside.

"Nothing in there, but I see a thick layer of dried blood. Best fetch the detectives."

"It's quite suggestive," Harry murmured.

"Of what?"

"Various possibilities, the most likely being that the killer attempted to conceal the murder weapon inside this shaft."

Clancy considered this. "Why didn't he leave it, then?"

"I don't know. Fear of discovery?"

"Or perhaps it didn't fit," John suggested.

Harry nodded. "Yes, that would make more sense. But it's quite large enough for a knife." She frowned. "Perhaps it wasn't the weapon at all." Her gaze fixed on the footprints. "Perhaps it was the shoes."

"I reckon a pair of size elevens would be a tight fit," Clancy agreed.

"If he was unable to get rid of them in the air vent, he had to stash them somewhere else," Harry said. She'd decided it was simply easier to revert to *he* for the purposes of theorizing. "Have the trash bins been emptied?"

"We checked those first thing yesterday."

"Someplace else then."

"I'll tell Detective Jones," Clancy said. "It's his case. But I imagine he'll be grateful for the lead."

Harry concluded her examination of the office by examining the door lock. It showed no signs of having been tampered with.

"I think we've discovered all there is here," Harry said at last. "Thank you, Officer Clancy, for your kind cooperation."

"Well, I'd say you earned it," he said. "I imagine they'll call for another sweep of the basement now."

"Have Holland and Sharpe both had access to this floor since yesterday?"

He nodded. "Afraid so. The search was completed so there was no reason to bar them, except from Sabelline's office."

"I understand. Perhaps you'd be kind enough to let me know if anything turns up?" She offered him a card.

"I'll do my best, Miss Pell." Clancy slipped it into his coat pocket.

Harry and John ventured down the dim corridor in the direction they'd been given. Unlike Nelson Holland, whose office on the top floor had sweeping views of the park, Davis Sharpe was also relegated to the museum's basement. They passed a number of doors with small brass plaques labelling them as storerooms or offices. As Holland had predicted, Sharpe's door stood open.

John stuck his head in and gave a courtesy rap with his knuckles.

"Mr. Sharpe? We're with the S.P.R. I'm John Weston, and this is my colleague, Harrison Fearing Pell."

"Oh, yes." He sat slumped in a chair and did not rise to greet them. "Come on in."

Davis Sharpe was in his mid-thirties, with a shock of brown hair and wide-set blue eyes that appeared slightly bloodshot. He wore a rumpled coat and scuffed boots. Harry's first impression was of a normally dapper man—his mustache had been neatly trimmed and the cut of his clothing was quite fashionable—who had lately grown careless of his appearance.

"I'd ask you to sit down, but I'm afraid there aren't any other chairs," he said ruefully. "I don't get many visitors down here."

The office was less than half the size of Sabelline's, little more than a broom closet. Untidy stacks of books and papers were crammed into every corner.

"It's quite all right," Harry said with a smile. "We don't mind standing."

"Feels a bit awkward. I'll get a neck cramp staring up at you. Perhaps you'd like a tour of the Alexandria exhibit whilst we speak?"

Harry looked at John, who shrugged.

"That could prove useful," Harry agreed. "Thank you."

Sharpe set aside the journal he'd been reading and stood up, turning sideways to get past John to the door. "I still can't believe someone murdered Julius," he said. "What a horrible thing."

They followed the corridor to the stairs leading up.

"How did you find him?" John asked.

"His wife, Araminta, came to my office. Said she couldn't get him to open the door. At first I thought he'd had a heart attack or stroke." Sharpe shook his head. "At the time, it was the worst case scenario."

"Could you hear anything inside?"

"Nothing. So after fruitlessly calling his name, we went for the guard. He had the only other key." Sharpe swallowed. "We found him outside, having a cigarette."

"So neither of you had stayed behind at Sabelline's office?" Harry asked.

"No." He gave her a look. "You think the killer could have been in there?"

"It's possible. What happened then?"

"The guard, Boot, found the key on his ring and opened the door. I remember the smell. I knew right away something terrible had happened. Boot saw the body and became ill. Araminta was just behind. She called her husband's name, tried to go to him, and fainted dead away."

"What did you see?"

Sharpe had grown paler as they spoke, almost greenish. "I saw Julius. He'd been stabbed. There was so much blood. But that wasn't the worst part." He seemed unable to continue.

"The eyes, you mean?" John prompted.

Sharpe shuddered. "I've seen some things in the jungle tribes, but it was the most horrific sight. I'll carry it in my mind until the day I die."

They were silent for a moment.

"Is there any significance?" Harry asked. "Any religious connection to his work?"

"Not that I'm aware of. I mean, there's the *curse*. But no one takes it seriously." He glanced at them and seemed to remember he was speaking with agents for the Society for Psychical Research. "At least most people don't."

They'd reached the east wing of the museum, where the Alexandria exhibit was in the middle of being finalized. Packing crates filled with straw and wool had been piled against the wall, their contents arranged on two long tables with paper tags.

"Julius was very interested in the underworld, the Duat," Sharpe explained as they meandered through the silent rooms, footsteps echoing. "The ancient Egyptians believed burial chambers formed portals between the everyday world of the living and the realm of the dead, and spirits could use tombs to travel back and forth."

"What about the stolen amulet?" John said, dropping his voice an ominous notch. "The key to the gates of Hell."

Sharpe smiled. "I don't think it's meant to be taken literally, Mr. Weston. Besides which, the Duat is not our Christian version of Hell, or even Heaven. More of a midpoint between earth and the afterlife."

"Would such an object be valuable to a collector?" Harry asked.

"It was to Julius's Hungarian count, that's for sure. And simply the fact that it was found in Claudius Ptolemy's tomb would make it worth a fortune, I suppose." Sharpe wiped his brow with a handkerchief. "Speaking of Hell, it's awfully warm in here," he said with a weak laugh. "Or perhaps I'm coming down with something." He stared into space for a moment, then seemed to pull himself together. "In any event, Julius was always convinced there was more to be found beneath Alexandria than anyone credited, and he was right."

"Why did he think there would be?" John asked. "If everyone else had written it off."

"I believe it began when he stumbled across the writings of the Flemish traveler Guillebert de Lannoy. In 1421, Lannoy was sent by Henry the Fifth to Palestine. He wrote an account of his travels, which was rediscovered and published in 1826. Describing Alexandria, he reported that underneath the streets and houses, the whole city was hollow. Julius was convinced it was true. He became obsessed with the idea. Eventually he got permission to tunnel down beneath the sewers."

"And what is your expertise, Mr. Sharpe?"

"Ancient languages. I did my graduate thesis on hieroglyphs." He pointed to a slab of stone. Harry noticed a slight tremor before he shoved the hand back into his coat pocket. "This is from the Book of Gates, describing the Fourth Division of the Duat. It says, *Open thou the earth, force thou a way through the Duat and the region which is above, and dispel our darkness; hail, Ra, come thou to us."*

"You seem very knowledgeable," John said. "Were you part of the expedition to Alexandria?"

Sharpe hesitated before answering. He rubbed the back of his neck. "No. I was supposed to go, but Julius made a last-minute substitution."

"Do you mind if I ask why?"

"We had a bit of a row, actually. Nothing serious, but I decided to stay. Julius could be touchy, obsessive even. Frankly, I didn't relish the thought of spending months with the man." He laughed. "Though had I known what he'd find, wild horses couldn't have kept me away."

"And yet you did go abroad recently," Harry put in. "South America, I'd say."

Sharpe gave her a startled look. "Did Holland tell you that?"

"No, but I notice that you have a suntan in December and a spider bite on your left wrist that I would guess came from one of the larger tropical species."

"Fair enough. But how did you deduce South America?"

"I noticed a bag of coffee beans with a Portuguese label on your desk."

Sharpe slapped his thigh. "Not bad, Miss Pell. Yes, I am recently returned from Brazil. When the Alexandria dig fell through, I managed to attach myself to an expedition going to the Amazon."

"I hope it was fruitful," John said politely.

"We brought back a few trinkets. Some prehistoric pottery shards. Nothing compared to the Egypt find."

Sharpe stopped before a globe encased in moveable metal rings with numbers indicating celestial longitude and latitude. "This is one of the prized pieces of the collection. An armillary sphere as described in the Syntaxis. Truly priceless."

"And yet it wasn't locked up in the strongbox," Harry said.

"No, only the amulet of Osiris. It belonged to Count Habsburg-Koháry. He'd personally requested an extra layer of security."

"Where was the count last night?"

"Waiting for Julius in the main hall, I believe."

"What do you know about him?"

Sharpe gave a shrug. "He's Hungarian royalty in exile. Fled after the revolution. A well-known collector of antiquities. Filthy rich. He'd been bankrolling Julius's digs for years." He sounded envious.

"It must be nice to have such a patron."

"I imagine so, although I hear he's a demanding taskmaster. But he let Julius have all the glory in the press. I got the distinct impression Count Koháry prefers to keep a low profile."

"I look forward to speaking with him." Harry examined an amulet. "Do you think it was robbery, Mr. Sharpe?"

He shrugged. "What else? There are people who'd sell their own mothers to get some of these artifacts, Miss Pell. It's a cutthroat business."

"And where were you after the party?" Harry asked.

"As I told the police, and no doubt you already know, I went back to my office." He suddenly seemed agitated. "Come now, haven't they arrested the night guard? Boot?"

"They did indeed," Harry replied pleasantly. "And released him this morning for lack of evidence. I'd say he's the *least* likely to have done it. Surely if Boot had murdered Mr. Sabelline, he would have claimed his copy of the key had been lost or stolen."

Sharpe seemed taken aback. "I didn't know that. So you think it's someone else?"

"I try not to speculate before all the facts have been gathered, but it seems certain."

"Then it would be one of us. The six who were inside the building."

There was a pregnant pause.

"If you had to guess, who would you pick?" John said cheerfully. "Gut instinct."

Sharpe hesitated a moment too long before answering. "Not a clue," he said with a tight smile. "But I'm sure the police will sort it out."

"Well, Mr. Sharpe," Harry said, offering her hand. "Thank you for speaking with us."

He gave it a firm shake. "Anytime. You know where to find me."

OUTSIDE, Harry turned to John. "What do you make of him?"

He thought for a moment. "Hard to say. He was definitely suffering from a hangover. I could smell the gin. And I don't think he's shaved since the party."

They began retracing their journey south along Central Park. The sun had come out while they were entombed in the grim basement of the museum. The white expanse of the park seemed like another world entirely, ringing with the exuberant cries of children on Christmas Day and the merry jingle of horse-drawn sleighs.

"Trembling hands, glassy eyes," Harry observed. "A habitual drinker?"

"He's a little young to show the most obvious ravages of alcoholism, though it's certainly possible. Don't forget, Harry, Sharpe did just undergo a traumatic experience. Seeing his colleague brutally butchered could make a man crave oblivion."

"Perhaps." Harry's eyes narrowed. "Did you get the impression he liked Dr. Sabelline?"

John considered this. "Actually, no. I don't think he was as sorry as he let on."

"Which is hardly conclusive, but isn't an argument in his favor either." Harry bit her lip. "So he has a dispute with Sabelline and goes off on another expedition that ends in failure, or at least nothing that would advance his career."

"While Sabelline returns covered in glory."

"Exactly. Add the financial motive if he can manage to sell the stolen amulet on the black market, and we've got ourselves a solid suspect."

"I agree there's something off about Davis Sharpe," John said. "He was almost certainly lying when he said the quarrel with Sabelline was minor. I wonder what it was really about, and whose decision it was for him not to go."

"I'd bet you anything Count Koháry would know. We'll have to ask him. Now, what did you think of Nelson Holland?"

"That one's a bit murkier. I don't know why he'd do it."

"Nor do I. But we know very little about the man, or his relationship with Sabelline. I do think it was interesting he called Orpha *a great friend of the museum*. That means she gives them loads of money. It's how you get invited to these parties." Harry thought for a moment. "Could you use your contacts at Columbia to look into Holland and Sharpe? Sabelline too, of course. I wonder if professional jealousies aren't at play here."

"Oh, all academic institutions have those in spades," John agreed. "I know a couple of graduate students in the history department. I can try asking them, though it's Christmas break."

"Go to their houses and bang on the door if you have to."

John groaned. "I'll be blacklisted."

"Tell them you're looking into Julius Sabelline's death. That ought to get the gossip flowing."

"You may be right. Once the news hits the papers, everyone will be talking about it."

They walked in silence for a block. "I've been thinking about the shoes," Harry said. "It explains the strange footprints. What if the killer simply slipped them off while standing in the blood, then stepped away in stockinged feet? If he avoided the other bloodstains, he'd leave no trail."

"But why do such a thing?"

"To confuse the investigators. And to cover his own tracks."

"Well then, I'd say you can write off Mr. Sharpe. What you're describing requires cold-blooded cunning, not to mention steady hands and nerves," John said dryly.

"You think he was too drunk?"

"I don't know. We should have asked Holland."

"If Sharpe had been blotto at the party, it seems unlikely he would retire to his office to work in such a state," Harry said.

"He might have gone to lie down."

"Lie down where? The room is like a closet. And why not just go home?"

"Too drunk, perhaps."

"Don't you find it curious that three of them went to their offices—separately, mind you—after midnight? Such dedication. A bit beyond the call of duty, especially two days before Christmas."

"We need to speak with the wife and son. Also that Count What's His Name."

"Yes, we do." Harry sighed. "Seven people, and not one of them has a solid alibi for the time of the murder except for John Boot, the only one with the key."

John shot her a significant look. "Even if they all hated Sabelline's guts, you have to admit, there are some strange aspects to the crime that point to something...otherworldly."

"The curse, you mean."

"Yes, the curse! Isn't that what we're supposed to be investigating?"

"I find it likelier that someone wanted it to *appear* as if a curse had been invoked. The staged footprints. The mutilation of the body to correspond with the phrase *struck blind*."

John looked unconvinced. Unlike Harry, he believed full-tilt in the supernatural. "Perhaps. Either way, it would be nice to know what the murder weapon was."

"With any luck, the post-mortem will clarify that. What time is it?"

John pulled out his pocket watch. "One-fifteen."

"Oh dear. We'll never make it by train now. Keep your eyes open for a hansom."

The temperature had risen a bit and the fresh snow was rapidly melting into slush. After being beaten to a cab by an old lady who menaced them with her black umbrella, John finally managed to flag down a driver at Seventy-Second Street. Thanks to the holiday, the usually nightmarish midtown traffic was sparse. Harry and John sped downtown to First Avenue and Twenty-Sixth Street in record time, where they found Mrs. Orpha Winter waiting for them in the Morgue at Bellevue Hospital.

CHAPTER 14

The Morgue was housed in a forbidding grey stone building at the edge of the East River. In imitation of the Parisian style, New York's dead house had a viewing room behind a glass partition, where the public could examine the day's fresh corpses in hopes they might be identified. If no one claimed them within a day or two, they would be sent to an unmarked grave in the pauper's cemetery on Ward's Island.

Some were visitors to the city who had died of natural causes, or just as often, been murdered for the coins in their pocket. Others were simply lost souls. Suicides fished out of the harbor. Prostitutes with no family who'd admit to knowing them. Their meager belongings were displayed on the far wall, in case anyone recognized an item of clothing or other personal effect.

The actual bodies lay on four stone tables beneath jets of cold water. This technique was supposed to slow putrefaction, but over the years, the odor of death had inevitably sunk into the foundations of the place.

White sheets covered the naked corpses, with only the faces exposed to public scrutiny. Neither Harry nor John cared to look too closely as they passed through the room. Their business was not here, in this sad, gloomy place. Julius Sabelline's body would be awaiting the post-mortem in a secluded area of the hospital. Still, Harry couldn't help but notice that one of the forms was tiny and could only be a young child. She felt a stab of pity. Untold hundreds of children died of illness, accident or parental violence every year, but to lie here, unclaimed by anyone, struck her as a particularly cruel fate.

They encountered Orpha just beyond the viewing room at the start of a long corridor leading deeper into the recesses of the Morgue. Mrs. Winter was an ethereally beautiful woman. She had milky skin and pale blonde hair that she wore twisted atop her head. Her dress was fashionable but tasteful, in dark colors somber enough for the occasion.

Orpha's green eyes lit on John, then moved to Harry. There was a crystalline hardness to them, like shards of jade. Not a woman to cross lightly, or without consequence.

It was the first time Harry had formally met her, although she'd watched her at S.P.R. functions with her husband, the banker Joseph Winter. He had the money and Orpha had the charm and connections. Together, they were a formidable pair in New York society.

"Miss Pell," she said with artificial warmth, clasping Harry's hand. "Such a pleasure. And you must be Dr. Weston."

John smiled amiably. "Only 'mister'," he said. "I'm a student at Columbia's College of Physicians and Surgeons."

"Of course. Well, it will be doctor soon enough, I'm sure. The coroner tells me they're running late for the post-mortem, so we have a few minutes to get acquainted. Have you come from the museum? I'm most anxious to hear your thoughts."

"It's rather early for theories," Harry said firmly. "I have three witnesses yet to interview. But I'm glad you're here. Perhaps you can tell us what you observed at the party."

"Of course. I believe there's a waiting area up ahead. We can discuss the case there."

They followed her down the hall to an alcove with two wooden benches facing each other. Orpha sat down and arranged her skirts while John and Harry took the other.

"Mr. Winter was on a business trip so I attended alone," she began. "The evening went off flawlessly. It seemed a smashing success for the museum. At around eleven forty-five, the staff began clearing the food and drink away. I suppose that's rather early, but it was nearly Christmas Eve and the guests had families to return to. I fell into conversation with Count Balthazar. We've known each other for years. A fascinating man, quite knowledgeable about the ancient world."

"I'd very much like to speak with him—" Harry began.

"Certainly," Orpha interrupted. "But you must allow me to arrange it. He's a busy man and we have no official authority in this investigation. It would be a personal favor if he met with you at all."

Harry nodded. "Sooner would be best."

"Of course." She smiled indulgently. "In any event, Count Balthazar was waiting for Dr. Sabelline to return from his office with the key to the strongbox. The count preferred to keep that himself. I wasn't paying a great deal of attention, but I eventually noticed the others had drifted off. Sharpe and Holland apparently went to their offices. It was nearly one a.m. and I decided to go home, but the front door was locked and the guard had left his post."

"He'd gone to smoke a cigarette?" Harry said.

"Apparently. We finally found him in the alley. He let me out the front door and my driver took me home. I heard what happened the next day."

"Were you in conversation with Count Balthazar the entire time?"

Orpha gazed at her. "What do you mean?"

"I mean between the time Julius Sabelline left to go to his office, and the time you decided to go home."

"I believe I went off for a few minutes to freshen up. You're wondering if I left the count alone at any point?"

Harry nodded.

"Really, my dear girl, you needn't waste your time thinking it was him. First of all, he owned the artifact. What reason could he possibly have to steal it from himself?"

"Perhaps it was insured."

Orpha laughed, long and hard. "You've no idea who you're dealing with, do you? Oh, I suppose it's not your fault. Kaylock should have explained. Count Balthazar Jozsef Habsburg-Koháry is one of the wealthiest men in the world. He descends from the House of Saxe-Coburg, and before that, the House of Wettin. His family tree goes back nearly a thousand years, to the Holy Roman Empire."

"That's all very impressive," Harry said. "But it hardly exempts him from murder."

"Don't be foolish," Orpha snapped. "I requested you for this case, but I can just as easily have you removed." She softened her tone. "We should go in now. But let me be perfectly clear. You have a bright future with the S.P.R. if you ally yourself with the right people. I believe you're clever enough to understand what I mean."

Orpha swept down the hallway before Harry could reply.

"Well *she's* a piece of work," John muttered.

Harry watched the retreating form. "I suppose she wanted us because she thought we were young and eager to please. Easy to manipulate."

John laughed. "Then she certainly doesn't know you at all, Harry. I'd say you're about as pliable as an iron bar."

Harry smiled back, but she looked troubled. "Don't make the mistake of underestimating Orpha Winter," she said. "We must tread cautiously. I fear there are treacherous undercurrents in this case, John."

THE POST-MORTEM EXAMINATION of Julius Sabelline was conducted in one of Bellevue's operating amphitheaters. The body lay on a steel table in the center of the room, covered with a sheet. Four men stood together talking quietly as Harry and John entered the room just behind Orpha Winter. The effect of her appearance was remarkable. They all stood up straighter like schoolboys before a favorite teacher.

"Gentlemen," Orpha said smoothly. "These are my new associates. I hope you don't mind if we observe the proceedings this afternoon."

She made brief introductions all around. A pleasant-looking man in his mid-forties with a slight German accent was the city coroner, Ferdinand Eidman. His job was to issue death certificates and, in theory, perform autopsies and inquests for all suspected homicides, suicides and accidental deaths in New York County.

However, Eidman wasn't a doctor, and in fact had no medical training at all beyond what he'd seen as a soldier during the Civil War, so he'd appointed a surgeon from Bellevue named Bernard Levis to conduct the actual autopsy. A tall, thin man, Dr. Levis wore a black frock coat with a gold pocket watch on a chain that he checked several times as though he had other places to be—which, considering it was Christmas Day, he probably did.

The last two men were detectives from the Thirty-First Ward, whose jurisdiction included the two-mile stretch from Sixty-Third Street north to One Hundred and Tenth Street, and the Hudson River to the western edge of Central Park. Despite the fact they clearly knew Orpha, their greetings for the pair of young civilian investigators were not warm. This was doubtless due in part to the fact that they had overlooked the grating and the key evidence it contained.

Harry, John and Orpha sat down on the second tier of

benches, which afforded a clear view of the gurney. The room smelled of carbolic acid and other chemicals, although they failed to mask the underlying scent of blood and decay.

"If we're all here, I suggest we begin," Dr. Levis said briskly. "Mr. Eidman will be taking notes." He drew back the sheet from the body. Harry swallowed hard.

You knew it would be bad, she thought, digging her nails into her palms and taking a deep breath. *The only way to help now is to catch the one who did it, and you won't manage that by fainting.*

"We'll begin with a visual inspection," Dr. Levis said. "The body is that of Mr. Julius Sabelline, stated to be sixty-two years old. Weight is one hundred and seventy pounds, height seventy inches from crown to sole. Rigor mortis is fixed, confirming that death occurred within the last twenty-four hours. The decedent is wearing a long-sleeved white shirt which is bloodstained. It has multiple tears that correspond with injuries consistent with sharp force trauma to the neck and back."

Dr. Levis leaned over the body for a closer look. "The decedent's eyes were removed post-mortem. There are scrape marks on the supraorbital ridges. Not a metal blade though, I daresay. There are no cuts to the malar bone. Some kind of blunt tool."

"Could it be the same that was used to stab him?" Eidman asked.

"Yes, I'd say that's possible."

With Eidman's assistance, Dr. Levis removed Sabelline's shirt and trousers.

There's nothing more bereft than a naked corpse in a room full of strangers, Harry thought. Sabelline looked both bloated and shrunken in that strange way of dead bodies. The terrible injuries he'd suffered only made it worse. There was no way of telling what his face had been like in life.

"I observe no deformities, old surgical scars or amputations," Dr. Levis said. "Before moving on to the stab wounds themselves, I would note that there are unusual defensive injuries to the right palm. Striated bruising in six parallel lines, three of which super-ficially broke the skin."

"What could cause that?" one of the detectives asked.

"I can't say. It appears he gripped something in his fist which caused the injury. An object with raised ridges." Dr. Levis let the hand drop. "We need to roll him over, Ferdinand," he said to the coroner.

Sabelline was not a small man and it took a minute or two of minor struggling before they got him on his stomach. Dr. Levis took a steel probe from a tray. "I count five stab wounds on the back, one on the side of the neck that penetrated the left carotid artery. This is a fatal wound that would have caused loss of consciousness within one to two minutes.

"The next is located twenty inches below the crown of the head and five inches from the front of the body. It is vertically oriented and measures five-eighths of an inch in length. Inferi-orly, there is a squared off or dull end approximately one-thirty-second of an inch in length. Superiorly, the wound is tapered to a sharp point.

"The pathway of the wound passes through the skin, the subcutaneous tissue, and through the right seventh rib. Estimated length of the total wound path is four inches, and as stated the direction is right to left and back to front with no other angula-tion measurable." He paused. "I would say this is also a fatal wound associated with perforation of the right lung."

"There is a second stab wound in the back, also on the right side, twenty-one inches below the crown of the head and two inches from the front of the body," he continued. "It penetrated the lungs without striking rib. There is fresh hemorrhage and bruising noted along the wound path as well as the hemothorax described above. The direction is right to left, with a total depth of four to five inches. In my opinion, this wound was also a fatal stab wound associated with perforation of the lung and hemoth-orax. Essentially, his lungs filled with blood."

Dr. Levis continued for another twenty minutes, meticulously measuring each stab wound as Eidman recorded the results. Any one of them would have been fatal.

"I conclude it most likely that the decedent was seated when his assailant came up behind him and stabbed him once in the neck, then five times in the back. Sabelline turned and seized the weapon at some point, possibly grappling with his killer for it. This would account for the bruising on the decedent's palms."

"But what was he stabbed with, doctor?" the older of the detectives asked. Orpha had introduced him as Michael Jones. "You said it wasn't a knife."

"No, the edges of the wounds are ragged and they taper to a very fine point. I'd say something more akin to an icepick."

"And the handle?"

"It will have sharp but shallow ridges."

The detectives shared a quick glance. At least they had a distinctive weapon to look for.

"Mr. Sabelline would have bled out quickly, within two or three minutes. Removal of the eyes occurred shortly after death, most likely with the same object he was stabbed with. It appears to have been done in a rushed, frenzied manner. The eyes were found approximately six feet from the body. The assailant did not cleanly sever the optic nerve, but rather tore the eyes from the sockets using brute force, with accompanying injury to the corneas and vitreous humor." Levis consulted briefly with the coroner. "We'll move on to the internal examination now."

The body was again flipped onto its back and Dr. Levis made the classic Y incision in the chest, using a bone saw to cut through the ribs. Julius Sabelline's organs were weighed and measured. The bloody fluid in his lungs confirmed the cause of death, but no other unusual findings were made. He had been a healthy, if slightly overweight, middle-aged man.

Dr. Levis and Mr. Eidman stayed to talk further with the detectives, who made it clear the civilian contingent from the

S.P.R had exhausted their welcome. Neither Harry nor John had any desire to remain. It had been a long day, beginning at the S.P.R. offices downtown and ending in this gruesome amphitheater. Catching whoever had wreaked such terrible destruction on the famous Egyptologist, now mercifully under a sheet again, would not be a simple matter, Harry feared. The killer was organized and cunning. If he was also mad, it wouldn't be the stark raving sort, but a quiet, twisted malice that was far more dangerous.

As they passed the table with Dr. Sabelline's personal effects, Harry had a final thought. She eyed his shoes intently, picking one up and reading the label inside. A disapproving harrumph from Dr. Levis made her drop it back onto the table.

Curiouser and curiouser, Harry thought, a hard gleam in her eye.

WHEN THEY REACHED FIRST AVENUE, Orpha Winter turned to them both with a peremptory tone. "Once you've spoken to everyone, please compile your findings in a report and submit it to me. Naturally, I'll share it with the police."

"Certainly. But the interviews are only the beginning of the investigation," Harry said. "There will be leads to follow up—"

"I'll make that determination. And Mr. Kaylock, of course. But we wouldn't want to put you in any danger."

"Why would we be in danger?"

Orpha studied her for a long moment. *Was that a spark of worry in her eyes? Or something else?* Harry couldn't tell if it was real or feigned.

"I think Dr. Sabelline may have waded into deeper waters than he intended. There are things in this world you know nothing of, Miss Pell. Matters that defy rational explanation." She held up a gloved hand. "I know. You're a skeptic, like Mr.

Kaylock. Don't believe in all that supernatural rubbish. And you think I'm a naïve fool because I do. But even Harland can't deny certain realities." Orpha's mouth curved in a tiny smile. "He'll have to come clean with you eventually if you're to work for the S.P.R."

Harry frowned and began to reply. Orpha cut her off.

"I've arranged for you to interview the Sabellines in the morning," she said, handing her a piece of paper. "Here's the address."

"And Count Koháry?"

"I'll keep you informed." Orpha stepped to the curb just as a shiny black barouche pulled up. The uniformed driver leapt down and opened her door. "My God, this has been the strangest Christmas," she said over her shoulder. "I do hope you enjoy the rest of yours."

They stood there watching the carriage speed away uptown, followed by the pathetic sight of an anxious-looking woman in tattered clothing entering the Morgue, her face a mixture of hope and despair. Hope that it wouldn't be the one she sought, despair because if he or she wasn't in the Morgue, they'd still be missing and their fate might never be known.

"What was that all about, do you think?" John asked.

"I've no idea. But she won't bully me off this case until I get a result. That I promise."

Harry was just looking for a cab when a loud squawk made her jump. A crow, perched on the lintel of the Morgue entrance. It was a large bird, dull black, with a sharp, curving beak. Something moist and red dangled from its mouth.

"Dirty carrion-eaters," John muttered. "Let's go, Harry."

She let him take her arm and lead her to a waiting hansom, but all the while, Harry had the peculiar sensation that the bird's unblinking gaze was fixed on them both.

CHAPTER 15

The sun hung in a red ball over the Hudson by the time they arrived at the Fearing Pell townhouse on West Tenth Street near Washington Square Park. Harry's motherly housekeeper, Mrs. Rivers, greeted them at the door in a cloud of delicious cooking smells.

"I thought you'd miss Christmas dinner," she said reprovingly. "It's been ready for half an hour." She sniffed. "You smell rather awful. Where have you been?"

"The Morgue." Harry hung her red coat on a peg by the door. "They just performed the post-mortem on Julius Sabelline."

Mrs. Rivers drew her shawl closer around her shoulders. "How perfectly morbid. Are you joining us for dinner, Mr. Weston?"

"If you'll have me."

"Of course, dear. But they're not expecting you at home?"

"We hold our family dinner on Christmas Eve," John explained with a wink. "And if that's your famous Apple Jonathan I smell in the oven, I'm not above celebrating the birth of our Lord and Savior twice in a row."

"I imagine you're not." Mrs. Rivers shot a harried glance at the kitchen. "The Butchers are here. I told Connor to round them up and give them a scrub. Nasty little rascals, but we can't have them going hungry on Christmas, can we?" This was said with fondness.

The Bank Street Butchers were Connor's old gang: Clyde, Danny, Two-Toed Tom, Kid Spiegelman, Little Artie and Virgil the Goat. Despite their fearsome moniker, not one was a day over eleven years old. The police in the Ninth Ward mockingly called them the Bank Street Bedbugs—pests who had proven impossible to eradicate. They lived by their wits on the unforgiving streets of New York, pooling various talents for pickpocketing (Clyde), defrauding charitable institutions for orphans (the cherubic Little Artie), larceny (Danny and Kid Speigelman), gambling (Virgil) and acting as a gopher for older delinquents (Tom).

Connor himself had been rescued from the streets by Harry's sister, Myrtle, who took him into her employ as an informant and general errand boy. He had saved Harry's life twice during the Hyde investigation, and now lived in a small garret on the top floor of the house. She'd come to think of him as a little brother and he'd done his best to fit into his new household, although when the Butchers came around, he tended to fall back into his old ways.

The boys greeted Harry and John with rowdy enthusiasm from the rear parlor, where they lay sprawled under the Christmas tree playing a fast-paced card game they called Jewish Faro.

"Hooked a new case, Harry?" Tom called out.

"Oh yes, and it's a humdinger," she said with a twinkle in her eye.

"It's got Egyptian mummies," John put in. "And fatal curses."

"Yer jokin'," Kid Spiegelman said, turning over a ten of diamonds to the groans of his companions.

"Not in the least," Harry said. "And there may be a job in it for you boys."

"Minus my ten percent commission," Connor added absently, copper curls gleaming in the lamplight. He eyed the thirteen cards laid out in a row on the carpet, muttering something about *the hock*.

"Call the turn, Spiegelman," Virgil said.

"Hang on, Clyde ain't bet yet."

Connor's nose wrinkled. "You smell pretty ripe, Harry."

"So I hear. Give me ten minutes to wash up."

Mrs. Rivers had raised all the leaves on the dining room table and they just managed to squeeze everybody in. She ordered John to say Grace, which the boys piously clasped their hands for, though they fell on the food like a school of piranhas before the final syllable of *Amen* had been uttered.

"I've been thinking about the removal of the eyes," John said, heaping buttery mashed turnips on his plate. "Don't you think it's telling they were ripped—"

"I won't have murder talk at the dinner table." Mrs. Rivers shot him a stern look. "I simply won't have it!"

"Sorry," he mumbled contritely. "Of course, it's perfectly savage of me. What about curses?"

That earned a disdainful sniff, but Harry could tell it wasn't a veto. Like John, Mrs. Rivers had a fascination with the occult.

"Pass the ham, would'ya pleeze?" sang out Two-Toed Tom from the far end of the table. Harry complied and the platter of meat traveled through a series of slightly grubby hands, growing a bit smaller with each encounter.

"What do you mean by *curses*?" Mrs. Rivers demanded.

"Oh, there's a doozy associated with the case," John said blandly. "But I wouldn't be so crass as to recite it now."

"I should hope not."

For many minutes, the only sounds were the clanking of

cutlery and enthusiastic chewing of the Butchers. Finally, Mrs. Rivers could no longer contain herself.

"Is it connected to a particular object?" she inquired. "I only ask because I just finished reading about Thomas Busby's Dead Man's Chair. Do you know of it?"

"Why, no." John leaned forward, a gleam in his eye. "By all means, tell us."

"Well," she began in a conspiratorial tone. "Thomas Busby, a Yorkshire man, murdered his father-in-law in 1702. Strangled him for daring to sit in Busby's favorite chair. I think there was some bludgeoning too. Well, just before they hung him from the gibbet, he put a curse on the chair."

"And?"

"Sixty-three people who have sat in the chair met with untimely deaths," she whispered loudly.

"Oh God," Harry said. "Where did you read this?"

"One of Connor's penny dreadfuls," she said, still in that booming stage whisper. "You know I confiscate them from the boy whenever I find them. Absolute filth!"

"Filth," John agreed, suppressing a grin. "In fact, the curse in the Sabelline case is connected to an Egyptian amulet. Claims that anyone who touches it will die in about a dozen unpleasant ways."

"Oh dear. Is that why the S.P.R is interested?"

"Partly," John said evasively. He raised his glass. "I must say, this is a smashing dinner, Mrs. Rivers. The glazed ham is a work of culinary art. I'd say we earned it, don't you think, Harry?"

"I'm just glad you're all here." She looked around at the eccentric gathering with a warm smile. "It would be awfully lonely otherwise."

"Indeed it would," the housekeeper said. "I know your parents are stuck in the Canary Islands, Harry, but far be it from Myrtle to send a telegram letting us know if she's dead or alive, let alone whether she'll be home for Christmas."

"No word from Paris then?"

Harry's older sister had departed two weeks before, hot on the trail of a jewel thief who'd been plundering the boudoirs of wealthy women in the exclusive 16th Arrondissement. She usually solved her cases within a few days; Harry wondered (with a degree of jealousy) if Myrtle had decided to stay and enjoy the sights. More likely, another case had come along to catch her attention and she hadn't bothered to send a letter home. Although she often complained that "there was nothing new under the sun" when it came to crime, Myrtle was always on the lookout for cases of sufficient complexity and weirdness to challenge her formidable intellect.

"Not a peep," Mrs. Rivers said.

"Just as well," John chimed in. "Myrtle would be second-guessing us every step of the way."

"True. But she might have some valuable insights." Harry stirred her oyster soup. "Do you think the police have a hope of solving it?"

"Of course not. Unless the killer has an attack of conscience and confesses, which seems unlikely considering the savagery—"

"Oh no, you don't." Mrs. Rivers put on a bright smile. "How about dessert?"

They talked of more cheerful things after that. John regaled them with stories about his brothers that had Mrs. Rivers red-faced and laughing. The Butchers cleared the table, bantering amongst themselves in street flash barely recognizable as English. Harry didn't mind, as she had a feeling their conversation touched on criminal activities she would prefer to be in the dark about.

Once the Apple Jonathan had been consumed down to the last sugary crumb and they sat before the fire in the drawing room, Mrs. Rivers relented and the talk turned once again to the strange death of Julius Sabelline.

"There are two possibilities as I see it," Harry said. "The theft of the relic in the strongbox was the reason for the murder, or it was intended as misdirection to make the scene *look* like a robbery, when in fact the true motive was entirely different."

"And the eyes?" John said quietly.

"Strongly imply a personal hatred. Punishment for some perceived sin."

"I agree. The stabbing had a clear purpose—to cause death, quickly. Six wounds. The killer didn't mutilate any other part of his anatomy. It wasn't torture, as Sabelline was dead already. Gouging out the eyes seems pointless."

"Clearly not to whoever did it. It required an extra minute or so to accomplish. Someone could have walked in at any time. Quite a risk, but one the killer was willing to take. The question is why."

"*Oculi quas fenestrae animi.* The eyes are the windows of the soul. Do you remember, Harry?"

"Bruno Alighieri, you mean. The demonologist we consulted in the Brady case."

"It's an odd parallel."

Harry kicked her shoes off and wiggled her stockinged toes at the fire. "It's useless to speculate until we know more about the amulet itself. I'll ask Sabelline's wife about it tomorrow. Any other ideas?"

"Here's one. What if it isn't an enemy of Dr. Sabelline, but of the museum?" John said. "Someone who wanted the exhibit to fail."

Connor had been listening quietly the whole time. Now he shook his head.

"Yer not thinking it through," he said patiently.

"What?"

He spread his arms wide. "Just pitcher it. Famous explorer gets his candle snuffed inside the museum just before the exhibit opens. Cursed object nicked! People will come in droves. They'll be beating 'em off with a stick."

"He's right," John said. "Which presents another possible motive."

"Nelson Holland killed Dr. Sabelline in a spectacularly gruesome fashion to revive the museum's attendance?" Harry asked with a smile. "Or maybe it was Morris K. Jessup himself?"

"I know it sounds far-fetched. I just think we should consider everything."

"Fair enough."

"What about the money? You ought to find out if there was an inheritance involved." Mrs. Rivers sipped her dry gin with a happy sigh. "At least half the murders in this city have profit as a motive."

"Half?" John snorted. "Try ninety percent."

"I've no idea if he was wealthy," Harry said. "The address Mrs. Winter gave me is in Brooklyn Heights. A respectable neighborhood but hardly Mansion Row." She grinned. "It's not far from that roller skating rink on Fulton and Orange Streets you dragged me to a couple of years back."

"Don't pretend you didn't have a good time," John laughed.

"I think I still have the scars."

Harry wandered into the kitchen, where the Butchers were drinking mulled cider and practicing some sort of cheating strategy that involved attaching a nearly invisible silk thread to the cards and dragging them to different piles in the faro deal. Virgil the Goat, the undisputed wizard of gaming sleight-of-hand, watched the others' efforts with a jaundiced eye, offering pointers in a bored tone.

"I have a job for you," Harry said. "All of you."

They perked up at this.

"There's a man named Count Balthazar Jozsef Habsburg-Koháry. I need you to find out where he lives and keep an eye on the place. Discreetly. That means without getting caught. We'll all be in the soup if you muck this up."

"Please," Little Artie said with quiet dignity. "Yer talkin' to professionals. We won't get nicked. What's the feller's name again?"

Harry repeated it, more slowly this time. There was no point in writing it down as she doubted any of them could read. "He's very rich."

"Probably lives uptown with the other swells then," Danny said. "Don't worry, Miss Pell. We'll track him down fer ya."

"Excellent. Keep me informed."

At ten o'clock, the Butchers thanked Mrs. Rivers for a "lov-er-ly dinner" and cleared out for their shared flophouse by the docks. Harry gave them each a quarter and a ham sandwich from the leftovers. She and Mrs. Rivers stood on the front stoop and watched as the six small forms melted into the shadows along Tenth Street.

"New York is no place for children," Mrs. Rivers said, an edge of anger in her voice. "Those boys can't be blamed for what they do, when they have no one to take care of them."

"No, they can't," Harry agreed.

When they went back inside, they found John going over his notes from the day, adding details while his memory was still fresh.

"What about Jeremy Boot?" he said. "I know the charges against him were dropped for lack of evidence, but that's not the same as being proved innocent. At the least it could be useful to get his story firsthand."

"Is that an offer?" Harry asked with a smile.

"His address is in the police report. I'll pop over tomorrow."

"Perfect. I'll see the Sabellines and we can meet afterwards for lunch at the St. Denis."

The clock chimed and Harry suppressed a yawn.

"Don't you think we ought to exchange presents now?" Mrs. Rivers said. "It's getting rather late."

"Oh no." John looked stricken. "This is so embarrassing."

"Ignore him." Mrs. Rivers gave John a playful swat. "He dropped them off days ago. Swore me to secrecy."

Connor passed the gifts around and they took turns opening them. Harry had bought John the latest edition of *Grey's Anatomy* and a cashmere scarf. For Mrs. Rivers, whose love of the macabre was only surpassed by her love of quackery, Harry had ordered a Dr. Scott's Electric Flesh Brush. Dr. Scott was a great favorite of Mrs. Rivers, and she seemed pleased with it.

"And this is yours." John handed her a rectangular box. Harry opened it. Her breath caught at the object inside, gleaming in its velvet lining.

"Oh, John. You shouldn't have. But it's lovely."

"Well, so are you," he said lightly. "A good match then."

Harry pointed the gun at the fireplace, admiring its sleek curves.

"It's a Colt Derringer," he said. "Walnut grip with an engraved silver barrel. Perfect for a stocking, muff or bodice."

She looked at him from the corner of her eye. "You're not afraid I'll shoot you with it?"

He grinned. "I'll just have to stay on your good side."

Harry laughed. "I won't have to swipe Myrtle's anymore. Oh, thank you!" She leapt to her feet and fairly bowled him over with an embrace. John grinned, his cheeks reddening.

"All right. I'm glad you like it. There's no point in telling you to stay out of trouble, so I figured you might as well be armed."

Connor received some useful but boring items such as new socks and coat, but his eyes lit up when John gave him *The Legacy of Cain*, Wilkie Collins' new horror novel. From the way Mrs. Rivers eyed it covetously, Harry had a feeling the book would end up among her extensive collection of confiscated penny dreadfuls.

John left at a little before midnight and they all toddled off to their rooms, warm and replete with food and camaraderie. Harry curled up in bed but as exhausted as she was, her mind kept running through the crime scene and the odd bits of evidence that didn't add up. Keys and shoes and missing weapons.

More akin to an icepick...sharp but shallow ridges.

Harry threw the blankets off, rolled over. Got cold and pulled them back on. She felt she was missing something. Something important. But what?

The eyes were found approximately six feet from the body.

They nagged at her, those eyes. Like John said, unsettling echoes of the Brady case.

Pervadunt oculus.

It comes through the eyes.

Harry felt a chill. She thought of the crow she'd seen outside the Morgue that afternoon. Just like the one that had perched on her windowsill when Elizabeth Brady came to visit that summer, staring in such a queer, un-birdlike way through the glass. They all looked the same. It couldn't possibly be the same bird.

Could it?

Don't, she ordered herself sternly. *Leland Brady is dead. You saw him die. The Hyde case is closed. You caught him in the act, about to kill Billy in the tunnel. Don't look for connections that don't exist.*

No, the simple truth was someone wanted Julius Sabelline dead, and that someone was almost certainly one of a small number of friends or acquaintances. She had only to eliminate them one by one, by gathering as many hard facts as possible. The amulet of Osiris seemed a promising line of inquiry. Why take that particular artifact when far more valuable ones would have been easier to steal?

Deep waters, Orpha Winter had said.

It was of water that Harry dreamt when she finally fell asleep. Dark and still and fathomless. Tall grey reeds swayed in the murk. Harry drifted among them, her bare toes brushing the muddy bottom. She had a strong sensation of being watched by hidden eyes. She flapped her arms to move quicker. Light shone in the distance, and in the way of dreams, she knew the edge of the queer forest lay not far ahead, if she could only reach it. But the not-water (for she breathed it easily) seemed to thicken the harder she tried to swim.

And then her heart froze as a larger shadow moved in the reeds. In an instant, the watchers scattered, a school of barracuda before a great white. She leaned forward, trying to dig into the muck, but every movement was painfully slow and labored.

He's been looking for you. The Hunter. The man named Hyde.

And now he's found you.

Harry opened her mouth to scream, and suddenly she was back in her bed. Paralyzed and sticky with sweat.

The night terrors.

Some part of her remembered, although she hadn't had them since she was a small child. The unshakeable conviction that someone—*a man*—was climbing the stairs and coming toward her room. She couldn't stir, couldn't draw breath to scream, and when he opened the door....

Harry woke up, truly this time. Her eyes flew to the doorknob, heart clawing at her chest. But it didn't turn. Ever so slowly, the panic ebbed. She lit a candle with shaking hand. She wished her parents would come home. At nineteen, she considered herself an independent woman, but the house felt awfully empty with just Connor and Mrs. Rivers.

Harry opened the drawer to her bedside table and confirmed that the gun John had given her lay inside, loaded and ready to fire. She took a drink of water and picked up the latest edition of the *Journal of Forensic Botany.*

Dawn was still hours off, but she knew there would be no more sleep that night.

CHAPTER 16

The Sabellines lived in a Greek Revival townhouse on Cranberry Street in Brooklyn Heights, with wrought-iron railings and a well-kept garden. A uniformed housemaid answered Harry's knock and seemed to be expecting her. The girl led the way down a short hall to a generously proportioned rear sitting room with tall windows that would have admitted wintry daylight had they not been sealed tight with heavy curtains. All the mirrors were likewise draped with black mourning cloths, giving the house the gloomy atmosphere of a medieval keep.

"Please to sit while I fetch the master," the girl said in a thick German accent.

Harry nodded and dropped obediently into a chair. The moment the maid left, she leapt to her feet and took a quick survey of the room, hoping to find some clue to Julius Sabelline's character. There were few souvenirs from the archaeologist's travels, but a framed photograph above the mantel showed two men standing shoulder to shoulder in the desert, the legendary Sphinx crouching in the background.

The first was rather severe-looking, with a harsh mouth and flinty eyes. He had thinning grey hair and a visible paunch.

Harry guessed this was Sabelline. The other man was much younger, no more than his mid-thirties, with dark hair parted on the side and combed back from his forehead. He wore a simple white shirt, open at the neck to reveal sun-darkened skin. Too old to be Jackson, Harry thought. There's something arrogant about him, but also a bit melancholy. A strange combination….

"Miss Pell?"

Harry spun around, trying not to look guilty. The photograph was on display, after all.

A young man in his twenties stood just inside the doorway. He was handsome, with a rugged build and thick, wavy brown hair, but red-rimmed eyes marked him as in mourning.

"Jackson Sabelline," he said, offering a hand by way of introduction. "Please do sit down."

"Thank you for having me. I hope it's not an intrusion. I suppose Mrs. Winter explained I'm from the Society for Psychical Research."

They took seats opposite each other. Jackson called for coffee. His demeanor was not precisely cold, but nor did Harry sense an enthusiastic welcome.

"She told mother you'd be coming, but perhaps you can explain," he said once the maid had left the coffee service on the table between them and closed the door behind her. "Forgive me if you find my question rude, but what exactly is the Society for Psychical Research? I don't see how it pertains to my father's murder."

Harry cleared her throat. "Well, the S.P.R. was first formed in London in 1882. The mission was to apply rigorous scientific principles to the investigation of supernatural phenomena. An American branch was founded a few years later."

"Supernatural?" he said in some confusion. "As in ghosts?"

"Among other things." Harry decided not to mention ancient reanimated mummies. "But I assure you, Mr. Sabelline, I have no intention of sensationalizing this tragic event. My sister, Myrtle Fearing Pell, is a consulting detective—"

"Oh yes, I've heard of her," he rejoined in a friendlier tone.

"She trained me according to the principles of logical deduction, which I intend to apply in this case as best as I can. I only wish to help the police, in an informal capacity."

He nodded slowly. "That sounds rather admirable, Miss Pell. I imagine they can use all the help they can get at this point. It's been two days and the only real suspect was released. I can't describe how upsetting it is to us that father's murderer is still out there, running loose."

Harry laid her empty coffee cup on the table. "Perhaps we can begin by going over what you remember from that night."

"Of course."

"I understand you weren't with your mother when the body was found?"

"No. I'd grown tired of waiting in the main hall for father to return, so I went off to explore the exhibits on the second floor. I'm studying anthropology at Harvard and the museum has a fine collection of pre-Columbian tools. I was only visiting for the holidays, you see."

The younger Sabelline sighed, his gaze falling on a single sprig of holly on the mantle. All other signs of Christmas had been purged from the house. Harry supposed yuletide decorations would only make the family feel worse.

"The next thing I knew, Mr. Sharpe was yelling for help. He sounded...well, panicked. I knew something was terribly wrong. I rushed down the stairs and found him in the main hall with Count Habsburg-Koháry. Sharpe told us what he'd seen, though not all of it. I didn't hear the worst of the details until later, when we were all questioned.

"I wanted to see my father but Sharpe wouldn't let me. I suppose I should be grateful for that. He said I'd regret it for the rest of my days and there was nothing we could do for him now except fetch the authorities." He swallowed. "We got the key from Boot and unlocked the front doors. There are always policemen in the park, even late at night, and Count Koháry found one quickly."

"Mrs. Winter had left at that point?"

"The last I saw her, she was speaking to the count. I suppose she went home sometime while I was in the upstairs galleries."

"And Nelson Holland?"

"To be honest, we'd forgotten all about him until he came wandering down from his office. The police had already arrived at that point."

"Did you see anyone else while you were on the second floor?"

Jackson shook his head. "I was gone perhaps fifteen or twenty minutes."

"And your mother? I understand she fainted."

"Yes, quite understandably, the poor thing. Boot and Sharpe carried her out to the hallway. Boot stayed with my father's body while the others went for help."

"So no one could have gone in or out after the murder was discovered?"

"Not without being seen. I'd say it was no more than ten minutes between the time Mr. Sharpe raised the alarm and we returned with a police officer."

"Thank you, Mr. Sabelline," Harry said. "You've been most clear and forthcoming in your answers. I wonder if it might be possible to speak with your mother?"

He hesitated. "She's resting. It's all been such a terrible shock."

"I understand perfectly. But—"

His face hardened a fraction. "The doctor has given her a sleeping draught. She's always been a fragile person, Miss Pell, and I fear the toll this will have on her psyche. Perhaps in a few days, when she's feeling stronger."

Harry nodded, sensing a lost battle and unwilling to impose on his grief any more than she already had. "Of course. I—"

"Jackson?"

They turned at a soft voice in the doorway.

"Mother." He stood immediately, looking stricken. "You shouldn't be up."

"It's all right." Mrs. Sabelline waved a pale hand. "I heard voices."

"This is Harrison Fearing Pell," he said with some reluctance. "She's informally involved with the investigation. I was just answering some questions."

Araminta Sabelline looked very much like her son, with the same generous mouth and lush hair, although her figure was small-boned and petite. Harry was a bit surprised to see she was a good twenty years younger than her deceased husband. She had pale skin, which looked even whiter against her long-sleeved black dress. There was something tragic about her features, as though she'd been born to wear a widow's clothes.

"Pleased to make your acquaintance, Miss Pell," she said. "I'm happy to assist in any way I can." She turned to Jackson. "Won't you open the curtains? It's so gloomy in here."

"Certainly, Mother." He crossed the window and threw back the heavy drapes. Thin light poured into the room.

"Is that your husband?" Harry asked, pointing to the picture above the mantel.

"Yes." She gave a trembling smile. "It was taken at Giza two years ago. They'd gone to meet with Gaston Maspero. He'd just embarked on an attempt to clear away some of the sand that had buried the Sphinx and to search for tombs beneath it."

"And the other gentleman in the photograph?"

"Is Count Balthazar Habsburg-Koháry."

"Of course."

"Tell me, Miss Pell." Her eyes shone with a piteous entreaty. "Have you any idea who could have done this to Julius?"

"Not yet, I'm afraid." Harry glanced out the window. Sparrows hopped in a patch of melting snow. For a moment, she remembered the crow and its beady, clever eyes. "Did your husband have any enemies?"

"I won't say he had many friends, but there are none I would call enemies. It's a cliché, but he was married to his work. Julius had been fascinated with ancient Egyptian culture since he read about Napoleon's campaigns as a child. *From these pyramids, four thousand years of civilization look down upon us.*"

"Had he behaved in an unusual manner in the days leading up to his death? Did he seem afraid of anything?"

"Not that I noticed." Her hand went to a plain gold crucifix hanging around her neck, twisting it nervously. "He was so busy preparing for the exhibit."

"Father did seem a bit distracted," Jackson put in. "I chalked it up to nerves about the party. He never enjoyed social affairs. I'm sure he would have found a way to beg off if his presence hadn't been required."

"My husband had a stoic temperament, Miss Pell. I doubt he would have let on if he was worried about something." Araminta threw a glance at her son. "I'm just grateful Jackson is here. I couldn't imagine staying in the house alone after what happened."

He took her hand and they shared a tender look.

"What about this supposed curse?" Harry asked.

A shadow passed over Mrs. Sabelline's features. "Oh, he didn't take it seriously at all. Though I wonder if he should have."

"What do you mean?"

"Only that I always wondered why Count Koháry insisted that the amulet be locked up at all." Her gaze fell on the photograph of the two men at the Sphinx. "He should have kept it himself if it was so valuable. Then Julius would still be alive."

Jackson laid a hand on his mother's arm. She didn't seem to notice. A long moment passed. Dark circles shadowed her eyes, which she'd tried to cover with powder. A tear etched its way down her cheek, cutting through the make-up like rain on a dusty window.

"I was feeling ill that evening," she said in a subdued voice. "Too much caviar. And I've never liked cigar smoke. It makes me light-headed. I left to freshen up in the first floor ladies room. Jackson had wandered off to look at some of the other exhibits." Her hands knit tightly in her lap. "When I emerged some time later, I encountered Mr. Sharpe in the hall."

"Of the basement level?"

"Yes, I very much wished to go home. It was a fair journey to Brooklyn and I was tired. I thought I'd see what was keeping Julius." She drew a deep breath. "He offered to escort me to my husband's office. You must know the rest."

"Yes, I saw your statement, you needn't repeat it, Mrs. Sabelline."

"Thank you."

"I'll only ask if you have any personal suspicions about who might be responsible. I assure you, I'll keep anything you say confidential. But since you know everyone involved, perhaps you have some instinct."

Araminta Sabelline shook her head. "For what I saw? I can't imagine any one of them committing such an act, Miss Pell." Her voice broke. "It was simply inhuman." Pale fingers twisted the crucifix. "Enough to make one believe the devil is real."

Jackson Sabelline frowned and put an arm around her.

"Perhaps you should lie down, Mother," he said. "You don't look well."

She shrugged weakly. "I'll be all right."

"No, really. I insist. Dr. Welles will never forgive me if I fail in my nursing duties."

Araminta raised a hand to her forehead and for an instant, her sleeve fell back. Five dark marks circled her frail wrist. Harry looked away before either of them noticed her staring.

She stood. "I've taken enough of your time. Please don't hesitate to contact me if you think of anything else." She put her new hat on—a miniature derby with a dark red velvet band—and gave Mrs. Sabelline a consoling look. "I'm terribly sorry for your loss."

Araminta barely seemed to hear her. She stared at the mantle, and the sad sprig of holly next to the photograph of her husband and Count Koháry.

"Berte will see you out," Jackson said, ringing for the maid. "Thank you for coming, Miss Pell."

As she walked to the door, Harry contrived to pass by the window. Something had caught her eye when Jackson threw open the drapes, and a quick glance confirmed it. *That's* interesting, Harry thought.

There was a gleaming new lock on the sash.

SHE FOUND John ensconced in a corner table of the St. Denis's elegant dining room, and he wasn't alone. An animated young woman sat across from him. She was a few years older than John, with a squarish face and short bangs. A black-and-white checked coat was slung carelessly over the back of her chair.

"Nellie," Harry said with genuine pleasure. "I should have expected you'd be mixed up in this."

"Harry! I understand you're coming from the Sabellines."

"Are you on her payroll now?" Harry asked John with a laugh.

"Pure coincidence," Nellie said airily. "I happened to be passing by and saw him through the window."

"I'm sure you did." Harry sat down and they ordered a round of drinks. "I thought you were busy planning for your trip?"

Nellie Bly was Joe Pulitzer's star reporter at the *New York World*. She'd gained a reputation for stunt reporting, pretending to be mad and getting herself admitted to the women's asylum on Blackwell's Island where she'd exposed the horrendous condi-

179

tions there. Her latest scheme, which her editors had recently approved, was to stage a race across the globe by train and steamship, with the aim of besting the time of the fictional Phileas Fogg in Jules Verne's *Around the World in Eighty Days*.

"I am, but we've got until next fall to put everything together. This museum murder is the big news now and John wants a story," she said, referring to her editor, John Cockerill.

"Perhaps we can trade information."

"You always were a little mercenary," Nellie laughed. "All right, sounds fair. Who goes first?"

"Can't we order?" John complained. "I'm starving."

A short time later, they were dining on wild duck and salmon, artichokes a la Barigoule, salsify au jus, and paper-thin slices of grilled eggplant.

"I suppose you've seen the police report?" Nellie asked.

"Better than that. We've been to the crime scene," John said. He gave a brief account of their time at the museum the day before. "Holland seems like an upstanding citizen. Sharpe is a bit of a drinker, but so are plenty of men."

"His story doesn't match Araminta Sabelline's," Harry said. "She told me they met in the hallway. He claimed she went to his office."

"Hmm. Could be an honest mistake," Nellie said. "Witnesses sometimes misremember details like that. Or they're in cahoots and got their lies mixed up. Wouldn't be the first time a wife offed her husband in this town. Do you think she's capable?"

"Impossible to say. She did seem genuinely grief-stricken. But I'll tell you one thing. Araminta was lying when she said her husband wasn't afraid. Someone put new locks on those windows, I'd say right around the same time Julius changed the lock on his office door."

"Perhaps she worried the killer might come after her," John offered.

Harry shook her head. "I think Mrs. Sabelline could hardly

have arranged for someone to come so quickly, particularly since it was Christmas. There was also an extremely fine layer of dust. The new locks must predate the murder."

"He was afraid of something."

"Or she was," John said.

In the pleasant, low-key hubbub of the St. Denis dining room, Harry recalled her nightmare and felt a chill.

"She also had bruises on her wrist, as if someone had grabbed her. No more than a day or two old, I'd guess."

"Her husband?"

"He's the likeliest one," Harry agreed. "Or the son, although they did seem to have a loving relationship."

"On the surface."

"On the surface, yes. I was only there for perhaps half an hour."

"Happy families are all alike," Nellie quoted. "Each unhappy family is unhappy in its own way."

"You should come to my house sometime," John muttered as he went in for a third helping of duck. "Even the Russians would shudder when they met Rupert."

Harry stared at them both blankly.

"Tolstoy's *Anna Karenina*," Nellie said. "I thought you were an avid reader."

"Only of forensics and chemistry journals," John said with a grin. "And the crime pages of the newspapers. Otherwise, she's practically illiterate."

Harry shot him a look. "What do you know about this Hungarian count?" she asked Nellie. "Sabelline's patron."

"Rather mysterious. Appeared on the scene about five years ago from somewhere in Central Europe. No one knows much about him except that he's terribly rich and an avid collector of anything more than a thousand years old. Unmarried, no children. His money must be old too because I can't seem to find out where it comes from."

"Speaking of which, I wonder who gets Julius's money. I didn't have the gall to ask the grieving widow," Harry admitted.

"I can answer that. There wasn't a great deal and it was divided evenly between the wife and son."

"Sounds like another dead end." John took a bite of salmon. "Well, I'll tell you what I found. The locksmith who made the keys has a shop on Seventy-Second and Broadway. He said there were only two and he gave them both to Mr. Sabelline the afternoon of the party."

"He could be lying," Nellie pointed out.

"He could," John agreed. "But why? I made a few inquiries in the neighboring establishments. He's been there for years and everyone vouched for his character without reservation."

Nellie gave a grudging nod. "You'd make a decent reporter, John."

He grinned. "Afterwards, I tracked down Mr. Jeremy Boot—who also seemed a polite, honest man, by the way. He confirmed that attendance at the museum has been way down since it moved from the Arsenal. You remember what a slog it was to get there, Harry. It's too far uptown with the elevated ending at 59th Street." He leaned forward. "Apparently, the trustees have been close to shutting it down. The Alexandria exhibit is critical to reviving the museum's fortunes. The publicity from the murder would be a sure way to make it a smashing success."

"What else did Boot say?"

"Not much we didn't already know. Said he went out for a cigarette sometime between one and one-fifteen. He stood in an alley adjacent to Seventy-Eighth Street. He'd only been outside a minute or so when Mrs. Winter came along loudly demanding to be let out. Boot complied, then went back to finish smoking. He was just returning to his post when Davis Sharpe and Araminta Sabelline came looking for him. He walked them down to the basement and unlocked the office door. You know the rest."

"Had he been in possession of the key all night?"

"He said it never left his pocket."

"Which leaves only the key belonging to Mr. Sabelline himself, and that was found in his desk drawer." Harry chewed her thumbnail. "We've spoken to six of the seven people who stayed after the party ended," she said. "The only one left is Count Balthazar Jozsef Habsburg-Koháry."

"I'd like to know why that particular artifact was locked up in the strongbox," John said.

"So would I. And if he has any idea what Sabelline was frightened of." She scowled. "But Orpha has me waiting."

"Your new boss?" Nellie asked sympathetically.

"You could say that. She won't let me interview the count without her permission."

John called for the check with a heavy sigh. "My God, I haven't eaten that much since I had two Christmas dinners in a row."

"Which was yesterday," Harry pointed out.

"I'm working on a respectable paunch. All the best-paid doctors have them."

Nellie eyed his tall, broad-shouldered frame with amusement. "I doubt you'll ever be one of those, John, and thank God for that."

"Fat or well-paid?"

Nellie laughed. "Take it as a compliment." She rose from the table and put on her checkered coat. "They'll want me at the office. I'll let you know if I discover anything interesting about our enigmatic noble."

"Don't worry, the Bedbugs are on the case." Harry grinned. "Count Balthazar Jozsef Habsburg-Koháry is about to have an infestation."

CHAPTER 17

A brief message waited when they returned to Tenth Street, summoning Harry and John to the S.P.R. headquarters next to Edison's new Pearl Street power station. Night was falling and the wind cut straight to the bone, so they decided to take a cab.

"What do you think it's about?" John asked as the driver fought the rush-hour traffic down Broadway.

"Let's hope Orpha Winter has finally tracked down the elusive count."

"Or perhaps she's luring us to our gruesome deaths to conceal her own guilt."

"That would only make sense if we'd found any real leads." Harry sighed. "I have a feeling Orpha's capable of almost anything if it involves self-preservation, but we're not exactly a threat, are we?"

"Unless you know something but you don't know you know it." John gave her a meaningful glance and Harry burst out laughing.

"What would I do without you, Dr. Weston?"

"Suffer unbearable tedium."

When they arrived, it turned out they hadn't been summoned by Orpha at all, but by Harland Kaylock. Mr. Kaylock was a rather severe person, tall and narrow with unruly brown hair and a sallow complexion. Before becoming vice president of the American S.P.R., he had been a professional magician. His current expertise was debunking fake mediums, placing him squarely at odds with Orpha Winter, who embraced spiritualism with open arms.

Harry and John were greeted at the door by the ancient butler Joseph, who escorted them to Mr. Kaylock's inner sanctum. He looked much as they had left him the day before, hawk-nosed and unsmiling in an impeccable dark frock coat.

"Do you have a progress report for me?" he demanded without preamble.

Harry recited all they'd learned, with periodic interjections from John. Mr. Kaylock laced his long fingers together and rested them on his desk.

"The police found the shoes," he said.

Harry smiled. "I thought they might. Where?"

"Hidden inside one of the stone sarcophagi."

"How heavy are those lids?" John asked.

"Extremely heavy."

"Could a single person have lifted it?"

"Not without a lever, and even then it would be difficult, although not impossible."

"Did the shoes have any distinguishing characteristics?" Harry asked.

"Size eleven, made by Lester Brothers in Binghamton. They appeared to be new. The police are canvassing shoe shops that carry the brand." He gazed at them with an inscrutable expression. "Do you have any theories?"

"A dozen, but they're all half-baked. Mr. Kaylock, we've

185

spoken to six of the seven people who were there. The only one left is the Hungarian count, and I believe he has critical information, but we're still waiting for Mrs. Winter to arrange an interview." She took a breath. "If you have any influence with her, can you press our case? Time is of the essence. You can't expect a result without—"

Kaylock cut her off with a wave of his hand. "I didn't call you here to rake you over the coals, Miss Pell. You've performed admirably. However, there have been new developments that alter the situation."

Harry frowned. "New developments?"

"You shall be fully informed of them. But first I would remind you both of the confidentiality agreement you signed yesterday." He patted the desk drawer.

"I'm still waiting for my copy," John said.

"And I'll see you receive it. But what I am about to tell you cannot leave this room. Is that clear?"

"Perfectly," Harry said. John nodded agreement.

"Very well then. First, I must inform you that the Brady case is now officially open again."

Harry frowned. "But he's dead. I saw him commit suicide."

Kaylock cleared his throat. "That may be true. But you will recall that your report alluded to the police doctor who attempted to treat Mr. Brady's gunshot wound."

"Dr. Clarence!" John shot to his feet. "I knew it, Harry! What did I tell you?"

Mr. Kaylock's brows drew together in disapproval. "Please sit down, Mr. Weston."

John fell back into his chair, but his eyes gleamed with excitement.

"As I was saying, Dr. William Clarence took a ship to England the day after Mr. Brady's suicide. That much you know."

Harry nodded. She had a sinking feeling in the pit of her stomach unlike anything she'd experienced before. It was worse than the day Myrtle returned from a job for the Pinkertons to discover Harry had been impersonating her for nearly two weeks.

"Thanks to your report, agents from the London S.P.R. located Dr. Clarence and took him into custody."

"Custody?"

"They committed him to an asylum for observation."

Harry stubbornly clung to ignorance. "On what basis?"

"That he was a suspect in the Ripper murders."

She stared out the window to Pearl Street, chest tightening as the implication of his words became clear. "But—"

"You should know that Dr. Clarence murdered an orderly and escaped nearly a week ago."

"That's terrible news, but I still don't see the connection," Harry said weakly.

Harland Kaylock looked genuinely sorry at his next words. "I like you, Miss Pell. You are rational and intelligent. We need those qualities in our agents, now more than ever. You may have deduced there is a struggle within the S.P.R. between those who champion science and reason, and those who blindly embrace the supernatural. Please be assured I stand firmly in the first camp." He paused. "However, there are also certain unpleasant truths in the world."

Harry forced herself to meet his level gaze. "Go on."

"There's no gentle way to put it." He tapped his long fingers on the desk. "I'm afraid monsters are real, Miss Pell."

"I knew it!" John looked as though he might leap to his feet again, but a quelling look from Kaylock nailed him to his chair. "I knew it," he muttered again.

"The Underworld is not a theoretical place. It exists. And there are spirits, undead spirits, that sometimes come back. Our colleagues in London call them ghouls."

"Ghouls," she repeated. "Surely you're joking. This is some kind of test—"

"I'm afraid not."

"Dr. Clarence is one of these ghouls, isn't he?" John asked eagerly.

"Worse than that. We don't know what he is exactly. Something infinitely more dangerous. In any event, the London office thinks he might be coming here. There's a connection to the Ptolemy exhibit. They're sending two of their agents to track him down. I expect your full cooperation."

"Of course," Harry said faintly.

If anyone other than Harland Kaylock had uttered such madness, she would have stood and walked out without a second thought. But she had researched the S.P.R. and its principal officers for years before being hired, and she had nothing but admiration for him, despite his chilly demeanor. If he claimed these things were true, they likely were.

"So it wasn't Mr. Brady's brain tumor that caused him to murder all those people?" she asked.

"No."

"You're absolutely certain?"

"Yes."

"What's the connection to the museum?" John asked. "It must be the artifact that was stolen."

"We don't know yet. The cable was rather terse, as cables tend to be. Mr. Sidgwick didn't go into detail. But the London agents are expected to arrive in the next day or two. Their names are Lady Vivienne Cumberland and Mr. Alec Lawrence. I'm sure they can explain in full detail."

"Going back for a moment," John said. "To be perfectly clear: This undead spirit possessed Leland Brady. And when he died, you're saying it jumped into Dr. William Clarence of the New York Police Department?"

Harry refused to look at him. Even worse than the fact of ghouls was the prospect of John's gloating. Throughout the

Brady case, he had argued that supernatural elements were at work. Harry had laughed at him.

"That would appear to be the case," Kaylock replied in a clipped tone. He clearly found the entire topic of ghouls to be distasteful.

Then the penny dropped. "Wait." John's mouth fell open a bit before he caught himself. "Was Dr. Clarence really the *Ripper*?"

"Undetermined," Kaylock said, in a tone that implied it was, in fact, highly likely.

"Could the ghoul, or whatever it is, be here already? Could it have killed Dr. Sabelline?"

"Well, that's the thing," Kaylock said slowly. "These creatures don't sprout wings or conjure magic carpets, Mr. Weston. London says it probably took a steamer, either on December 18th or 19th. The Transatlantic crossing has never been made in less than six days."

"And Dr. Sabelline was killed on December 23rd. Yes, I see your point." John thought for a moment. Then he pulled out his notepad and a nub of pencil, rolling up his sleeves in a workmanlike fashion. "So how does one stop a ghoul? Holy water? Crucifix?"

"They can't stand iron, that's all I know. Oh, and it's best to cut their heads off."

"Heads, got it." He scribbled on the pad. "Is New York quite infested?"

"No. It's much worse in London. Scotland Yard was forced to create a special branch just to deal with them."

"So Becky Rickard summoned this thing with *The Black Pullet* grimoire?"

"We don't know how it came through, actually."

"Through from Hell, you mean?"

Kaylock sounded funereal. "The official term is the Dominion. It's a sort of limbo."

John nodded. "What about werewolves?"

"Not real."

"Vampires?"

Kaylock hesitated. "Well, ghouls do consume the blood of their victims."

"Vampires: real," John whispered to himself, writing frantically on his pad. "Mummies? Please say yes."

"Not real."

"Fairies?"

"All right, Mr. Weston." Kaylock leaned back in his chair. "I'll admit, I'm still coming to grips with the news about Dr. Clarence. The cable only arrived today. Apparently, there was some mistake and it was supposed to have been sent nearly a week ago. Mr. Sidgwick couldn't understand why I hadn't responded."

He turned to Harry, who had been staring out the window in a daze for the last few minutes. "I understand your reluctance. The mind simply rejects. I felt the same when I was first informed of the existence of ghouls. In the end, I decided there was still room for reason in our work. In fact, it is a necessity. I very much hope you'll continue with the S.P.R., but I'm afraid I'll have to recall you both from the Sabelline case. It's simply too dangerous."

She blinked as the import of his words sunk in. "Recall us? But we're just getting started!"

"I understand your frustration, but it's only sensible to hand the case over to London at this point. They have the expertise in this sort of thing." He added, not unkindly, "I'll have them contact you when they arrive. You can bring them up to speed."

Angry tears pricked her eyes. Harry blinked them away. "So that's it?"

"Yes, that's it. I won't mince words. We're in over our heads, Miss Pell. I've never dealt with one of these things before and therefore cannot give you adequate guidance on how to protect yourself." He shuffled the papers on his desk and glanced at the clock. "Frankly, it's a miracle you survived the Hyde investigation at all."

"But this monster will be arriving in New York any day now. What if the agents don't get here in time?"

She had a sudden vision of Anne Marlowe, lying in the harsh glare of the police arc lights, her face mottled purple and black. Of Raphael Forsizi, the teenaged organ grinder whose body had been dumped at the base of a statue in Washington Square Park, along with his dead monkey. Of Becky Rickard, the first victim, stabbed thirty-one times and badly bitten on her face and neck.

Mr. Kaylock stared at her. The solemn expression on his face said he knew what Harry was thinking. "Let us pray they do."

"DON'T SAY IT," Harry snapped at John the moment Joseph closed the front door behind them.

"But I wasn't—"

"Yes, you were. And I'm not in the mood."

John narrowed his eyes. "When *you're* right, everyone hears about it in excruciating detail."

"Excruciating?"

"That's right. You're worse than Myrtle sometimes."

They glared at each other.

John blew out a breath. It clouded white in the frigid darkness. "I'm sorry you got sacked."

Harry shrugged, trying to ignore the hard lump of disappointment in her chest. "So am I."

"Are you really going to quit the case?"

"What else can I do? Kaylock's right, John. We're out of our depth." She turned away. "Let London handle it."

"And if they don't get here in time? If the thing that was in Brady, and then Dr. Clarence, comes for the amulet?"

Harry rubbed her forehead. "It's like a third-rate story by

Edgar Allen Poe. I can't believe we're actually having this conversation."

"And I can't believe there's a special branch of Scotland Yard just for ghouls. My God, when I tell Rupert—"

"You can't tell anyone, John. Remember that contract we signed?"

"Right."

He looked crestfallen. For some reason, it made her angry. "It's easy for you," Harry muttered. "You believed all that nonsense to begin with."

He gave her a tight smile. "And it's not nonsense after all. Well, maybe the bit about mummies. I'm not giving up on were-wolves though."

Harry sagged against the brick wall, the wind going out of her sails.

"I joined the S.P.R. to expose the fakers, John. Charlatans like the Fox sisters who fleeced desperate people seeking reassurance their loved ones had gone to a better place. I never thought any of it would be *true.*"

John patted her shoulder. "I know, Harry."

"Well, aren't you going to gloat?"

He assumed an angelic expression. "Gloat? That would be redundant, don't you think? We both know I was right."

She considered kicking his ankle but just didn't have the energy. "I can't believe Mr. Brady was actually...."

"Go on. Say it."

"Possessed."

"Was that so hard?"

Harry's mouth twitched. "I hate you. Can't even let a girl wallow in self-pity without cheering her up."

"I'm a right bastard that way."

"Ghouls." She barked a laugh.

"Poor Mr. Brady. It's a good thing you didn't get close to him in the tunnel, Harry." John extended his arms, hands hooked into claws and eyes rolling back in his head. "He might have turned you into Jane the Nipper."

"That's not funny."

He let his arms fall to his sides. "I suppose it's not. But are you really going to back down?"

She sighed. "If I disregard a direct order, I might never work for the S.P.R. again. And it's not what I signed on for."

"Chopping off heads?"

"That's right. I'm a consulting detective. I don't belong on this case anymore."

John grew serious. "Do what your heart tells you, Harry. You know I'll take your side."

She forced a smile. "I know. And it's all that matters in the end."

* * *

THEY FOUND a cab outside the Astor House and shared it to Tenth Street, after which John continued on to his family's home on Gramercy Park. He always managed to lift her spirits, but once his cheeky grin was out of sight, they plunged again. As Harry slowly trudged up the front steps, she began to question everything Mr. Kaylock had said. How well did she know him anyway? Who's to say he wasn't mad, or simply deluded? He'd offered not a shred of proof to back up his wild claims.

No, she decided, the entire thing was preposterous. As unhappy as it made her, Harry resolved to tender her resignation the next morning. It was time to move on. If only women could apply to be New York City detectives. They would never take her, though, not in a million years, even though she was smarter than most of the men on the force. It was all abominable! Perhaps she should put her talents to work with the suffragette movement.

But I don't like politics, Harry thought glumly, as she hung her coat on a hook. *I like crime, in all its infinite, grotesque varieties. I like the thrill of the hunt. The satisfaction of unearthing a clue others have overlooked. I like the speech at the end, where I've got the killer dead to rights and he—or she—listens in dumb amazement as I explain exactly how they carried out the murder. My God, do I like that part...*

Harry's gaze fell on a small black beret sitting on the table next to the front door. She took a deep breath and went into the kitchen. Myrtle lounged in a chair, smoking a cigarette.

"Harrison." Myrtle had always refused to call her by her nickname. "You look downright melancholy."

The sight of her elder sister inspired the usual awkward mix of feelings: fear, envy, love and a desperate craving for approval. She'd long ago learned not to show any of this, of course.

"Myrtle," she said, giving her sister a stiff embrace. "You're back."

They looked nothing alike. Myrtle had long black hair and porcelain skin bordering on deathly. Her features were not classically beautiful, but she had a definite magnetism, a kind of manic mental energy that made her fascinating to watch. Her grey eyes were constantly roving, assessing, weighing, analyzing.

"As of this afternoon. I hear you're with the S.P.R. now."

"Sort of."

Myrtle gave her a rapid once-over and raised an eyebrow.

"Please." Harry held up a hand. "I don't want to hear about what I ate for lunch, every location I've been to today, and that my dressmaker is a morphine addict."

Myrtle smiled. "I was going to say I like your new hat."

"No, you weren't."

"Let's have it then. What's happened with the S.P.R.? I know you've wanted that job for years."

Harry dropped into a chair and rested her elbows on the kitchen table. She thought of the confidentiality agreement, and how she'd just admonished John about honoring it.

"I can't discuss it."

"Kaylock made you sign a contract, eh?"

"Iron-clad."

"Yes, the Pinkertons require something similar." Myrtle's thin lips twitched. "If it was simply a difficult case, you'd never admit that to me. You would have pretended everything was roses. So it's something else. From the look in your eye, I'd say you've just learned something very unpleasant, something that goes against all you've ever believed in." She blew a series of perfect smoke rings at the ceiling. "Mr. Kaylock told you about ghouls, didn't he?"

Harry stared at her sister. "You already knew about this."

Myrtle let out a peal of merry laughter. "Oh, Harrison, you poor dear thing. Of course I did. It's hardly a secret."

"It was to me!"

"I don't mean that great herd of lowing cattle referred to as the general public." Myrtle waved a slender hand. "But yes, I've known of ghouls for some years now. Do you mean you're unfamiliar with the Buckingham Palace incident?"

Harry stonily shook her head.

"It was July 1886. A ghoul nearly took Queen Victoria in her own chambers. Scotland Yard created the Dominion Branch after that. They specialize in keeping a lid on the undead. It's not my area of interest, but I've heard they're reasonably competent."

Coming from Myrtle, this was high praise.

"Have you ever seen one?"

"A ghoul? No. I've never seen a Bolivian anaconda either, but it doesn't mean they don't exist."

Harry sighed. It was too much. "And how do you reconcile logical deduction with the supernatural?"

"Look at Uncle Arthur. He believes in Cornish pixies, for God's sake, but he keeps them out of his detective stories. He understands how to put things in boxes." She gave Harry a look. "If you're thinking of quitting, don't be an idiot. There are agents of the S.P.R. who are trained to deal with the Dominion and its spawn, but there is a place for us as well."

"Not for me," Harry said glumly. "Kaylock's pulled me off the case."

"Why?"

"Two of those trained agents are coming from London to handle the situation."

"I see. Names?"

Harry told her.

"I've heard of them. They're good."

"I hope so. Otherwise we'll have more bodies on our hands, very soon."

"So Brady was a ghoul?"

"No. *Something infinitely more dangerous*, quote unquote."

"That's what Kaylock said?"

Harry nodded.

"Nasty business." Her gaze took on an intensely focused quality Harry knew well. "Now tell me about this case of yours."

"Julius Sabelline?"

"Yes. Every detail. Omit nothing—"

"No matter how small or seemingly irrelevant. I know."

So Harry told her. And as she talked, she realized she and John had actually gathered a fair amount of information in the last two days. Murder cases were like puddings, she thought. Keep stirring, add a little heat, and they start to congeal into something solid.

Myrtle fired off a barrage of questions—most of them horribly patronizing—but Harry didn't mind. She was feeling much better, partly because at the end of her recital, Myrtle frowned and lit another cigarette. She did *not* say, "Dear God, Harrison, it's painfully obvious who did it. Have you no imagination? The solution is elementary."

Instead, she smoked furiously, threw the butt in her coffee dregs, and said, "You must interview this Count Koháry. It's a devilish problem, with at least thirty-two possible solutions as far as I can see."

"Thirty-three," Harry corrected, fervently hoping Myrtle wouldn't ask her to explain any of them. "But I'm off the case, remember?"

"You're off the *Sabelline* case."

"Right, that's what I said."

"But the Brady case is yours. It didn't come through the S.P.R." Myrtle smirked. "If anything, I could argue that it's *my* case, since you took it pretending to *be* me."

Harry thought for a moment. "And you're saying it's no longer closed so I owe it to my client, Elizabeth Brady, to pursue a solution?"

"She paid you a fee, did she not?"

"A rather generous one." She grinned. "That's diabolical logic, Myrtle, but I like it."

"As long as there's a clear connection between the two cases, you're well within your rights to interview the count. If Mr. Kaylock takes exception to that, refer him to me." Her grey eyes grew flinty.

"Thanks, but I'll fight my own battles," Harry said mildly, feeling pleased Myrtle cared enough to threaten on her behalf.

It also pleased her that Myrtle had said "a place for us," meaning she considered Harry to be a real consulting detective and not simply her grubby, half-bright little sister. That was as good as it got with Myrtle as far as compliments went, but Harry didn't complain.

When Mrs. Rivers came home from her sister's house later that evening, she found the two of them in Myrtle's laboratory setting fire to a stuffed moose head to see how long it took for the glass eyes to melt.

"I'm writing a monograph on the use of accelerants by arsonists in the context of taxidermy," Myrtle announced. "There's probably six people in the world who'll read it, but I don't really care."

"I'll read it," Harry said stoutly, brushing a bit of singed fur from her dress.

Mrs. Rivers wiped away a tear. "How lovely to see the girls together again," she said.

CHAPTER 18

THURSDAY, DECEMBER 27

H arry awoke the next morning determined to follow
Myrtle's advice and get her interview with Count Balthazar Jozsef Habsburg-Koháry. It was obvious he held the keys to
certain inexplicable aspects of the Sabelline case. Since Orpha
Winter had failed to arrange it, she would simply call on him
unannounced and see what he had to say.

I'm within my rights to pursue the case, she told herself firmly.
*Even if it turns out I was hired by an undead monster with a thirst for
human blood. Who may be arriving in New York at any moment.*

The museum murder was now splashed across every front
page. As Nelson Holland had predicted, reporters pounced on the
curse angle with unbridled delight. *The World, Herald* and *New
York Times* all ran sketches of the museum's president, Morris K.
Jessup, which they probably had on file. Nellie's article was the
most thorough and accurate, although the headline hardly took
the high road: DISCOVERY OF CURSED TOMB ENDS IN MUSEUM
BLOODBATH!

Harry ate breakfast with Connor. Myrtle had retreated into
her laboratory with several buckets of water and a bag of
sawdust.

"I want you to round up the Butchers," she said. "Tell them I'll pay them for whatever they've found on that Hungarian count, including his address. I want results by tonight."

"Sure thing, Harry. I'm meeting the lads shortly anyway."

"Do you miss the old life, Connor?"

He considered the question for a moment. "Well, I hate school. And I hate wearing those Little Lord Fauntleroy suits Mrs. Rivers stuffs me into. But I don't miss being cold, and I don't miss being hungry."

"What about the other boys? There ought to be a way we can help them too."

Connor shrugged. "They got each other. And you help 'em out with the odd job, like this one. The lads are all right."

Harry didn't see how a bunch of little boys could be "all right" living on their own in the streets, but she let it drop for now. "Well, tell them to come by later."

Connor had barely swallowed the last bite of toast before he was out the door. Harry had a feeling he wanted to dodge Mrs. Rivers, who probably had errands for him to run. At the least, she didn't approve of him hanging around with the Butchers, even if classes were on break until the following week. Quite accurately, Mrs. Rivers assumed Connor would be tempted by the multitude of sins on offer. Harry herself had once caught the boy with a bottle of something he called Rattle-Skull that smelled absolutely lethal.

A knock on the door raised her hopes that it might be word from Orpha. Instead, Jackson Sabelline stood on her doorstep. A brisk west wind tugged at his chestnut hair.

"I'm sorry to drop in on you like this," he said. "But I've found something I thought you might be interested in."

"Of course, please do come in." Harry stood aside and took his coat. "Would you like some coffee?"

"No, thank you. I don't have much time. The funeral is this afternoon."

"Oh." Harry wasn't sure what to say. She hated clichéd words of comfort, their false familiarity and empty sentiments. She thought Jackson Sabelline must be tired of hearing them himself. "Won't you come sit down for a moment?"

They went to the front parlor and Harry put more coal on the fire.

"I was going through Father's things and I found this." He took a piece of paper from his pocket and handed it over. "It was balled up in his shaving kit. I don't know what to make of it."

Deep creases lined the paper as though Julius Sabelline had crushed it in a fist. Harry smoothed it out on her lap and began to read.

Dear Sir,

I write this from the most wretched place one can imagine. I suppose you would say I deserve my fate and that my Everlasting Soul is going to Hell. That is the truth and I do not pretend to have a chance at Salvation, but you must believe me. You must! If you would only come to hear it from my own lips, you will hear the ring of Truth.

I have done a terrible thing, Sir. Not the one they put me here for, something else. It cannot be undone, but I hope my warning to you will go some way to make amends. For now, I can only say that there is an object in your possession of certain particular value to my Master. This is a most urgent matter. If you would be so kind as to arrange to visit me, I can explain matters further. If you will not, at least throw it away. You know what I speak of. Throw it away, sir, or the consequences shall be dyre.

Yours,

Mary Elizabeth Wickes

HARRY SAT STILL for a long moment, trying to make sense of it.

"What do you think?" Jackson asked. "I've never heard of this woman. But it's a queer letter indeed."

"Yes, it is. Was there an envelope to go with it?"

"No. Only the letter."

"Why did you bring it to me and not the police?"

"Mother wanted to come to you first. She knows you solved those awful murders over the summer." He gave a somewhat bleak smile. "I think she believes you stand a better chance of catching Father's killer."

Harry nodded. "I'm flattered. But I also don't want to be accused of obstruction. If you'll allow me to keep this for a day, I'll return it and you can hand it over to the police."

"That seems reasonable."

"I see the letter is dated one week before Dr. Sabelline's death. I don't suppose you know if he acted on it?"

"That's why I came, Miss Pell. I don't know if he went to see this woman or not." He gave her a hard look. "You know who it is, don't you?"

"I have an idea."

"Then you must tell me!"

Harry held up a hand. "Give me one day. I will look into it and report back to you all I discover. But I don't wish to speculate now."

Jackson twisted his gloves in his hands. "I suppose I can agree to that, though I don't like it much." He stood. "I hope you'll keep whatever you find confidential."

"Of course, although I think you'll need to share it with the police."

"You'd best come to me first. Poor mother's been having nightmares. I don't wish to upset her further."

Outside the door, he turned back to Harry. The unguarded sorrow and desperation in his face made her feel sorry for him.

"A dark shadow has fallen over our house, Miss Pell. As if the

Sabelline name is indeed cursed in some way. I only pray you can help us."

The next hours passed with excruciating slowness. Harry waited impatiently for Connor to return, then sent him straight back out again with a note for John, asking him to come to Tenth Street as quickly as possible. She paced up and down in the parlor, thinking furiously. The case was taking a strange turn and she wasn't sure what it meant yet, only that they might be close to discovering the source of Julius Sabelline's fear.

The clock was just striking four when John arrived.

"What's happened?" he asked. "I'm sorry it took me so long. I was out with Bill—"

"Look at the signature," she said, thrusting the letter into his hands.

John read it and shrugged. "Sorry."

"You don't remember?"

"Afraid not."

Harry paced to the window. "Assuming it's the same person, this letter was written from one of the death cells at the Tombs."

"What?"

"Mary Elizabeth Wickes murdered more than a dozen children in her care. Poisoned them over long periods of time with arsenic."

John frowned. "Wait. That nanny? What did they call her?"

"The White Rose."

"Oh God, yes. I remember now."

"She would bring her poor charges to the brink of death, then nurse them back to health. When the game grew tiresome, the child would take a sudden turn for the worse. After he or she died, Mary would move on to the next household. She got away with it for longer than you'd imagine possible."

John nodded. "Death from arsenic can be difficult to detect if the coroner isn't looking for it. It often imitates the effects of a natural disease like cholera."

"Yes, the timetable is different in each victim. Some succumb in days, others can linger for weeks. You can't smell or taste it either. That's why it's so popular with poisoners."

"So what happened?"

"Mary's luck finally ran out at the Clinton home in Staten Island. She was recognized by a family friend as the same caretaker who had been present at the death of another child the year before." Harry stared out the window. "After the police arrested her and started looking into her background, they found her parents had also died under suspicious circumstances."

"She was from a wealthy home herself, wasn't she?"

"Yes, and I believe it's one reason she got away with it for so long. No one thought an educated, well-bred young lady—and a tragic orphan to boot—could be capable of such monstrous acts."

John shook his head. "Why did they call her the White Rose again?"

"She wore one pinned to her dress every day at the trial. It was held in Albany because they were afraid they wouldn't be able to control the angry mobs outside the courthouse if she was tried on Centre Street. Anyway, the evidence against her was fairly iron-clad. When the police exhumed the children's bodies, they all tested positive for arsenic. The jury returned a guilty verdict and sentenced her to death in less than two hours."

"Let's see that letter again."

Harry handed it over.

"The object she refers to. Could it be the amulet of Osiris? But why on earth would Mary Elizabeth Wickes be writing to Julius Sabelline?"

"There's only one way to find out."

"It won't be easy." He gave her a hard stare. "And I thought we were off the case."

"Myrtle talked me back in."

"She did, did she? When did she get home?"

"Yesterday. Listen, John, we can't just sit around. I've been thinking about Brady's victims. All those murdered women in London and what was done to them. We both know there will be more when this thing in Clarence arrives in New York."

"You'll get no argument from me."

Harry felt a rush of warmth at his loyalty. She took his hand. "We'll just quietly follow the leads we have. Like Myrtle said, it's all connected to the Brady case anyway, which was ours. And when the London agents come, we'll give them everything."

"So we're off to see the White Rose. I'm sure that'll make for a pleasant afternoon. Will they let us in?"

"Let's ask Connor. I'll bet he has some idea of how to go about it."

They found the boy up in his room, reading a penny dreadful about Spring-Heeled Jack, a devilish figure from English folklore with claws and fiery eyes.

"You want to go to the Tombs?" he said. "Whatever fer?"

"We need to speak with one of the prisoners there," Harry explained.

"Shouldn't be too difficult. They're allowed visitors."

"The person we wish to see is in one of the death cells."

Connor's eyes widened a fraction. He scratched his head. "That's a wee bit more complicated. Which one?"

"Mary Elizabeth Wickes."

Connor let out a whistle. "The one that poisoned all them kids?"

"The very same."

"I heard she's due to be hung in a week."

"Just tell us who to bribe," John said impatiently.

Connor laid the magazine aside and scrambled to his feet. "I'd best go with you."

Harry laughed. "Not on your life."

"Good luck, then."

They stared at each other for a moment.

"Fine, but you wait outside while we see Miss Wickes," she

said. "Mrs. Rivers would skin me if she knew I'd brought you to such a place."

Connor laughed. "I been there plenty of times, in the boy's wing. The Tombs ain't no mystery to me."

"We'd best go straightaway then." Harry tucked the letter in her dress pocket.

There is an object in your possession of certain value to my Master.

"It's either a sick prank or the break we've been waiting for," she muttered.

John nodded absently.

"What is it?"

"I was thinking Mr. Kaylock was right when he said monsters are real, Harry." He put his Homburg on. "It's just that some of them are perfectly human."

CHAPTER 19

They took a streetcar downtown to the grim building on Centre Street formally named the Halls of Justice, but known to all as the Tombs. Constructed of granite and occupying the entire block, the Tombs had sat at the intersection of Leonard and Franklin Streets for fifty years. To the east stretched the crumbling tenements of the Five Points, that most infamous of New York City slums.

Over the decades, the Tombs had become crowded, dank and decayed, housing twice the number of prisoners it was built for. Now it was widely considered one of the worst prisons in the country.

"It does look like a mausoleum, doesn't it?" John observed as they walked up to the main entrance.

"That's what the architect intended," Harry said. "Myrtle told me he modeled it after an Egyptian tomb described in a memoir called *Stevens' Travels*. I must say, the overall effect is certainly bleak."

They ascended a wide flight of steps into the shadow of a massive portico supported by towering columns with lotus flower capitals. Just beyond the entrance doors was a large rectangular courtyard. The male prison sat in the middle of it, and was connected to the main building by a covered passage.

"The Bridge of Sighs," Connor said in a low voice. "Them poor buggers condemned to death must cross it on their way to the gallows. I reckon they'll be putting the scaffold up for Miss Wickes soon."

The outer building held the female prisoners. It was dark and gloomy, with mere slits for windows that let in so little natural light that gas jets were required even during the day. Connor took them straight to the Sisters of Charity, who ministered to the women and boys at the Tombs. Although more than a year had passed since Connor began living at Tenth Street, they remembered him well and with a good degree of fondness. The matron of the prison, a woman who clearly took guff from no one, chucked him under the chin. She was about fifty years old with dark hair showing threads of grey and the sort of strong, large-featured face that would politely be called handsome.

"In school, are you? I never would have imagined it, young Connor Devlin. But I'm glad to see you looking well." She turned to John and Harry. "All too often, the men awaiting trial in the main prison first came to us as boys in the detention house, scrubbing floors and doing laundry."

Connor made a face. "I thought my hands had gone to prunes for the rest of my days, Sister Emily. The sight of a pail of soap and water still gives me nightmares."

"So what is it you're here for?" she asked, a slight sharpness to her words. "I somehow doubt this is a social call."

Harry laid a hand on Connor's shoulder. "Time for you to head home."

"But—"

"Now."

He scowled but didn't argue. "Nice to see you again, Sister Emily."

"I hope it's the last time," she said with a smile, watching as the boy left her office. "Now, what's all this about?"

"We'd like to see Mary Elizabeth Wickes," Harry said.

The matron's eyes narrowed in sudden suspicion. "Who are you, reporters? I thought you lot would have had enough by now. What are you after, her last words? Repentance? Well, you won't get it. The creature hasn't a human emotion in her."

"We're with the Society for Psychical Research," Harry said, displaying her badge. "We're investigating the death of a man whom Miss Wickes recently wrote a letter to. We'd like to ask her about it."

"A murder?"

"I'm afraid so."

The matron frowned. "Do you think Mary had something to do with it?"

"Not directly. But she might know something."

"Either way, she's headed to her maker in a week's time. What's another stain on Mary's conscience? Not that she has one." She sighed. "I suppose you're welcome to ask. Her family's all dead. No one comes to see her. But we frown on men entering the women's side unless they're husband or son."

"Mr. Weston is a medical doctor," Harry said. "Perhaps we can compensate you for the inconvenience?"

The matron had no strenuous objections to this proposal. Ten dollars changed hands and Harry and John followed her toward the far end of the corridor. The cries of infants and general hubbub of more than a hundred women echoed through the courtyard, clanging off the wrought iron railings and damp stone floors. They continued past the first turning to the far side of the building, a walk of about three city blocks.

"Here she is," Sister Emily said. "You can have ten minutes."

The cell they stood before measured ten by six feet. Besides a single cot, it contained a water closet, with a pipe sticking out of the wall several feet above to flush the waste away. There was neither table nor chair.

"Visitors for you, Mary," she said. "Mind your manners."

Mary Elizabeth Wickes sat on a straw mattress, picking at her skirts with feigned disinterest. She was nineteen years old but looked fifteen. Her mouse-brown hair was neatly parted in the center and pinned into a bun at the nape of her long neck. Nothing about her stood out in any way, Harry thought with a slight chill. Not a hint of the aberrant personality lurking behind those grey-blue eyes.

"Hello, Mary," Harry ventured.

She looked up then and smiled, revealing a set of oddly small but even teeth. "I know you."

"Do you?"

"You're the one that caught Mr. Hyde, aren't you?"

"We both did," Harry replied. "This is my associate, Mr. John Weston."

Mary nodded thoughtfully. "Killed himself before they could bring him here and hang him." She paused. "Too bad. I would have liked to see that."

The matron shook her head wearily. "I've things to do. Bang on the door if you change your mind and wish to come out early. Otherwise, I'll be back in ten minutes."

Harry and John entered the cell. The door closed behind them. Matron locked it. The space suddenly seemed much smaller. Mary Elizabeth Wickes had murdered her victims by stealth, preying on the small and weak. Her keepers didn't seem to consider her an immediate physical danger to others. Still, Harry kept her back against the bars and was glad to have John at her side.

"We'd like to speak to you about a letter you wrote," John said. "To Julius Sabelline."

Mary didn't respond for a long moment. A certain wariness entered her eyes, though she held herself perfectly still.

"What's happened to him?" she said at last.

"Why do you think something's happened to him?"

"He's dead, isn't he?" The matter-of-fact tone raised the hair on Harry's arms.

"Yes," John replied. "Two days ago."

"I warned him." Mary's mouth twisted. "I told him to get rid of it."

"Get rid of what? The amulet?"

Mary said nothing, staring at the stone floor. It glistened with a foul dampness that seemed to pervade every inch of the prison. Harry didn't wonder so many sickened and died here.

"Please, Mary." John crouched down so they were eye to eye. "Won't you help us?"

She lifted her face and studied him. "Nice-looking, aren't you? Pretty eyelashes, like a girl."

John held her intense gaze without flinching, which Harry found impressive. "What do you know about Mr. Hyde?" he asked mildly. "Has he something to do with Julius Sabelline?"

She lifted her chin. "Why should I talk to you?"

"You've nothing to lose."

"You think not? How stupid you are."

"You said in the letter that you wanted to make amends," Harry said. "This is your chance. What did you feel remorse about, Mary? You said it wasn't the thing they put you here for. What was it?"

They locked gazes for an instant. Mary looked away. A full minute passed, and Harry didn't think she would answer.

"I let him through," Mary said at last, her voice empty of all emotion.

"Who?" Harry demanded.

"The master. The one you call Hyde."

Harry's fingers tightened around the letter in her pocket, unconsciously crushing it into a ball just as Julius Sabelline had done.

"He spoke to me from the other side. Came to me in dreams. He showed me such terrible, awful, *wonderful* things." She twisted her skirts in her hands. "God help me, I let him through."

"When was this?" John asked.

"Last summer. It was dreadfully hot."

"What do you mean by *let him through*?"

Mary's eyes grew distant. "There was a girl here, always crying. Night and day. She wouldn't *shut up*." An edge of barely suppressed fury entered her voice. Harry wondered how many of Mary's young victims had annoyed her with their wailing. "She'd killed her husband and was sure she'd be sent to the gallows. It's not always a clean death, you know. People shit themselves. If your neck doesn't snap from the drop, you suffocate slowly. I told her that. It wasn't hard to convince her to end things herself. She used a hairpin to open the vein in her wrist."

Harry and John shared a look of mutual revulsion.

"You talked her into committing suicide?" he asked.

"Someone had to pay the blood price."

"What was this girl's name?"

"I don't remember. What does it matter?"

"What's the blood price, Mary?"

She turned her face away and refused to answer.

"Did Dr. Sabelline answer your letter?"

Mary shook her head. "He never came. He didn't listen. And now he's dead."

"Do you know who killed him?" John asked. "Was it your master?"

"Shadow and flame," she muttered. "Flame and shadow. It comes for us all." She gave John a sly smile and tapped the corner of her eye. "*Pervadunt oculus.*"

Harry's skin prickled as a cold draft swept through the tiny window. She hugged herself, rubbing her arms for warmth.

"Did your master want the amulet?" he pressed.

Mary Elizabeth Wickes looked at them. She drew herself up,

suddenly haughty as a queen on her throne. "He's coming and he will take what's his. You can't stop him now. *It is loosed.*"

"Whoever killed Julius Sabelline tore his eyes out, Mary," John said. "I think you know who it was. Tell us, for God's sake."

With startling abruptness, her demeanor changed. The imperious woman became a frightened girl again. "He'll come back for me too, sure as sunrise. I begged them to move up my date with the gallows, but they won't do it." A sob tore from her throat. "I've seen what waits beyond the veil. Oh, sweet Jesus, have mercy on my soul."

There was an awful silence. Harry heard footsteps approaching in the corridor.

"Did the master tell you to kill those children?" John asked.

Mary wiped her nose with her sleeve. "No." She gave a bark of brittle laughter. "I did that on my own."

A key turned in the cell door. "Time's up," Sister Emily said briskly.

"But can't we—" Harry began.

"I'm afraid not," she interrupted. "I've bent the rules for you enough already. It's time for Mary to take her exercise."

The girl seemed not to hear, or even to be aware of the matron's presence. Her eyes looked like black holes in her thin face.

"*Abyssus abyssum invocat,*" she hissed. "The master comes for what's his."

"I see she's having one of her spells." Sister Emily sounded almost pitying. "She wouldn't be any good to you anyway."

They left Mary alternately giggling and weeping on her straw-covered cot. Harry had a thousand more questions she would have liked to ask, but it was a relief to get out of that dank cell. The Latin phrase—*deep calls to deep*—brought back half-buried memories of the terrible summer she and John had hunted Mr. Hyde. For the first time, she felt truly afraid.

"I used to wonder if she wasn't faking madness in hopes of

clemency," the matron remarked as they headed back toward the prison entrance. "Her crimes didn't seem to have an ounce of passion in them. Just cold-blooded viciousness. It took planning and cunning to get away with it as long as she did. And when she first came to us, Mary seemed as lucid as anyone. But the girl's been strange lately. Likely she's realizing there won't be any more appeals. She's going to hang in a week and that's all there is to it."

"Was there a suicide on the ward over the summer?" John asked. "A woman awaiting trial for killing her husband?"

"Aye. Sally McBride. She was in the cell next to Mary."

"When did it happen?"

"I'd have to check the records."

"Would you mind?"

She sighed. "Wait here."

Ten minutes later, Sister Emily returned.

"It was during that heatwave," she said. "Sally McBride died on August 6th."

CHAPTER 20

"I'm not sure what to think, except that Mary is tied up in this business somehow," Harry said as they walked down Centre Street toward Broadway. "August 6th is the same day Brady killed Becky Rickard."

"Mary said she *let him through*. There has to be some connection to the séance and *The Black Pullet* grimoire, don't you think?"

"I suppose so, though I can't imagine what, since Mary was locked up at the time. One thing did strike me, John. She said the master would come for what was his. That means he doesn't have it yet."

"The amulet of Osiris."

"Someone else is still in possession of it. Whoever killed Julius Sabelline."

They chewed on this as they cut across the trolley tracks bisecting the open plaza past the courthouse. To the right lay City Hall and the towering baroque Post Office the newspapers had dubbed "Mullett's Monstrosity" because it was widely considered a hideous eyesore.

"Maybe she gave the grimoire to George Kane," John said.

Kane was the dissolute son of one of the oldest and wealthiest families in New York. He'd been romantically involved with the medium Becky Rickard, Brady's first victim, who'd conducted the ill-fated séance that ended with her vicious murder.

"George said he got *The Black Pullet* from a gentleman at his club, but he could have been lying," Harry replied. "I can't imagine how he'd cross paths with Mary though."

"She might have been a nanny for one of the rich families who were friends with the Kanes."

"I suppose it's possible." She frowned. "But it doesn't seem to fit somehow. George was a cad, but Mary's not his type. I doubt he'd even notice her existence. And there's the matter of the blood price, whatever that is, and Sally McBride's suicide."

They reached the bustling artery of Broadway and turned south toward the Ninth Avenue elevated stop at Dey Street, where they bought tickets for a nickel apiece.

"Oh, I nearly forgot," John said as the uptown train rumbled into the station with a great clatter and screech of brakes. "I received a cable this morning from a friend at Yale. We went to St. Andrews together. His anthropology professor was connected to the expedition to Brazil."

"And?"

"Rumor has it the real reason Sharpe was dropped from the Alexandria dig is that he was having a torrid affair with Araminta. Her husband found out somehow. That's the row Sharpe mentioned. Sounds rather major to me."

Harry felt a pain behind her left eye. "Another complication. I can't for the life of me see how all of this fits together, John. It's like two entirely different cases!"

"I know. What if the two of them decided to do him in? Make it look like a robbery?"

"And gouge his eyes out? Mary used the phrase *pervadunt oculus*, John. I don't know about you, but I found it extremely creepy. That's what Brady scribbled on the walls of the Beach tunnel."

"I remember. *It comes through the eyes.*"

She sighed. "So what do we do about Mr. Sharpe?"

The tide of humanity on the platform swept them into the car.

"Only one thing for it," John said. "I say we go ask him ourselves."

IT HAD ONLY BEEN three days since the discovery of Julius Sabelline's body, and one since the story made the newspapers, but the museum was already overrun with visitors. No one seemed to care that the Alexandria exhibit wouldn't be opening until after the New Year—they just wanted to gawk at the general vicinity of the crime scene.

Harry and John elbowed their way through the crush and slipped through the door leading to the basement. They found Davis Sharpe in one of the storerooms, labelling shards of pre-Columbian pottery.

His blue eyes seemed to darken when he saw them. There was no pretense of warmth this time. "What is it you want?"

"We have new information we hoped you could verify," Harry said.

"I'm rather busy at the moment. Why don't you make an appointment?"

"That's a fine idea," John said lazily. "But seeing as we're already here, I'll just ask you now. Sorry if this is an indelicate question, but were you having an affair with Araminta Sabelline?"

Sharpe's face turned the color of a brick. He opened his mouth and closed it again. "Indelicate? I'd say that's damn rude."

"Perhaps we should speak with the detectives at the Thirty-First Ward," Harry said with a polite smile. "Sorry to impose on your time."

Sharpe watched them turn toward the door. "Wait!" he called. "For God's sake, I'm sick to death of talking about it, but I see you're leaving me no choice. Just close the door behind you."

John did so. Sharpe set aside the paper tags he'd been filling out and ran a hand through unkempt brown hair. He took a deep breath. "Julius thought the same. Five months ago, just before the expedition was to leave, he accused me of engaging in a dalliance with his wife. I hotly denied it because it wasn't true."

"He didn't believe you?" John asked.

"Of course he didn't. Julius was a sour, vindictive man. He threatened to ruin my career. I voluntarily dropped out of the expedition." He scowled. "Araminta *was* having an affair, just not with me."

"The count?" Harry guessed.

Sharpe gave a bitter laugh. "Nelson Holland. I walked in on them once, in his office. Araminta had come to see Julius, but he wasn't here. So she'd gone up to say hello to Holland. Quite a hello it was."

"Did you tell Dr. Sabelline?"

"How could I? It's as much as my job is worth. Holland would have known it came from me. All I could do was deny my own involvement."

"Do you think Dr. Sabelline might have discovered the truth?" John asked.

"I don't think so. Five months in Alexandria did nothing to calm his jealous rage. He was still barely speaking to me by the time of the party." Sharpe rubbed his mouth in that nervous way Harry remembered from before. "I'll tell you, I was tired of it. I was going to insist that Araminta do something about the situation or I'd have to tell Julius myself, but I never got the chance. He died that same night."

"Do you think Holland suspected you were going to reveal their secret?"

"I'm honestly not sure he would have cared. Oh, of course he had a reputation to consider. But who would believe me? I have a reputation myself—for drink." He laughed hollowly. "If you're looking for motive there, it's a bit thin. Holland might be physically capable, but I simply can't picture him cutting Julius's eyes out. It's too bizarre."

He glanced away. "If you take a hard look at anyone, it should be that Count Koháry. He collects ancient weapons, you know, among other things. Holland told me Julius wasn't killed with an ordinary knife. That you have no idea what it was."

Harry and John shared a look.

"And how did Holland know?" she asked.

"How else? Orpha Winter. They're thick as thieves."

Harry sighed. "Thank you, Mr. Sharpe, you've been most forthcoming. I apologize for the intrusive nature of our visit, but it couldn't be helped."

"Don't tell anyone what I said, for God's sake." He wiped his mouth with the back of his hand. If anything, the tremor had gotten worse. "Holland would ruin me."

Dark had fallen by the time they left the museum. The crowds of visitors were thinning out, most of them drifting downtown towards Columbus Circle. One by one, the new electric lamps in the park pushed back the dark shadows under the trees.

"Did you believe him?" John asked.

"Unfortunately, yes."

"So Holland's back in the picture."

"It would seem so." Harry rubbed her forehead. "I need to think. This case is a vipers' nest."

"Fine. Just promise you won't do anything rash without me."

"I promise." Harry fussed with the new scarf she'd given him for Christmas, tucking the ends snugly into his coat. "I've been meaning to thank you, John. Most people wouldn't want to get involved in the sorts of things I've dragged you into. They'd run the other way. But I couldn't do this without you."

He studied her face. "Well, you *could*. It just wouldn't be as much fun."

"No, it wouldn't." She smiled. "I'd like to walk alone for a bit. Is that all right?"

"Of course."

"Goodnight then."

"Goodnight, Harry."

John flipped his collar up and set off down Central Park West, whistling *O Come, All Ye Faithful*. For an instant, the clouds parted and a full yellow moon appeared, sailing across the sky. Before he looked up, the rift sealed again and darkness descended. A scattering of raindrops struck the pavement. John ducked his head and walked quickly for the downtown elevated.

A storm was coming.

CHAPTER 21

FRIDAY, DECEMBER 28

H arry woke to the biting odor of lye soap. As she did every year, Mrs. Rivers had gone into a lather of scrubbing and baking, sewing and broiling. Tradition dictated people visit each other on New Year's Day and she firmly believed in a top-to-bottom overhaul.

It was also a tradition for Connor to make a desperate bid to dodge forced conscription in her campaign, not that it did him any good. Mrs. Rivers had an uncanny talent for ferreting him out of the deepest, darkest hiding places.

Harry could hear her in the dining room, humming some martial tune as she polished the silver. Myrtle had locked herself in her laboratory. It was the only room in the whole house to escape the mid-winter sanitizing. Ever since a memorable occasion several years back when Mrs. Rivers had nearly been stung by a Javanese scorpion the size of a feather duster, she'd refused to enter.

Harry wandered blearily down to the kitchen, where she found Little Artie sitting at the table, a newsboy cap pulled low over his butter-yellow hair.

"Been waitin' for ya," he said. "Got the address of that royal."

"Bless your heart." She dove on the coffee pot and poured a cup. "Want some breakfast?"

"The missus fed me already. She's some pumpkins."

Harry assumed this was meant as a compliment. "She is indeed. So where does he live?"

"Uptown. Sixty-First and Fifth. And he's home right now."

Harry took a sip and felt the fog in her head begin to clear. "What else have you learned?"

Little Artie smirked. "Lots of lady visitors."

"A rake, eh?"

"Regular Romeo. We been watching from the park cross the way. Ain't seen many servants though. Just one who looks like trouble, but he ain't savvied us."

"You're sure?"

"Yep."

"Good. Go fetch Mr. Weston and bring him here. He lives on Gramercy Park. Number 15. I'll pay you when you get back."

Little Artie tipped his hat and slid off the chair.

Upstairs in her room, Harry put on a forest green silk dress and dug out matching gloves with pearl buttons and ivory lace trim. If she had to venture into the lion's den, she might as well look her best.

Harry's pale reflection swam in the vanity mirror. Her freckles had faded since last summer, leaving a scattering across the bridge of her nose. She'd been named after her paternal grandfather. His Scots-Irish blood had bypassed Myrtle completely, but Harry had gotten it in spades. She dusted a bit of powder across her face and examined the results in the mirror.

Does it really matter, Harry? A little voice asked. *You'll be permanently sacked after this stunt anyway. And then what will you do? Sit around in the upstairs parlor while Myrtle goes off solving cases, just like you used to. John will become a doctor, he'll marry some nice girl—not one of the Sloane-Sherman monstrosities, please God—and Connor will grow up and leave, and then it will just be you and Mrs. Rivers.*

You can sip dry gin and read the penny dreadfuls together, won't that be lovely?

Harry sighed and ordered the voice to shut up. She could always travel with her parents, they'd be thrilled to have her along. Wouldn't they? Well, of course they would. Except that her well-meaning mother would find any opportunity to introduce her to suitable young men and Harry didn't want to get engaged, let alone married, maybe not ever. She wanted to continue doing what she was doing now, even if meant the rabbit holes she'd stumbled across during the Brady case were deeper and darker than she'd ever imagined.

There's a shadow world, Harry. Right alongside our own but hidden just out of sight. Most people don't know about it until it's too late. But now you do know. Can you really walk away?

She arranged a mother-of-pearl comb in her blonde hair. Then she went to the table beside her bed and took out the gun John had given her for Christmas. She studied it for a long moment, her heart beating a touch faster. She slipped it into a pocket.

Harry found Connor scrubbing the second-floor hallway.

"I'm going to need you today, if you're willing. Go to that livery stable on McDougal Street and hire a carriage."

He pushed a sweaty lock of hair from his eyes. "But Mrs. Rivers—"

"I'll explain it to her. But you do work for Myrtle. I'm sure she wouldn't mind if I borrowed you for the morning. Official business." She winked. "We're going to go interrogate that count. Unless you'd prefer to stay here and wash floors?"

Connor grinned and threw his brush into the pail of hot water. "No, Miss!"

AN HOUR LATER, she, John and Connor pulled up before a grey

limestone mansion on the east side of Central Park. A fresh wind had blown in overnight from the south and the day was unseasonably warm, with temperatures hovering in the mid-fifties. A heaviness to the air promised rain.

"Not Vanderbilt excess, but not shabby either," John remarked as they climbed down from the carriage.

In fact, the palace—and there really was no other word for it —built by the second Cornelius Vanderbilt sat only four blocks away on Fifth Avenue and Fifty-Seventh Street. By contrast, the abode of Count Balthazar Jozsef Habsburg-Koháry looked downright tasteful. It was only two stories with little ornamentation except for a wrought-iron fence. Light spilled from tall French windows.

"Are you sure about this, Harry? Orpha will be furious if she finds out, and I can't imagine Kaylock would be pleased either. He specifically ordered you to back off until London gets here."

"I know. And I don't care anymore." This wasn't entirely true. Harry *did* care, quite a bit. But she'd come too far to sit on the sidelines now. And they couldn't punish her if she exposed Dr. Sabelline's killer, could they?

"If we're not out within an hour, summon the police," she told Connor.

"Do you really think this aristo is the one who done it?"

"I don't know. But I won't underestimate him." She gazed at the house. "It's often the people with the most to lose who will do anything to keep it."

A youngish man in a blue morning coat answered John's knock. He had close-cropped hair going prematurely grey at the temples. An old scar, faded nearly to white, bisected his jaw. This must be the manservant Little Artie said looked like trouble, Harry thought. He eyed them coldly.

"May I help you?" He had a gruff voice, with a hint of a French accent.

"We're here to see Count Habsburg-Koháry," Harry said pleasantly.

"I'm afraid he's not in at the moment."

"I was given to understand that he is."

"Begging your pardon, but I fear you're mistaken."

At that same instant, a peal of delighted feminine laughter erupted from somewhere inside the house. A deeper voice, silky as mink, said something too low to make out.

Harry smiled at the servant. She handed him her card, which he accepted with obvious reluctance.

"Please inform the count that we will wait on his doorstep until he invites us inside. Tell him we're acquaintances of Mrs. Orpha Winter who humbly request a few minutes of his time."

The man scowled and closed the door in her face. Footsteps retreated down the hall. Several minutes passed. Harry was starting to think her bluff had been called and they'd be left standing there when it opened again.

"The count has just returned," the manservant said with a wintry smile. "If you'll follow me, please."

They entered a cavernous entrance hall. The mansion was much larger than it appeared from the outside, with soaring barrel-vaulted ceilings and stained glass windows, as if an Old World castle had been dropped into the middle of Manhattan. The décor was unremittingly gothic, dominated by dark oil paintings and heavy claw-footed furniture.

After plodding down miles of thick carpeting, the servant opened the door to a mahogany-paneled library. A fire crackled in the oversized marble fireplace. There were no windows at this end of the long, rectangular room, which was lit only by a series of lamps with green glass shades. A man sat in a leather chair before the flames, a glass of amber liquid in his hand.

"Hello. Do come in." He rose to greet them with a small bow. Harry recognized the velvety voice she'd heard through the door. "I've heard of you, Miss Pell. And you, Mr. Weston."

The count looked exactly as he had in the photograph at the Sabelline house. No more than thirty-five, with broad shoulders and a slightly crooked aquiline nose. Dark hair and an olive complexion completed the picture. He wore evening clothes, impeccably tailored if somewhat rumpled.

He's been up all night, Harry thought, though he doesn't look tired. The guest he'd just been entertaining must have slipped away. The count met Harry's gaze and she had to admit he had an unmistakable magnetism it was easy to imagine women finding attractive.

"I'm sorry I didn't extend an invitation sooner," he said. "But the last two days have been rather hectic. As you can imagine, I am extremely anxious to have my property returned to me. And to find Dr. Sabelline's killer, of course."

His English was flawless, his welcome seemingly genuine. Harry suddenly felt awkward. She hadn't expected him to be cordial.

"Of course. Thank you for seeing us. I didn't mean to barge in on you, but I've been tasked by the S.P.R. to investigate this case, and there are questions we believe only you can answer."

He nodded. "I'll do my best. Would you care for coffee or tea?"

Both Harry and John demurred.

"You may leave us, Lucas."

His manservant gave a deep bow and backed through the door.

"Please." The count gestured to a pair of matched wing chairs by the fire. "I blame myself for Julius's death. As I told the police, that amulet was a rare and valuable object."

It was just the opening Harry had hoped for. "Why is it so valuable, Count Koháry? I understand it came from Ptolemy's tomb, but so did other objects in the exhibit."

He gazed at them for a long moment. "You're with the S.P.R. so I assume you have knowledge of certain sensitive topics and we can speak frankly."

"Oh, you mean ghouls," John said casually, as if he'd known about them for years.

The count drained his glass. "And other things. The amulet of Osiris is very old, far older than Claudius Ptolemy. I'm not sure how it fell into his hands, but it's a most dangerous object." He stared into the hearth. "I never should have permitted it to go on public display, even with the extra precautions we took."

"Dangerous?" Harry repeated. "In what way?"

"I think I can guess," John said. "It truly is a key to the gates of Hell, isn't it?"

The count gave him an appraising look. "Who told you that?"

"Nelson Holland."

"Of course. He believes it's all myth and metaphor. Sadly, it's not. There are twelve gates to the Dominion, Mr. Weston. They're all locked, have been for centuries. Only one key existed and it's in safe hands. Until now."

"So the amulet you dug up in Alexandria is the second key," Harry mused. "Who has the first one?"

"The London S.P.R."

John gripped the arms of his chair. "Do you think whoever stole the amulet means to open these gates?"

"That's the question none of us wish to contemplate, although we must."

"I assume the undead would come through?"

"By the boatload."

"Have you ever seen a ghoul yourself?"

The count smiled, though there was little humor in it. "More than you can imagine."

"Where?"

"Europe, mainly, and the Near East. The North American continent never had a gate so it's been spared." He spun the empty tumbler in his hands. "They're all in cities of the ancient world."

Harry and John exchanged a quick look.

"I don't mean to be rude," she said, "but I'm curious how you know so much about all this, Count Koháry?"

"Please, call me Balthazar. It's a hereditary title and one that's not much use since the revolution." He glanced at an oil portrait over the fireplace of a man who looked strikingly like the count, but in a dark velvet doublet and cloak of the medieval era. "That is my great-great-grandfather, Count Ferenc Jozsef. For generations, the House of Koháry has devoted itself to protecting the world from the undead. To safeguard the talismans that bestow the power to travel between worlds. I wanted the amulet of Osiris not to use it myself but to keep it from others who would. There is evil in the world. I do my best to oppose it."

"Do you have any idea who took it?" Harry asked. "Or what they intend?"

"If I did, I would already have it back, Miss Pell," he said in a steely tone.

Harry decided to take a chance and trust him. "There's an additional complication. Mr. Kaylock told us that something from the Dominion might be searching for the amulet. Worse than a ghoul, he said." She drew a breath. "We fear it's the same creature that committed the Hyde killings last summer. It went to London in the form of a doctor named William Clarence. The Ripper murders began shortly after and might be his work as well.

"Now Kaylock says it's taken a ship for New York and agents are coming from London to track it. A Lady Vivienne Cumberland and Mr. Alec Lawrence."

A strange expression crossed the count's features, there and gone in an instant. It looked almost like guilt.

"I know of them. They're quite capable."

"Well, that's good, but what if they don't arrive in time? It seems to me rather urgent to find the key before this thing gets here."

"I couldn't agree more." The count didn't sound the least bit surprised.

"You knew this already," Harry said flatly.

"Orpha Winter told me," he admitted. "I believe the creature you refer to is known as a daemon."

"You mean like a...devil?" John asked.

"Not in the Christian sense. It's an undead spirit, but one that is ancient and powerful."

"How is it different from a ghoul?"

He thought for a moment. "Ghouls aren't difficult to identify. They react strongly to iron. It burns them. And while they might superficially appear human from a distance, they rarely speak and wouldn't pass even moderate scrutiny. Daemons have no corporeal body themselves. Rather, they must possess a living host."

Harry thought of Leland Brady. How perfectly normal he'd appeared until the mask fell away.

"Yes, I think I see. Mr. Kaylock also said there was a connection between this particular daemon and the exhibit. Do you know what it is?"

"I know a little. My European sources say the daemon has obtained a set of rare maps revealing the locations of the gates. Now it needs a talisman of opening."

"The amulet of Osiris."

"Precisely."

"And once it has both—"

"It can open one of the gates," John finished.

"Or all twelve," Balthazar said grimly.

They were silent for a moment.

"There's something else we need to ask about," Harry said. "It pertains to your collection. Davis Sharpe said it was quite extensive."

He stared into the fire. "I like old things. They speak to me.

My family goes back a long way, Miss Pell. A very long way. Perhaps I live in the past too much, but I feel at home there."

"Mr. Sharpe said you also collected weapons," John said.

The count's dark eyes narrowed a touch. "Indeed I do."

"We still don't know what was used to kill Mr. Sabelline, but it's something exotic. The doctor who conducted the post-mortem described several peculiar characteristics of the wound. Perhaps you can shed some light on what the weapon might have been."

"I'm happy to be of assistance in any way possible."

"It wasn't a metal blade. Whatever it was tapered to a sharp point, and the rest of it had rough edges that abraded the wounds. Dr. Sabelline also had unique bruising on his palms. Parallel lines. I believe he might have seized the hilt or shaft of the weapon in grappling with his killer."

Balthazar thought for a long moment. "What you are describing sounds like a madu."

John leaned forward. "I've never heard of that."

"Few people have. It was used by Indian fakirs primarily as a defensive weapon, although it can be quite lethal. A madu is constructed from two antelope horns connected perpendicularly by a crossbar. I'll show you a drawing of one." He strode to one of the bookshelves and chose a volume bound in grey cloth with two blades crossed on the cover. *"The Book of the Sword* by Richard Francis Burton." He flipped through the pages and turned it around so they could see the illustration. "Here it is."

John studied the drawing. "That could certainly have made the wounds. I'd say it's consistent in every respect."

Something flickered in Balthazar's eyes.

"Do you own such a weapon?" Harry asked quietly.

He stared at her for a long moment. "I do."

Harry felt the hair on her arms rise up. Had they unwittingly walked into the lair of a murderer? She thought of the manservant. He was young and strong. More of a bodyguard than a butler.

But then why would the count admit to owning it?

"May we see it?"

"I don't have it anymore. I lent it to Jackson Sabelline for study several months ago." He rose and walked to a writing desk. "I have the paperwork to prove it, if you think I'm lying. I lend items from my collection frequently and I keep meticulous records." He shuffled through the drawers. "Ah, here it is. You'll note the date and his signature at the bottom."

"Jackson! Why didn't you tell the police about this?"

"It was one of more than two dozen items. And I wasn't told about the post-mortem. I had the impression Julius was stabbed with a knife."

"Jackson Sabelline," John said slowly. "But why would he kill his father?"

Balthazar frowned. "I thought you knew."

"Knew what?"

"Julius wasn't Jackson's natural father. He married Araminta as a widow. Her first husband died in the war for the Union when Jackson was an infant."

John shot Harry a look. "We had no idea."

"How did Jackson feel about his adopted father?"

"To be honest, I don't think they were particularly close. Julius was a brilliant archaeologist but not a very kind man. He ignored the boy mostly, although he paid for his schooling and did his duty by them both."

"Did you know Araminta Sabelline was having an affair with Nelson Holland?" Harry asked.

"No," Balthazar said dryly.

"When I spoke to her, she had a bruise on her wrist. Could Julius have confronted her about it? Gotten physical? If the son saw, he might have felt a need to protect his mother. They seemed close."

Balthazar looked dubious. "I don't know Jackson Sabelline well, but he struck me as a decent young man."

"I'd say it's rather damning that he borrowed the murder weapon from you," John said with feeling.

"That's hardly been proven beyond the shadow of a doubt."

"Well, it's highly persuasive. Don't you think so, Harry?"

She nodded absently. She still had the crumpled letter from Mary Elizabeth Wickes in her pocket. Jackson had never returned to ask for it.

"If you find the amulet, I want it back," the count said frostily.

"Of course you do," Harry replied in a soothing tone, which wasn't quite the same thing as a promise to return it. "Well, I must say, it's been enlightening to speak with you, Count Balthazar."

He nodded brusquely. "Give my regards to Mrs. Winter."

Harry suppressed a smile. "We shall indeed."

THE SKY HAD OPENED up while they were speaking with the count. Rain fell in torrents, sweeping across the park with Biblical intensity. A small river already raged at the curb. They dashed out of the townhouse and clambered into the carriage. Harry called out a Brooklyn address to Connor.

"Where are we off to?" John demanded, shaking water from his coat.

"The Sabellines." She rubbed her hands together. "I knew the count would be the missing link."

"Did you notice the medieval fellow in the portrait had the same crooked nose? As if they'd both broken it just the same way?"

"I did. There's something strange going on there, but we've no time to worry about it now. The threads have come together, John."

"The stepson, eh? Oughtn't we go to the police?"

Harry patted her coat pocket. "Don't worry, I have the revolver you gave me. We'll be fine."

He winced. "I'll just let you go first. When we get there."

Harry made a noise of irritation. "You're worried I'm going to shoot you again."

"Don't be ridiculous."

Connor shook the reins and they lurched forward.

"It was an accident, John. At least I missed your vital organs."

He clasped his hands and gazed heavenward. "A blessing indeed...."

BALTHAZAR STOOD AT THE WINDOW, watching the carriage speed off into the rain. A moment later, his manservant, now in a long oilskin coat, slipped out of the house, leapt into a dog-cart and followed.

It never ceased to amaze him how one could simply stick a title before one's name and it went unquestioned. As long as you had money and an aristocratic manner, people saw what they expected to see.

He wasn't even distantly related to the Habsburgs or any other European royalty. He had lived in Hungary, but he had lived in many places. His true birthplace was Karnopolis, a city long buried beneath shifting sands. Balthazar was largely indifferent to verse, but he'd always enjoyed those lines by Shelley that began thus: *I met a traveler from an antique land....*

The poem appealed to his sense of irony. Everything fell to dust eventually, except for himself.

Well, it was done. There was nothing now but to wait. When the moment came, he would act.

He opened a teak box and examined the object inside, coiled

and gleaming, though he didn't touch it. The sight of the talisman stirred ancient memories better left alone.

Lady Vivienne Cumberland and Mr. Alec Lawrence.

The names were different but he knew them nonetheless. He made it a point of keeping track of everyone who wanted him dead. If Vivienne had any idea he still lived, she'd go to the ends of the earth to find him.

He still thought of her as Tijah, her daēva as Achaemenes. Along with Cyrus and Cassandane, the oldest bonded pairs on the planet. And yet they'd let this daemon leave England. It had outwitted them, just as it had outwitted his own mistress two thousand years ago.

Did they understand what it was they hunted? Balthazar very much doubted it. That it had somehow escaped its prison in the Dominion shook him to his core.

A creature of shadow and flame.

I know your name.

He turned away. Lucas would be his eyes and ears. The Devereaux family had served him for generations, their loyalty and devotion unquestioned. He understood the amulet must be recovered at all costs. Balthazar touched the ouroboros he wore on a chain around his neck. A serpent devouring its own tail.

He hated himself for what he did to survive, but he feared the prospect of dying even more. There were special levels of Hell reserved for his kind.

Unwillingly, his mind conjured up the image of a fey palace in the Dominion. The House-Behind-the-Veil. In the gardens, a stone well of pure darkness waited. He had seen the thing that lived inside. It called itself—

"Balthazar."

He turned at the soft purr behind him. Evangeline waited, embroidered robe provocatively dangling from one bare shoulder. She wore a ruby necklace underneath and nothing else. Evangeline Martin was very rich, or at least her husband was.

"You left me abruptly," she pouted. "The bed's gone cold."

"I'll be there in a moment," he replied absently.

"Who were those people?"

"Business associates."

"Who arrive without an appointment, demanding to see you like common peddlers?"

She was starting to irritate him. "They had one. I forgot about it."

Evangeline crossed the room to stand beside him at the window. Rain coursed down the glass, blurring the street beyond. She tangled her fingers in his dark hair. "Do all the Koháry men look like you? Every portrait in this house has the same eyes." She touched his lips. "The same mouth."

"Our blood runs thick."

"Very thick." Her eyelids drooped seductively. The pulse at her neck fluttered.

Heat flared in his groin and he felt a wave of self-loathing. *You do what you must.*

He'd tried to mend his ways.

There is evil in the world and I do my best to oppose it.

Not a lie. But not the whole truth either.

You see, Miss Pell, some would say I'm evil myself.

Evangeline ran a hand along his arm, light as a feather. He picked her up and she let out one of her throaty laughs.

"Count Koháry." She gave him a frank green-eyed stare. "Have you ever made love to a woman in your library?"

"Never," he lied.

"Then you must do it quickly because my husband will be home in less than an hour."

He inhaled the scent of her, so young and alive. "I'm not afraid of your husband."

"Well, I am. He's a jealous lunatic."

Balthazar carried her to a chair by the fire. The gold ourobouros glinted in the light of the flames, each jeweled scale perfectly lifelike. He removed it from his own neck and hung it around Evangeline's so the talisman dangled between her small breasts.

"I don't wish to hurry," he murmured.

When she cried out in pleasure some time later and he felt all that life flow into him, all that precious time, Balthazar inexplicably thought of another face. Smooth brown skin, hair shorn to the scalp. A scimitar in her hand. So young, but she'd been formidable even then.

He'd tried and failed to have her killed.

What did she look like now? And why did he even care?

PART III

Hell is empty and all the devils are here.
— William Shakespeare, *The Tempest*

CHAPTER 22

Two steamships arrived in New York on the afternoon of December 28.

The first was the White Star Line's R.M.S. *Oceanic* out of Liverpool. She had been due to arrive two days earlier, but one of her boilers overheated and the ship hit rough weather, delaying her progress. The nor'easter tossed the steamer around like a tin can; anything that wasn't nailed down became an airborne missile. Even some of the most seasoned sailors suffered from violent seasickness.

That wasn't the worst of her troubles, however.

When the *Oceanic* departed on December 19, she'd carried one hundred and sixty-six first-class passengers and a thousand third-class passengers, along with a crew of one hundred and forty-three men. By the time she limped into New York Harbor over a week later, six of the passengers and two of the crew had vanished. They were officially presumed to have fallen overboard during the storm, but everyone knew that eight casualties was an unprecedented number for the voyage, weather or no. Rumors abounded, each wilder than the last.

There was a wild animal aboard the ship, or a crazed killer.

Some whispered that it was Saucy Jack himself. An aura of fear and paranoia hung over the ship like a pall. For the last several days of the voyage, most of the passengers stayed locked inside their staterooms. The lavish dining rooms and salons sat empty. Those who did move about did so in groups of three or four.

The afternoon the *Oceanic* arrived in New York, a rising wind had whipped the surface of the harbor into whitecaps flecked with great webs of spindrift. A light rain fell, but even darker clouds mounded on the horizon. The passengers hurried down the gangplanks the moment the gates opened. They were relieved to be disembarking from the *Oceanic*, which some muttered was cursed.

Only a few noticed the large black dog that leapt straight from the deck to the wooden pier. They assumed someone's pet had slipped its leash. A child cried out and pointed, but by the time her mother looked over, the dog had disappeared.

It loped along the docks to the cobblestones of Christopher Street, pink tongue lolling. In fact, the dog had once belonged to a Mrs. Aloysius Bellemore of Philadelphia, one of the vanished passengers. It was something different now. Neither alive nor dead, but a strange amalgam of both.

The dog skulked beneath the tracks of the Ninth Avenue elevated line. In the shadow of a ramshackle wooden warehouse, the creature paused, sniffing the air. It padded down a narrow alley that smelled of rotten fish and other even worse things. Muscular haunches rippled beneath matted black fur.

The old woman watched it come with trepidation. Her name was Alice Carstairs and she was a rag picker. Her feet had grown sore from wandering the city with her cart and she knew this alley as a quiet place out of the wind where she could rest for a bit.

"Here now," she said in a calm voice, though her heart beat faster. "Here, boy."

The dog stopped a few feet away, looking at her with intelligent eyes.

"Poor thing. Haven't eaten in days, I'll wager," the old woman said. "I'll give you a crust, my dear."

She cautiously extended a hand and patted its massive head. The dog licked her hand.

THE SECOND SHIP to dock was the *Etruria*, which arrived precisely seven days, two hours and forty-one minutes after she had left England. Rain fell in sheets by the time she made port at the Cunard Line's Pier Forty-Eight, just three blocks south of the *Oceanic*.

Vivienne Cumberland and Alec Lawrence took a hansom cab downtown and left their luggage at the once fashionable but now slightly decrepit Astor House, which they had chosen mainly for its location. Then they went straight to the offices of the S.P.R. on nearby Pearl Street. Dark had fallen by the time the aged butler led them up to Mr. Kaylock's office.

He rose from his desk to greet them. Kaylock's normally unflappable demeanor was fraying around the edges. He'd forgotten to shave that morning and ink stained his long, simian fingers.

"Thank God you're here," he said quietly. "We have a situation."

Harland Kaylock proceeded to inform them of what had transpired at the American Museum of Natural History during the week they were crossing the Atlantic.

"The stolen amulet is likely a talisman," Alec said. "A true one." He looked at Vivienne. "It was our worst fear, Mr. Kaylock. The daemon already knows the location of the Greater Gates."

"Daemon?" Kaylock interjected. "Could you perhaps…."

"Explain? Of course, sorry. That seems to be the nomenclature for this particular entity. We found a reference in a letter from a necromancer who had traveled to the shadowlands. He described its lair. *A deep, dark hole.* In other words, a lower level of the Dominion. He made a pact and tried to bring it through to this world but couldn't manage it."

"Are they similar to ghouls?"

"Superficially. Both possess a living host. But daemons can wield fire." Vivienne produced her cigarette case but didn't open it. "From what we saw of Dr. Clarence, they're stronger and far more sophisticated."

"I see." Kaylock glanced at the case. "Go ahead, if you like. I don't mind."

"Thank you." Vivienne took out her Magic Pocket Lamp. She clicked the button and a flame jetted from the wick. She lit the cigarette and exhaled toward the window.

"Fascinating device," Kaylock murmured. "And how is this daemon killed?"

"We're not sure it can be, not in any meaningful sense," Alec said. "But we believe it can be banished."

Vivienne shot him a look. "We've had a week to think of little else, Mr. Kaylock. Its weakness is that is has no body of its own. Ghouls don't actually possess anyone. They consume flesh and blood to mimic the appearance of their victim. To absorb them, in a way."

"Daemons are different," Alec said. "The necromancer described the one he met as shadow and flame. I don't think they can survive for long outside of a living host. The one we've been chasing went straight from Leland Brady into William Clarence. Then from Clarence into someone else, we don't know who. It enters through the eyes, or perhaps even by touch alone. But if the host body dies before it can find another—"

"It will be vulnerable," Vivienne finished. "We know how to open a temporary gate. Send it back to the lowest level of the Dominion and hope it takes a thousand years to find its way out again."

Kaylock nodded. "I don't mean to be contentious, but what's to stop it from just possessing one of *you*?"

"Before he fled England, Dr. Clarence attacked Mr. Lawrence." Vivienne tapped her cigarette on the edge of a crystal ashtray Kaylock had pushed across his desk. "It could have killed him but didn't. I think it was trying to take him and our bond repelled it."

"I was told about that," Kaylock said carefully. He cleared his throat. "I've never met a...."

"Daēva?" Alec said, watching his reaction.

"Indeed. I must say, you look perfectly, ah, human."

"Only on the outside." Alec smiled wolfishly. "Now, Mr. Kaylock, we just have to corner this thing. Any ideas?"

"To be perfectly honest, I'm not sure it's even here in New York yet. Julius Sabelline was killed two days before Christmas. Our agents have been investigating his murder, but we can't blame that on the daemon."

"Because it can't have crossed the Atlantic so quickly," Vivienne agreed. "Someone else must have stolen the talisman."

Alec drummed his fingers on the silver falcon of his cane. "It can't be a coincidence. I think we should speak with Miss Pell right away. Where is she?"

"I removed her from the case until you arrived," Kaylock said. "It was too dangerous."

"Well, get her back," Vivienne snapped.

"If you don't mind," Alec added in a milder tone. "She seems to know more than anyone at this point."

"Of course," Kaylock replied distractedly. "I'll send my messenger boy."

He dug out a piece of paper and scrawled a note.

"I'm sure she'll be at home in this foul weather," he said with a confident smile, yanking on the bell pull. "We should hear back shortly."

CHAPTER 23

The torrential rains slowed traffic to a crawl. It took more than an hour to get downtown and the same to cross the mile-long span of the Brooklyn Bridge. Harry sat quietly, lost in thought. John stared out the carriage window at the turbulent grey waters of the East River, muttering to himself as he ran through a dozen new theories.

"Even if Jackson despised his stepfather enough to kill him, I still don't see how it all fits," he finally exclaimed as they inched down the exit ramp to Sands Street. A forest of black umbrellas clogged the pedestrian walkway to the right as some of the early-shift commuters made their way home from Manhattan. "How did he lock the door without a key? And why on earth would a promising young student from Yale want to unleash hordes of undead on his fellow man?"

"It's an exceedingly peculiar and complex case," Harry said. "But I believe there is only one explanation that fits all the facts."

"Well?" John demanded. "Let's have it."

She adopted what she hoped was an enigmatic smile. "Don't fuss, you'll find out shortly."

"You're doing that supercilious thing again, Harry. Smug and awful."

She laughed. "I could be entirely wrong, and I don't wish to embarrass myself by bandying about pure conjecture."

"Fine. My wager's on Jackson then." He searched her face for any sign of affirmation. "Wait, no, the whole madu weapon thing is too obvious. I'll say Holland. Holland *and* Araminta."

Harry just gave him her Cheshire Cat grin.

"You're a horrible girl, do you know that? Davis Sharpe, and that's my final answer! Perhaps he's the illegitimate son of Jeremy Boot and they conspired together." He pulled out his notepad and began flipping through the pages. "I know it's in here somewhere," he muttered. "It always is. That needle in the haystack of utterly irrelevant and misleading information."

"Poor John," she murmured. "You mustn't forget Orpha. Despite her initial appearance at the post-mortem, she hasn't been all that helpful, has she? Almost obstructive. And she has a strong interest in the supernatural. What if her true affiliations are darker than anyone imagined?"

"Be quiet," he snarled. "I'm trying to think."

Two blocks before they reached No. 17 Cranberry Street, Harry called out to Connor.

"Let us out. We'll walk the rest of the way."

The boy pulled on the reins and the carriage juddered to a stop in front of a series of identical row houses. "In the pouring rain?" he asked.

"I don't wish to announce our presence. Not until we know who's at home." Harry turned to John. "You don't mind getting a bit wet, do you?"

He looked with resignation at the deluge outside the window. "Go for a swim, you mean? Of course not. December drenchers are my favorite. Especially without an umbrella."

"I'll take that for a yes," Harry said, buttoning her coat.

"Should I wait fer ya here?" Connor asked.

"No. Go straight to the S.P.R. offices. It shouldn't take long. The bridge ramp is only a few blocks from Pearl Street and traffic should be lighter heading back to the city. Tell Harland Kaylock where we've gone. Tell him it's nearly over."

Connor hesitated. "Yer sure, Harry? Seems a bit reckless to leave you two here alone."

"Maybe you should listen to the ten-year-old," John said. "He's actually making sense."

Harry gripped the Colt in her pocket. The feel of the cold metal gave her courage. "There's no time, Connor. Just go as fast as you can. We'll look after ourselves."

"What about the police?"

"There's things they wouldn't understand."

"If you say so." He gave them an encouraging nod, though doubt was plain to read in his young face.

They jumped out. Within moments, the carriage was speeding back toward the river. John turned his collar up, tugging the Homburg low over his eyes. Harry shivered as chilly droplets slid into the neck of her gown and straight down her spine.

"What's the plan now?" John asked. "Storm the castle with torches?"

"We'll go round to the back garden."

They hurried the two blocks to the Sabelline house, splashing through small lakes at the corners. The cobbled street was deserted, though cracks of light could be seen through the heavy curtains on both the first and second floors. Harry and John slipped through the front gate and crept around to the side. They crouched beneath a window. It was closed, but they could just make out voices inside. One belonged to a woman. Harry felt certain it was Araminta. The other had a cracked, whispering quality.

"Can you tell who that is?" John whispered.

Harry shook her head.

"Jackson?"

She pressed her back against the bricks and risked a quick peek inside. The room was empty. Whoever had just been there was gone.

"Let's give it a few minutes. Maybe they'll return."

The eaves of the house offered partial shelter from the rain. No sparrows today, but no crows either, which Harry took as a good sign. The last of the daylight bled away. They heard nothing more from inside the house, which was still as a grave.

"I'm going to knock," Harry whispered.

"But—"

"Just follow my lead."

She seized John's hand, dragged him around to the front door and gave it three smart raps. When no one came, Harry banged again, harder this time. They shared a quick glance as tumblers spun and the door swung open.

"Miss Pell?" Araminta Sabelline clutched the doorframe, her face pale as chalk. She wore the same black dress as before. She seemed surprised to see them, but not angry or upset.

"Good afternoon, Mrs. Sabelline. I'm sorry to trouble you but I have some news. This is my colleague Mr. John Weston, also of the S.P.R."

John touched his hat in greeting. Araminta smiled uncertainly.

"May we come in?"

"Of course." She stood aside so they could enter. "What foul weather we're having. You can hang your coats over there." She gestured to a small mud room off the hallway, with racks for boots and pegs for outerwear. "Our maid Berthe's taken sick. She lives with her mother in Williamsburg. It's just as well she stayed home today, I imagine the streets are a mess."

"It took ages to get over the bridge," John said, hanging up both of their coats. "I must say, this is a charming house."

"Thank you. We bought it when Jackson turned five. I prefer

Brooklyn to the bustle of the city. A much healthier environment for children."

Somewhere in the depths of the house, a clock chimed five. The echoes faded into perfect silence.

"Is your son at home?" Harry asked.

"I'm afraid he's gone out." She looked at them anxiously. "Did you follow up on the letter he found, Miss Pell? Is that the news you've brought?"

"I did. And we've discovered some other things as well. Perhaps we should sit down to discuss it."

Araminta took a steadying breath. "I wish Jackson were here. He said he had to meet someone, but wouldn't tell me who. I'm certain he keeps things from me, simply out of natural protectiveness, you understand. He means well. But the not knowing is maddening too." Araminta rubbed her arms as though she felt a chill. "This whole tragedy has shattered my nerves. Nothing seems quite real anymore."

She led them down the hall to the same sitting room at the rear of the house. Araminta lit the lamps. It was nearly dark as night outside. Rain beat against the windows in a soothing rhythm. Beyond them, the garden was a misty blur.

"Can I offer you anything?"

"Thank you, no," Harry said, settling herself in an armchair. Araminta took the sofa, and John stood by the mantle, discreetly examining the photograph of Julius Sabelline and Count Habsburg-Koháry.

"I'll begin with the author of the letter, Mary Elizabeth Wickes. She's a prisoner at the Tombs."

"The Tombs?"

"The city jail on Centre Street. She's due to be hanged for murder in a week."

Araminta drew a sharp breath and put a hand to her throat, fingering the crucifix. "Whatever did she want?"

"To warn your husband about the amulet of Osiris. She knew

it placed him in danger and that someone would kill to get their hands on it. Mary told us he never replied, but I think her letter frightened him enough to put new locks on the windows and to change the one on his office door."

Araminta looked away. "My husband didn't order those locks," she admitted. "I did. The ones on the windows, at least."

"Why?"

"I thought I saw someone looking in. A man. It frightened me."

"When was this?"

"About a month ago. I told Julius. He was dismissive. I've always been high-strung and he thought it was my imagination." She passed a hand across her eyes. "I can't be sure it wasn't."

"You didn't recognize him?"

"No. I'm certain it was a stranger."

"Not Nelson Holland?"

Araminta gave her a sharp look. "Why on earth would it be Mr. Holland?"

Harry let the silence lengthen for a few beats. "I may as well be blunt. Davis Sharpe said he saw you together in Mr. Holland's office."

"Oh." Araminta's voice was barely audible, but she didn't bother trying to deny it.

"Did your husband give you the bruise on your wrist, Mrs. Sabelline? Or was it Mr. Holland?"

"Neither," she said dully. "It was Davis. He confronted me after the party. He must have been waiting in the corridor when I excused myself to freshen up. He was very upset, and of course, he'd had too much to drink as usual."

"What did he want?"

"He said he was tired of being falsely accused by my husband. That it was ruining his career. I begged him to keep quiet. Not that it mattered in the end."

"What happened next?" John prompted.

"He stormed off to his office. I went to the ladies' room. I was rather shaken by the encounter and stayed in there for ten or fifteen minutes. I didn't want Julius or Jackson to see me that way. They would have known something was wrong." She stood and walked to a sideboard. "Are you sure I can't offer you anything? I don't usually drink before dinner, but I could use one now."

John opened his mouth. Harry answered for both of them.

"No thank you, we're fine," she said.

Araminta poured herself a glass of red wine and took a long sip. It seemed to steady her.

"I know you must think me an awful person, but my husband was a cold man, Miss Pell. I'm not sure he ever really loved me. I suppose I should be grateful he took us in."

"After Jackson's father died?"

She nodded. "Julius was a good provider. I hoped he'd be more—a father figure—but he simply wasn't capable." She set her glass down. "I don't care if you believe me or not, but I held no ill will toward Julius. And I certainly didn't kill him."

"No one says you did." John sounded sorry for her. "Do you know when Jackson is returning?"

"He didn't say." She took another sip of wine.

"It's a strange case," Harry remarked. "Nearly everyone involved has lied about something. But it all comes down to two facts. The rest is window dressing."

Araminta stared out at the rain-soaked garden, now shrouded in darkness. "I fear there is devilry at work, Miss Pell. Forces beyond our understanding."

"That may indeed be so, but it was clear to me from the very beginning that this case revolved around the key and the seemingly impossible fact that the door was locked from the inside after the deed." She leaned forward, blue eyes bright. "Let us say for the sake of argument it was not Jeremy Boot. We will rule him out."

Araminta Sabelline tilted her head and nodded.

"Nor was there a third copy of the key. The locks had been changed that day and the reputation of the locksmith is above reproach. So how could it be done?"

"I can't imagine."

"We all know the order of events prior to the discovery of the body. Your husband left first, followed by Holland and Sharpe. Shortly after, Jackson claims he went to view the second floor exhibits, though no one actually observed him there." Harry looked at Araminta. "You left and encountered Mr. Sharpe in the hallway. The count and Orpha Winter were the only ones remaining in the main hall. Am I correct so far?"

"I believe so."

"At some point during this time, your husband was murdered and his strongbox looted. The act itself would have taken no more than five to ten minutes. Let us now arrive at the discovery of the body by yourself, Mr. Sharpe and Jeremy Boot. Before this moment, all is clear. The facts are unchallenged. But now things become a bit murky."

Araminta bridled ever so slightly at this. "How so?"

"Well, we have poor Mr. Boot vomiting on his shoes. Mr. Sharpe standing in the doorway, no doubt transfixed by the scene of horror before him, and perhaps going to Boot's aid. And you, Mrs. Sabelline, taking several steps into the room and fainting."

"Your point?"

"We all made an erroneous assumption from the start." She turned to John, who knew just what she was up to and was watching her closely. "That since the key was found in his desk, it had been there all along."

"Oh damn." He slapped his thigh. "You mean someone put it back afterwards?"

"Precisely. It's the only possible explanation."

Araminta didn't speak, but her face had gone deathly pale.

"If that's the case," Harry continued, "it could only have been done by one of the first people to enter the room. We know Mr. Sharpe didn't actually come inside, but instead went for help. Mr. Boot was busy getting sick at the sight of the mutilated body. He also had his own key. Replacing the one that belonged to the victim would only cast suspicion on himself, which is just what happened." Harry smiled unpleasantly.

"Which leaves you, Mrs. Sabelline. When you pretended to faint, you no doubt caught yourself on the edge of the desk. It would only be a matter of seconds to return the key to the drawer before anyone noticed."

Araminta laughed dismissively and placed her empty wine glass on the table. "That's where you're mistaken. Mr. Sharpe did come inside. Both he and Mr. Boot assisted me into the hallway. Assuming all this wild supposition is even true, he could easily have returned the key himself."

"But Mr. Sharpe didn't have access to the murder weapon," John interjected, light dawning in his eyes. "We've learned what it is. A madu. Quite an exotic item. And we know Jackson borrowed one from Count Koháry's collection."

"Perhaps you thought that in the unlikely event the police figured it out, suspicion would fall on your son."

"I'd say that's a bit cold," John muttered.

Araminta lifted her chin. Dark purple stains streaked her lips from the wine. "You have no proof of anything."

Harry ignored her. "The ruse with the footprints makes sense if it was someone who had small feet and wished to throw off the investigation by wearing a large pair of shoes. Your husband was also a size eleven. I wonder if you recently purchased dress shoes for him? I think you did, and I also think they'd be missing from his closet." She leaned back in the chair and steepled her fingers the way Myrtle did. "As for the proof, you must have the amulet stashed away somewhere. The police are on their way and I have no doubt they will find it."

"Bravo," John said under his breath.

Araminta snorted. "You're a fool, Miss Pell."

"I'm not sure why you did it, or why you cut out his eyes. Further misdirection, I suppose," Harry said, although the certainty in her voice faltered. "Perhaps you intended to sell the amulet on the black market. Perhaps he refused to divorce you—"

"You know nothing."

"Or perhaps you had an accomplice," John said. "We heard two voices through the window. Who's here, Mrs. Sabelline? Is it Jackson?"

"I sent him away." A shadow crossed her face. "It's not safe."

"Why?" Harry frowned, her mind racing through parallel possibilities. "Is it Nelson Holland?" She wished she hadn't given John her coat. The Derringer was in the pocket. *Sloppy, Harry.*

"The police are on their way," she repeated in a louder voice, wishing it were true.

That's when Araminta Sabelline began to chuckle. It was a horrible sound, half-mad and full of despair.

"Nelson Holland? Why, it's the master who's come." She smiled coyly. "You know him, don't you? *Mr. Hyde.*"

Somewhere upstairs, a floorboard creaked.

"I've dreamt of him. He promised me eternal youth and beauty. Everlasting life. Oh, the things he showed me." She cocked her head. "The master tried to show Julius things, but he wouldn't listen. Wouldn't look. Kept his eyes shut tight. We didn't like that, so we took them. The eyes are the windows of the soul, you know."

"Where is the amulet?" John said, grasping her arm. "Where?"

Araminta looked at the ceiling. She slowly raised a pale hand. "Upstairs. In Julius's study." She grinned and yanked free. "Come and get it."

John staggered back as she gave him a hard shove and ran from the parlor. Footsteps pounded up the stairs to the second landing. Harry made to follow but John blocked her way.

"Are you mad?"

She squared her shoulders and tried to look down her nose at him, which wasn't easy since he was about a foot taller. "We have to get that amulet, John."

He shook his head in amazement. "Something's up there, Harry. A *daemon*. The same one that possessed Mr. Brady. We've no idea how to stop it."

"James Moran shot it before," she said stubbornly. "Bullets do have an effect. The thing is in a mortal body. We'll just have to stay back." She looked at him. "Give me one moment first."

"What?"

"I left my gun in the mud room."

John sighed. He was swigging from the bottle of red wine when she returned.

"Want some?"

"No, thank you."

John took a last gulp and tossed the empty bottle aside. "So the plan is we take the keys to Hell and walk out of here?"

"Yes. Run, probably."

He sighed again. "Hang on."

John disappeared. A moment later he came back with a heavy iron frying pan in his hand.

"Only thing I could find, but it's better than nothing. Lead the way then."

They ascended the stairs to the second floor. The hall was dark save for a door at the end, which showed lamplight through the crack.

"I expect it's in Dr. Clarence," Harry whispered, cocking the pistol. "Just don't get in front of me, I'd hate to shoot you again."

"Yes, that would be inconvenient."

Harry put her hand on the knob. "Ready?"

John nodded, eyes huge and frying pan poised to swing.

Harry eased the door open. Julius Sabelline's study was more cluttered than his office at the museum. Boxes of books and papers were stacked haphazardly around the room. A single standing lamp in the far corner cast a dim pool of light. The windows had all been thrown wide open and the curtains fluttered as rain swept inside.

A figure sat behind the desk. It seemed shriveled, shrunken, its face hidden in shadow. Araminta crouched on the floor next to it like a faithful dog. Harry brought up the pistol and aimed it at the faceless thing in the chair.

"I will not hesitate to shoot you," she said, trying hard to keep her hand steady. "We're agents with the Society for Psychical Research, fully trained to deal with your sort. Where is the amulet of Osiris?"

The creature leaned forward into the light. Harry drew a sharp breath. It wasn't Dr. Clarence at all but one of the oldest women she'd ever seen. Even her wrinkles had wrinkles, like the underbelly of an ancient sea tortoise. She wore a ragged dress that had been washed so many times it seemed to have no color at all. Stringy white hair drew back into a tight bun atop her head.

"Harrison Fearing Pell," the thing said in a paper-thin voice. "And Mr. Weston."

Harry felt vaguely disappointed when she failed to add, *So we meet again.*

"Where is it?" John demanded, brandishing the frying pan.

"The key? It belongs to us." This time, the old woman and Araminta spoke in simultaneous, overlapping voices.

"It belongs to Count Balthazar," Harry said.

The old woman made a wheezing sound that might have been laughter.

"He paid someone to dig it up. That doesn't make it his."

"It doesn't make it yours either," John said.

Light glinted in the hollows of her eyes. "Claudius Ptolemy promised me passage in exchange for knowledge, but he abandoned me. He was a liar and a cheat." The daemon sounded almost petulant. "Few men travel to the Dominion and fewer still leave. He owes me a debt."

She raised a claw-like hand. Harry saw a flash of gold. The amulet.

"The thirteenth gate will open," Araminta said in a strange, hollow voice. "The dead will walk."

"Look," John said. "You've had your fun. Time to crawl back to purgatory. Let's not overstay our welcome."

The old woman bared her broken teeth in a grin. "Those whores in London were merely a prelude, John Weston." It tilted its head, considering. "Perhaps I'll wear your skin next. You can watch through my eyes. We'll hold the knife together." That amused wheezing again. "I am the Dominion made flesh. *Abyssus abyssum invocate.* Do you remember? Hell calls to—"

Harry pointed the gun at its heart and pulled the trigger. The sound was deafening in the small room. The old woman fell backwards, vanishing behind the desk. Araminta let out a high-pitched screech. She seized a letter opener and lunged forward. John swung the frying pan, but she twisted like a snake, easily dodging his blow.

"Get the amulet, Harry!" he cried.

She nodded and cocked the hammer of the pistol. Then she crept forward and peeked around the corner of the desk. Blood stained the carpet, but the old woman seemed to have vanished into thin air. John's scream made her whirl around. The letter opener was buried to the hilt in his right shoulder. Araminta wrenched the frying pan from his grasp and brought it down on his head with a horrifying crunch. John fell to his knees. Another blow and he collapsed bonelessly on the carpet. Blood trickled from the corner of his mouth.

White-hot rage scoured Harry's bones. She got the gun up and fired, but she'd never been a good shot. The bullet went wild, smashing into the desk. Araminta's face was perfectly blank and

Harry had a sudden vision of her cutting out her husband's eyes with the same chilling calm.

Harry was about to squeeze the trigger again when the old woman skittered out of the shadows and grasped Araminta's skirts. Blue fire raced from its fingers. Within seconds, she was ablaze. Araminta staggered to the window, beating futilely at the flames. The heavy velvet curtains went up like a torch. Glass shattered as a dark shape hurtled through the window into the rain-soaked night.

Araminta's screams seemed to go on and on. The sickly odor of burning flesh and hair filled the air. Orange flames streaked up the wallpaper, quickly spreading to the boxes of books and paper. Harry crouched down, seeking clean air. She still had the pistol in her hand, but the metal was growing hot. She tried to get her bearings in the smoky darkness. She crawled across the floor, groping blindly. Finally, she found an arm.

You're a fool, she thought. *An arrogant fool.*

Harry's throat burned. She dropped the gun and cradled John's still form, stroking his hair, wet with blood.

"I'll get us out, don't worry," she whispered.

Flames licked the ceiling. Sweat poured down her face and her scalp tingled from the intense heat. Mercifully, Araminta's hoarse cries had finally stopped. But Harry's heart sank as she saw the fire had already spread to the doorway and hall beyond. The window was the only possible escape route, but the blazing curtains created a barrier and John was too heavy for her to carry. She tried to shield him with her body, pressing her nose and mouth into the thin pocket of air on the floor. *Shadow and flame*, Mary had said. *Flame and shadow. It comes for us all….*

Wood splintered as the door flew open. The fire roared like a live thing at the fresh oxygen. A beautiful woman with brown skin and hard eyes grabbed Harry like a sack of potatoes. Behind her, a slender man lifted John in his arms. John had to weigh at least a hundred and eighty pounds, but the man handled him like a child. They dashed into the burning hallway and down the stairs. Harry dimly heard a crash as part of the roof caved in behind them. And then cool night air hit her face, and glorious rain. She blinked red, watery eyes, coughed violently. Outside, a crowd was gathering.

Her savior set Harry on her feet. "Are you burned?"

"I don't think so." She coughed again. Her lungs felt scalded. Araminta's screams still echoed in her ears, but even worse was the sound of the frying pan striking John's skull. It had to be fractured. *Oh dear God….* "He needs a doctor." Tears clogged her voice. "Immediately."

"It's being handled," the woman said cryptically.

"How?" Harry looked around. "Where are they? *Who are you?*"

The woman opened her mouth to reply when Jackson Sabelline came rushing out of the darkness. "Where's Mother?" he asked frantically.

Jackson turned to run inside the inferno but Harry seized his arm. "She's dead."

His face crumpled and she knew she could never tell him what his mother had done. It would be too cruel.

"How could you leave her?" He tore at his wavy brown hair. "How could you?"

"She was already gone." Harry hesitated. "I'm terribly sorry."

The crowd fell back as a pumper truck drawn by three enormous draft horses tore around the corner. Firemen in long, heavy coats leapt down and started unspooling a white cotton hose. Jackson gave her a last despairing look and ran over to speak with them. Harry scanned the faces lined up across the street, searching for John and the man who had rescued him. Rain and smoke stung her eyes. Most of the gawkers sheltered under umbrellas, but then a brief space opened up and Harry caught a glimpse of a man with grey streaks at his temples. He wore a bowler hat that cast his upper face in shadow but something about him struck her as familiar. Was it Count Koháry's manservant?

She blinked and the crowd swirled together again. Harry was about to run across the street when the tall woman next to her spoke.

"I'm Vivienne Cumberland," she said in an upper-crust English accent. "My associate Alec Lawrence is seeing to your friend. I don't suppose you managed to get the amulet."

Harry stared at her, understanding dawning. "You're from London."

She nodded. "We came as soon as your boy brought his message to Mr. Kaylock." Her voice hardened. "The daemon was here."

"Yes. It got away with the amulet. I think I shot it, but then it set Araminta on fire. *With its hands.*" She shuddered. Even at this distance, she could feel the heat of the flames. "Everything happened so quickly. I heard a crash. It must have jumped out the window." Harry forced herself to meet Lady Cumberland's cool gaze. "We've made a terrible mess of things, haven't we?"

Vivienne sighed. "There's no time. We need to leave before someone starts asking questions. Come."

They ran past the firemen. One of them gave Harry's soot-covered face a sharp look but made no move to stop her. Despite the downpour, the blaze had already spread to the adjacent houses. The Sabelline home was made of brick, but its neighbors were wood. Flames erupted from every window and the entire street was bathed in reddish light.

The carriage waited at the curb a block away. "Harry!" Connor called out when he saw her. "What happened?"

"I'll tell you later," she said with a wan smile. "But you brought help just in time. Thank you."

"It's a habit of mine," he responded cheerfully.

They crowded into the carriage. John lay slumped against the seat, his eyes closed. Vivienne signaled to Connor and he urged the horses into a trot away from the chaotic scene.

"Mr. Weston needs a hospital," Harry said. "Araminta stabbed him with a letter opener and bashed him on the head. Twice." She leaned over and took his hand. A lump of guilt lodged in her gut like a stone. "Poor John. He always seems to get the worst of these encounters."

Vivienne laid a reassuring hand on her arm. "I told you, Mr. Lawrence will see to him."

Harry studied Alec Lawrence for the first time. He was young like Lady Cumberland, perhaps a decade older than Harry, but both of them had an ageless quality. A slight strain was evident around the eyes, as if he too carried pain but had learned to live with it. A cane with a silver handle sat propped between his knees.

Alec Lawrence looked at Vivienne.

"You can let me go now," he said mildly. "We're far enough away."

Harry didn't understand what he meant since Vivienne wasn't even touching him, but a moment later his expression softened. Something like satisfaction stole across his features. He turned to John and gently cupped his face, watching him intently. Harry frowned, but the hair on her arms rose up as if a breeze had swept through the carriage. The raindrops coursing down the window seemed to shiver. Alec gritted his teeth. Whatever he was doing, it was unpleasant. Harry suddenly wanted desperately to stop it. She opened her mouth, unsure of what she planned to say, but Vivienne gave a sharp shake of her head.

Moments later, John stiffened. He gave a low gasp, back arching beneath Alec's hands. His eyes flew open, wide and startled.

Alec released him. He looked exhausted. "It's done."

"What's done?" Harry demanded.

Vivienne ignored her. "Are you all right?" she asked John.

He raised a shaking hand to his eyes. "I think so. Who are you?"

Harry stared at him in wonder. Blood still matted his hair, but he was sitting up now.

"These are the agents from London," she said. "They just pulled our fat from the fire. Literally." She squinted at Alec. "What did you just do?"

"Mr. Lawrence has special abilities," Vivienne said, her tone discouraging further questions.

John gingerly tested his shoulder. "Miraculous, I'd say."

Harry leaned over and gently probed the spot where he'd been struck on the head. There wasn't even a lump.

"Miraculous," she repeated faintly.

Alec smiled at them, though there was something grim in it. "You're both lucky to be alive."

"I know. Thank you."

He waved a hand dismissively. "We read your report on the Hyde case, Miss Pell. It seems you've caught another killer, but I'm guessing this one met her own brand of rough justice."

Harry nodded. "Araminta confessed to murdering her husband. She thought she'd be rewarded with eternal life. Instead, it sacrificed her to get away."

"Demonic pacts do have a way of turning on one," he said dryly. "Any idea where it went?"

"I'm afraid not. It jumped out the window."

"We need to review everything we know. There must be some clue." Alec banged on the roof of the carriage with his cane. "Pearl Street!"

CHAPTER 24

Both Harland Kaylock and Orpha Winter were waiting at the S.P.R. offices. They sat on opposite sides of a large drawing room on the first floor, Mr. Kaylock perched on the edge of a divan like some dark bird of prey and Mrs. Winter elegant in a high-necked blue silk gown the precise shade of her eyes. They might not have liked one another, but their stony faces made it clear they were united in disapproval of their newest agents. Not even John's bloodstained clothing seemed to generate much sympathy.

Harry held her tongue while Alec Lawrence gave a brief accounting of his and Lady Cumberland's arrival at the Sabelline home. Had Connor not driven like a maniac back across the bridge, they would have been too late. Her rescue was a blur of heat and darkness, but Harry remembered the crash of the roof coming down just seconds before they ran out the front door.

John sprawled in a chair by the grate, still seeming a bit dazed. He nursed a brandy poured for him by the butler, Joseph. Vivienne Cumberland paced up and down, smoking distractedly. When Alec explained that the amulet had been lost, Orpha Winter made a small sound of genteel disgust. Harland Kaylock briefly closed his eyes. Smelling blood in the water, Joseph shuffled to the far end of the room.

Overall, the atmosphere at Pearl Street crackled like one of Edison's electrical turbines. When Alec finished, Mr. Kaylock's gaze settled on Harry.

"It was fortuitous indeed that the agents from London were here when your boy came rushing in," he said in a flat voice.

"It was, sir," she agreed, resisting the urge to wring her sweaty hands together.

"And that they were kind enough to go to your aid."

"Very kind."

"I'm rather confused on one particular point, though. Perhaps you can enlighten me?"

"I'll do my best, Mr. Kaylock."

He leaned forward, his blade of a nose stabbing the air. "I expressly told you not to pursue the case any further. You were to wait for Lady Cumberland and Mr. Lawrence. Was any part of my instructions ambiguous, Miss Pell? Because you appear to have disregarded them completely."

Harry withered under his vulpine stare, but managed to keep her chin up. "I had no intention of doing that, sir. But Jackson Sabelline came to me yesterday with a letter he'd found in his father's effects. It was from Mary Elizabeth Wickes."

"The child poisoner?" A flash of surprise crossed his face.

"Yes. She warned him he was in danger. Sabelline took her letter seriously enough to change the lock on his office door, but it wasn't enough."

"You should have brought the letter straight to me."

"I promised Jackson Sabelline I would pursue it myself."

He frowned. "That was a rash promise."

Harry cleared her throat. "It seemed to me there was a direct connection with Brady's crimes, which you'll recall was *my* case. With all due respect," she added hastily. "If the Brady case has been reopened, I'm within my rights to pursue closure on behalf of my client."

"Your client?"

"Elizabeth Brady, sir. She paid my fee."

"You're splitting hairs rather finely, Miss Pell," Kaylock said. "If you had only come to me first, I could have sent Lady Cumberland and Mr. Lawrence with you to the Sabelline house. The daemon wouldn't have gotten away with the amulet. It's even possible that Araminta Sabelline might have lived to face a jury."

"Yes, I do see that," Harry said in a small voice. "I didn't realize they'd arrived. Time seemed of the essence."

"I'd say it still is," Kaylock said, biting off each word. "The daemon now has what it came for. A talisman to tear open the veil to the Dominion. To unlock the gates Lady Cumberland and Mr. Lawrence have spent their lives guarding. So it's impressive you solved the little mystery of who killed Julius Sabelline, but I'd say we're in rather a worse position for the knowledge, wouldn't you, Miss Pell?" His gaze raked over John. "How about you, Mr. Weston? Anything to say for yourself?"

John opened his mouth, then flushed red and closed it again. Vivienne and Alec appeared embarrassed at witnessing the dressing-down but as foreign agents, it wasn't their place to interfere. In the end, rescue came from unexpected quarters.

"Oh, leave off, Harland," Orpha Winter snapped. "The girl defied me too. I told her to wait to approach the count and she went ahead and showed up on his doorstep, demanding an interview."

"How did you know—" Harry began. Then she saw Connor edging toward the door. "*You* told her."

"Well, ya never said I shouldn't," he muttered.

Orpha gave Harry an unpleasant smile.

"If you'd only asked him, I wouldn't have had to," Harry said sullenly, feeling like she was eight years old again and Mrs. Rivers had caught her sucking the lemon meringue out of a freshly baked pie with a paper straw.

"I did, foolish girl. More than once." She gave Harry and John an icy look. "I agree that our newest investigators require some reining in, but now isn't the time to do it. At least Miss Pell had the brains to figure out it was Araminta. Without her, we'd be chasing our own tails. Now, I suggest we find out exactly what they've learned, every scrap, and then we can determine a course of action."

Harland Kaylock pursed his thin lips but refrained from comment. Joseph poured everyone brandies except for Connor and Alec Lawrence, who took tea. It was still raining hard outside, blowing in sideways gusts that made a soft hiss against the windows. The others listened in silence as Harry related the series of events at the Sabelline house before the London agents arrived, and how she had deduced that Araminta was the killer.

"She had access to the madu Jackson had borrowed from Count Koháry," Harry said. "He showed us a drawing of one. It's not a large weapon and easily concealed. After the party, she waited for her husband to go to the strongbox. Then she followed him. I do believe she had an altercation in the hall with Mr. Sharpe over the affair. After he stormed off to his office, where he probably had another bottle stashed, she carried out her grisly task."

"And the footprints?" Orpha asked.

"Araminta wore her husband's shoes to throw off the police and keep her own shoes clean. But that meant she had to get rid of them. First she tried hiding them in the air duct, but they wouldn't fit. So she slipped upstairs and placed them in one of the sarcophagi."

"And she lifted the lid alone?" Kaylock asked skeptically.

"Daemons confer superhuman strength on their mortal victims," Alec put in quietly. "I saw it when I encountered Dr. Clarence in Oxford. He nearly bested me."

"What about the eyes?" Orpha asked. "What drove her to such grotesque lengths?"

"She said her husband refused to look when the daemon tried to show him things. I wonder if it didn't seek to possess Julius first," Harry replied. "Everyone we spoke to described him as cold and strong-willed. Perhaps he simply wasn't as susceptible to the magic of the Dominion as Araminta, who was already prone to morbid fancies."

"I remember her exact words," John said, taking a bracing gulp of brandy. "They gave me a chill. *He kept his eyes shut tight. We didn't like that, so we took them.*"

"Dear God." Orpha shook her head. "I wouldn't have thought she had it in her. She always seemed rather mousy. Although I suppose it wasn't Araminta, not really." She idly toyed with an emerald bracelet. "I had no idea daemons could influence a person through their dreams. Fascinating."

"It did the same with Mary Elizabeth Wickes," John said. The spirits had put some color back in his face, which he'd scrubbed clean of blood and soot with a damp towel provided by the butler. "When we visited her at the Tombs, she said she let it through. Something about paying the blood price. Do you know what that is?"

Alec nodded. "There are two ways to open a portal to the Dominion. Talismans like the amulet can unlock a Greater Gate. But a lesser gate can be conjured by shedding the blood of an innocent. It won't stay open long, but even a few seconds is enough if something is waiting on the other side."

"Mary talked the girl in the next cell into cutting open her wrist. It was a few months ago—the same day this daemon possessed Mr. Brady and killed Becky Rickard."

"That would do it, if Mary knew the words of opening."

"So we know how it came through." Harry turned to Orpha. "The count said you told him it was a daemon. That would have been useful information to share."

She looked confused. "But I didn't. I only learned that fact from Mr. Kaylock an hour gone."

Vivienne's eyes narrowed. "Who is this man?"

"He's the last descendant of the House of Habsburg-Koháry in Hungary," Harry replied. "He told us his family has known of the Dominion for generations. That he's fought ghouls."

"I find it strange we've never heard of him."

"Necromancer?" Alec said to Vivienne.

"Possibly." She snicked her lighter open and shut. "But he's not our immediate problem. We need to track down this daemon before we do anything else."

"Are the gates being watched?" Kaylock asked.

"Of course. And none of them are nearby. It will have to take a ship again. And whichever gate it chooses, we'll be ready. Cyrus Ashdown has sent cables to all his agents. They'll come out in force. If the body it takes can be killed before it switches to another, it will be banished back to the Dominion."

"But which gate will he choose?" Kaylock asked. "There are twelve, correct?"

"Yes." Alec ticked them off on his fingers. "One in Afghanistan and another in the ruins of Memphis, Egypt, just south of Giza. Then you have Rome, Damascus, Jerusalem, Babylon, Karnopolis, Samarkand, Athens, Luoyang, China, and Kush, now called Karima in Northern Sudan. And London, of course."

John broke the silence. "Begging your pardon, but are you certain there are only twelve?"

Alec turned to him, mouth quirked in mild amusement. "We've already established that this daemon came through a lesser gate by inducing a human familiar to pay the blood price. But every reference we've ever found to the Greater Gates says there are twelve. Without exception."

"I'm sure you're correct. But just before the daemon started the fire, it was complaining about Claudius Ptolemy. That they'd made some kind of bargain, but Ptolemy betrayed it. And Araminta said, *The thirteenth gate will open.*"

"He's right," Harry said. "I heard it too."

"A thirteenth gate." Alec's eyes narrowed in thought. "I don't suppose either of them was kind enough to say where it was."

Harry and John looked at each other. They both shook their heads.

"What if it's here in New York?" Mr. Kaylock said.

"One we never knew about?" Vivienne asked doubtfully. "Then why isn't the city plagued by ghouls?"

They were all silent for a moment.

"Perhaps it's a new gate," Orpha said. "Would that be possible?"

"I don't know. There's nothing says it couldn't be," Alec said. "The Dominion is a strange place. In many ways, it's alive. Organic. We don't know why the first gates appeared, but it's a fact that they attract human settlements. And New York's a relatively young city."

"The de Lusignan letter we found at Cyrus's said the gate rejected the daemon and wouldn't let it pass," Vivienne pointed out. "That neither blood nor talisman sufficed."

"But if it *was* a new gate, it wouldn't be warded. Or not as strongly as the others."

"Goddess," Vivienne breathed. "A thirteenth gate. The question then is where."

"There's one consistent fact about gates," Alec said. "They're always in water."

"That hardly narrows it down. Manhattan is an island," Kaylock said.

"Still water, not running. Which rules out the rivers and harbor."

"I'll fetch some maps," Kaylock offered.

He returned a short time later and unrolled a large map of the city across his desk. They all crowded around.

"There are two obvious locations," Kaylock said. "The reservoirs in Central Park and on Forty-First Street."

"But they're manmade, aren't they?" Alec said. "Gates are always in natural water sources. The one in London is beneath the lake in Hyde Park. In Rome, it's a pond in the Villa Borghese. And so on."

"Wait. I'll fetch the 1874 Viele map." Kaylock dashed off. He returned a minute later with a long rectangular map that showed the topographical features of the city. "Egbert Viele used surveys and historical maps to reconstruct the original hydrology of Manhattan Island. It's become absolutely indispensable for building engineers. They call it the 'water map.'"

It was hand-drawn in exquisite detail, with shaded lines to illustrate the island's original contours. Most of the map was colored in hues of tan and green, but a few splotches of blue indicated water. Harry easily recognized the twin squares in Central Park labelled *Receiving Reservoir*. At Fifth Avenue and One Hundred and Sixth Street, a river snaked east from the edge of the park. The orderly grid of streets and avenues had been superimposed over the natural features, creating the impression of a phantom world of marshes and meadows now displaced by bricks and cobblestones.

"What's that?" Vivienne pointed to an unmarked blue splash on the map only a few blocks from the S.P.R. offices.

"The old Collect Pond," Kaylock said. "It was drained and filled in eighty years ago."

"What's there's now?"

Harry and John looked at each other, eyes widening. "The Tombs," they said in unison.

John slapped his forehead. "Of course! It's where it all began. The prison is only a few blocks from the flat on Leonard Street where Becky Rickard was murdered. Mary Elizabeth Wickes said she'd brought something through. What if it wasn't through a lesser gate but one of the Greater Gates?"

"And that gate is somewhere in the prison itself," Harry finished. "I have to say, it does fit the facts."

"Tell me about this Wickes woman." Alec leaned forward. "Mr. Kaylock said she was a poisoner."

"Yes. She murdered children with arsenic, beginning when she was only sixteen."

"Such a person might well be susceptible to dark communications from the Dominion," Orpha Winter said in a theatrical whisper. "The spirit world is only visible to those with *sensitivities*. Many mediums are no strangers to traumatic death. If Mary was already corrupt, she would have attracted the most dangerous entities that roam the shadowlands."

John nodded fervently. Mr. Kaylock examined his fingernails as though they were the most fascinating thing he'd ever seen.

"By all accounts, Mary was sane when they first brought her to the Tombs—or as sane as a repeat killer of children can be," Harry said. "A jury thought so. They found her accountable for her actions and sentenced her to hang. But when we visited her, she seemed to have been driven half mad. She rambled about the master, just like Araminta."

"But if the Collect Pond was drained, how can there be a gate?" Connor asked. He'd been listening quietly from the shadows.

"Gates persist no matter what people build over them," Vivienne explained. "They can't be destroyed, only warded. If there truly is a Greater Gate at the Tombs, I promise you it will be standing in water somehow."

Alec used his cane to push himself to his feet. It was an oddly graceful gesture.

"We must go immediately," he said. "The daemon might start with the gate here, but I've no doubt he'll try to open all of them. And I don't have to tell you how disastrous that would be." He looked at Harry and John. "Speaking personally, I find you both to be highly competent agents."

Harry flushed at the praise. John straightened his collar.

"Would you be willing to take us there?" Alec continued. "If you visited Mary once before, it might make it easier to get inside."

"Of course," John said immediately. Harry nodded her agreement.

"I would only ask that you let Lady Cumberland and myself deal with this creature when we find it."

"Understood."

Vivienne swept a hand across her skirts and produced a wicked-looking dagger, which she examined and then caused to vanish. A moment later, it had been replaced with another. Harry watched in fascination as the process was repeated several times. She realized Vivienne had sewn secret compartments all over her gown. They must have been designed by an expert seamstress, as nothing unusual was visible when she moved. Finally, Lady Cumberland seemed satisfied that her armory was in good working order.

"How will you proceed?" Mr. Kaylock asked.

"We corner this daemon in whatever body's it's taken and cut its head off," she said, heading for the door. "If that doesn't work, Alec and I will drag it through the gate and hand it over to the Shepherds."

"Shepherds?" John asked, hurrying to keep up.

"The creatures that keep order in the Dominion. They herd the dead along to their final destination and have no fondness for souls who try to return to the living world."

Harry and John's coats had been lost in the fire, so Orpha Winter found a pair of blankets they could wrap around themselves for the short ride. Harry wished she had her pistol, but that too had been left at the Sabellines. John's gift had only lasted three days, she thought ruefully.

"Count Koháry said you have another key," John said to Alec

as they waited for Connor to bring the carriage around. "Is it true?"

"Yes. I always thought mine was the only one in existence."

"May I see it?"

Alec slipped a hand in his pocket and pulled out a smooth grey stone. "It may not look like much, but it's a powerful talisman. We've used it to close all twelve of the Greater Gates. And I can use it to lock the thirteenth as well if we don't manage to get the amulet."

Darker striations made a whirling pattern on its surface. They bent the eye in a queer fashion. John found himself looking away after only a few seconds.

"Makes one dizzy," he said with an uneasy laugh.

"Most talismans have that effect."

"How is it used?"

"Words can be spoken, but they aren't strictly necessary. Incantations are merely a tool to focus the will of the user. The only thing that matters is that one has the spark." He slipped it back into his pocket. "Very few mortals can wield talismans, Mr. Weston. One in a thousand, perhaps less than that now."

The carriage jolted to a stop before them on the deserted street. Connor leapt down and opened the door for Lady Vivienne. Harry went next, then John and Alec.

Orpha Winter and Harland Kaylock huddled under umbrellas at the curb. Before closing the carriage door, Mr. Kaylock leaned in and gave them each a brusque nod.

"Good luck," he said, his black eyes resting on Harry and John. "Particularly you two. Despite any prior lapses of judgment, you're quite valuable to this organization. And I'd say your nine lives are nearly used up."

CHAPTER 25

That a portal to the underworld existed beneath Manhattan's most notorious prison made a strange kind of sense, Harry reflected as the carriage raced east on Fulton Street.

She'd read enough local history to know that the Collect Pond had been a focal point of human misery for quite some time. One of the first gallows in New York was erected on an island there by the British before the war for independence. As the city grew, it became a convenient receptacle for waste from factories and tanneries. When the pond (not surprisingly) turned into a breeding ground for disease, it was filled in and transformed into the worst slum in America: The Five Points.

Now she understood why the tenement buildings leaned so drunkenly against each other as they sank into the muddy, uneven streets. Apparently, the underground spring that fed the Collect Pond continued to flow. And something else had emerged there. Something even worse than the cesspool that lay above.

At Broadway, the carriage turned north and passed City Hall Park, where Harry and John had stumbled over the entrance to Brady's lair in the Beach Transit Tunnel. In fact, most of the key locations of the Hyde case were within walking distance of each other—and of the Tombs prison.

Though full dark had fallen on the city, the unseasonably warm weather was only intensifying. It rained like a monsoon now, utterly cockeyed for the end of December. Water rushed and ran, dripped and drummed. The sewers overflowed, turning the streets into a dirty brown morass. By the time they arrived at the Tombs, water lapped at the bottom steps of the entrance. Connor let them out, then moved the horses down to the corner to wait.

The massive front doors were locked tight and repeated pounding failed to rouse any guards. In fact, there was no one in sight at all, though lights burned in the upper windows of the fortress-like structure.

Alec closed his eyes and pressed a palm against the door. A look of concentration sharpened his features. Heavy tumblers spun. He dropped his arm and pushed. The door silently swung open.

John gave a low whistle. "That's a neat trick. Another of your special talents, Mr. Lawrence?"

Alec smiled briefly and went inside. A deep, quiet chill greeted them beyond the threshold. The usual rustles and mutters of more than fifty women were completely absent.

"Where are all the guards?" Harry wondered aloud.

"And where are the inmates?" John added.

Alec and Vivienne exchanged a quick glance.

"We'd better find Sister Emily," Harry said. "She's the matron in charge of the women's prison. The offices are on the Centre Street side."

"It may be too late for that," Vivienne said. "Where's Mary's cell?"

Harry pointed to the left. "That way. The other side is Bummer's Hall, where they put the vagrants and drunks."

They started down the long corridor leading to the Leonard

Street wing of the Tombs. Water condensed on the stone walls and coursed down like blood from an open wound. The prison had been bad enough during the day, Harry thought, with the smell of unwashed bodies and sounds of soft weeping. But this perfect silence was much worse.

They'd just reached the end of the first tier when Sister Emily strode around the corner. She gave a short gasp of surprise when she saw them, one hand flying to her mouth.

"Miss Pell! However did you get in here?" She glared at Vivienne and Alec. "And who are these people?"

"Lady Vivienne Cumberland and Mr. Alec Lawrence," Harry said, ignoring the first question. "Mr. Lawrence is with Scotland Yard."

"Scotland Yard?" The matron blinked in confusion.

"We need to know if anyone's come to visit Mary Elizabeth Wickes today," Alec said in the calm but forceful tone he'd heard D.I. Blackwood use on reluctant witnesses. "Someone claiming to be a relative? A grandmother, perhaps?"

"No, and I wouldn't let her in if she had," Sister Emily said briskly. "Visiting hours are long past. I can't imagine who'd be out on a night like this anyway." She squinted at them with suspicion. "The water's been rising steadily for the last several hours. All the women have been moved up to the boys' reformatory on the second tier." She sighed. "All except Mary. She hissed and spat like a wildcat when anyone tried to get near. I suppose I shouldn't care, she'll be dead in six days anyhow and no one will mourn her passing. But I thought I'd check on the girl. Most likely I'll have to send some guards from the men's wing to move her by force."

"Is she still in her cell?" Harry asked.

"She's in there all right. Won't budge." Matron shook her head. "You'll have to go now. Come back tomorrow during visiting hours if you must speak to her."

"That won't do," Alec said. "I'll give you $500 right now for five minutes with your prisoner."

He removed a roll of bills from his coat pocket and held it out. Harry wondered if Orpha had given him the cash for precisely this eventuality.

The matron's mouth dropped open. When she realized she was gaping, she shut it with a click. It was an exorbitant sum, possibly more than she earned in a year. Still, she hesitated. *The woman has a decent heart*, Harry thought.

"Why would you offer me such?" she demanded. "What do you want with Mary? I'm not defending her crimes, but she was convicted by a jury and the State of New York will carry out the sentence those men handed down. If it's vigilante justice you're after, I can't oblige."

"We've no desire to do Mary any harm," Vivienne assured her. "Only to ask her a few questions. You can stay outside the cell if you like."

The matron considered this, her eyes fixed on the money. She licked her lips. "All right. Are the lot of you going?"

"No." Vivienne cut a look at Harry and John. "Those two will wait in your office."

Harry bit her tongue. She didn't like being relegated to the sidelines, but she'd made a promise and Lady Vivienne obviously wasn't a woman to cross.

"We'd best be about it then," the matron said, tucking the cash into her dress. "Water's rising."

HARRY AND JOHN took seats on the hard wooden chairs before Sister Emily's desk and settled in to wait. The room was tiny, with a battered wardrobe occupying the rest of the space. A plain wooden crucifix on the wall completed the décor.

"Do you think it's a coincidence the weather seems to have gone insane?" she asked.

"I thought you didn't believe in coincidences."

"Generally speaking, I don't."

"And now?"

She shifted in the chair. "I can feel it, John. Something's wrong and this place is at the heart of it."

He studied her. "You've changed. I can't imagine you saying that a week ago."

"What do you mean?"

"Listening to your gut."

Harry smiled. "Myrtle despises hunches, intuition—whatever you want to call it. If it can't be observed, it's irrelevant."

"And yet she accepts the existence of ghouls."

"Yes. She said one of them almost ate Queen Victoria."

"You're not serious."

"It's a new world, John—to us, at least. I wonder what Myrtle would think of Mr. Lawrence. All this talk of talismans and special abilities. What they really mean is magic." She sighed. "I'm certain you had a cracked skull, John. I *heard* it when Araminta bashed you on the head."

He rubbed a spot above his ear. Blood still stained his collar, though thankfully Sister Emily hadn't noticed in the dim light of the corridor.

"I just remember the look on her face, Harry. Like she was squashing an insect."

"The point is you might never have woken up. Mr. Lawrence did something. I've no idea how. But did you notice that he and Lady Cumberland wear matching gold bracelets?"

"No. Your eyes were always sharper."

"I don't think she can work magic. Only him. She's deferred to Mr. Lawrence on that score every time. But there's a connection between them that runs deeper than the S.P.R."

"Another gut feeling?" John smiled. "No, I get that impression too. You can see it in the way they look at each other. I'm just glad they're here. They know what they're about."

"I wonder what's happening in Mary's cell." Harry shivered in the damp. "Do you think we ought to—"

"My God, this prison is leaky as a sieve," John exclaimed. "Do you hear that dripping? It's driving me half-mad."

Harry cocked her head. "Faintly."

John paced to the wardrobe and pressed his ear against the wood. He tried the knob but it was locked.

"John." Harry pointed to the bottom right corner of the wardrobe. A red stain oozed from under the door.

John swore and kicked it hard. Once…twice. On the third try, the door popped open. Harry screamed as the body of the old woman tumbled out. She landed on her back, eyes staring glassily at the ceiling. Though her sagging skin had already turned grey, John pressed a finger against her neck. He waited a moment, then shook his head.

"Superficial bullet wound on the arm," he said, quickly examining the body. "You did graze her, Harry. But cause of death is a stab wound to the back. A long, tapered wound, just like Julius Sabelline."

"So she did come to the Tombs and someone murdered her," Harry said in puzzlement. "But why?"

"Perhaps because the daemon didn't want that body anymore," John replied slowly. "It shed her like a snake sheds its skin."

Harry's eyes widened. "And moved on—"

"To Sister Emily."

They stared at each other.

"Ah, Christ," John said.

VIVIENNE FOLLOWED the matron down the long, empty corridor.

Alec limped at her side, the familiar sound of his cane clacking on the stone. The gate had to be here somewhere. Even if it was still warded, it would be visible. She knew what to look for. And yet the signs weren't there.

"Is there a lower level to the prison?" she asked Sister Emily, who strode purposefully ahead, her black skirts swishing against the slick floor.

"Oh no, the water table is much too high. It was built on top of marshland, you know. They drained it to lay the foundation, but the damp tends to seep back in, especially in weather like this. The city's forever sending in masons and carpenters to shore it up." She glanced at them over her shoulder. "The prison itself sits on a platform of hemlock logs. It's been sinking into the muck since a few months after they built it, which was nigh on fifty years ago."

Vivienne nodded, only half listening. She would have guessed the gate lay somewhere beneath their feet. Mary would know exactly where it was. But if she didn't....

"What if we're wrong?" she whispered to Alec. "What if this daemon is on the other side of the city, in some other location, opening the gate right now?"

"We're not wrong." His eyes glowed green like a cat's in the semi-darkness. "Can't you feel it? Power is gathering in this place."

Vivienne couldn't sense such things the way Alec did, but if he said they were in the vicinity of a Greater Gate, she believed him. And she could feel the temperature dropping as they made their way deeper into the prison. At first, it was perceptible only as a growing chill in her bones. But then Vivienne realized she could see her breath, pluming like white fog. And the gas jets illuminated not condensation on the stone walls, but a thin veneer of ice.

"Here we are." Sister Emily stopped before a cell door. "Ask your questions quickly." She shivered and rubbed her arms. "It's colder'n the bottom of the sea down here and I have a nice cup of hot onion soup waiting for me upstairs."

She unlocked the cell and opened the door. Alec and Vivienne stood still, startled into silence by what they saw inside.

Glacial blue ice coated every surface. It stabbed down from the ceiling in sharp fangs and formed thick ridges along the walls that gleamed like glass. Vivienne let out a foggy breath and half-expected the moisture to tinkle into ice shards on the ground. The corridor was cold, but the air in the cell had to be thirty degrees colder.

Mary sat on a cot, knees drawn up to her chest. The sheet and blanket lay in a tangle beneath her, drooping down over the sides of the rusty frame. She wore only a thin nightgown. Her hair had come unpinned and hung across her face in a stringy, ice-coated curtain. She seemed oblivious to their presence.

"You see?" Sister Emily said, a hint of exasperation in her voice. "I told you she was having one of her spells. I doubt you'll get much from her that makes any sense." She squinted into the cell. "Goodness, it's like the frozen wastes of the far north in there. We'll have to move her upstairs straight away once you're done."

Vivienne took a step inside, watching Mary the way one might a viper drowsing on a flat rock.

"Let me speak to her first," she told Alec quietly, one hand slipping into the fold of her dress where she kept a six-inch iron blade. The memory of Dr. William Clarence luring the guard at Greymoor into his cell by pretending to be catatonic—or harmless, at least—was still fresh in Vivienne's mind.

"The boy didn't want to take his medicine," Mary muttered in a rapid monotone, the words running together without pause. "Said it gave him hot needles in his bowels. How he cried. She had to hide it in the porridge. She promised him extra sugar and he finally ate it, the greedy thing." She shook her head, dark hair whipping around her face in stiff pieces. "Puked it up, he did. She had to clean the bedclothes before the mother came back. Mary takes care of them, the dirty little angels. She holds them tight as they go."

Vivienne swallowed her distaste for the creature on the cot. "Mary," she said. "Look at me."

"A miracle, it's a God-blessed miracle, how Mary nurses them back to health." Her voice took on an edge of childish glee. "How they adore her. She has all the power, doesn't she? They're too stupid to see the truth. Just like Mother."

Vivienne could hear the subtle change in emphasis immediately. Not *the mother*, but Mother.

"Too stupid to see what Father does while she's dreaming her laudanum dreams. Too weak to care. So Mary bakes them a nice apple cake. Such a good, thoughtful daughter."

Dear God, Vivienne thought. "Where's your master, Mary?"

The girl hugged her knees tighter, as if trying to fold in on herself. "When he came through, she smelled the blood of the gate. Sharp, like a woman's womb."

"Where is the gate?" Vivienne's temper snapped. She leaned down and shook her. "Where?"

Mary's hair flew out of her face. Vivienne recoiled at the hollow eyes that stared up like bruises. Blank and yet shiny with terror.

"The devil is real. The devil is real. The devil is—"

"This is getting us nowhere." Alec laid a hand on Vivienne's arm and drew her back. "We'll have to search the prison top to bottom."

"I hope we're not too late. I think—"

Urgent shouts rang out in the corridor. Vivienne spun around just in time to register a blur aimed at her head. She ducked and it whistled past. Sister Emily bared her teeth in a savage grin. She slashed again and Vivienne felt a stinging pain across her forearm. Something jutted from the matron's fist. It almost looked like it had grown horns....

The madu. Vivienne had one in her own collection. Metal-tipped blackbuck antlers designed for goring an opponent. Nasty, but no match for a skilled swordsman like Alec.

Out of the corner of her eye, she saw the New York agents splashing toward her down the corridor. Icy water surged around her shoes as the flood surpassed the top step of the entrance and poured into the prison. Vivienne could no longer deny the magic of the Dominion at work, pushing outward like a bubble of darkness. The gas jets flickered.

She whipped her knife out, the weight reassuring in her palm. Alec stepped smoothly between her and Sister Emily, who crouched against the opposite cell, wearing that fixed grin. Vivienne held his power tight through the bond. He couldn't work the elements—it was too dangerous—but he would still have his strength and speed.

Vivienne almost smiled. The daemon was cornered now. It had been foolish to show itself. She didn't know how Miss Pell and Mr. Weston had figured out it was hiding inside the matron, but she and Alec would banish it back to where it came from. When they fought together, it was like one mind in two bodies. Nothing from the shadowlands could stand before them.

Alec flicked the catch on his cane and bared his sword. Vivienne knew he meant to take its head, and she felt a moment's pity for Sister Emily. When Vivienne was young, she'd faced similar creatures called wights. Once they entered a person, there was no saving them.

Alec tossed the cane-sheath aside. Then he spoke to the daemon in some old, musty dialect of Tuscany.

"I' vegno per menarvi a l'altra riva ne le tenebre etterne, in caldo e 'n gelo."

I come to carry you to the other shore.

Into the eternal darkness. Into fire and into ice.

Vivienne thought it might have been a line by Dante Alighieri.

She didn't read many books, but she'd always enjoyed *The Divine Comedy*.

The daemon's lip curled. Its voice was the rasp of steel on leather.

"I've been waiting for you, *daēva*."

Miss Pell and Mr. Weston had stopped a short way down the corridor. Vivienne flung out an arm to signal they shouldn't come any closer. Before her eyes, the ice crept outward from Mary's cell, coating the door and walls. She moved cautiously to the right, flanking the daemon so it couldn't escape.

The next events happened both terribly fast and with the inertia of nightmare. Alec raised his sword, poised on the balls of his feet. Sister Emily feinted an attack, but he was ready, sweeping it in a lateral stroke that grazed her collarbone. Alec was bringing the sword back around when her left hand shot out and grabbed the blade, heedless of how it bit into the flesh of her palms. Then she threw herself on the sword, forcing her way toward the hilt. Too late, Vivienne had an inkling of what it intended.

"Drop your blade!" she screamed, rushing forward.

Alec tried, but he was pinned against the stone wall. The daemon grasped the sides of his head, thumbs pressed against his eyelids to hold them open. A foot of iron jutted from Sister Emily's back, but still she wormed her way forward until they were close enough to kiss. Vivienne saw something flash between them, dark as midnight. It all took seconds. Alec's eyes rolled back in his head, mouth falling open in a silent scream.

As Vivienne reached them, both Alec and Sister Emily collapsed to the ground.

"Dear God." Miss Pell ran up. "Is he hurt?"

She moved to crouch down beside Alec but Vivienne grabbed her arm.

"Don't touch him." Her voice nearly broke.

They stood over Alec and Sister Emily, limbs twined together in a macabre embrace. Red water swirled around the two motionless figures. Sister Emily lay on her side, still impaled on Alec's sword. The falcon hilt pressed against her black dress just above the navel. Alec's face looked peaceful, as if he had simply fallen asleep, but Vivienne imagined she felt something. Clammy fingers brushing their bond.

She pointed to the sword and John Weston nodded gravely. She would try to pull it out. Her mind wanted to spin in circles. *One thing at a time. Get his sword. Cut off that thing's head.* She would deal with the rest afterwards.

Vivienne knelt down, water soaking her skirts. Sister Emily still gripped the madu in one hand. If the New York agents hadn't shouted a warning, it would be embedded in her throat.

Vivienne reached for the weapon, her mouth dry as dust. She pried Sister Emily's fingers loose from the crossbar and tossed it away. The matron's eyes were open and glassy, her pupils dilated so far the irises appeared black. The current tugged at her hair. Vivienne placed her right hand on the hilt of Alec's sword. She began to slide it free. Blood flowed from the wound and Miss Pell made a muffled choking sound, one hand clamped over her mouth.

"Is it dead?" Mr. Weston whispered.

"No," Vivienne replied. "We'd know. A lesser gate would open to claim it."

Alec lay on his side, right arm pinned beneath the shoulder. His left hand was curled into a loose fist, the fingers perfectly still. Vivienne could feel his heart beating. He faced Sister Emily, their foreheads only inches apart. Vivienne slid the blade past his hip. It was halfway out now.

"You shouldn't be here," she said to her fellow agents. "It's too dangerous. I don't know—"

She frowned as the sword caught on bone. Vivienne tugged harder.

Alec's eyes flew open.

Before she could draw a breath, he sprang to his feet. His left leg buckled slightly, then jerked straight. Vivienne backed away, scanning his face for any sign. All the shared sensations she normally felt through the bond vanished.

"Go, my lovely," he said.

For a moment, Vivienne thought he was talking to *her*. Then she realized the words had been directed over her shoulder.

Mary. She'd kept so quiet, they'd forgotten all about her.

Quick as a ferret, the girl darted through the open door of her cell. A pale hand delved into the neck of Sister Emily's dress and fished out a gold object on a chain. Mary gave a hard yank and the chain snapped.

"She's got the amulet!" Vivienne cried, unwilling to take her eyes from Alec for more than a second.

The New York agents dashed after Mary, faces grim. Vivienne expected the girl to make a run down the corridor, but she retreated back to her cot. Mary dragged it aside, revealing a wide crevice beneath that had been concealed by the nest of blankets. Water poured into the lightless crack. Mary dropped to hands and knees. A moment later she was gone.

John crossed the tiny cell in two strides. Without hesitation, he turned sideways and lowered himself into the hole.

"Mr. Weston!"

He looked back over his shoulder.

"Take this."

Vivienne threw one of her iron blades down and kicked it across the floor. John's hand shot out and grasped it by the hilt. He gave her a terse nod, then dropped into the crevice.

With a heartfelt curse, Miss Pell followed.

CHAPTER 26

Harry trailed her hands along the rough stone walls of the fissure as they descended into the earth, feeling her way through the blackness. Water poured down from the flooded prison above. It soaked through her clothing and sent her into fits of shivering. She'd always hated tight spaces. The hole Mary had bolted into was less than two feet in diameter, like a sloping, ruggedly hewn mineshaft. Harry could barely stand upright and the ceiling lowered the deeper they went. The first stirrings of panic scratched like a trapped animal in the back of her mind.

It could be worse. To get into the Beach Tunnel where Brady held poor Billy Flynn, I had to wiggle on my belly like an eel.

This thought did little to reassure her. In fact, it had the opposite effect. The memory of that terrible crawl through a ventilation shaft under City Hall Park brought back all the old feelings of helplessness and confinement. The certainty that she and John would die in some dark pit came back in full force. At least she'd had an idea where the other shaft went. This one could lead to the center of the earth for all she knew.

Stop it, Harry. You're not alone. John's just ahead. He was always more brave than sensible, but he'd probably say the same about you.

"John," she called in a hoarse whisper. "Wait for me."

"I'm just here, Harry," he replied, his voice much closer than she expected. A pause. "Are you doing all right?"

He knew about her claustrophobia. Stubborn pride steadied her voice. That, and the thought of her sister Myrtle, who didn't seem afraid of anything.

"Oh, yes," she said with false cheer. "Don't worry about me. Is Mary still up ahead?"

"I think so. I can see a faint glow. It must be the amulet."

Harry swallowed. "Where could she be going?"

"Not a clue. But it can't be much farther. We'll hit bedrock eventually."

It was too dark to see much of anything. The crevice jigged left and then right, taking a steep angle that gradually leveled out. Harry wished for a lantern, although perhaps it was better not to see too clearly what sort of Hell they were descending into—figurative and possibly literal. After some minutes, she felt a whisper of air against her skin that signified a larger space.

Far ahead, a spark of light bobbed unsteadily in the darkness.

"John," she hissed. "I see her."

"Watch your footing," he warned from somewhere off to the right. "It's squishy."

As if to confirm this statement, she heard a wet sucking sound.

"Damn," John muttered. "I think I just lost my shoe."

Harry took a step and felt her feet slide on some slick, slightly curved surface. She windmilled her arms like a drunken tightrope walker. One of them struck John, who gave a soft grunt of surprise.

"What are we standing on?" she whispered once she'd regained her balance. "It feels strange."

"Logs, I think," he replied in a low voice. "Must be the foundation of the building. Try to stay on top of them, the stuff beneath is worse."

Their voices sounded very small in the cavernous blackness.

"What is this place?"

"I don't know, Harry." He groped for her hand and gave it a squeeze.

"Poor Mr. Lawrence," she said bitterly.

John was silent for a moment. "He'd want us to go on. To get the amulet back."

"I know." Harry squeezed his hand back. "Let's keep going then."

The great logs made for treacherous walking. Some were planted firmly in the mud of what must once have been Collect Pond, but others had a tendency to shift when one put weight on them. Several times, Harry nearly sprained an ankle when her foot slipped into the cracks between the logs. With the water up to her knees, the going was slow. But she had the satisfaction of knowing that Mary faced similar difficulties. Every so often, the glow of the amulet would suddenly dip down and she would hear a muffled curse.

I hope she breaks a leg, Harry thought darkly.

The walls receded into pitch darkness, but Harry realized she could see the rough outlines of things. Stone pillars rose out of the muck, slimy and dark with age. Around them swirled a thick white mist. It had swallowed Mary without a trace.

"We're losing her, John," Harry hissed.

She tried to go faster and immediately slipped on a patch of rotten wood. Harry threw out a hand to catch her fall, but she still cracked her knee on the trunk. Pain lanced through the joint.

"Drat," she muttered, tears stinging her eyes.

"Are you all right?"

"No, but I'll live." Harry clenched her teeth and used John's offered hand to pull herself up.

They continued on. The mist grew denser, brushing chill tendrils along her cheeks.

"Mary Elizabeth Wickes!" John shouted.

The rough stone walls threw his voice back in mocking echoes. Harry thought she heard a faint peal of laughter from somewhere ahead in the mists. She didn't wish to go a single step further, but she knew John would never turn back now. He'd always had a surplus of physical courage—the result of growing up with four rowdy brothers—but it wasn't just that. John had an innate decency that wouldn't permit him to let someone like Mary run loose in the world. And, Harry thought with a mental sigh, she supposed she did too.

As they moved forward, the mists parted slightly, revealing patches of dark, still water. Harry began to have the unpleasant sensation of being in two places superimposed one over the other. The pillars stood sentinel over the cavern like a forest of petrified trees. But at the very edge of vision she glimpsed another, even stranger landscape. Colorless reeds swayed in an invisible current. She turned her head and they vanished like distant stars, but part of her felt certain she stood on an abyssal plane that stretched into dimness in all directions. Her inner ear tilted dizzyingly.

"Do you feel it, John?" she whispered.

He nodded. "Keep your eyes straight ahead. It seems to help."

They kept going, picking their way across the platform of decaying logs. The water rose to Harry's waist. She couldn't see the surface at all now through the layer of mist, which only contributed to the creepy-crawly feeling that unseen things moved in the subterranean pond.

"What is that, John?" Harry whispered.

At first it was just a dark blur. But then the outline resolved itself into two vertical wooden beams connected by a crosspiece. A noose dangled from the center of the scaffold. Mary sat on a small platform beneath. Water lapped at its edges, making hollow echoing sounds that immediately made Harry think of the raft at her grandmother's lake house in the Catskills. Harry used to swim out to it and bask like a turtle when they visited in the summers.

"It's pretty Mr. Weston," Mary said in a sing-song voice. "Come to watch me swing?"

The bizarre tableaux stopped them in their tracks. Harry wondered if it was truly real, but she could see the grain of the wood, smell the fresh sawdust. A bit of Mary's skirt had caught on a nail that hadn't been pounded in all the way.

"Or perhaps it will be *you* who takes the final step into air," Mary said. "The abyss is always waiting for the unwary."

She stared at Harry as she said this, her eyes dark and unknowable.

"It's not too late, Mary." John took a step forward. "Don't let that creature use you. It's not your master unless you allow it to be."

Mary turned the amulet in her hands. It glowed with a sickly green light. The wet nightgown clung to her thin body. Harry could see the tendons in her neck, taut as bowstrings.

"I told you the dead will walk," she said, her feet swinging back and forth, heels drumming on the platform. "My dear little angels will come back to their Mary. Would you like to meet them?"

She paused as if awaiting an answer. Harry felt ill. A shiver worked its way up from deep in her bones. She could barely remember a time when she'd felt warm and dry. It seemed another lifetime.

"I've always liked children." Mary scratched her lank hair. "Don't know why I did it. The excitement, I suppose. Poor, unloved creatures. If their parents had cared, I might have spared them, but no one did, not really. No one but me. I always held them as they crossed over. The fluttering heart. The little sigh. It was a lovely thing."

She studied the gallows above her head. "This would have

been my end if the master hadn't come. A cruel fate. But if I serve him faithfully, I need never die. Not ever."

"He promised the same to Araminta Sabelline," Harry said quietly. "Before he killed her."

Mary frowned, turning the amulet over and over in her hands.

"You wanted to make amends," John said. "That's why you wrote to Julius Sabelline."

A tic contorted her face. "It was a mistake. But *that* Mary is gone now. She was always weak and timid. I made her take a dose of her own medicine." She gave a sly smile. "Would you like a nice cup of hot chocolate, Mr. Weston? I'll put cinnamon in it. No one makes hot chocolate like Mary does."

"No games." He'd been steadily moving towards her. "Give me back the amulet and we'll help you. You said your everlasting soul couldn't be saved, but it's not true. You can still end this before it's too late."

"But it is, Mr. Weston." She smiled sweetly. "The gate is already open, you see."

The mist shivered like a candle guttering in a draft of air. The undulating reeds in the corners of Harry's vision grew more solid. More real. This was the sea of her dream, she realized. The Dominion. Not hellfire but someplace cold and dark.

Mary tilted her head. "They're coming." She grinned, but there was an uncertain edge to it. "They loved their Mary. You'll see."

"John," Harry hissed. "I think we should...."

She trailed off as the mist slowly peeled away from the gallows. Little ripples marred the still surface of the pond. The air thickened. An oppressive feeling of dread stole over Harry, as paralyzing as the night terrors. Mary seemed to feel it too, for her gaze darted around.

Something was moving under the water. Harry couldn't see it, but she felt faint pressure as it brushed against her skirts. The temperature dropped sharply. Mary's breath streamed out in white bursts. Her eyes grew huge in her face.

"The master promised," she muttered. "He *promised*. The children can't be angry at Mary. She was only helping them." She clutched her belly, as if at a sudden pain. "Mustn't hold a grudge now. Mary's let you out of the cold place. She knows how *hungry* the poor dears must be. She'll feed you well. Help you grow strong again."

Harry gave a little shriek as a white face flashed in the depths, there and gone in an instant.

Mary swallowed. She raised a trembling hand to head. It came away with a hank of hair. She examined it blankly for a moment. "Perhaps best to close the gate," she whispered. "I promised the master, but—"

She started to scoot backward from the edge of the gallows when a small, pale fist closed around her ankle. It had dirty black nails shaped like fishhooks. They dug into the skin. Mary's eyes bugged out as a thin line of blood trickled down her foot.

Harry's tongue froze to the roof of her mouth. Her legs felt numb. She watched, transfixed, as more hands seized hold of Mary's skirts, dragging her into the water. Mary clung to the edge, nails raking the wood, hoarse cries coming from her throat. The amulet fell from her hand.

John lurched forward, trying to catch it, but he was too far away. The moment the talisman touched the water, suffocating blackness fell on the cavern.

Mary screamed a final time. It became a watery gurgle as her head went under.

Then all was still.

CHAPTER 27

Vivienne backed out of the cell, her attention fixed on Alec Lawrence.

Except it wasn't Alec. Not anymore.

How foolish she'd been to think the bond protected them. Maybe the daemon hadn't taken him on the tower in Oxford because it didn't have sufficient time. She'd interrupted it. Or maybe it was simply playing its own game. Either way, they'd made a fatal miscalculation. Now she faced something new.

A daēva with a daemon inside.

She could feel it leaking through their bond like a sickness. An ancient, evil intelligence. Vivienne's skin crawled. If Alec was there, she couldn't find him. But she refused to admit he was dead. If she did, she knew it would break her.

The daemon grinned with Alec's mouth and Vivienne felt a hatred so pure, it was like freedom.

Fight filthy. There aren't rules anymore. All that's done now.

So Vivienne did something she'd never done in all the years they were bonded. Something she'd never even contemplated because it was so morally indefensible. She sent a white-hot lance of pain through the cuff.

Only the human of the pair had the power to do that. It was the way one administered punishment to a disobedient daēva and it should have knocked Alec to his knees. Sent him writhing on the ground in agony. But his face remained smooth. Unreadable.

Not possible.

"You can't hurt us," he said. Wet hair was plastered across his forehead in dark clumps. His face looked the same, yet the lines of it were alien somehow. "Well, I suppose you can hurt *him*. But your tricks won't work with me."

The sound of his voice was a knife in her heart. Still well-educated, faintly accented but with no definable nationality. A voice made for laughter and poetry and bad jokes.

"What is it you want?" she snarled, backing away to give herself room.

Alec's eyes tracked her, a leopard stalking a mouse.

"We want our power back," he said.

She snorted. "Do you take me for a complete idiot?"

"It's ours."

"No, it's not. It's *his*."

The power belonged to Alec. It had always belonged to Alec. The cuffs themselves were a remnant of a dark period in human history when the daēvas had been forced recruits in a war with the undead. Now Vivienne was just grateful she still held his leash. Alec was stronger and faster, but at least he couldn't tear her apart with air or make her blood boil.

She backed down the corridor, empty, locked cells to either side. The gas jets flickered fitfully. She wondered how long it would be before they failed.

Daēvas could see in the darkness like cats.

"We always loved you," Alec said, slowly approaching as Vivienne backed away. His arms hung at his sides, deceptively loose. She knew he could strike faster than she could blink. "But you know that, don't you?"

"There is no *we*," she said. "You're just some dead thing that won't admit it's dead."

"We were your faithful hound and you kicked us in the ribs."

"Shut the bloody hell up!"

Vivienne switched the sword to her left hand and wiped cold sweat from her palm on her dress. She switched it back to her right hand. The daemon had her over a barrel and they both knew it. Even if she miraculously found an opening, she couldn't kill him. She'd be killing Alec. Maybe Alec was already dead, but maybe he wasn't. Maybe there still was a way to save him. She didn't know. And as long as there was any chance at all, she wouldn't risk it. A hopeless situation.

"Poor crippled hound," he said, fingers trailing along the bars.

"Alec was never a cripple."

"That's a matter of opinion. I feel his pain, Tijah. Or should I call you Vivienne now?"

"I don't give a toss what you call me."

"Oh, I think you do." He grinned. "You hurt us. Took a piece of us and trapped it in the cuffs. What does that make you, Tijah?"

Vivienne said nothing. She was watching the daemon's hands.

It's an interesting thing to fight at a man's side for centuries. You learn all his secrets. All his tells. And she knew Alec's left ring finger would twitch just before he attacked.

"Is he alive?" she asked, to buy time. She didn't expect an honest answer.

"Oh, he's here somewhere." As if Alec was a misplaced sock. "I have his memories. All the way back to the day you camped with Alexander's army on the shores of the lake in Bactria. You ran from him. Do you remember that, Tijah?"

She did. Alec—Achaemenes then—had healed her. He'd also wanted her desperately and she'd almost lost herself in that desire. It wasn't a memory she cared to dredge up.

"Who knew the undead could be *so* feckin' tedious?" she asked.

Alec's expression darkened. He removed his jacket and threw it to the side. Another familiar gesture she'd seen a thousand times. Vivienne kept her face smooth but her gut tightened.

She couldn't kill Alec, but the daemon wanted her dead. *Needed* her dead. That was the only way to break the cuffs. To free Alec's elemental power. And while Vivienne would never succumb to old age or disease, she could die from violence—just like her bonded.

She stopped, poised on the balls of her feet. "You know my true name, daemon. It's only fair you tell me yours."

Alec stopped too, leaving ten feet between them. Despite the taunting, he was wary of her.

Now he laughed softly. "Proper introductions before you die, is that what you're after?"

The tone was wry, sardonic. Vintage Alec Lawrence. She realized with dreamy horror that it was already assuming his personality. Sifting through two thousand years of memories, learning the man inside and out. If she hadn't seen Alec taken with her own eyes, if she didn't feel the *wrongness* of him through the bond, Vivienne had no doubt this thing could have fooled her into believing he *was* Alec.

"You're nothing but a parasite. A bloody great tapeworm."

"Catherine doesn't think so." His lips curled in an amused smile. The cat that devoured the canary in one savage bite.

Oh, it knows where the soft bits are, Vivienne thought. *The unguarded belly. Bastard.*

She lunged forward, testing his defenses, hoping against hope the thing inside Alec would be even a hair slower. The sword whistled through air as he slipped easily out of reach.

"All you do is lie, daemon."

"Am I lying when I say he's half in love with her but won't admit it, even to himself?"

Vivienne stayed silent.

"An intriguing woman, Catherine de Mornay. A whore, but

our gallant Mr. Lawrence doesn't care." He stared at her. "She likes to comb his hair before she spreads her legs for him. Did you know that?"

Vivienne watched him move. The limp was still there though he tried to conceal it. Alec's infirmity was her only advantage. She needed to hamstring him. Hurt him badly enough that he'd stay down. For a normal person, a few broken bones would put them into shock. Not Alec Lawrence. He could absorb an ocean of pain with no discernable effect. She'd seen it hundreds of times. Thousands.

"I'm looking forward to meeting our lovely Catherine." His eyes grew flat. Reptilian. "I wonder how she'll look with her womb on the outside."

Alec's ring finger twitched.

Before he moved, she was already pivoting on her right foot. Without that split second head start, Vivienne knew beyond the shadow of a doubt that she would have been dead. She spun and landed a ferocious kick to the side of his bad knee, then followed it with a punch to the ribs just as he'd done to her in the sparring room at St. James. The punch might have cracked a rib or two, but it was the blow to the knee that brought him down. His leg buckled like an unstrung puppet. The backwash of pain through the bond made her gag.

It was the first time she'd ever exploited Alec's infirmity.

Alec screamed and she kicked him in the face. Now he lay on his back, the tip of her sword drawing a pinprick of blood at the juncture of throat and jaw. One quick thrust and she'd lay open his carotid artery. Vivienne's heart hammered in her chest. Their eyes locked.

"Please," Alec whispered. "Viv...."

"Shut up." Her teeth ground so hard they creaked.

"It's me, Vivienne. I just can't—"

"*Feck!*" She increased the pressure by a fraction. A line of blood ran into his collar.

"We both know you won't do it," he whispered.

"Then you don't know me."

"Of course I do."

He sounded so much like Alec at that moment, Vivienne couldn't stop the tears from streaming down her cheeks. She barely noticed them. The daemon was much cleverer than she'd given it credit for. It had taken the one person on the face of the earth she couldn't bring herself to kill, even if it meant her own life.

But there was still a way.

"Take me instead," she said. "Take me, or I swear to the Goddess Innunu, I'll kill you and then I'll kill myself." She slid a small triangular dagger into her palm and placed the tip beneath her own jaw. "You know I'm telling the truth. I'd rather die than let you have him."

His eyes darkened. Something gathered there, in the irises.

"You give yourself to me willingly?"

"Yes."

"His life for yours?"

"Yes."

"I would control his power through the bond."

She nodded.

And I hope he kills me the first chance he gets.

Alec looked up at her, considering.

"Touch me, Tijah."

Vivienne held out a hand, biting back her revulsion. Alec took it and twined his fingers with hers. His lips parted slightly. Heat radiated from his palm, warming her frozen limbs. It slowly built in intensity and Vivienne felt a bead of sweat roll down her neck. Alec watched her, hazel eyes locked on her face. The daemon was enjoying the sensation, she realized. The powerful pleasure of two bonded touching each other. He would feel her reaction, the echo of her emotions.

It sickened her. And yet part of her couldn't help herself.

Not Alec. *Not Alec.*

She bit the inside of her cheek, tasted blood.

"Just take me," she whispered. "Please."

He watched her for a long moment, dark lashes beaded with water. Vivienne waited for that vile consciousness to slither into her mind, to make her its puppet, but all she felt was searing pain in her hand. The skin began to blister. Vivienne smelled burning flesh and tried to pull away. He wouldn't let go.

Betrayed.

Before she could stick him with the sword, he gave a hard yank. The breath left her lungs as she slammed onto her back. Alec knelt on her chest. He shoved her face to the side. She sputtered, dirty water filling her nose and mouth.

"Sorry, love," he whispered. "But your daēva is already dead."

CHAPTER 28

Harry spun in a circle, her feet sliding on the treacherous logs. She held her arms in front of her face, palms out. Not a sliver of light could be seen in any direction.

"John!" she cried.

No answer came.

The last she'd seen, he was diving after the amulet. But there were other things in the water too. Her mind shuddered away from the thought.

Small white hands tugging at Mary's dress....

She listened intently for any sign of movement. The water still sloshed and echoed beneath the platform of the gallows, so she knew which direction it lay. Part of her wanted to swim to it and climb up. Anything was better than standing waist-deep in the gate. But if she did, she knew she'd never have the courage to climb down again.

She could wait there. Maybe Lady Cumberland would find her.

Or maybe Lady Cumberland was dead too.

Harry didn't want to think that, but it was a possibility.

"John!" she cried again.

Still, there was no answer.

Without a light, she'd never find him. He should have come up for air by now. If he hadn't, it must be because *they* had gotten him.

Harry covered her face with her hands and drew a ragged breath. She had no idea how to find the crevice leading back to Mary's cell. In the blackness, it would be next to impossible.

What would Myrtle do?

The thought came unbidden, but it wasn't the first time. During the Hyde investigation, when Harry had posed as her older sister, she'd asked herself the same question on an hourly basis. In fact, though Harry didn't care to admit it, she'd been emulating Myrtle since she was old enough to toddle around the house behind her. For years, Harry had hated her own blonde hair and freckles, her shortness and rounded hips. She wanted to be tall, thin and saturnine.

The darkness weighed on her now, thick and suffocating. How easy it would be to simply stand there forever, afraid to move. Afraid to give herself away. Harry took a steadying breath.

For starters, Myrtle wouldn't panic. She'd examine the situation from a logical standpoint and choose the best course of action.

Harry couldn't see anything, but she could still *feel*. After probing a bit with her feet, she realized they had been walking across the logs lengthwise, and if she just proceeded slowly, she could stay on a single log. With any luck, it would lead her to the edge of the cavern near to where they'd entered.

She didn't want to think about what else was swimming in the pond with her.

I'll get a light and come back for you, John—that I swear, even if I have to follow you into the Dominion itself.

Harry started along the log. With her sight extinguished, other senses rushed to the fore. The briny scent of the water. The harsh rasping of her own exhalations. The copper taste of adrenaline. She estimated she'd gone about thirty feet when the water stirred off to her left. It was such a small sound, she'd never have heard it if she hadn't been listening so hard.

Harry froze. Her mind conjured up an image of pale things with fixed grins silently coming toward her in the darkness. She launched forward, swimming as hard as she could. Her heart clawed at her ribcage. A hand grabbed her foot and she lashed out with a wild kick, connecting with something solid.

"Ow!" came a muffled voice behind.

"John?" she cried.

Sudden light bloomed, and she squinted, momentarily blinded.

"Thank God," he whispered.

He held the talisman in one hand. It lit the planes of his face with an eerie green glow. A shock of wet hair fell into his eyes and he shook it impatiently away.

"It's rather nasty down there. I think I touched a dead rat."

She laughed aloud, shaky with relief. "However did you manage to get it back?"

"Honestly, I think I just got lucky." He sounded dubious. "It was very odd, Harry, I didn't need to hold my breath. It's not water, really. Anyway, I just crawled around, groping on those slimy logs until I found it. Thank Christ Mary and…the others seemed to be gone."

Harry stared at the amulet in fascination. "May I see it?"

"Of course." John pressed it into her palm. The amulet felt heavy—solid gold, she reckoned. The moment he withdrew his hand, it winked out. Darkness rushed in on all sides.

"What happened?" Harry whispered in alarm.

"I don't know." His fingers trailed along her arm. When they brushed the amulet, it sparked to life again.

"Oh!" Harry said in surprise. Then she screamed, for not three feet behind him stood Mary Elizabeth Wickes.

She looked the same except for her eyes, which had gone yellowish, and her hands. The nails were ragged and filthy and curved into sharp talons.

"Stay with us." She gave Harry a red smile. "We'll show you such *terrible, awful, wonderful things.*"

CHAPTER 29

Vivienne's mind drifted as the daemon's boot ground down on her neck, forcing her head beneath the floodwaters. She'd been close to death before, but the closest had been the day Achaemenes bonded her. It was an act of extraordinary generosity.

He had nothing to gain and everything to lose.

When Tijah met him, he was seventeen and she was twenty. Her first daēva, Myrri, wasn't even dead a fortnight. Tijah had sought her own death, courted it with reckless indifference. She'd found it on the sword of a necromancer. Then Achaemenes had bonded her with a set of cuffs he found inside the prison fortress of Gorgon-e Gaz. It was done while she was unconscious. He'd seen no other way to keep her alive. When she'd woken up and discovered what happened, she'd thrown a water jug at his head.

It had taken her years to get over Myrri. Once she accepted him, the thought of losing Achaemenes was unbearable. Now Vivienne was just thankful she would be the one to die first.

Her lungs burned as she resisted the urge to take a great, gulping mouthful of water. It was habit. Reflex. The body didn't want to die, even when the mind gave it permission. Even after all these years, more than she was meant to have.

Darkness pressed at the edges of her vision. Her skirts billowed in the water, heavy and tangled. Vivienne's fingers scrabbled for a hidden slit that gave access to a sheath around her thigh. Her last knife. So many layers of clothing in this age. Tijah had worn a simple tunic and trousers. She would have been out of this mess already.

Her hand finally brushed a metal hilt. The knife caught in her skirts so Vivienne worked the edge like a saw, slicing through multiple petticoats, a chemise, and finally the gown itself. When the blade broke free, she stabbed it into Alec's bad knee. With the other hand, she pressed her own cuff against the bare skin of his forearm.

That, at least, still had an effect.

White-hot pain rebounded through the bond. Alec screamed. It gladdened her and broke her heart at the same time. She tried to roll away, but he was on her again in an instant, wrenching the knife from her hand.

"Oh, you poxied bitch," he growled.

He adjusted his grip for a gutting slice. Images of the White Chapel women flashed through her mind, the things Dr. Clarence had done to them before and after death. Vivienne fought back but knew she was no match for him. The fact that it wasn't Alec didn't matter. It was *his* body. His daēva physiology, superficially human but so much more. She'd never bested him without weapons. Not even once.

The knife came down in a descending arc. Vivienne shut her eyes. She didn't want to see Alec's expression as he carved her up.

"Farrumohr!"

The hand pinning her tensed. She heard Alec draw a slow breath.

The voice seemed to come from miles away, echoing down

the stone corridors of the Tombs. It was accented, the *R* slightly rolled. *A Russian?*

"Do you remember me?" Louder now. Closer.

Alec emitted a bestial growl of hatred. The weight on Vivienne's chest shifted. She blinked, trying to make out the speaker's features. He was tall and dark-haired, handsome in a wolfish way. He was also dressed for a party, in a formal tailcoat, starched shirt and white cravat. She felt certain she didn't know him. She had an excellent memory for voices and she'd never heard this man's before.

Vivienne scooted away. Pain flared through her body. Her right arm was swelling and wouldn't move right. It felt broken, although at least the bone hadn't pierced the skin. The hand burned like fire where Alec had touched her. She used her left to scrub dirty water from her eyes. A sharp *snick* of metal jerked them open.

The man had snapped an iron collar around Alec's neck. Chains led from the collar to a bracelet around the man's wrist. They clanked as he jerked them tight. Alec let out a wail of fury. His fingers clawed at the collar.

What madness was this?

"I should have killed you before," the man said to Alec. He gave a strange laugh. "We went our separate ways, you and I. And yet here we are, together again."

Sounds of inarticulate rage bubbled from Alec's throat. He writhed and bucked, tearing at the collar. The man watched him without emotion for a long moment. Then he jerked the chain again. This time, a look of blank dullness fell across Alec's face like a curtain. A thread of drool dangled from his lower lip.

A necromancer.

Did he help summon the daemon? If not, how had he found them?

Vivienne's pulse raced. She had to do something before he collared her, too. It was a fate far worse than death to be a necromancer's slave. She would become an automaton, subject to his will as surely as if the daemon had taken her. He would drain her life force, quickly or slowly depending on the temperament of the necromancer. Sometimes it was very slowly indeed.

Seeing the thick collar around Alec's neck made her physically ill. She groped in the water for her knife.

"Don't interfere," the man said, shooting her a warning glance. "I won't harm him. Trust me, Lady Cumberland, this is the only way."

Trust him?

Vivienne almost laughed. She ignored the pain shooting through her arm and kept rooting around for the knife.

The man dragged Alec away from her by the chain. Then he took out a straight razor. Her breath caught in her throat, but he used it to open a shallow cut on his own palm. Blood dripped into the water. He muttered to himself. Not Russian, she realized. Hungarian. A dialect from the Transylvanian Plain, or possibly Székely. She had an ear for languages, and once Vivienne heard an accent, she never forgot it.

Still gripping the chain in one hand, the man used the other to remove an object from his coat pocket. It looked like a shell, the edges twisting so that they blurred the eye. Vivienne recognized it as a talisman of Traveling. He spoke more words, this time in a language far older and harsher, a stream of guttural consonants and jagged syllables that made her think of a snapping dog.

The words of opening for a lesser gate.

"I suggest you hold onto something," he said without looking at her.

Vivienne swore under her breath. She knew what was coming. She managed to pull herself to standing and locked her uninjured arm around the bars of the cell.

The floodwater began to swirl, slowly at first but quickly gathering speed. Wind howled down the length of the corridor. The gas jets blew out, leaving only the fey light of the talisman.

"*Agzardamon*, Farrumohr!" the man cried. "*Dhest kundixighan!*"

Alec's jaw clenched, every muscle tensing. Black fog oozed from the corners of his eyes. It hovered in the air for a moment, a writhing ball. Then a single hair-thin tendril stretched toward the whirlpool of darkness at the man's feet. The substance of the daemon fought, but the thread grew into a thick tentacle. A low, moaning wind battered against the walls of the old prison.

Vivienne's ears popped as the daemon vanished through the lesser gate and it winked shut. Alec slid into the water. She crawled over to him, the collar ice cold beneath her fingers. Almost as cold as his skin.

The man leaned down until his face was close enough to touch. He reached for Alec and she knocked his hand away.

"Don't, or I'll kill you myself," Vivienne snarled.

The man took a deep breath. His eyes had a hunted look.

"I'm sorry," he said softly.

The man's hand slipped around the back of Alec's limp neck. Vivienne slapped him across the face. When she tried to do it again, he grabbed her wrist. She heard a click and the collar fell open. He'd been feeling for the catch. One smooth movement and he was on his feet, the chains trailing into the water.

"Who are you?" she demanded. "What's your name?"

He stared at her for a moment. Then he strode away down the corridor.

"Who are you?" she screamed at his back.

He didn't turn around.

It didn't matter. She'd find him if it took the rest of her life.

Vivienne pressed her face against Alec's icy cheek.

CHAPTER 30

John spun around, the iron knife materializing in his hand. Mary hissed when she saw it. She swiped at him with clawed fingers and John pressed the flat of the blade to her cheek. The skin sizzled and smoked. Mary made a thin whining noise and scrabbled backward. There was neither fear nor fury on her face. Just a kind of mindless hunger.

"Come *on!*" Harry urged.

She grabbed John's shirt and dragged him toward the edge of the cavern. The rough stone walls loomed ahead, but she couldn't see the crevice they'd emerged from and the current kept pushing them back. It was like swimming against an incoming tide. Harry dug in with her toes on the slippery log. She could hear John breathing hard next to her.

"Come, my angels," Mary cried. "Come feed and grow strong!"

Harry risked a glance over her shoulder. Mary had recovered from her brush with the iron blade and was wading after them, her jaundiced eyes flat and reptilian. Somewhere in the darkness, Harry heard a childish giggle.

And out of the mist, the children came. White, shiny faces with black holes for mouths. Sixteen of them, the taller ones carrying the littlest in their arms. The girls wore pretty white dresses with ribbons in their hair. The boys had been combed and looked ready for Sunday School. Harry guessed with a sick feeling that they had, in fact, been dressed for church, but by hands accustomed to carrying out a more macabre task.

The children were clothed for their own funeral services.

The cavern wall rushed up to meet her. Harry pressed her back against the jagged rock. It looked unbroken. They must have gotten turned around in the middle of the pond, for the exit had vanished. Cold water crept toward the neckline of Harry's gown—the green silk dress with pearl buttons she'd worn to Count Koháry's house. It seemed a lifetime ago.

Mary had paused to wait for her "angels." Now they advanced together in a tight semicircle, undeterred by the current and rapidly rising water. Only the children's eyes could be seen, black stones beneath white smudges of forehead. John put his arms around Harry, drawing her close. She pressed her face against his chest. His heart pounded like surf in her ear.

"The will of the user," he muttered. "The *will*…."

Even with her eyes closed, Harry flinched at the sudden flare of light. A great cracking sound followed and dust rained down from above. The surface of the water churned.

"I think I see it," John cried, pulling her past the momentarily stunned ghouls—for that is what they were, Harry knew. "The way out!"

What she had taken for a shadow resolved into narrow crevice. They dashed inside just as chunks of the ceiling smashed into the water behind them. John held the amulet up for light, but it dimmed the further they went from the gate. Water still cascaded down from above. It was like climbing up a sewage pipe, Harry thought, while someone repeatedly flushed the water closet. When the amulet finally went dark, they made their way by touch.

The main problem was that the crack seemed to be slowly

sealing itself up again. Every few seconds, the stone would shudder beneath their feet. When it stopped, Harry felt certain the walls had shifted even closer together.

"There's a branching," John muttered.

"Do you remember which way we came?"

"Not a clue."

The crevice had grown very tight. Harry had a sudden vision of getting stuck while the undead children crept up behind them on cold bare feet.

"Would it do any good to call for help?" she asked, despising the squeakiness of her voice.

He hesitated. "Well, if it's Mr. Hyde up there, we're in trouble anyway. If it's not, maybe Lady Cumberland will hear us. So let's try it. We can't be that far from the top."

They called out, their voices sounding both too loud and oddly muffled in the confined space. Harry's spirits lifted at faint answering cries.

"This way!" John seized her hand and dragged her into the left-hand tunnel.

They stumbled and crawled, the rough rock walls scraping skin from palms and John's shoeless foot. After a minute, Harry detected a glimmer of light. The foundation groaned around them, contracting like a giant stone fist. At last, they squirmed out of the crack into Mary's cell. Two lanterns had been hung from the bars of the tiny window.

"Well, aren't they a sight," a deep voice declared in a thick Irish brogue.

"Is that Mary?" another voice said doubtfully. "Don't look like her."

"One of t'others, I suppose."

Hands grabbed Harry under the armpits and yanked her to her feet. She tried to pull free and earned a rough shake that rattled her teeth.

"Let her go!" John objected, himself in the clutches of three large men wearing navy guard uniforms.

"I don't know how the hell you got down there in the first place, laddie, but you won't be leaving again." A guard with a stringy blonde mustache unhooked a set of handcuffs from his belt. "Don't make it harder on yourself."

"But we're not prisoners," Harry said indignantly.

"Sure you're not, Miss. That's why you're crawling around in the Tombs." His face hardened. "We found Sister Emily floating down by the end of the ward. If one of you did her, you'll swing for it."

Nasty laughter erupted. "Or maybe you'll be one a' the first customers for the new electric chair they're building up at Auburn Prison," another guard said.

"You don't understand—" John began.

"Shut yer gob!" The mustachioed guard brought his club back.

"I wouldn't do that," a cool voice said from the doorway of the cell.

The men spun around.

"And who the hell are you?" Mustache demanded.

Something in Lady Cumberland's eyes seemed to give the men pause. She was soaking wet from head to toe. Blood stained her beautiful dress and one arm hung at an awkward angle. Her face could have been carved from granite.

"Touch him with that club and you'll regret it," she said.

The guard stared at her in open-mouthed astonishment. "Who is this mouthy negress?" he said to the others.

Blood rushed to Harry's face. She opened her mouth to cut him down when Orpha Winter strode into the cell wearing a hat with enormous soggy-looking ostrich plumes. She carried an umbrella in her gloved hand, which she pointed at the guard like a spear.

"I very much hope you're not speaking of the Marchioness," she said icily. "Assuming you value your job."

"Out, boys," said the middle-aged man next to her. "Let 'em go."

The guards exchanged puzzled glances.

"Now," he repeated firmly.

"Yes sir, Warden," Mustache said reluctantly.

Even in her chilled and bedraggled state, Harry felt a spark of interest at meeting the man newly appointed to run the Tombs. Charles Osborne had taken over in April when Thomas "Fatty" Walsh, a Five Points crony of Mayor Hewitt, was forced to resign after being denounced in the editorial pages as a gambler and general lowlife. Osborne was widely viewed as a respectable alternative; he'd been deputy warden for years both at the Tombs and the penitentiary on Blackwell's Island.

"Remove his handcuffs at once," Orpha said. "My God, have your men nothing better to do than harass honest citizens?"

After a nod from Osborne, one of the guards produced a key and opened the manacles. John rubbed his wrists. The guards pushed past them, avoiding eye contact with Vivienne.

"They did break into the jail, Mrs. Winter," Osborne said uncomfortably. "And someone killed the keeper of the women's prison."

"Mary Elizabeth Wickes did that, did she not?" Orpha gave Harry and John a look that dared them to say otherwise.

They both nodded.

"There's another body down here!" one of the guards called.

"Stay away from him!" Vivienne rushed down the corridor, her face a thundercloud.

Harry moved to follow but Orpha laid a hand on her arm and gave a brief shake of her head.

"But Mr. Lawrence—"

"Let her handle it," Orpha said in a low voice.

"Where is Mary Wickes?" Osborne asked.

"We followed her down there," John said, pointing at the hole in the floor. It had narrowed to less than a foot across. The cavern below was submerged completely now, and the crevice sat under several inches of dark water. "She…she drowned before we could reach her."

"I see. I'll have to send men down to verify that." He shook his head wearily. "What a night. Maybe the legislature will finally do something about the fact that this prison is sinking into the muck. Frankly, it should have been torn down years ago. I've been telling them that, but no one listens."

"Thank you, Charles," Orpha said. "Perhaps Mr. Winter can exercise some influence in this matter." She glanced at John and Harry, who stood shivering near the door. "Are we free to go? I'd like to give my agents some blankets and hot coffee."

He waved a hand. "You're free. I need to organize a search party. Better you're not here when they arrive, Orpha."

She nodded and signaled to Harry and John. Harry threw a last glance at the crevice, half-expecting a small hand to reach out, but the water remained still.

"First things first," Orpha said briskly as they waded down the corridor. "What's the status of the gate?"

"I'm not entirely sure, but it seems to be closed again," Harry said. "You should warn Warden Osborne though. He oughtn't send anyone down there who isn't trained to deal with…that sort of thing."

"Indeed. Charles is a man of the world. I'll find a way to explain it to him. It helps to have friends in high places," she added airily. "Mr. Kaylock doesn't seem to grasp that fact."

"What about Mr. Lawrence?"

Vivienne and the guards were nowhere in sight.

"We'd best leave him for Lady Cumberland. London takes care of its own."

"But—"

Orpha cut her off. "Mr. Osborne was right. We should leave while we still can. This place will be crawling with officers in just a few minutes. There will be awkward questions I'd much prefer not to answer. The warden will keep our presence here quiet, but not if we announce it to the world."

"Is Mr. Lawrence dead?" Harry asked quietly.

Orpha shrugged. "If he is, there's nothing we can do. If he's not, Charles Osborne will make sure he's taken to a doctor."

Harry could see the doors to Centre Street. She longed to get out of the Tombs, to breathe the fresh night air—or what passed for it in lower Manhattan. What Orpha Winter said made logical sense.

It was also utterly wrong. Harry stopped walking.

"No."

"What?"

"No, we're not leaving her. Are we, John?"

"I was about to say the same thing."

They turned and began running back down the corridor.

"Miss Pell!" Orpha cried, her voice brittle. "Mr. Weston! Come back at once!"

They found Vivienne just past the first turning beyond Mary's cell. She was trying to lift Mr. Lawrence over her shoulder with one arm. Harry could see the other was broken. Alec's eyes were closed. He looked ashen.

John pressed his fingers to Alec's neck and let out a breath of relief. "He's alive, but we've got to get him out of this cold water before he succumbs to shock." He glanced at Vivienne. "And you have a nasty fracture of the radial bone. Here."

He removed his suspenders and created a makeshift sling. It had to hurt to like hell, but Lady Cumberland didn't even wince as he maneuvered the sling into place.

"Osborne sent for men to help, but he can't wait," she said, her gaze fixed on Alec.

"Of course not." Harry lightly touched her shoulder. "Agents of the S.P.R. stick together, don't we? Come on, John. You take his legs."

Vivienne seemed so lost, Harry didn't want to ask her any

questions about what had happened. She understood all too well. Their last case had ended with John in the hospital undergoing a risky blood transfusion. She'd sat in the waiting room with his parents and four brothers, waiting to find out if he was alive or dead. It was the worst three hours of Harry's life.

Mr. Lawrence was still alive, though for how much longer was anyone's guess. At least they could take him someplace warm. She lifted him gently under the arms and together she and John carried Alec out of the Tombs. His body hung limp, his head lolling on his chest.

Orpha Winter waited next to the carriage, impatiently slapping her gloves into her palm.

"Hop to it, boy," she said to Connor when they appeared at the top of the stairs. "Get the door open! Can't you see we've got an injured man?"

Connor rolled his eyes but leapt down from the driver's seat and helped them lift Alec inside. It was a tight fit, but they managed. John rode up top with Connor. Harry and Orpha sat on the rear-facing bench, while Vivienne and Alec occupied the other. He slumped against her, pale and motionless.

"We can go straight to New York Hospital," Harry said. "It's the closest. They treated John when—"

"There's nothing they can do for Mr. Lawrence," Vivienne interrupted in a tone that brooked no argument. "We're staying at the Astor House, though I suppose it would cause a scene to carry him through the lobby. The Pearl Street offices are best for now. I'll see to him myself."

Orpha relayed their destination to Connor. Vivienne stared out the carriage window. She didn't look at Alec again, but the hand not in a sling gripped her skirts like a drowning woman clutching a lifeline.

Lady Cumberland was a proud woman, Harry sensed. She wouldn't indulge in grief before strangers. Better to distract her with the tale of Mary and the amulet.

"You'll want to know that John Weston closed the gate," Harry said. "At least, I think he did."

Vivienne's eyes sharpened. "Tell me what happened."

"We followed Mary down to the foundations of the prison. It had flooded, forming a kind of lake. And in the center....well, it sounds mad, but there was a gallows."

Vivienne nodded. "I've seen queer things manifest in the vicinity of a gate. In simple terms, I believe they're places where the boundary between our world and the Dominion has grown thin. The Tombs is a site of executions. It doesn't surprise me that such a potent symbol would be reflected near to the gate itself."

Harry told her all that happened next. Lady Vivienne stayed silent for a moment, considering. Then she gave a smart rap on the roof. The carriage jolted to a stop. Vivienne opened the door and leaned out. The rain had lightened to a fine mist that made yellow haloes around the gas lamps.

"Mr. Weston?"

He looked down at her from the driver's bench. "Lady Cumberland?"

"Do you have the amulet of Osiris?"

John flushed. "Of course." He rummaged in his pocket and produced the gold talisman. It gave a brief flicker of light as he passed it down to her. "I never meant to keep it."

She smiled. "I know. You did well, Mr. Weston. Very well."

He reached into his belt and withdrew the iron knife, extending it toward her hilt-first.

"And thanks for this as well. It came in handy."

Vivienne gave him a small smile. "It's yours, Mr. Weston. I have others. And you never know when you might need it again."

He smiled back and touched his forehead in a brief salute. "Thank you, milady."

"Just Vivienne will do." She glanced at Alec. "We'd best get moving. Mr. Lawrence needs a bed." She tucked the amulet into a pocket and shut the door. The carriage resumed its journey to the S.P.R. headquarters.

"He has the spark," she muttered.

"What?" Orpha Winter asked.

A faint smile touched Vivienne's lips. "Mr. Weston has the spark. He can use talismans."

"What does that mean?" Orpha demanded, leaning forward.

Harry batted a limp ostrich feather away from her face. Orpha's hat seemed to take up half the space in the carriage.

"He has the blood." Vivienne sighed. "Ask me later. I'm too tired to talk anymore right now."

Orpha sniffed, irritated, but let it go. "Can you at least tell us what happened to the daemon?"

A shadow crossed Lady Cumberland's face. She pulled out a crumpled, waterlogged packet of cigarettes, looked at it, sighed, and tossed it out the window.

"In the universe, there are things that are known, and things that are unknown, and in between, there are doors." Vivienne ignored Orpha, turning instead to Harry. "Mr. Weston closed one, but someone else opened another and I'd give anything to know who."

CHAPTER 31

Snow dusted the entrance of the American Museum of Natural History as John and Harry bought their tickets to *Ptolemy's Tomb: The Secrets of Alexandria.* The line to get in snaked around the corner. The exhibit was already shattering attendance records, and the abrupt resignation of Nelson Holland only added to the public speculation.

Dr. Julius Sabelline's murder had been closed. The official conclusion was that Araminta had killed her husband during a violent argument and committed suicide by burning their house down. Harry had heard through Nellie Bly that Jackson was back at Yale, seeking solace in his studies. She felt truly sorry for him.

That night at the Tombs still seemed like a fever dream. Mary's body was never found, but no one seemed overly concerned about the fate of a girl who was going to be put to death, and although it couldn't be proven, few doubted she had murdered Sister Emily during an escape attempt. Charles Osborne managed to keep the S.P.R. agents out of the matter completely, sparing Harry and John being called as witnesses at the inquest.

The old woman whose body had tumbled out of the wardrobe

was never identified. John hectored Orpha Winter until she reluctantly paid for a burial plot in Greenwood Cemetery, so at least the woman wouldn't go to a pauper's mass grave.

With the mayor's blessing, Charles Osborne sent in an army of workers to seal up the cracks in the prison's foundation. A few of them (discreetly on the payroll of the S.P.R.) carried iron knives, but no one reported seeing anything untoward. The ghouls had vanished—though Harry still got a funny feeling when she walked over sewer grates.

"Show me the sarcophagus where they found the shoes," John said, offering his arm. She took it, and they spent the afternoon drifting through the rooms of the museum and hoping to understand the man who had traveled to the Dominion and met the daemon called Farrumohr.

"So Claudius Ptolemy had the spark too," John mused.

That's what Mr. Kaylock had called it when they'd met with him the previous afternoon.

The spark. An inborn ability to use talismans like the amulet of Osiris. It was very rare. Mary Elizabeth Wickes had it. So, it seemed, did John Weston.

"Ptolemy likely went through the Greater Gate in Memphis," Harry said. "It was the closest to his home in Alexandria. He met this daemon, pumped it for information about the Dominion, and then fled. I can't really blame him."

"But where did he get the amulet in the first place?" John mused.

"We may never know."

"Well, he should have destroyed it. Once he realized what it could do."

"That's easier said than done, apparently. I suppose he thought the next best thing was to stick it in a box with a nasty curse. It worked until Julius Sabelline came along and dug it up."

"Do you believe what Mr. Kaylock said about Alec Lawrence?"

"That he's not human?" Harry shrugged. It was a measure of how far she'd come that being told one of the London agents was not a man at all but something called a *daēva* had barely fazed her. "After everything else, after all we've seen, how can I doubt it?"

Kaylock hadn't wanted to tell them, that much was obvious, but felt he'd had no choice. Still, he'd forced them to sign a *second* confidentiality agreement, this one even more draconian than the last.

Harry thought she understood why Alec's true nature was such a closely guarded secret. There were people who would call him witch—or worse—even in this day and age. She still didn't fully understand what he was, only that he could do impressive things and shared a connection with Lady Cumberland through the gold bracelets they each wore.

Lady Vivienne Cumberland had the spark as well. It's why she could wear the bracelet. If Harry put it on, she wouldn't feel a thing. Kaylock had given the impression that both Lady Cumberland and Alec were older than they looked, although he was vague on precisely how *much* older.

When the jostling of the crowds became tiresome, they left the museum and walked east across Central Park. The weather had grown colder again. A chill wind swept through the bare branches of the trees. Harry kept one hand firmly on her new hat.

"Uncle Arthur wrote me a letter," she said. "I sent him a copy of our report on the Sabelline case."

"Kaylock didn't mind?"

"Kaylock didn't know."

"Ah. Of course."

"He says it just might inspire him to write a story about mummies and Egyptologists. He already has a title. *The Ring of Thoth.*"

"I'd hoped he might write another story with that detective and his sidekick."

"Sherlock Holmes and John Watson?"

"Yes, them." He grinned. "You don't mind being the sidekick, do you?"

Harry swatted him with her hat.

"What else did your Uncle Arthur say?"

"He already knew about ghouls, of course, living in England. It's a bit of an open secret, apparently."

The Seventy-Ninth Street Transverse followed the edge of the Croton Reservoir. A few hardy souls were out walking their dogs, collars turned up against the wind that raised small white-caps on the surface of the water.

"Arthur says we should come for a visit. There's an open invitation from the London S.P.R. as well."

John lit up. "I'd like to see England. There's something called a lubber fiend that's been sighted up around the Scottish border. We could conduct a little inquiry."

"A lubber fiend?"

"Big hairy fellow with a tail. Bit like a brownie but uglier."

Harry shook her head in fond resignation. "I suppose I should have expected you to have an aptitude for this sort of thing. If we do go to England, you can hunt lubber fiends all you like. I plan to visit Scotland Yard. There's a brilliant surgeon there named Henry Faulds who claims every human finger mark is unique. Imagine the implications, John."

They took one of the southern drives and exited through the Children's Gate at Seventy-Second Street and Fifth Avenue. A few blocks later, they stood across the street from the townhouse of Count Balthazar Jozsef Habsburg-Koháry. The windows were all dark, the blinds drawn.

"It's been put up for sale," she said. "No one knows where he's gone."

"Do you think the man Lady Cumberland saw at the Tombs was really the count?" John asked.

"I don't know, but the description certainly fits, right down to the crooked nose and white tie." She frowned. "In fact, I thought I saw his servant outside the Sabelline house, when the fire trucks came. But then Lady Cumberland said something, and he seemed to disappear and I forgot all about it."

"There you are. He must have had us followed. And here you thought *you* were pursuing *him*." John chuckled. "I can't believe we had tea with a necromancer." He sounded inordinately pleased.

"They're quite evil," Harry admonished him. "They summon ghouls and use talismanic chains to suck the life from their victims in order to prolong their own."

He blew out a slow breath. "Yes, that's rather unpleasant. But this one saved their lives. He banished the daemon back to the underworld. Why would he do that if he's the one who called it up?"

"I've no idea," Harry admitted. "He must have had some reason."

"Maybe he wasn't a necromancer at all."

"Then why did he have the chains?"

John had no answer for that. The mansion gave off a desolate air, with drifts of dead leaves skittering through the front garden.

"I was thinking, Harry. I might start keeping a record of our cases. For posterity."

She gave him a sideways glance. "You know you can never publish it. Mr. Kaylock would sue us in an instant."

"I know. But when I'm old and grey, I want to remember everything."

Harry smiled. "And what would you call this one?"

John thought for a moment. "*The Adventure of the Cursed Amulet.*"

"How about *The Adventure of the Thirteenth Gate*?"

He frowned. "That does have a certain ring to it. Or simply, *The Thirteenth Gate?*"

"Too cryptic. It sounds like one of those gothic melodramas…"

Harry took his arm and they wandered down Fifth Avenue, leaving the deserted mansion and its secrets behind them.

CHAPTER 32

Alec Lawrence rested his leg on a pile of cushions in the conservatory. Vivienne had done some damage when she stabbed him in the knee. The joint was already arthritic; now it felt like a live coal. The doctor had offered him morphine, but Alec declined. He didn't like opiates. They dulled his ability to touch the elements and he'd had quite enough of that to last a lifetime.

Cyrus had come down on the train with Cassandane. It was the first time he'd left Ingress Abbey in three years. Cassandane had told Alec he'd have to get himself nearly killed more often.

"You're lucky, you know," Cyrus said, sipping a cup of black Assam tea.

It was a very un-English morning. Bright sun poured in through the wall of glass windows.

"I know."

"It all puts rather a new spin on things."

"What?"

"The fact that new gates can spontaneously appear in metropolitan areas."

"Oh, that."

"Vivienne says you remember nothing."

"I don't."

Which was a lie. Vivienne wouldn't tell him in any detail what had happened, but he had a fair idea. Both of them were pretending things were the same as before, and they were—but they weren't too. Because Alec wasn't the same. Not exactly. He had a kernel of something inside him, chafing like a pebble in his shoe. A darkness. An *affinity*. With what, he didn't yet know.

Alec hadn't sorted it out, but he knew he needed to get away from Vivienne. Not forever, just for a little while. It was impossible to think straight with her emotions clouding the bond. And he was afraid she would sense the change in him. Demand answers.

"I suppose that's for the best." Cyrus folded bearlike paws in his lap. He had the face of a scholar and the hands of a dock-worker. "I've been looking into this Count Koháry. My guess is our boy is old, Alec. Very old. He's been *dying* and leaving himself a fortune for hundreds of years."

"How many hundreds?"

"My agents in Hungary have traced him back to the 13th century. The trail before that is cold but they'll sniff it out. They're good."

"Is he one of the Duzakh?"

"I don't think so. I know them all."

"You just can't find them."

Cyrus made a noise of irritation.

"Well, whoever he is, I'm grateful for his intervention." Alec laced his hands behind his head.

"He probably stole the Ptolemy maps."

"They could have been lost in the flood."

"They could have. But I have a feeling our count took them. He was a collector. If he's connected with the Duzakh, we'll have a world of trouble."

"What makes you think the necromancers don't already know where all the gates are?"

Cyrus sighed. "They probably do."

"So it makes no real difference. And Koháry will turn up eventually. Now that we're looking. Personally, I hold no special ill will toward him. He saved my life."

Cyrus frowned. "The bond saved your life."

"So I gather."

"Without it, your soul would have been driven out. But it worked like a tether, holding you in your body even though the daemon had taken possession."

"Can we talk about something more pleasant?" His gaze fell on a pot of hot pink Phalaenopsis. "Orchids, perhaps? You should grow them, magus. Give that frigid old pile you call home a splash of color."

Cyrus looked around, as if noticing the riot of flowers for the first time. "Cass would never remember to water them. What are you going to do now?"

"I might go to Wales. Just for a bit."

"Holy Father, it's like a frozen tundra this time of year."

"The south of France then."

Cyrus smiled. "That's more like it."

They talked of insubstantial things like food and weather and first-rate hotels on the Côte d'Azur. When late afternoon came, Cyrus went to take a nap. He said being in the City tired him out. Vivienne had gone out for a walk with Cass; they'd finally received word from Vivienne's ward, Anne. She was still in the Carpathians. The villagers were reflexively superstitious, fanatically religious, and nursed an inborn distrust of outsiders, so it was rather slow going. But she'd hinted in her letter that strange things seemed to be afoot in this wild, isolated corner of Europe —stranger even than usual.

She hadn't asked for their help; Anne wouldn't. But he knew

Vivienne was itching to go to her. As much as it tore him apart, Alec might let her handle this one alone.

Dusk arrived at the house at St. James, creeping on little cat feet. Alec bathed and shaved. He put on his best suit. He was on his way out the door when Vivienne appeared. Her left arm was in a sling. She'd refused healing from Alec, claiming she didn't want to tire him out. He suspected her sense of honor wouldn't permit him to suffer alone.

Tonight, she wore a shimmering gown of pale green silk that left her shoulders bare. A strand of pearls looped twice around her long neck. She looked beautiful and untouchable.

"Going to a party?" he asked.

"The new Lyric Theater. I'm in the mood for something light."

"What's playing?"

"*Dorothy*. It's starring Ben Davies and Marie Tempest."

"You should come with us, Alec." The Marquess of Aber-vagenny came bounding down the stairs like a handsome blonde puppy.

Alec hesitated. "I'm rather tired."

Nathaniel gave him a brisk once-over. "You look much too nice to be staying home. Confess."

"Just going for a walk."

"It's too far," Vivienne said decisively, as if she knew exactly what he intended. "I'll have Henry bring the carriage round. Nathaniel and I can take a cab."

He studied her but sensed no jealousy. Only a tinge of sadness. "All right. Enjoy the theater."

"It's a comic opera. Mistaken identity and silly plot twists." She smiled. "How can we go wrong?"

ALEC ASKED Henry to stop at Covent Garden, where he bought a bouquet of yellow and white moss-roses from a tattered little girl. Her eyes widened when he gave her eight silver pennies.

"Thank the kind gentleman!" she exclaimed.

Alec tipped his hat to her and she giggled.

The climb up to the front door took him a full minute. By the time he knocked, his leg was on fire. His heart beat slow and steady in his chest, but it picked up when he heard footsteps. The door swung open.

"Mr. Lawrence."

"Miss de Mornay."

She examined him, green eyes inscrutable. "You haven't called me that since the first time we met."

"I thought we were being formal."

She wore a violet dress today, with thin grey pinstripes and a row of tiny buttons down the front.

"I got your note," Catherine said.

Alec waited, trying not to lean too obviously on his cane. He badly needed to sit down.

"*Splendid supple thighs* indeed."

"You said you liked Swinburne."

"I do." She smiled. "Very much. Do you want to come inside?"

Something loosened in his chest. "I wasn't sure you'd have me, after last time."

She held out a hand. "Give me the flowers first."

Alec did. The knuckles of his right hand were white from gripping the cane. This did not escape Catherine's notice. She frowned.

"What have you done to yourself now?"

"Fell off a horse."

"Really?" She raised an eyebrow. "You're very accident-prone, Mr. Lawrence."

"I told you I was graceless."

"Not the word I'd choose. You move like a dancer when you're well."

329

"You may have to carry me upstairs."

She stepped onto the landing and put an arm around his waist. She smelled of that same lilac soap. "Come along now, poor invalid. I'll make you some tea."

"Only if you let me brush your hair, Catherine. It's an absolute disaster."

The door closed on her laughter.

EPILOGUE

The woman slept, her raven hair fanned out against the silken pillows. She didn't look any older than she had an hour before, but her life had just been shortened by an indeterminate amount of time. It might have been hours or days. It might have been months or years.

He justified it by telling himself that he didn't take too much from any one of them, but there was no way to objectively know if that was true. The ouroboros wasn't designed for precise measurement. It had a single purpose: to prolong the mortal life of its owner by stealing from others at the instant of sexual release.

He had tried to stop countless times. To simply let it end. Sometimes he was so weary of living, he almost didn't care what waited for him after death. Almost.

But fear always dragged him back in the end.

Balthazar had done unspeakable things. It mattered not that they were in the distant past. The man he had been was beyond redemption. He knew because he had spent lifetimes trying to atone. To gather all the talismans he could find and hide them

KAT ROSS

from the Duzakh. But the stains on his soul ran too deep. When he did die, he had no doubt the Pit would be waiting for him.

And so he bedded them, always a different one. The women sought him out. He knew he was attractive, but that wasn't why they wanted him. Nor was it for his wealth, although that made things easier. No, they wanted him because they sensed his wounds. His self-hatred. And they thought they could fix him.

"Lucas."

Balthazar stood at the balcony of his villa in San Sebastián. He'd pulled on a pair of trousers but left his shirt unbuttoned. The sun warmed his skin.

"Yes, my lord?"

Lucas Devereaux had spent his childhood at an elite boarding school in Switzerland. He spoke seven languages fluently and had impeccable manners. He was also a master swordsman and expert in various Eastern arts of hand-to-hand combat. Balthazar had known him since he was a small boy, orphaned and alone. Sometimes he felt more like Lucas's father than his employer, although they looked only a handful of years apart.

"Pack our things and close up the house."

"Very good, my lord. Where are we going?"

"London. I have some matters to settle there."

Lucas's expression didn't change, but Balthazar knew he was surprised. They'd never once been to England, although Balthazar kept a townhouse in the City. In truth, he liked New York and was sorry to leave it.

No choice now. Even if they don't know who I am yet, they'll figure it out eventually.

"Saddle my horse. I'll go on ahead and meet you at the station."

Lucas understood he didn't wish to see Doña Higuera de Vargas when she woke up. The lady would be miffed at her abandonment, but she was married and unlikely to kick up much of a fuss.

332

Balthazar padded barefoot to a writing desk and removed a sheaf of papers, carefully rolled up and tied with string. He'd found them with Sister Emily's corpse, which had drifted down the corridor until her foot caught between the bars of an empty cell. He'd nearly tripped over her on his way out of the Tombs.

It was only fair. If the S.P.R. intended to keep his amulet, he would keep their maps. The fragile pages had sustained water damage from the flooding, but most were still legible. Balthazar resolved to have copies made as soon as possible.

He had met Claudius Ptolemy in Alexandria, at a dinner party in honor of the Roman Emperor Antoninus Pius. At the time, he'd thought the man a bit of a bore. Balthazar laughed softly. And here the old astronomer had been consorting with daemons and secretly making maps of the twelve Greater Gates.

If they ever fell into the hands of the Duzakh....

Balthazar thrust the papers into a leather valise. He buttoned his shirt and let Lucas help him put on a coat. He buckled on his sword and went out to the stables. There were bandits in the mountains and he'd learned it was always better to be armed than not. One of the primary lessons of a long life.

She didn't remember me, he thought, as he swung a leg into the stirrup and mounted his black stallion. *But she hated me nonetheless. Understandably.*

"May the Holy Father keep you, my lord," Lucas said, fingers brushing forehead, lips and heart in the sign of the flame.

Good thoughts, good words, good deeds.

Balthazar repeated the gesture. "And you, Lucas."

He paused for a moment under the scorching Basque sun. Insects buzzed in the cypress trees. He could smell the salt tang of the ocean. The Bay of Biscay lay just over the hills, a stretch of cobalt water notorious for its sudden, violent storms.

Through the open French doors, Balthazar heard the crash of something breaking. Doña Higuera de Vargas stalked out to the balcony wearing nothing but a sheet and unleashed a torrent of heated Spanish in his direction.

"Nincs drágább az idönél," he murmured.

There's nothing more expensive than time.

Balthazar spurred his mount up the narrow, winding road that led into the pass.

AFTERWORD

Dearest Reader,

The next book in the Gothic Gaslamp series, *A Bad Breed*, comes out on May 31, 2019 and is now available for preorder.

It also features Alec, Vivienne, Nathanial and Balthazar, but introduces two new characters and flirts with being a magically Gothic retelling of Beauty and the Beast — though I promise not the same tale you've heard a thousand times :).

Without giving away too much, I can tell you it begins in the Carpathian mountains with a series of vicious attacks on a remote village that bear all the hallmarks of a *pricolici* (yes, that's what werewolves are called in Romanian folklore).

Sign up for my newsletter at www.katrossbooks.com so you don't miss any new releases! I also run sneaky price promotions that I only advertise on my mailing list.

In the meantime, if you're curious about how Vivienne Cumberland met Alec Lawrence, the history of the daēvas, and Balthazar's checkered past, you can take a journey back to ancient Persia in the Fourth Element Trilogy where these characters first appear. Book #1 is *The Midnight Sea,* I hope you'll check it out.

Cheers, Kat

ACKNOWLEDGMENTS

A huge thanks as always to my brilliant editors, Christa Yelich-Koth and Jessica Therrien, who caught so many problems, large and small. To Laura Pilli, for her constant encouragement and guidance on an early draft, and Pilar Erso, for her many virtual cups of tea and awesome Sherlock GIFs. Seriously, they kept me going during a truly brutal rewrite.

To the warm, wonderful and talented crew at Acorn Publishing.

And lastly to Mom, for everything.

ABOUT THE AUTHOR

Kat Ross worked as a journalist at the United Nations for ten years before happily falling back into what she likes best: making stuff up. She's the author of the Fourth Element and Fourth Talisman fantasy series, the Gaslamp Gothic mysteries, and the dystopian thriller Some Fine Day. She loves myths, monsters and doomsday scenarios.

Made in United States
Orlando, FL
23 May 2025

61543527R00204